Where's Annie?

Also by EILEEN BASSING:

Home Before Dark

Where's Annie?

EILEEN BASSING

Random House

New York

This is a work of fiction. No character or event in it derives from any living person or actual occurrence.

To my husband, with love

Contents

1	THE ADMIRAL	3
2	VICTORIA	29
3	ABEL	59
4	VICTORIA	70
5	NED	99
6	VICTORIA	124
7	THE BEAUTIFUL PEOPLE	160
8	VICTORIA	179
9	DR. OBREGÓN	195
10	VICTORIA	218
11	CHARLES	237
12	VICTORIA	267
13	NED	299
14	VICTORIA	316
15	HARRY	351
16	VICTORIA	376

Where's Annie?

1

The Admiral

ANDREW CUNNINGHAM was a retired admiral.
He and his young wife, Annie—oh, and she was beautiful, with
long, slightly curling, rich brown hair and wide green eyes—
came to the village and rented a house just beyond the yellow
and white towered church, on the rise of the hill near the highway.

Annie ran around excitedly, flinging open doors, calling out,
"Oh, see the darling tin-framed mirror over the dressing table in
this bedroom! And here, look how charming the patio is! Did you
ever see such flowers?"

He beamed at her, which was what he usually did, his lined
tanned face going bright with pleasure. He was satisfied with

the house himself. He checked the bathroom and found that here, when he pressed the lever, water flowed as it flowed in the United States. In the kitchen, when he held a lighted match to the burner on the stove, flame appeared. For these multiple conveniences, after having lived for a year in a series of Mexican villages, he was grateful.

He was aware that his preoccupation with comfort and convenience was typical of his age, and he did not call it to Annie's attention. He did not want to spoil her pleasure in any way, not even by showing her that the things he cared about were not the things she cared about. Anyway, this trip was for Annie. They had been married three years and when he was retired from the Navy they decided finally to settle down in Florida, but Annie said she wanted to travel first, and he'd agreed to that, even when she said that where she wanted to travel was through Mexico. He had always thought of Mexico as a rather ridiculous country, and he was confident that after a few months of it, she'd feel the same way and they could go home to the land of sanitation, comfort and progress. Annie, however, had loved it all. He had been homesick the whole time, at first in Baja where the heat was dreadful and then in Mazatlán. There Annie had been enchanted with the beauty of the curving coastline and did not, as far as he could tell, notice that it was hot. He, having seen a lifetime of coastlines, was really aware only of the constant sweat he was in and how hard it was to sleep in the long muggy nights. In San Miguel de Allende, while Annie was exalted by the beautifully carved doors, the handsome buildings and the view of the mountains from their high windows on the top floor of the hotel, he was unpleasantly conscious of the fact that the milk and butter had a goaty taste, and that there was sand blowing in minute particles which found their way into his food as well as his nostrils. The constant blowing desert wind irritated his sinuses and made his old joints ache wretchedly in the chill dry nights.

As they traveled, he found new problems besetting him everywhere—bathrooms without water—failing electric power—filthy kitchens and careless maids—cockroaches, scorpions and fleas. The list of annoyances was endless. In Guadalajara, just before they came to the village, he had become acutely aware of just how poor were the poor Mexicans in contrast to the blatantly rich ones, and it made him uneasy. He'd known, from his reading, that it was this way, but he wasn't prepared for the daily impact upon himself of this contrast. He found that instead of looking at the noble profile of an Indio woman, he looked at the aboriginal poverty in which she lived; instead of seeing the beautiful sprays of bougainvillaea over a crumbling adobe wall, he saw the crumbling wall, and the garbage dumped beside it.

This village was a great relief to him. It was different. The climate was gentle and the people were not poor. They were hardly to be considered well off by American standards, but they owned and farmed land, and they were fishermen and tradesmen, and their houses were solid adobe which, from time to time, they not only repaired but even, in accord with a local law haphazardly enforced, painted once a year. There had been many Americans and other foreigners living in the village for such a long time that the Mexicans were Americanized. The Americans ran the village, or so it seemed to him; the Mexicans were happy to take advantage of American know-how, up to a point. Bathrooms usually worked, the cobblestoned streets were comparatively clean, the sun shone down on tropical plants which were pruned and clipped in a way the admiral considered neat and sensible. For the first time, in Mexico, he had a feeling of safety. He had not known until he felt it again, here, that he had not felt it in a long time.

The lake made a difference. The village was grouped along its shore, its houses overlooked the water, its gardens ran down to the water's edge. The purple mountains on the other side of the lake stood staunch against the incredible blue sky, and a frequent breeze rippled the water and moved moistly among the trees on the shore. It was a beautiful lake, and its colors shifted from shimmering mauve to deep tawny yellow in a single morning, turned turquoise, coral and finally scarlet and lavender in the late afternoon.

The admiral and Annie spent their time in this village much as they had in the other places. Annie stayed indoors until after siesta and then there was usually a cocktail party or tea party or what in his mind he called "a bun fight"—which was what his father used to call a ladies' tea or luncheon—to which she went. For him the day began earlier. He had always been an early riser and the village was noisy with awakenings in the morning. Most Mexicans arose in the dark and began the day's work before the sun leapt into the sky. The admiral, restless after the years of naval discipline, forced himself to remain in bed until it was light, but then it was his habit to get up, shower, dress, and go for a walk along the lake shore before breakfast.

He enjoyed these walks. The mornings were cool and clear and because of the slight altitude—the village was about five thousand feet, a relief after Tepoztlán's seven thousand—the mornings, no matter how hot the day might become, were fresh and sparkling. He walked briskly, touching his cap in a friendly way when he passed a Mexican man, carefully looking preoccupied when one of the women passed him on her way to the *molino* with a bucket of corn to have ground into *masa* for the day's tortillas.

The admiral was shy, especially with women. He rarely saw any Americans on these early morning walks since most of them were asleep. Once, as he strolled down the steep street to the lake, he came upon a group which, in the early daylight, was on its way home after some sort of drunken party. There were four or five of them and one of them was a girl. They were very drunk and tired, and working hard at the task of getting to their houses. He looked into their pale young faces, not knowing that he scowled in disapproval. The girl wore an evening coat, which hung from her shoulders as though somebody had put it there when she didn't notice, and she swayed, so that it hung loose and unbuttoned as she walked. Her face was white and strained and there were circles under her eyes. The young men with her helped each other, but even so they staggered and lurched against the adobe walls of the houses from time to time. Just before they came abreast of the admiral, the girl slipped on the treacherous cobblestones and fell down. One of the young men slowly pulled loose from his friend and stood swaying over the girl.

She whimpered. "My ankle," she said, rubbing it, staring at it.

"If you've broken your leg, I'll shoot you," the young man said.

They all laughed at this, including the girl, who gave up rubbing her ankle, rolled over and lay relaxed on her back on the stones, laughing. The young man who had spoken, bent over her, almost fell on top of her, righted himself and pulled her

up. She stood there swaying, still laughing, and they moved
past the admiral up the street.

The incident disquieted him. He'd seen plenty of drunks in
his life, and in his twenties he'd made a hearty but unsuccessful
effort to become one, but there was a disturbing quality about
these particular drunks that he couldn't explain. Perhaps it was
because not one of them saw him or spoke to him, or perhaps
it was because they looked very unhappy in their intoxication.
Or maybe, he thought, resisting the idea without knowing why,
it was the sight of their youth which shut him out as though he
were suddenly invisible, without presence, without importance,
so that as he walked along afterward he felt unreal even to himself. He looked determinedly at the lake, and the green velvet
mountains beyond the lake.

The lake gave the village a reason for being there. Everywhere else in the world, the admiral had been conscious of why
a city was where it was—except in Mexico. San Miguel and
Guanajuato, for instance, seemed to him simply to be there
through some capricious accident, to have stood there until people came and lived in the houses. There were other towns and
small villages dotting the countryside whose reason for existence
he could not understand. In the United States he always knew
the reason a town became a town—it was a crossroads of trade
routes, or built on a railroad line, or on the edge of a power-
giving river; but in Mexico often he was bewildered, for there
was no reason for half its towns being where they were instead
of some place else.

The lake made the village beautiful and was probably the
reason the foreigners came here. The Americans who were real
empire-building businessmen went to the big cities of Mexico,
where they found a new economic frontier, equivalent to the
United States at the turn of the century. They were the money-
makers, whose hearts strained always toward the moment of
going home, laden with booty, to the world of country clubs and
baseball games and new cars every year. But living in big
cities cost more, and the artists who did not yearn to go home
and who came for the cheap living on their meager incomes—
and because Mexico begged to be painted—found small villages
such as this one and settled down. Traveling through San
Miguel, the admiral had met a number of artists, large ladies in
floppy hats who set up easels in the open and painted happily

like children. There were many artists here, too, and he
thought that if he were an artist he might want to live here a
long time and paint what he saw.

The ideal climate in the village, plus the rate of exchange,
was what probably attracted the nuts—the folk singers, and
those women who wore full black skirts and tight black jersey
tops, who made raffia mats, or fired their own ceramic ash trays,
or worse still, hand-loomed cloth which they then mistakenly
wore. These were the same ones who went in for blackstrap
molasses, yoghurt and raw foods, who, at the same time they
added this false fastidiousness to their lives, were trying to be
primitive, back to the soil and the simple life, "of the earth,
earthy," as one of them said to him. The bearded crackpots
drifted here from Mallorca or Tahiti, along the route the bums
of the world take, with women, or with other men, or both,
harmless enough most likely, but to the average American mind
just no damned good. Looking at them, the admiral always felt
a hot wave of pity for their fathers, thinking what a legion of
solid citizens there must be, dismayed and bewildered by what
they had begotten. He was, he thought, no Babbitt himself, but
he couldn't help thinking about these fathers and feeling sorry
for them. For example, homosexuality didn't bother him, as a
spectacle or as a reality—he'd kept up with things since he left
Princeton, and he'd read *Time* and he was neither uninformed
nor righteous—but he sorrowed with the fathers, who didn't
know what that was all about. That, he told himself, must be
tough.

There was a great deal of drinking among the foreigners in
the village. Liquor was cheap and there were many parties—
parties before lunch, which at this altitude was the heavy meal
of the day and at home would be called dinner, parties before
supper and parties after. There were parties at the Posada, the
beautiful inn on the lake shore, almost every evening, and the
tourists were always there and the residents attended these parties upon invitation. Annie liked these, and he went with her to
several of them, but he didn't enjoy them. They seemed to work
out so that Annie became involved with the younger residents
of the town, while he found himself surrounded by tourist
schoolteachers. These fluttered around him cooing like excited
pigeons and automatically excluded him from the gayer group
around Annie. Everyone else ignored the traveling teachers, ex-

cept for the few couples who lived in town and operated shops and who, therefore, bohemian though they might be, were also compelled for practical reasons to be nice to the temporary visitors. The admiral thought of these bohemian business people as real expatriates, for most of them spoke Spanish as fluently as they spoke English and had no intention of ever returning to the States. These formed a clique which was the social core of the village, since they were permanent, and the other cliques— the artists and writers and retired rich people—circled around them.

There was one group which Annie told him was pretty disreputable. It was made up of ex-servicemen for the most part, some of them living on disability compensations from the U. S. Government, some of them making a pretense of getting an education at American government expense at the nearly defunct University of Guadalajara which, from all reports, did not know what to teach them on the rare occasions when they did show up there, but also did not want to give up their share of the money paid for the purposes of educating them— so there was a kind of tacit diplomatic agreement in effect that if at all possible these "students" should stay at home in their village and not bother anybody. They were young, and seemed peculiar and rather brazenly dirty. They did not talk to each other in G.I. slang, which the admiral would have understood, but in a strange, mumbled, unintelligible jargon all their own, which he had never heard before.

Among the English-speaking population, there were many jargons, but most of them were just the precious artistic stuff he thought was a lot of baloney. The painters and the nuts used a lot of foreign phrasing—French usually—and talked, he thought, like undergraduates. The writers had an entirely different way of talking. They were the unhappiest-looking people in town. They seemed frightened and worried and talked with false bravado about despising commercial success. Some of them only talked and didn't seem to write at all; others worked constantly and said less than the others. These latter were usually at the post office when the mail came in the afternoon, posting manuscripts off to the States in big manila envelopes and, just as regularly, getting them back. The admiral had a lot of respect for real writers—the old boys like De Maupassant and Balzac, Virgil and Homer, Wordsworth and Pope—but he found it impossible to associate the writers he met in the village with those great names. He thought these were mostly goof-offs, small talents, desperate kids who probably should be selling shoes. What did they know about life and what in hell could they have to say?

There were exceptions—Lawrence Creighton for instance, who'd left the advertising business to write the great novel, who might, just possibly might, get to be something as a writer. There was Victoria Beacon, who'd been pretty famous and, he supposed, since she was a professional, an exception. He'd never read any of her novels; he didn't go much for contemporary fiction; it all seemed pretty tortured to him, except for detective stories which he liked, stupid as most of them were. But Annie had a high opinion of Victoria and talked about her and said she'd loved her last book. It had been a best seller and Annie had read it some time before their marriage three years ago. She was fan enough to be thrilled to be in the same village with Victoria, she said.

Victoria puzzled him more than anyone else there. He saw her often on his morning walks. He thought at first that she was Mexican. She was a chunkily built little woman who wore her long dark hair in two Indian-style pigtails, braided, tied with bits of colored ribbon or yarn, the way the Indio women did. Her skin was dark and at first when he heard her speaking voluble Spanish to the grocer one day, he was sure she was Mexican. But after a while he noticed the typically American way she walked, erect, almost martial in her carriage, rapid-gaited and precipitate. And then one evening in the Posada he heard the Americans talking about "Victoria," and finally somebody said something which told him that this was the name of the little woman he'd seen who puzzled him. People spoke of her with tolerant affection, as though she were somehow fascinating and important to them, a beloved eccentric whose remarks could always be quoted, being clever, brilliant or absurd. People talked of how unfriendly she was, as though it were an achievement, and how she constantly refused invitations, as though it were proof of her value. One woman said, "I asked Victoria to come tonight and she said, 'Get away from me. Get away from my house. Don't knock on my door. Don't invite me places. What time is the supper being served?'" There was a shout of laughter. "She'll come if she's hungry," somebody else said, and they all laughed again.

The admiral usually saw her when he got to the lake shore. She walked in the mornings straight down the hill to where the cement pier extended like a thick frozen finger out over the shore. Once the lake waves had billowed and broken here, and now, because the lake had shrunk, the end of the pier was several yards from where the water began. Victoria walked to the end of it and sat down under the sign facing the water, which said BIENVENIDO, as though ships could come in and sailors alight to be welcomed, and as though she, like the sign, were waiting for them.

One day the admiral almost bumped into her when she stumped swiftly around a corner directly into his path.

"Out of my way," she said, not looking up.

"Sorry," he said, and stepped aside.

Afterward he found that he was angry at the way she had treated him, but at the time he had automatically obeyed the urgent voice of command.

There was something familiar about it, the ring to her voice and the fire-eater look of her, and he realized, thinking about it afterward, that she reminded him of Hazel, his first wife, dead now six years. That was partly why he'd obeyed so automatically. Hazel had had a way of bluntly saying what she meant which, when it wasn't turned on him, he respected and enjoyed and now missed. Strictly on the level was Hazel, with no damned nonsense about her, and the first year of his marriage to Annie he'd kept up a running argument with Hazel in his mind, trying to justify to her his marrying a girl twenty-five years younger than himself. But he lost the argument because he remembered too well, and could not help himself from conjuring up, the wide-eyed cynicism and the mocking grin with which, he knew, she would listen to his rationale. He wasn't fooling her and he wasn't really fooling himself. Now, except in the moments when it seemed to him it would have been a great comfort to be here with Hazel, who'd have seen it all pretty much the way he did, and made short shrift of it at that, he had successfully banished her from his mind. She mocked him with her honesty no more. Until he saw Victoria, and that revived the disapproving ghost of Hazel again.

He resolved to avoid Victoria after that, but if he couldn't avoid her and did meet her, he'd put her in her place. Probably, for all her being famous, she was just a nut like the rest of them down here.

But the next time he saw her, and braced himself for the meeting, she looked full into his face and her wide dark eyes were smiling and her mouth widened in a friendly urchin grin.

He was surprised into touching his cap and saying to her, "Good morning, ma'am."

Her smile dwindled; she stood still; she tugged at her ear and removed a rubber earplug. "What did you say?" she demanded, the smile gone as though it had never been. "Is something the matter? I'm plugged up. I'm working, do you understand, I'm *thinking*. What is it you want?"

He felt his neck go red and he said, with his voice grating in his suddenly dry throat, "I beg your pardon. I just said—good morning, that's all."

"Oh," she said, and put the plug back in her ear. "Christ! Good morning." She brushed past him muttering to herself.

After that whenever he saw her coming, he turned the other way, crossed the street, avoided her no matter how inconvenient it might be. It wasn't difficult; now, imperceptibly, he had begun to avoid all the Americans. He touched his cap to Mexicans, but when he saw Americans, he pretended to be greatly preoccupied and walked past them staring at the ground, cloaked in his thoughts. It worked, as it had worked when he stood on his bridge, not looking at his officers.

Which is how it happened that the day Charles spoke to him, he walked on a few steps automatically before he realized what had happened. Then he turned back at once, not wanting to seem rude. Charles was a very tall, very thin young man, who drifted lazily around the village wearing an old pair of Marine Corps pants, his manner half-insolent and half-propitiatory, his eyes heavy-lidded and cynical. The admiral had seen him many times, often with some of the others of the ex-G.I. group, often alone. Charles was the cleanest of the lot and the admiral had been struck by his laugh, which had a rare sound for laughter, of spontaneous, whole-hearted enjoyment. When the admiral had heard Charles laugh, his own lips had twitched and he had been unable to keep from smiling.

He turned back. "What?" he said. "Did you say something to me?"

"Yeah. I'm out for a walk and you're out for a walk, and I thought we might walk along together," Charles said.

The admiral looked at him in surprise. Charles was smiling as though he had told only the first part of a joke and the rest was about to come now, but he didn't say anything more. The admiral thought the smile was probably an index of the boy's embarrassment.

"Fine," he said, trying not to sound hollow. "Let's do that."

Charles fell in beside him and they walked along together to the shore and turned without speaking onto the path along the lake. Charles carried a stick and he whacked at the bushes with idle viciousness as they went. The admiral wondered what in the world he could talk to Charles about. Not the Marine Corps, certainly . . .

Charles said, "I got nothing against anybody who was brass. Some people do. I could never understand it. I figure you guys were victims, too. You didn't set it up and you couldn't knock it down. You didn't want to be there either. Hell," Charles said, "I'm hip. It's just stupid to blame the guy who's playing boss, like it's stupid to blame the guy working for you." He looked at the admiral. "You agree with that, sir?" he said.

"More or less," the admiral said.

"You don't talk much to anybody."

"No, I don't." He told Charles about Victoria. "I said good morning to her," he said. "She smiled at me, you see, and I was being polite."

"Ah, Vickie's a flip." Charles laughed. "She wasn't smiling at you. Maybe one of her inner voices told a joke." He looked sideways at the admiral and laughed again. "She's a real flip."

They walked along for a while unspeaking. The *chicharras* in the trees buzzed and clacked like angry schoolteachers; roosters crowed, and somewhere in a house near by a radio chattered metallically. Their shoes crunched on the stony sand.

"Vickie's pretty wild," Charles said. "You ever read any of her books?"

The admiral shook his head. "No, but my wife has. She seems to think she's a pretty good writer."

"Yeah," Charles said. "Vickie had it made."

A Mexican riding on a burro came along the path toward them, his long legs hanging down almost to the ground, his broad hat tipped forward on his head. They stepped aside for him, but he steered the burro off the path and went by them, head down, not looking.

"A *crudo*," Charles said, chuckling.

"*Crudo?*"

"That's what they say in this village. Boy, am I ever *crudo*! they say. Hung over. *Hombre*, they say."

"Oh." The admiral had thought the man simply did not want to greet them.

They passed the fishermen spreading their nets out from pole to pole along the beach, and together regarded the line of black *canoas*, like so many triangles, moving slightly with the ripple at the lake's edge.

"I'd like to sail one of those," the admiral said. "That one with the red sail."

Charles looked at the *canoa*. "Yeah?" he said. He stood still. "No jazz?" he said.

The admiral shook his head. "Very interesting craft," he said.

"Want me to fix it up for you, sir?"

A little surprised, the admiral nodded amiably, and waited while Charles sauntered off and talked to one of the fishermen.

He came back and said the admiral could take the boat out tomorrow afternoon if he wanted to; the fisherman would rent it to him for fifty pesos. The *canoa* had been freshly caulked and by tomorrow the tar should be completely dry.

"Splendid," the admiral said slowly. "Care to come along?"

Charles smiled. "Crazy," he said indifferently. "I'll go tell Nacho it's okay for tomorrow, sir." He loped off again and the admiral stood there pushing at the coarse dark sand with his shoe, feeling the sun hitting down hard on his head now, and tried to think of a pleasant way to ask this gaunt young man not to call him "sir" in that aging, respectful manner. He could tell him his name was Cunningham. Or Andy? No, Andy was too boyish and he hated "Andrew." He was afraid if he said anything, Charles would just begin to call him admiral or something worse. He decided to wait until tomorrow and see how they got along when they were out in the boat together.

The next afternoon he put on a yachting cap and wore white

ducks and an Italian striped T-shirt and cork-soled shoes. He felt young, lean and seaworthy and he kissed Annie good-bye and set off for the lake. When he got to the shore the fisherman was there, squatting on his heels beside a big rock, but there was no sign of Charles. He paid the man the fifty pesos. The fisherman said something which he could not understand, touched two fingers to his sombrero, slid his brown feet into his worn huaraches and walked away.

The admiral waited three-quarters of an hour and when Charles did not come, decided to go alone. He pushed the boat farther out into the water easily enough, and waded along until he was in to the waist. He did not like the feel of the lake bottom, which was not clean like the bottom of a mountain lake, nor the ocean floor, but muddy with slime which eddied thickly about his calves. He got into the boat and began to pole the boat away from the shallow beach. He was caked with drying mud and the tropical sun was very hot.

He could see Victoria hunched down under the sign at the end of the pier, as usual. It seemed to him that she was watching him, but he wasn't sure because it was hard to tell where she looked from behind her enormous dark glasses until she waved at him. When she did that, he looked quickly away, not wanting to return her salute, flushing again with remembered embarrassment. There was no sign of Charles anywhere on the shore and he admitted to himself that, along with being annoyed at the boy's irresponsibility, he was also disappointed; he had rather liked him.

He soon discovered that the boat was ridiculous. It shipped water at an amazing rate. It was built high and sharp, with its prow off balance, and the colorful red sail was insecurely fastened to the mast. He looked at the hand-hewn mast in bewilderment; it wasn't even straight.

He had thought, looking at the water from the security of its sandy edge, that this was a pleasant lake, something like Arrowhead in California. But he saw, now that he was out on it, that it was riddled with cross-currents and strange tides; the waves were choppy and ugly-looking, unpredictable; he was the only living thing afloat for miles and miles. Looking at its turgid, chaotic flow, he decided that it was an abnormal lake altogether, which didn't even have honest-to-God fish in it, just some kind of whitefish so thin you could see through them, and catfish.

He'd never liked catfish. But the water was so loaded with silt, he guessed nothing much could live in it.

The boat was moving along but there was something peculiar about its motion which troubled and puzzled him, and he was just deciding to give up and go back to shore when it happened. He did not know then, and was never to know, what it was that happened. All he knew was that one moment he was looking at the swirling opaque waters and the next instant the sail luffed and flapped and he turned quickly to look at it. The boat swung sharply about as though it were beginning to spin. He felt no shift in the wind, but suddenly he was flung against the spindly mast and heard a cracking noise and a tearing sound and the sucking of waves. Abruptly he was sinking in the shocking cold water. He opened his eyes, looking about him in the dark water, and began to kick his legs. He felt no panic but only a kind of enduring amazement.

The water was not at all buoyant, but his old legs kicked sturdily as they had learned to do in the cradle, and he rose fast and smashed his head into the *canoa* above him. The blow dazed him and now all he thought of was getting air. He turned over on his stomach and began swimming hard under water.

At last he came up into the sunlight and tried to gulp in a breath. His lungs would not open at first and when at last they did, they wheezed like a pair of old bellows. The pain of breathing left him giddy and half-conscious. But he sucked in the air, a little at a time, and became conscious of his eyes, which pained him sharply and felt as though they had popped. He blinked and thought he was blind but after a while he could see light through the red haze of blood. When at last the red faded, he began to look about him for the *canoa*. It was not there. It had sunk and was now no doubt settling heavily into the ancient layers of slime beneath him. Blood was making a red stain near his face and he put up his hand and felt the cut on his forehead. It was a wide gash.

He rolled over onto his back and tried floating, but he soon found that even with moving his hands and feet constantly, he could not stay on the surface. He took a big breath and went down in a jackknife position and got his shoes off and began to tug at his pants. They were caked with mud and he sank low getting them off. Then he was air-hungry again and tired. He came up. He wished that he had waited for Charles and discovered that his eyes were filling with hot tears and that unexpectedly he had thought of and wanted his mother.

But it couldn't be that he would drown in this little, forgotten lake in Mexico after all the oceans and the wars, could it?

He spotted the white line of the pier. He was close to the middle of the lake, about a mile and a half, he estimated, out from the pier. He blinked up at the rolling white sun. It was going to be a long hard swim and he probably wasn't going to make it. He turned over and began the sidestroke, long slow motions which he assumed propelled him through the water, but he had no sense of progress, of passing anything.

He had swum about half a mile, pausing often to rest, when he remembered the Navy doctor in San Diego saying to him, "Andy, you have the heart of a lion. It won't come to you that way." But he could swim in the lake until his lion's heart burst. He knew it. He felt his heart tiring right now, pumping hard, forcing him more and more often to lie on his back and drift and lose the yards he had gained by swimming.

He grew overpoweringly sleepy. His skin burned with blood, his head ached and his eyes, irritated by the silty water, closed and closed, and it was hard to hold to a direction. His legs slowed and he forced his arms to pull harder, dragging the lower three-quarters of his body. His head kept sinking down under the curling waves and he kept swallowing the damned, hateful water.

He was thinking, it's too lonely, I don't want it this way, I feel awfully sick, this is enough now, when he got his head up a last time and sucked in air. Then he saw the boat coming toward him with what looked like Victoria standing up in the prow of it waving her arms, and he heard faintly over the noise of the motor, like the distant crying of gulls, the voices which shouted to him.

They pulled him into the speedboat, and once he was lying on the bottom and they had covered his twitching purple legs with a blanket, the fat man who owned the boat kept patting him here and there and shaking his head and saying, "For God's sake, Admiral!" in a frightened, reproachful way. He knew all this, was aware of all this with a single point of bright perception in all the bewildered, delirious numbness of himself, which shone in his chaos with the single steady beam of a pencil flashlight, and showed him whatever caught in its beam and nothing else.

When any one of them moved out of it the voice was lost to him, and blurred into a sound like the cawing of birds. In the middle of hearing that sound, he had an abrupt dream, of the kind he had only when he was deeply asleep, in which he was lying under a blanket in bed and itching terribly all over but when he scratched himself the scratching made a bird-cawing sound, which in turn scratched his inflamed red brain and made him cry out. He awoke from that dream in the grip of a terrible nausea, which was so vivid he was truly conscious for the first time. He was afraid he was going to be sick. One of the birds was cawing distinct words . . .

Victoria was saying, "He was showing off. He may not know that's what he was doing, but it was. I know these men who have had glory and lost it. I tell you I *knew* he was going to sink that boat today. *Knew* it. The water must always have been the arena for him where he could prove himself, demonstrate himself so to speak . . . A retired admiral, you know. Water, you know . . ."

"Aw shut up, Victoria!" a man's voice said. Was it his own voice? No, he couldn't have spoken. There ought to be a way he could tell them he was going to be sick. With a tiny, sharp click, the pencil beam of the flashlight went out, and he rolled down into nauseous depths of dark.

They carried him into the patio of the Posada—it was the hotel speedboat which had brought him in—and sat him down in a leather chair. A gigantic grapevine grew over the bare beams above and gave the patio a weighted, grapy shadow which made it as cool as a mountain cave. They rubbed his legs and arms and his chest and they poured brandy down his throat and when he was fully conscious—although still gasping for breath and with his eyes rolling—they bandaged his head and smeared iodine on his bleeding shins. He was grateful for the sting and burn of it because it seemed to wake him up more, but there was still the sound of bird voices, raucous, crowlike and distant . . . and ringing around his head an ever-deepening halo of darkness. He could hear but he thought he couldn't, and because of the blackness telescoping his vision, he thought he was blind. He stood up and said he was able to walk to his house, but they shoved him down into the chair again and he fainted.

When his eyes rolled open, seeing again, but still with the black rings outside of everything, he looked into Victoria's face.

Her eyes were enormous and luminous and he looked deeply into them and it was as though he could see into the black pupils, as though they were stages in the distance, and there were small white figures writhing there, in some kind of agony. He saw them distinctly and sharply, but as infinitely small. He watched them, and fear crept through him and he thought his first really coherent thought—that this was the most frightening of all the things that had happened to him. Hazel's eyes had once presented that look to him, and he had peered into them in the same helpless, sucked-in way, and seen small figures writhing, and it seemed possible now that this was Hazel; in fact it seemed impossible for it not to be Hazel . . . She moved away, closing up her eyes as she did, and his head fell back. He listened, wondering what was it in her face that he had seen?

She said, "He's awake now." Her voice dropped until it was miserable. "I saw great fear in his eyes now. He knows he will live."

There was a silence and then a brisk clatter and he lifted his head, knowing that this was the clacking of her heels on the tile floor, and he looked and saw her marching down the corridor and out the door, her back sturdy and small, her head held high. Now that she was gone, full consciousness began to return to him. He struggled to sit up straight.

Carl Rogers, who had a shop near the Posada—he was one of the businessmen-bohemians—brought out his big blue Cadillac to drive the admiral up the street. A huddle of small Mexican children watched as they helped the blanket-wrapped admiral into the car, and then Carl, a big-faced man with a scraggly mustache and whose hands and feet were dirty, drove him the two blocks to his house.

"You feel all right?" Carl asked.

"Yes, thanks."

There was a pause while the Cadillac spongily moved over the deep ruts. Then Carl said, "Somebody said you're a retired admiral."

"That's right," he said.

"U. S. Navy?"

"Yes."

"No fooling," Carl said, incredulously. "Probably a Pentagon admiral, huh?"

"No." The admiral sighed. He swallowed, and pain stabbed

in his throat from the retching. "I sailed ships. *Not*, however, homemade canoes."

Carl glanced over at him. "Yeah, that's a mistake all right. I could have told you. Well, the natives get a kick out of it when a *gringo* sinks one of them. Happens every so often." He paused and bit down on his pipe. "Never with an American admiral on board though. They'll have a great laugh over that one." He shook his head.

Before the car jolted to its stop, the admiral had the door open. He got out and stood in his bare feet on the cobblestones, tugging the multicolored blanket closer about him.

He said, "Thanks for the lift."

He turned and strode furiously toward his house, fighting off the closing circle of blackness, scrabbling at the door and getting it open, stepping into the refuge of his home.

Annie was sitting in the flowering patio with the handsomest young man he had ever seen. His eyes were blue, his brows sharp and black, his hair dark and curly, and his skin pink with the glow of youth. He rose from his chair, staring at the admiral in his blanket.

Tears burned into the admiral's eyes and the blackness was closing in. He came forward, looking through the black for Annie.

"I almost drowned, Annie," he said.

For the next several days the admiral took it easy. He resented his tired body's need to rest, and when he called it "take it easy" in his mind, another part of his mind smiled superciliously at his euphemistic choice of phrase. The truth was that he was full of fear and a sense of being old; the soreness of his ropy muscles and the way his heart labored when he took his slower walks—now they were promenades—argued for admission of his age. But even while he observed the change in himself and knew that in one day he had aged very abruptly, he held the knowledge away from himself. "I'll just lie around the patio today," he'd say, as though it were a decision for today only and not for the shrinking future. "Just take it easy and get some sun." And he lay in the sun, his brain bewildered by its eyelid-reddening heat, by the blaze which assaulted him, and did not—lest Annie notice—let himself check his racing pulse by putting his hand on his wrist.

When he shaved he avoided the mirror's summation of his

face, and saw it a section at a time, seeing and shaving the beard in this one place, not seeing his white hair—listless now, strawlike, not burnished, handsome silver—not observing the shadowy puffs under his eyes, ignoring the oddly raffish bandage on his forehead. At the table he tried to keep his suddenly tremulous, big-veined hands out of sight as much as possible, and once in the living room when he caught himself gazing at his edematic ankle, he lifted his gaze slowly to the height of the mango tree in the patio and did not look down again. He had begun to move rather carefully, and to avoid unnecessary activity. He had always dashed about a lot. Well, perhaps not always, but certainly since he married Annie. Then he did it when he didn't need to, because he liked the feel of himself hurrying through a room on his way somewhere. Now he stacked things and carried them in one slow trip, and did without things he wanted instead of rushing off after them. He did not like to ask Annie to fetch and carry. Not yet, he told himself; he didn't have to take her youth and use it as he would use a servant's youth, or a nurse's.

Anyway, these days, Annie was not always available. She was, in fact, seldom available. She was busy going places with the handsome young man who had been sitting in the patio with her the day he almost drowned. His name was Clay Patton. Sometimes she didn't go any place with him but stayed home and then Clay Patton visited her. The admiral couldn't decide which was worse. He lay on a mat in the sunlight on the upper patio, hidden by a bush, listening to the lunge and beat of his heart, hearing Annie's laughter. Annie laughed a great deal lately, and her voice was becoming different, a little affected, breathier, younger. She sounded, when she was with Clay Patton, like a stage ingénue, fun-loving and a trifle silly.

Either Clay Patton was a very amusing fellow or Annie was getting feeble-minded. He didn't really believe there was anything wrong with Annie's mind, so he began to strain to hear what it was Clay Patton said. But he never heard him say anything funny when he was eavesdropping. He assumed that Clay Patton must be different when he was alone with Annie, because when the admiral was around, Clay Patton behaved as though he were in a sickroom, or dealing with an august personage of great age. The way Clay said "sir" every few minutes was infuriating. It did not carry the gibe that Charles' "sir" carried;

it was gravely delivered, super-respectful. It was the sort he once or twice had gotten from junior lieutenants—young men, who thought him so old he must be incompetent and who, while they were scrupulously polite, with shining, scrubbed faces showing nothing of what they felt, nonetheless had a certain light look in their eyes he considered mutinous. It was necessary to show them that he was no fictional inept officer who could be given a sop of respect and otherwise safely ignored. He managed to reduce them to utter humility in a very short time. He was quite good at it; it was part of his job and it gave him a stubborn, ignoble satisfaction.

But Clay Patton was not in the Navy and neither was he. They were in Mexico, under a democratically pagan blue sky, at the mercy of the golden sun, the balmy nights, breathing the same scented air, in unfortunate equality, gazing at the same beautiful girl.

No, not the same beautiful girl. A beautiful girl of a wife with a slim body and green eyes and long, curling brown hair— that was the admiral's Annie. But what was Clay Patton's Annie? A princess in a tower, guarded by an enfeebled ogre? Or was Clay Patton's Annie a tramp? A pushover who stayed near him as much as she could, brushing his hand with hers, tipping her soul into his eyes when she looked at him—and found him handsome—spilling infatuation and innocent-animal-sexual hunger upon him, as though she poured them from a cup.

In the old days there used to be advertisements in the magazines for Arrow Collars, featuring an extraordinarily handsome young man with a perfect profile and a pretty, girlish mouth. Many times in nightmares and daytime fantasies during the three years he and Annie had been married, he had imagined a young man he called "Arrow Collars," knowing, with the cold hackles of dread rising on his skin, that one day such a young man would certainly appear—perhaps blond, perhaps dark, perhaps in a cable-stitched tennis sweater, but in any case, irresistible, to steal his Annie away from him. He knew he could not forever hide Annie away from the world, nor from Arrow Collars, not even in Mexico, and time worked against him.

But because he was so tired and so unable to do anything, really, without his heart's increasing its rising drumbeat, he told himself for the first couple of weeks that Clay Patton was just a jerk, and all right for Annie to play with while he rested and got strong again. But gradually he found it impossible to keep

on thinking this, and the unwelcome, heart-jolting thought came
more and more often into his mind and would not go away. . . .
Was Clay Patton Arrow Collars?

The admiral sighed and reminded himself to stop sighing.
It was old and sick and sad to sigh that way. His mind showed
him Gauguin-like pictures of the two, beautiful as Polynesians,
in bright colors, and when his imagination evoked the memory
of Annie's cone-shaped breast with its delicately pink tip, there
came almost at once Clay Patton's hand moving onto the canvas
to cup the breast, and he shuddered. Deadlier than a tarantula,
that hand. He gritted his teeth and his heart thudded within
him so that the bones of his body shook with its bound.

Finally, one morning at breakfast he suggested to Annie
that they go into Guadalajara for the day, do a little shopping,
have lunch at the Copa de Leche, see a movie—all things Annie
loved to do. But now she shook her head no, so that the shining
brown hair slipped from side to side in a kind of dance, saying
she had the day planned. ("Tennis, anyone?" said Arrow Collars in his mind.) She and some people were going to climb the
mountain and have a picnic lunch at the waterfall and come
back in time for a late siesta. (He'd been almost right.) He sat
there, thinking of taking a chance and going with them, knowing he must not do it, not only for the sake of his tired, trip-
hammer heart, but because he'd be short of breath, wheezing,
perspiring, his legs rubbery, looking like an old man with a
ridiculous bandage on his forehead to remind everyone of his
ridiculous accident, while Clay Patton bounded effortlessly up
the grade, probably singing with all that extra breath he'd have,
or making his hilariously unfunny comments. As he sat there,
thinking, his hand closed involuntarily on the yellow flower near
his plate, and tremblingly began to tear the petals loose so that
there was a little golden shower of light yellow dust on the
tablecloth and the cool wet of the wrinkled, torn petals on his
fingers.

"No, no," Annie said, staring at the flower with a horror that
astonished him. "You're destroying it. That lovely flower! Look
what you're doing, Andrew!" and he looked and saw his old pulpy
fingers smeared with the flower's yellow, stained and shaking. He
took his hand away. Annie began to cry. She got up from the table
and hurried from the room, her negligee clouding around her
slim running legs.

He felt a monster, cruel, an absent-minded murderer. He

hadn't known he was doing it. But it was only a flower . . . there were others; it was nothing to get hysterical about. He supposed that to her the act had had some significance and that he must try to understand . . . she acted as though he had committed murder. He had been thinking, concentrating so hard on Clay Patton, on getting her away with him for a day, and feeling so wearily disappointed to learn that she was committed to a program which excluded him, that his hand had struck out on its own, living its own destructive life. He stood up, frowning, shoved his hands out of sight in his pockets and, even while he said to himself sternly, no sense encouraging Annie in this kind of adolescent behavior, he walked with his guilty hands hidden, into the bedroom where she lay, not sobbing now, but rigid and blank-eyed on the bed.

He explained, and apologized and was tender with her and pampered her and won her over to him again. And even as he kissed her forehead lightly, and felt the silken brush of her lashes against his cheek, he was counting the beatings of his heart, observing the new rhythm they were developing, so that every few strokes the whole heart seemed to lift and grate against his chest wall as it dropped down again more heavily against his stomach. Finally, he permitted himself to lie beside her on the bed, but not flat, not without pillows pushed up under his head, and she jumped up and said with what must have been false gaiety that she must rush and dress, and he told her to go ahead and he lay there watching her lay out her clothing, while his heart lunged and grated within him.

"Who's going?" he asked her.

"Oh—some people," she said. "That new couple from Ohio who are staying at the Posada, and the German artist." There was a pause. He listened to it. "And Clay, I think."

The next morning after he was dressed, he stood at the foot of the bed and looked for some time at Annie's sleeping, dimpled face and the shining nimbus of her hair. Then he came out into the dining room and seated himself and rang the little bell and waited for the maid to bring him his coffee and orange juice.

Last night after her long visit with Clay, he had heard her come to bed finally, watched her as she stood at the window breathing in the flower-scented, moonlit air, and he thought he saw a new arch to her body, heard, as she came to bed, a new lightness in her step, sensed an excitement in her. He had pinched his eyes shut tight until sleep had mercifully blacked him out. But now he knew something must be done.

He looked at his hands folded on the table before him in the quiescent posture of age. Even if by some miracle she had not yet fallen in love with Clay Patton, the picture of his face and the sound of his voice now existed within her and whenever he placed his old hand upon her in a husbandly way, her wayward imagination could summon the image, the perfect face and lean young body of Arrow Collars.

When Annie strolled into the dining room, stretching like a kitten so that her firm breasts rose under the peach silk negligee, he stood up and bowed to her with the formality he habitually used to hide his passion. She came to him and kissed his cheek sweetly and he waited for her to sit down before he spoke. He had decided to use surprise.

"I want," he said levelly, looking straight into her green eyes across the table from him, "to leave here."

She yawned. "All right," she said placidly. She rang the bell for the maid. "When?"

"Tomorrow," he said, watching.

"The day after," she said with no evidence of dismay. "I promised everybody a big party tonight. The *mariachis* are hired to come and sing and I've ordered the liquor and Deetsy is bringing her marvelous hot chicken salad. I just know I can't be ready to go in the morning after that. And we really do owe these people a party—they've all been so nice." She tilted her head a little to one side and looked at him like a little girl asking for a present. "Day after?"

"All right," he said gruffly, amazed that she bothered to wheedle, asking himself didn't she know he'd have to stay here forever if that was what she wanted? asking himself how could she possibly be so calm about leaving the day after tomorrow if she were interested in Arrow Collars? asking himself if it could be that she was capable of a duplicity he could not even imagine?

It was after twelve o'clock. The *mariachis* were stationed in the patio, their wide sombreros stark white against the bougainvillaea, their bright red jackets like larger flowers blooming along the curving white wall. They sang what seemed to the admiral to be a series of identical songs, and he wondered wearily through his headache why, since every song was the same, they had not learned to sing it on key. But the guests clapped tirelessly and Nicolás, the fat one who played the guitar, and Jesús, who played the trumpet, smiled around during each cannonade of applause with huge, immodest satisfaction.

An American named Harry, one of Charles' clique of ex-servicemen—a big fellow with a broad face and lank blond hair—had brought his clarinet, and from time to time he played it, standing beside the *mariachis* and joining in with them, but with his back to the guests, sending the music like a ball to bounce against the curving white wall. The admiral listened attentively to Harry's music and found it melancholy and spiritless, and when the guests clapped hard after one of Harry's solos, he felt as though somebody had told a joke he hadn't understood.

Through the filter of the music he heard Deetsy talking. Her voice had a nasal twang which had become more pronounced with each drink. The combination of the twang and the lurid Southern accent made her speech oddly compelling. It seemed to penetrate the very walls. ". . . but he coulda washed," she was saying. "Mah gawd, ah tol' Challs, ah said, 'Now damn Sukey, you make that Harry *wash*, heah? Ah doan cayah how good he plays that theah stick, he shouldn't come ta Annie's pahty smellin' lak a goat. . . .' "

He looked at the lacquered hair and full face, once pretty with its cupid-bow mouth and handsome black eyes, now showing fifty years of hard drinking and marrying and spending her Daddy's tobacco fortune. Her tongue, long and pink, flicked from her wet lips.

"Wheah *is* Annie?" she said and her voice narrowed to a sharp whisper. "And *wheah's* that pretty Clay-boy? Ain't he the cutest thing you evah saw?"

He walked deliberately away from the sound of her and into the bar. He looked around at the faces there and it seemed to him that the faces regarded him expectantly, even while they talked to each other. He did not know what it was the faces expected of him. He adjusted the bandage on his forehead—it was little more now than a big Band-Aid—and looked everywhere in the bar for Annie, but she was not there. He took a glass and strolled, with careful indifference, toward the living room. He paused in the doorway and looked at the group of women seated in a row on the long couch. Annie was not among them.

"Get me a drink, son," Victoria called out to him and then, before he could move toward her, abruptly got up and stumped over to the door. "No," she said to him when she reached him, "I'll get it myself." He looked at her, thinking in a puzzled way that she had rather peculiar clothes on, so the blouse didn't seem quite right with the skirt. Her braids were black and shining and she was wearing lipstick and she looked handsomer than he'd ever seen her look and he supposed with some really nice clothes on, she'd look pretty good. But she was stamping around in an irritating, unfeminine way and she brushed past him as though he were a footman . . . with one difference, he reminded himself. She'd called him "son." That was like Hazel.

He searched, walking slowly and deliberately, through the entire house. Annie was not there and Arrow Collars was not there.

He went back into the bar and stood with one foot on the rail and drank straight rum and thought about Annie and the fact that Annie was not there.

It seemed to take only a minute or two, the drinking that he did, and he would have said he'd had only about a full tumbler of rum in all, when he heard himself suddenly cry out drunkenly into the lull between the *mariachis*' songs, "Where's Annie?"

They all looked at him and his voice kept echoing in his ears saying that, and it was all he could do not to say, I take it back, don't listen to me, I didn't mean it. Victoria stared intently into his face for a second and then turned around again quickly and continued talking to Charles. Charles glanced over at the admiral and shook his head slightly. The admiral watched the two of them with heightened perception. He was not, mystically, surprised when Victoria set her drink down on the bar and walked away from Charles and came toward him.

She said, "Come along and dance with me, sailor."

He laughed at that. Something about the way she said it, with a tough little jerk of her head, like a dime-a-dance girl. He went with her, thinking that she was more and more like Hazel, and he wished to God Hazel hadn't died, and wished that an American orchestra would suddenly be there playing "I'll See You in My Dreams" and he could dance with this little woman and remember Hazel.

Victoria led him onto the tiled floor of the *corredor* and took hold of him and began energetically to dance, sawing her elbows up and down and sliding her feet around on the floor. He swung her in a pirouette and the world kept revolving around him when he stopped and he warned himself not to try that again. He clung to her and tried not to step on her feet. Once his shoe scraped her instep and he heard her suck in a quick whistling breath but when he apologized she smiled up at him warmly and pressed his hand and he realized with astonishment that she was not cross with him.

When the music stopped, she moved back from him and clapped her hands. He looked around again in the moving confusion of people and from his mouth again came, unbidden and very loud, the cry, "Where's Annie?"

Victoria reached out and gripped the shoulder of a girl who was passing them and the girl stopped and wriggled the hand from her shoulder and put her hands on her narrow hips and eyed Victoria defensively.

"Well?" the girl said.

"Alma," Victoria said, smiling, "you must dance with the admiral. He's wonderful. So . . . so artless, you know."

Alma looked up into the admiral's seamed, unhappy face.

"Dance with him," Victoria said.

The girl twitched her head around, tossing the coarse black mane of her hair, and looked at Victoria.

Victoria's eys were fixed upon her, hypnotically.

"I'm really not very good," the admiral said, but the music started, Alma moved close to him and then he was dancing.

2

Victoria

VICTORIA pushed through the crush of people blocking the way to the bar. She was looking for Charles. She strained up on her toes and angled her body first one way and then the other, trying to spot him. He was very tall and, unless he were sitting down, she should be able to see him. She couldn't imagine his sitting down in this press of people and enduring the noise of so many raised babbling voices, but he might. The volume of sound in the room had moved up decibel by decibel, drink by drink.

Through the din she heard somebody calling her name persistently and she listened to the voice long enough to be sure it wasn't the admiral. Since it wasn't, she ignored it, looking past

the comic-tragic drunken faces around her, looking instead at
a series of images of the admiral, which flashed through her
memory. There he was, looking surprised the day she had snapped at him to get out of her way . . . surprised, not with the
small-boy-hurt look of so many American men, but with the real
male look of gentleness affronted by a rude woman. And here
was the dignity with which he somehow met her viciousness
the day he had mistakenly interrupted her to say a civil good
morning. That was memorable.

All right. Find Charles. Save the admiral.

She pushed, jabbing with her elbows, through the bodies,
ignoring the possibility of inflicting lasting injury—who mattered? who the hell mattered now?—the way she had once
pushed and jabbed in the subways of New York, grateful that,
like swimming, it was a technique which, once learned, was
never forgotten. She got out to the roofed-in section of the patio.
The night air was sweeter here, and, because the *mariachis* had
stopped their moronic music for a minute, quieter. She wondered if Charles could hear her if she shouted his name, but just
when she decided that was a good idea, there was a loud hand-
clapping to encourage the *mariachis* to play more. She glared
around at everybody but nonetheless the music began again.
Jesús, the trumpeter, was not a hopelessly bad carpenter and his
two little boys were nice, and it might be a good, kind thing to
go tell him to settle for that and give up trying to be a musician;
after all it could only be a favor in the long run since he played
so badly. Nicolás too, the fat one who plucked at the guitar and
—great God Almighty!—sang, was a bricklayer and good to his
mother and she could warn him, too. One day somebody would
surely get a mob together and stone them out of town.

But the potential mob listened now in drunken approval to
the dreadful cacophony, for it was a party and one had to have
music at a party. Suppose instead there was a silence? Suppose
silence crept through a crack in the wall, like a great gray rat,
and sat there frightening everybody? The gray rat of silence at
the feast?

That was a good metaphor . . . and that was the trouble
with the way her mind worked, writing everything that happened as it happened, and then going sterile when she was at
the typewriter.

That was where she should be right now, at the typewriter,

not meddling in the admiral's life, not running around looking
for Charles. She shouldn't have come here at all.

In the beginning when Annie first sent her the invitation,
she'd written simply in reply, "I'm not coming." That was all she
had to do. Everybody knew that when she was working, holed up
in her house, she did not accept invitations. She was a good
third of the way along in the rewrite of the novel . . . the come-
back novel, the one that would halt the tides, make the rivers
run uphill, absolve her from guilt and shame and turn her from
the stony paths of self-betrayal, make the world run right, the
stars reverse their courses, and give life back to her again. She
lived behind her locked doors like a medieval maniac. Every
day she got up from the rope springs and sagging mattress of
her bed, bathed, drank scalding coffee, bitter and black to sting
her awake, walked alone and in silence along the lake shore,
with plugs in her ears, wooing the creative spirit, evoking her
timid self-confidence. Some mornings she awakened anxiously
with her hair soaking wet with perspiration, as though the wet
sponge of melancholy had been pressed into her face the whole
night, with her eyes gritty still from crying in her sleep, sick with
the fear that came in shuddering cramps through her body and
brightly lighted her mind with despair. She forced herself up,
dragged to the typewriter, driving her blurred, gray, hopeless,
despicable self to the typewriter, focusing her feeble strength
onto the story, into the people and the world which must be
made to exist on these pages, if she was to exist in any world at
all.

There had been a few times of victory and exaltation, the
long-missing sense of the divine to pit against the times of despair. She had, fortified by these few instances, resisted all the
familiar demons—sex, alcohol, hunger and physical gratifica-
tions of all kinds, not letting herself sink down into the velvet
memories of past successes or, most dangerous of all, drift onto
the eerie reefs of withdrawal where fantasy became reality and
reality fell downstairs and disappeared.

Then the temptation about the party began. The writing
was suddenly blocked and through the vacuum of these days
came the excited talk about the party, voices discussing what
would be worn and who was taking whom, as though she cared,
for the love of Christ! Of no use now the shuttered windows, the
plugs in her ears; she heard the voices and abruptly there came

the old treacherous sense that, outside her thick walls, Life strolled irremediably past and if she did not now, this minute, run and follow it, she would emerge too late upon an empty street, clutching her tattered, still imperfect pages, to find herself the only living thing in a world long dead.

She began to feel choked, to suffocate. She leapt up from the typewriter, not looking back at it once in the moments that followed, and scurried to her closet to find something acceptable to wear, muttering, "Just for one drink . . . just for a few minutes . . . just to pay my respects to pretty Annie . . . then back to work, refreshed . . ."

Remembering this now, in its full absurdity, she felt her neck stain with hot shame. There was an abandoned glass on a table and she went over to it. She picked it up and drained it. It was *aguardiente* and she had been drinking martinis, but no matter. It burned her throat. But she deserved it; she was a ridiculous woman. It was not nice to know you were a ridiculous woman. For that was not Life which she thought strolled past her window, playing his seductive pipes . . . that was Death.

She thought she heard Charles laugh, and she peered about her. Deetsy's voice, threaded with a heavy innuendo, needled in and out of the talk on the patio. Her nostrils twitched as though she smelled something unpleasant, and so she did. She did not permit herself to hate Deetsy. That was too good for Deetsy, raised her to false estate, *honored* her, in fact. She was nothing more than a cheap ten-cent-store edition of Scarlett O'Hara. No, that didn't really say it . . . She was nothing more than a cheap second-rate ruin of an imitation Scarlett O'Hara —yes—who lacked the wit to know that the book ended before Scarlett approached the hanging wattles, blue-veined legs and slack-eyed bloat of ugly age.

She hurried around a large group of Mexican men standing together, watching the *gringos* at play, and spotted Charles slouching along the far wall of the patio toward the steps. She ran to him quickly and caught at his white shirtsleeve.

He looked around at her.

"About the admiral," she said. She could not hear herself against the noise of the party, but she could see that Charles heard her and she pleaded urgently with him, telling him what to do, and as he listened to her, he turned his head and looked off in sleepy disinterest at the blue night sky.

"You lushed, Vickie?" Charles said.

"It doesn't matter," she told him, speaking more loudly. "I'm telling you that a man is in torment. *Torment*, do you un-derstand?" Looking up into his averted face she saw no under-standing. Her hand twisted desperately on his sleeve, pulling on it in a way she supposed was hateful, but hateful was better than ineffectual. "Torment is a *simplicity*. One can ignore a *com-plexity*. One cannot ignore a *simplicity*. I ask you to think of tor-ment and remember how it feels. You remember how torment feels, don't you, Charles? You remember torment?"

"I remember Mama," he said, laughing.

"Boy . . . listen to me." She took a breath and ignored the way he was trying to get out of her grasp. "You must help the admiral. He is a good man. There are not many good men, did you know that? Not many kind, good men. You must find Annie for him and bring her back here. After all that he has endured in this village . . . the cruel loss of dignity . . ." She felt the tears coursing down her cheeks (. . . ask not for whom I cry, I cry for me . . .). "Ah, the poor man! The miserable wretch! The tor-ment in his eyes! How could you not lift your hand?"

He said coolly, "It's got nothing to do with me, Vickie. Or you either."

"It has, it has!" she cried. "It's my torment and yours. Do it for me . . . do it for yourself." She saw that he was about to walk away from her. She gave his sleeve a wrench and forced him to look at her. He was annoyed. "*I* ask you, Charles. Will you refuse me?"

"Jesus," he said. He reached down and got hold of her hand. "Will you let go of my sleeve?" She did. The annoyance faded out of his eyes and the cynical indifference came back. He gave a little laugh and said, placatingly, "I'll brace Harry . . . see what he says . . ."

He strode off. Harry! He probably had no intention of men-tioning it to Harry. He was just getting rid of her. She tightened her hold on her shoulder purse and followed after him. He took big strides with his long legs and she had to take three or four to his one. Hurrying after him, she saw a man's foot in her way, one of the dancers doing a fancy twirl. Hating him and his foot and everything that stood in her way, she kicked the foot aside. She heard as from a distance his outraged complaint, and con-tinued on her way.

She was almost up to Charles. It was dreadful having to

rely on him. But who else was there? To whom could she turn?
At least Charles listened to her, even if then all he did was con-
sult with his gang boss. What was the matter with these boys
. . . these hipsters or whatever they called themselves, who
lived in a world where they were absolutely incapable of individual action, so that they were endlessly consulting each other?
What made any one of them think that the other might be
wise? Only if, in their strange and constant discipline, the others elected to act, would one of them act. They were like guerrilla
fighters drawing straws to see who'd assassinate somebody, forming a kind of cell, with Harry usually at the motionless center,
and the rest of them like arms and legs put forth from the
parent body, achieving whatever small thing they had agreed to
achieve. But was there a war on? Were they at war? Who was
the enemy? Who the ally? Was it the army which had, with its
mass, divisional thinking, done this to them? The regimenta-
tion of schools? No, no. Gangdom? Juvenile gangdom? They
were always too frightened to do anything, think anything. They
were strait-jacketed in their incomprehensible code of what
was hip and what was square, like children playing criminals
. . . They acted like prisoners, talking with their lips motionless
as though they were in a prison yard . . . but what was their
crime? Who convicted them, sentenced them? Who was the
warden, who were the jailers?

She slipped on the stairs, and damned them all in a groaning voice, reminding herself that the admiral had to be saved at
any cost . . . and wasn't this worse in a way than the day
she'd seen his *canoa* sink and had to run to the Posada and alert
the stupid Mexicans and persuade the idiot who ran the Posada
to put the boat out? Yes, because there she had had only stupidity
to deal with . . . it was said that the idiot who owned the
Posada was an embezzler from the States, a fugitive, but she
had never believed it. He hadn't the intelligence to have stolen
money and made it across the border . . . (She could see him
now, picking up the wrong suitcase, the one with the bricks in it,
and rushing headlong to Juárez and getting stopped by a
machine-gun barricade at customs . . .)

Charles looked around and saw her. He smiled, patiently,
and waited for her to catch up with him. Stupidity was one thing
but perhaps fear was worse, and Charles and the whole lot of
these boys were fear-ridden, as immobilized by fear as though

they were bedridden with disease. Ah, poor things, poor young things . . . not that all they had to fear was fear itself, a statement she had always thought to enclose only a terrifying half-truth . . . but that along with whatever else they feared—reality, life, their anonymous enemy, themselves, each other, Time, Death, the warden, incipient homosexuality, or a middle age and old age of attrition—they also had fear itself to fear.

But this was a time of half-truths, half-lies, wasn't it? Of sloganized, philosophical premises, of shadowy, one-dimensional thinking, which left out the heart, forgot the emotions, ignored the hungers of the mind . . .

Harry was hunched over the clarinet with his back to the party—typical . . . it would delight a newly diplomaed psychologist, this spectacle of antisocial withdrawal—playing into the curving ear of the white wall. While she waited, Charles came close to him, suddenly uncertain, standing back, as though afraid of the moment when Harry must be interrupted. Harry was like a wild beast which had killed something, pulled it into his lair and now picked over it, insatiably hungry, but moaning with grief at what he'd done . . . That's stupid. There's no guilt and no grief and animals don't mourn. Charles hesitated, but he moved into Harry's range of vision and then stood still. Harry saw the lower half of him but did not look up, and Charles put a gentle hand on Harry's shoulder. Harry pulled the clarinet from his mouth and swung quickly around. His broad face was smooth, but he said in a low voice, "You got a hand like a cop, man." He wiped his mouthpiece on the sleeve of his big dirty jacket. When he moved, it was possible to smell him. He was unwashed and there was a stale, rank odor of tequila coming from him. He looked from Charles to Victoria. "Hey, Vickie," he said. "Whatcha say?"

Victoria pointed to Charles.

Charles said, in his stiff-lipped, prison-yard diction, "Vickie wants me to go find the brass's broad. She says the brass is flipping because his broad ain't here. She cut out with Clay. You think we ought to get his broad back for him?"

Harry stared at him incredulously. "What's come *over* you, man?" he said.

Victoria stepped nearer. The guitar was close to her ear and she raised her voice over it so that she was almost shouting. "Please, Harry," she said. "Please. Say yes." She closed her eyes, ran around the empty corners of her mind, trying to find the words which would reach Harry, make him see. "The admiral can't stand it. He's gotten old and sick since he almost drowned. He's like glass. He's ready to shatter. He can't endure it if Annie's doing this to him . . . Be Christlike, Harry . . . save him. He's as close to death as he was in the lake . . ."

Harry leaned against the wall and yawned. He did not look at Victoria. He looked at Charles. He said calmly, "I don't care whose chick balls what stud," he said. "*You* care, man?"

Charles shook his head.

"We don't care, Vickie," Harry said. He lifted his clarinet, ready to blow some more.

Victoria reached up and grabbed him by the shoulders and turned him around. "Look down there," she told him. "Look at his *face!*"

"I've grown accustomed to his face," Harry said. He stared obediently at the admiral revolving slowly past with Alma. "Yeah," Harry said. "The brass is suffering. His face is a mask of drunken suffering. Suffering is an ennobling experience . . . Did you ever read the *Confessions* of Saint Augustine?" He stood straighter in his baggy clothes. "I got no use for the brass," he said sadly. He bowed to Victoria slightly and lifted his clarinet again. He smiled derisively. "Right now I got to blow. I'll blow something sad for the brass . . ." He turned his back to her and began to play, a haunting, lilting phrase of defeat.

She reached toward him, not caring now if she made him mad, but Charles caught her hand and pulled it back.

"Don't bug him," he said softly.

"But Charles . . ."

"Don't . . . bug him." He drew her away from Harry, holding her by the hand. He was singing softly under his breath, the tune Harry was playing, which wasn't part of what Jesús and Nicolás were playing but fitted in with it, turning his head from side to side in rhythm, with his eyes almost closed.

Victoria stood still, biting her lips in frustration. Now what? Now what? She jerked at his sleeve.

Charles eyed her with exasperation. "You're real juiced up, Vick," he said. "Can't you see how gone Harry is?"

She shook her head. "Oh what shall I do?" she said.

Charles sighed. He said, "We'll talk to Jim."

She thought, Oh my God, I've got to go through it again, and she said, "Jim isn't here. *You* do it, Charles? Just go find Annie . . . Bring her back here . . ."

"Jim's here," Charles said.

She saw that he hadn't even admitted to his group-minded consciousness her suggestion that he do it alone.

He led her toward the *corral*. As they passed through the squeaking wooden gate, she could smell the marijuana smoke. She looked toward the back of the walled-in land and she could see the lighted cigarette passing from hand to hand, moving like a slow firefly in the deep darkness under the mango tree.

Charles called out, "Don't kill the roach . . . we ain't The Man," and somebody laughed in the darkness. She watched where she walked because this was a field where animals had been kept, thinking that she never knew what it was these boys were saying to each other in their peculiar language, never, and she didn't really want to know. She had no connection with them and they had none with her and in any other place in the world she wouldn't know them.

She could see better now as they drew closer and she saw Jim's almost handsome face turned toward them, and she thought that he had never been handsome really, but he always looked as though he might have gone through a handsome phase, the way some young girls do who suffer from an early blooming and then wash out and look like memories of themselves the rest of their lives. But perhaps Jim had never been handsome and never would be, and it couldn't matter anyway because who was going to look at him and care? Life was not a beauty contest, and he'd been buried in Mexico for three years, not buried really, but bottled for three years, like an almost handsome foetus in a jar of alcohol. It was not likely that he'd ever get out, ever live, ever walk again on the streets of the world.

Charles took the cigarette when Jim handed it to him, and dragged on it and talked without letting the smoke out of his lungs, so that he sounded like a man in extremis, or like one who'd had a larynx operation and learned to talk with his throat. She was getting more and more nervous, standing there, with the little night breeze tugging at her hair and wisping it about her forehead, and her eyes growing large so that she could feel them stretching back her stiff eyelids, with her lips taut and ready for speech, no, not speech, a scream . . . He was talking about using the London *Times Literary Supplement* paper to make their cigarettes out of, saying in that sepulchral, operated-on voice that it was tissuey and thinner and finer for rolling the pot than this thick stuff.

"Please, Charles," she said. Her voice shook.

He had forgotten that she was there. Now he turned his head after a second or two and looked at her and, slowly, the others looked at her, too.

"You gonna turn Vickie on?" somebody said in a sly voice, and there was a little laugh in the group.

Charles looked at her and raised his eyebrows, questioningly. He was very slowed down now, even his breathing was slow.

"No," she said impatiently, "I don't want it." It sounded harsh and she sensed how the others stiffened. Of course this was not the way to get them to do what she wanted. They were very easily offended; she had noticed that before. She made herself laugh a little and look around with as charming a smile as she could manage. "I don't need it, really," she explained. "You know . . . I am self-propelled . . ."

The interest in her subsided, shifted away, and somebody said conclusively, wistfully, "She'd make a great head." This was one of the things they did, ignoring her, really forgetting that she was there, discussing her as though she'd just walked away from them.

Charles said, "Harry said nobody should turn her on until he's there, anyway. He wants to dig it."

There was a silence then and the cigarette went on to somebody else. She said, throwing her voice like a rope into the silence, "Charles, about the admiral. You promised . . ."

Charles said, "Sure, sweetie." He moved closer to Jim and explained. Jim listened impassively, only turning and looking at Charles the way Harry had done, as though he couldn't believe Charles cared about the admiral.

"Lush him up," Jim said. "He won't know what's happening."

"No," Victoria said. "He's drunk now, but he keeps shouting about Annie. Oh, don't you see?"

Jim cut in. "What does Harry say?"

Charles slowly moved his head from side to side. "Harry's stoned."

Jim said, "Well, you know, I like to watch. But I don't want to mix in . . ." His speech was thick, coming from a dry throat. "Who's the square Annie's cut with?"

"Clay Patton."

Jim thought about that, staring at the ground, his lips moving in an infantile way. "I put that mother down the most," Jim said with sudden emphasis. "You?"

"You know it, man," Charles said.

Victoria realized they had come to some sort of decision. They were going to help her. The three of them came back to the party together and they told her to go stand near the *mariachis* and watch the front door. Charles and Jim drifted through the press of people—louder and drunker now—and along the *zaguán* out onto the street.

Victoria stood near the *mariachis*, staring at the ground. She felt hopeless, caught in a wash of melancholy, helpless. She leaned against the wall and the party sounds racketed around her. "I hate everybody," she said in a whisper. "I hate them all."

Then the music stopped and Harry passed her on his way out to the *corral*. He said, "City Mother. Little City Mother. The admiral's little City Mother. Why do you act like advice to the lovelorn, chickie, when you've really got a heart as big as a peanut?" He began to sing breathily, with his eyebrows raised and his eyes mocking her. "Oh that little City Mother Machree . . ."

She laughed, in almost a spasm of laughter because, although he was making fun of her, there was something comic in the baggy burlesque look of him. His question was a question she could not answer. But even laughing, she was thinking that Harry was despicable; there was something mean about him; he was a destroyer . . . she didn't like him. Probably, if she thought about him, she hated him, but she didn't know yet. She looked at him with her eyes still half shut with laughter, thinking, do I hate you? Would I hate you if I had time to think about you? And then the admiral's voice came to her like the far bellow of a buffalo, demanding, "Where's my girl? Where's Annie?"

"Oh my God," she said, abruptly not laughing, and pushed past Harry and went looking for him.

For a moment Victoria hesitated at the bedroom door. She had not seen Annie yet. Jim and Charles had brought her back and escorted her to the bedroom, pushed her in and shut the door. Then they strolled to the bar, like two hoods, one on either side of handsome Clay Patton. Clay was pale and he kept shrugging the collar of his white linen jacket high on his neck and looking nervously from one to the other of them. She did not know what had happened, nor where Jim and Charles had found them, only that they had brought them back.

She pushed the door open and saw Annie seated on the bench in front of the dressing table, with her arms folded on the table and her head on her arms. Victoria stepped in and closed the door softly behind her. She came toward the girl, who did not lift her head and whose face was hidden by the shining shower of soft brown hair. Victoria saw herself in the mirror and saw with a little shock how really frightful she looked in her shabby dress, with her unhappy face.

She stood behind the girl, erectly, waiting, like a governess. The girl kept crying, making sounds that were desperate and distressing. Victoria tapped her shoulder. Annie turned her head and looked up at Victoria, her beautiful eyes lighter green through tears, her skin pale, blanched of life. Victoria picked up the handkerchief from the dresser and put it into Annie's hand. Annie lifted it to her eyes. She sat motionless, staring at nothing.

"Lipstick," Victoria said and put it into Annie's hand. Annie looked at it vaguely. "Use it," Victoria said sharply. "Put it on your mouth."

Shakily Annie shaped her upper lip with it. Their eyes met in the tin-framed mirror. "So you know all about it, too," Annie said in a choked voice. "The whole town knows it, I suppose. Did they tell you? Did they come back and tell it all over the house? Did they tell *him*?"

Victoria watched as Annie colored her lower lip, then glanced up at herself in the mirror. She not only looked like a governess, she felt like one . . . standing over the girl, telling her what to do. But, when you were this young and you let emotion run away with you like this, when you just said whatever you thought and when you thought such young things, you turned other people into governesses. You maneuvered them into playing the part opposite your part. We're all playwrights . . . only some of us have no talent . . .

Annie blotted her lips with a tissue, spoke through the paper bitterly. "Those two . . . crumbs," she said. "Those dirty crumbs."

Victoria heard herself sigh. Was she going to have to go every slow-footed, laborious step of the way with this girl, while she worked it out that really she was not a crumb but Charles and Jim were crumbs instead, because they had caught her doing what she was doing, whatever the hell it was?

Annie looked at the other mouth on the tissue as she took it away from her lips. "What a filthy place this is! What a filthy little town . . ."

Trying to sound amiable, Victoria said, "My dear, you're very pretty." But then when she looked at the mirror to see how that speech affected Annie, she saw herself instead, the dark smudgings life had thumbed in under her eyes, the line of melancholy between her brows, the eyes themselves, large and strained . . . and there came, like cards falling, a memory of many mirrors and many times when she had looked at herself, evaluating like this, with abrupt clarity of vision, and each time it happened, each time she looked, it was worse and there was no stopping the relentless march of Death, and of course Death had already subtly marked her for his own, here with this shadow, there with that gauntness under the cheekbones. She looked away from the mirror and drew herself up. Hers was a perfect face to have said my-dear-you're-very-pretty.

She put forth a hand and struck an attitude of prophecy. Oh, she knew what to do and how to hold the attention of a wandering, shocked intelligence like Annie's! "I understand you," she said, speaking hollowly and slowly. "I also understand the importance of timing. Do you know what timing means? It is the essence of successful living. It is one of the simplicities." She let her hand drop and her voice dropped with it. She picked up the compact of rouge and handed it to Annie. "You need color," she said. Annie stared at it unmoving. She nudged her impatiently. "Put it *on!*" she said, hating having to hover around with psychological aspirin for an immature personality which would always be less than her own. To what are we reduced by the exigencies of our lives? Hadn't the admiral been reduced by this less than heroic girl to less than heroic behavior, but with an embittered, paralyzing self-knowledge? "Listen," Victoria said, "if the admiral had not sunk that ridiculous boat on that ridiculous lake so that he had to be dredged up out of it practically dead, he would not be without dignity with which to meet this moment . . . this, I might say, looking at the flaccid lines of

your lips, the weakness in your eyes, the loosening of the flesh of
your face . . . *inevitable* moment." She fixed a look upon the
girl, meant to be wise and portentous. "This is what I mean by
timing. T-i-m-i-n-g. If the episode of the lake had not happened, if that destruction to his personality had not just taken
place . . . But it did. He almost drowned. He looked at Death
the other day. It just happened. That's timing."

Annie closed her eyes and tears shone in her lashes. "But
you see," she said, whispering, "I didn't know. I thought I loved
him. I didn't know. This *happened* to me. I didn't mean it to happen. . . ." She choked and grabbed the handkerchief and dabbed
at her eyes. "He's . . . so old," she said.

Victoria drew back, shaking her head. "Please," she said.
"No confidences. No confession-story confidences. I cannot
stand that."

Annie sobbed in a strangled way.

"I do not know what happened. I do not know whether you
were caught in . . . *flagrante delicto,* or whether you and the
false young man were exchanging the maiden kiss of your inevitable affair, and I do not care. Nor do I care whether you
now believe you do not love your husband, and you do love this
other fool, or anything. I do not want to know. I do not, you see,
care at all about you. Therefore, no confidences." She reached
up with both hands and smoothed her braids. "I do not stand
against nature," she said. "What is natural happens. This too
is a simplicity. It will happen again. Can you hear me?" She bent
over and pulled back the girl's hair so that she could see her suffering face. "All I am saying to you, my dear, is . . . wait. You
have time. He has . . . almost no time. He went out upon that
lake a man and he came back . . . something quite different.
He is a hero, you know, a hero. You are nothing and Clay Patton is nothing. I beg you, for the admiral's life. Let him live a
little longer. . . ."

The door burst open and she straightened up and looked in
the mirror and saw the admiral standing in the frame of the open
door, his blue eyes bright in his face. "*There* she is!" he cried delightedly as though surrounded by a host of people who had
doubted that she would be there, ever again. "There's my
Annie-girl!" he said.

He staggered a little coming toward them, but then he held
himself more carefully and he got across the room and got his

arms around Annie and cradled her against him, rocking her a
little. "Knew you were here," he said, rocking her, "knew it all
the time. Knew you weren't gone. Asked everybody. 'Where's Annie?' I said." He kissed her forehead and Annie did not move out
of his arms although she sat very still and her tears spilled on
the sleeve of his coat. "Looked for you," he said. "Everywhere."
He waved his arms to include the universe, and the joy twisted
and fell abruptly out of his voice. "Where were you all that time,
Annie?"

"Next door," Annie said huskily, in tones of truth. "Lying
. . . down."

He patted her hand. "Aw there," he said. "My girl was all
tired out trying to give this big party and everything . . ."

Victoria adjusted her shoulder bag and turned toward the
door.

"Hey," the admiral said to her, and she did not answer him,
but she stood still for a moment. "Annie, did you know this little
lady was the one saved my life?"

"Yes," Annie said, looking at Victoria.

"I owe her a lot," he said. He smiled, a warm, gentle smile,
drunk but loving. "She even . . . liked my dancing," he said.

Victoria turned and marched out of the room and closed the
door behind her. She stood in the *zaguán* staring down at the big
green leaves of the plant bordering the wall, and fished a torn
wisp of Kleenex out of her pocket and wiped her mouth with it
very hard.

When she looked up, she saw Charles leaning against a
corner of the wall, watching her. He smiled. She went to him.

"Buy me a drink, son," she said. "One for the road."

He straightened up and they walked together into the bar.
The noisy wave of the party broke over them and as they walked
she fished the plugs out of her purse and stuffed them into her ears.

It was not yet light, but the baby next door was crying, as it
did every day, as though to summon the dawn. Few Mexican babies cried, and fewer were left to cry, but the one next door was
an exception. Victoria pressed the pillow tightly against her ears
to shut out the sound, but it was no use. She let go of the pillow
and lay with it over her face. The woman next door called in a
voice hoarse with sleep, *"Calle te!"* and then her huaraches
scraped across the brick flooring to the kitchen and she began

slapping the tortillas into shape. The radio, which must lean against the echoing adobe wall—adobe was a marvelous amplifier of sound; it should be used in hi-fi sets in the States—burst into life, shouting about *Cocomalt, Cocomalt, instantáneo bueno* . . . Ugh. She stared, agonized, into the pillow; the hangover twisted in the middle of her forehead, like a spike. A man in the street called, "Huh, burro!" like a matador; there was the crack of a stick against the burro's hide, and a staccato spattering of burro hoofbeats. . . . The Mexican day was begun.

What did she drink last night? But she'd gone home . . . put her plugs in her ears and gone home . . . No. "One for the road," she'd said to Charles and then . . . but it had only been a short time, hadn't it? A drink or two, at most? No, there was a long talk with Clay Patton, sitting on the low brick wall of the patio, thinking in the beginning that he was a villain but then deciding he was really enchanting and being pleased with him . . . charming. Wasn't he charming? No, later he got to be a bore. An ordinarily silent man, who should remain silent and look profound. He had a one-dimensional personality, busy with its good looks, pleased with itself, like a girl on a television commercial. Then, all of a sudden Deetsy, who had gotten very drunk and very loud, gave a great scream of laughter—or was it the Rebel yell?—and fell over backward, chair and all, in a flurry of lace and tulle petticoats . . . and that was a good excuse to get away from Clay Patton and his logorrhea . . . but not to go home. No.

She pushed the pillow aside and got up. A ranchero song on the radio, complete with wolf calls, filled the room. Damn the tone-deaf Mexicans! It would be bad enough if the radio were tuned on-station. She scratched at her head furiously. Their radios were their secret weapons, deadlier than amoebic dysentery. It was growing light. The furniture in the room seemed to move forward, taking larger shape with the coming of dawn, and a delicate pink, like the light of a boudoir lamp, flushed the white walls. In the corner on the table the typewriter loomed large. The light pointed at it, pink and directional as God's finger. . . . No, you couldn't write that. The noise pulled hard on her headache.

She made a tour of the house looking for her earplugs, found one in the bathroom and jammed it into one ear and found the other inexplicably enough in the kitchen. Once they

were both in place, the noises outside her head furred away into
an unidentifiable, undemanding blur. She came back into the living room and stood by the typing stand. The admiral and Annie
would leave the village today. She would not see them again.
Almost certainly she would not see them again. She had gotten
drunk and meddled in their lives, but now they were gone, taking
yesterday with them, damn them for that, and here she was beside some empty pages. She pulled some of the latest pages toward her and began to read them indifferently, with her head
aching, and gradually she took up all the pages, one by one, and
read them until there were no more to read.

She set the pages down—were they good? were they bad?—
and lit a cigarette, shuddering at the first harsh bite of the smoke.
They put dung in the cigarettes in this country. Her legs ached
and trembled. From standing so long? Or dancing last night . . .
capering and cavorting like a court fool? She pulled an *equipali*
close and sat on it, hunched in her nightgown . . .

Empty-minded, with a hangover, and guilt like a crown of
thorns on your head for having lived other people's lives instead
of your own, you are an emotional parasite, living in a village full
of crackpots, tosspots, madmen, cut off from the world, consort-
ing with drifters, bums, exiles without charm.

In her nightgown she went out to the well in the patio and
hauled up two buckets of water and carried them into the corner
of the garden and set them down. She pulled off her nightgown
and slung it over the low branch of the mango tree. Naked, she
stalked back into the bathroom and got a cake of soap and a
wad of abrasive straw, so harsh it was ordinarily used just to
clean pots, and came back into the yard. She took the rubber
plugs out of her ears and almost staggered under the onslaught
of sound upon her suddenly unprotected eardrums. She had forgotten just how much din was going on in the village. There was
a loud-speaker system in the Plaza, where records were played
every day and the sound relayed in all directions, all over the
village. Just now they were playing "Laura" in mambo style.
She knew, from other days, that every so often they would play
"*Las Mañanitas*," which was the Mexican birthday song, an-
nouncing first that it was being played for some idiot's birthday
at the request of her family—this was for Lupe, or Carmen, or
Jesús—and it was always the same poor record, loaded with surface noise. But they deserved it for not knowing the difference.

They thought of themselves as music lovers. But they were tone-deaf, all of them.

She poured half of the first bucket of streaming cold water over her nakedness, and gasped with the shock of it. She soaped herself and scrubbed herself all over with the punitive abrasive until her skin stung and she could see that it was mottled pink. Then she poured the rest of the first bucket of water over herself and all of the second. The water, at first soapy and then clear, sluiced around the rooty base of the mango tree. She had no towel. She stood in the sun, growing hot by now, and exercised gently to keep warm while the sun dried her. She began to feel better. She walked flat-footedly back into the nearly empty bathroom, waiting while a lizard scuttled out of her way, and took up her hairbrush and brushed her long black hair furiously, until her head felt as though it would ache its way off her neck altogether, and then she braided her hair, making the plaits pinchingly tight.

She dressed in an old drawstring blouse and a wide wool skirt and fastened a leather belt at her waist, got into her T-strap sandals with the wedge soles and went into the kitchen. The cracked tin-pan bell in the Plaza church tower was being rung. It must be noon. The morning had gone by while she read her pages.

There was a dented percolator of coffee steaming on the stove. While she had been shut unaware in the living room, the *niña*—the little girl who worked for her, who ran errands and came in and did what she was told once in a while—had come in and made the coffee. There was also a small ugly embroidered cloth folded and laid on the sink board. She opened it and found two fresh tortillas. She poured the coffee into a cup, liberally spooned some coarse gray sugar into it and stood, eating the tortillas, drinking the scalding black thick coffee and stared out the door at her nightgown hanging on the branch of the mango tree. She grinned. Looked as though there'd been a lynching, or a rape. The rape of Lucrece.

When she was a child how she had circled that line in the poem about "the nightgown muffling up around her throat." How she had considered that, like a child poking at a small crab at the seashore, sensing in the never quite complete innocence of childhood that this was a clue to some of the mysteries of life, to what perhaps happened nightly to her mother. . . . Her mother, on angry days, with her brows pulled into a sullen line over her fleshy nose, made oblique references to her father's habits and ways, no doubt thinking the child did not understand her, but nonetheless, implying something—shameful, bestial. Hysterically, she had not gone further in pursuit of the mysteries, not wanting to have anything that happened to her mother someday happen to her . . . But she hated her so, and she had always, when she looked at her mother, deliberately dissociated herself from the shabby, bulky figure which moved through a tenement kitchen in carpet slippers, wearing an old sweater pinned at the neck over a cotton wash dress . . . sagging breasts and swollen stomach and varicose veins in the legs and the lumpy feet bulging over the flattened sides of the slippers . . . Hating her, denying her with pity at the same time like a worm at the apple of her heart . . . hating her without pity when her mother laughed because, how dared she laugh when she looked like that, was like that? But there was always the fear, because this was her mother, that she might be like that herself, might contain in the very genes of her being a likeness to her mother, and so she had to get away from her mother when she was sixteen. (I'm not like that; I'm thin and young and I wear high-heeled shoes and silk stockings and lipstick on my mouth, and I walk with a swing to my young body and hold my head up, stand erect, act proud, and they're never going to think I'm like her, speaking broken English with a thick Slavic accent, laughing at old-country jokes, full of peasant fear of the world, the landlord, the high-school principal, the man who worked in the market, the census taker.)

She had to get away from her father too, because in those days she thought she hated him . . . although now she understood a little better about that sick little lustful hatred . . . and she thought she never wanted to see another slim, dark man in the world, with delicate Eastern features and a slim hand shaking, with nicotine stains deep brown on the bony fingers, and the cigarette always dancing in the small shaking hand . . . How could he stand her mother? How could he look lovingly upon her mother's neglected bulk and ugliness when, although he was nothing to be proud of with his shiny vest and baggy pants and the shirt worn without a collar, he at least had a thin body and his shirt was always clean, and he loved good music and

managed to read a newspaper now and then? How could he keep
from despising her mother, who was, although he was nothing,
so much less than he? But the important thing then was running away from both of them, getting away from them into a
different world, running into the marriage with Brady, whom she
thought of as being as different from them as anyone could be.
That was his value . . . that difference . . . his red hair and
blue eyes and light, light skin, and the fact that he was Celtic
and occidental. She knew that marrying Brady had something
to do with the rape of Lucrece, and that first night she had
backed away from him into the shabby corner of the shabby
hotel room and waited in dread for the rape of Lucrece to begin.

Not so wrong either when you remembered Brady's big
freckled hands with the red hairs on the backs of them, coming
at you; his look of shamed determination, which brooked no plea,
and took no time, but which would now take what it had a right
to have . . . Ah, but she had made him ashamed all right. Poor
old red-haired beast! It was not really Lucrece who had been
raped, but Brady the Rapist who was raped of his pride and his
self-love. And there was something strange about the way in
which, although she had thought he would be unlike her mother
and father because he was Irish, he became almost like their
representative to her. He was not at all what she imagined "Irish"
to be, which was to her mind, needing to find the difference, a
kind of cheaper grade Englishman in tweeds, with a roguish
twinkle in his eyes and a ready laugh. His red hair looked kinky
and ugly, and she discovered that his voice was high, thin and
breathy, and in his thin, high, breathy voice, he said things which
showed him to be a man of uncertainties, of brooding temperament, melancholy as any Slav, only worse, because there was
never any wild compensatory lift of spirits. He almost never
laughed; he whined; his feet never danced dazzlingly fast as her
father's sometimes could when she was little so that she could
not even see them but saw only a blur where each foot should be.
. . . No, no. At best, his sullen small mouth would yield up a
tight, reluctant little smile. He loved her in his worried, brutish
way. Oh, and was it because she was to him the most different
thing he could find from his own family, from the images he
longed to escape when he married? What a clumsy joke on them
both . . . He'd be easy for Hemingway to write, his conversation being clipped, cryptic . . . inhibited was the word. He

hated himself and his own concupiscence, and hated her for in-
spiring it in him and then, having inspired it, rejecting him,
running from his grasping hand, making excuses, dodging and
hiding and that first night, hiding in the bathroom away from
him and locking the door against him, and sitting in there on the
floor with her flushed cheek pressed against the cold white tile of
the wall. . . .

He wasn't smart either. If he'd had the wit to wait, to walk
away, she'd have come out of there and gradually, out of her
loneliness and fright and when she had gotten him separated
from her mother and father and the rape of Lucrece, she'd have
gone to him, because she needed him, too. But he hadn't the wit
to know that, or if he had the wit, it was dulled by his rage and his
frustration. He had yelled—"squeaked" was what she thought at
the time—outside the door, threatening to break it down, and
she'd sat on the floor with her eyes closed and been afraid, but
she hadn't believed him.

With the first crash against the door—absurd, like a ram
who wanted to mate—she was sure she was right not to believe
him, but gradually she sat up and interestedly observed that when
he rushed the door again and again, battering it like a ram, he
made it shake, though he was not breaking it down. Then the
noise changed and became, if anything, more violent because she
could hear his hard, enraged breathing with it, and she realized
he was kicking at the center panel of the door. Suddenly there
was a splintering of the wood and she saw his foot crash through
the panel, and stay there for a minute with its big black un-
polished shoe on it. She looked at it in disbelief, and at the same
time began to feel a terror of him and his violence which was different from what she had felt before, because now it was a
terror of him and not a ghost-terror out of the past. She wanted
to stop everything she had begun now, and somehow come out of
there and start over with her new knowledge that he was a violence to be feared, but she could not. She scrambled to her feet
and stood there, biting at her knuckle, as his foot kicked in more
and more of the wood and then his hand, disembodied, came
through the opening and turned the lock, and the door opened
and she was confronted with the full spectacle of him, of his
rage-engorged face. He came toward her relentlessly, and she
backed against the wall until his swollen face swam like a balloon above her. . . .

His hands as he grabbed her were like hams, huge, reddened and very strong. He picked her up, muttering something in a strangled voice, and brought her into the bedroom and threw her down on the bed, and fastened her there with his hands. "Is this what you want?" he said. She meant to say "No," but said nothing, only kept writhing to get away from him. The full weight of him fell on her then, surprising her too, and until that moment of feeling his physical weight on her—the weight of his body—she had not known that he was real. Knowing it now, with a shock, she attempted to pull up her knee but he moved quickly, and as he did, he put the heel of his hand on her throat and bore down until the pain was intolerable and blackness was coming into her eyes and she began to see that if she kept on fighting he would probably kill her, not even meaning to, not wanting her dead, but not willing to give up now and not even knowing that her life hung in the balance. She stopped fighting and abruptly lay flat and lifeless as stone. Slowly he lifted his hand from her throat and she fixed her wide terrified look on his swollen distorted face as though her glance could hold him back where her fighting had failed. Her body tried to pull back and away from him at the same time and her legs locked rigid, holding him out. His fist burst against her jaw and her head cracked against the wall, her shoulders were against the wall now, and she was scrabbling to get back and away. Things blurred and she began to be sure this was some kind of nightmare and not true, and with no hesitation, and no kindness, he invaded her, and there was a terrible tearing pain . . . Then he gave a kind of miserable groan and she became aware that he had ceased to move, that the agony was dying out, and his body grew heavier on her. His mouth was on hers, and almost experimentally, she bit his lip, and when he did not move away, bit it again viciously. He jerked his head back and she saw the horror and shame in his face. Blood trickled from his lip and he put his fingers to it and looked at them. Then he got up awkwardly and, moving clumsily, went out of the room. She turned on her side after a moment, pulled her knees up and lay still, abruptly feeling the soreness of her body but not feeling anger and not fear. She was dazed, so that if she'd had the strength to say anything, she'd have said, what was that all about? What was it for? After a while he came out of the bathroom, dressed, and went out.

When he was gone, she lay flat again, thinking she had not known that there was all this violence involved, where one

human being went into another human being's body in a way
which, if you didn't just accept it as natural and the way things
were, was absolutely monstrous.

She sat up and saw the bloodstains on the sheet and she
stared at them, and then she saw the black marks his shoes had
made at the foot of the bed. He wore his shoes, she thought. Her
throat throbbed painfully and her jaw was sore. She stood up,
swaying a little, wrapped herself in the spread and went into the
bathroom. She looked at the broken door in amazement as she
passed it, for at this point she was already dreaming it all away
as though it were a bad dream which could be undone, the way
motion pictures could be run backward, so that the diver went
slowly and gracefully up out of the water, feet first, to land on
the diving board again. But the broken door and the shoe marks
on the sheet and the flowing of her own blood made it impossible
to undream. She looked into the mirror but she couldn't cry; she
hated herself and thought herself a fool. And when she thought
of him, she thought that no matter what the differences between
them, the basic physical difference, he could not have enjoyed
that, either. Wasn't it, she thought with her mind sliding down
into a whirlpool of fear, supposed to be more than that? Wasn't
something supposed to happen when the invasion was accom-
plished, that would give him and her pleasure? But he had
groaned and collapsed. He had been ashamed. She did not hate
him. She thought that he was a fool too, as though there had
been a third person in the room who had made him do what he
did and made her do what she did . . .

When he came back, much later, she was packing her clothing. He ignored that and sat miserably on the bed and talked
about having to pay for the broken door, and about how the
pimply-faced bellboy would know he had broken the door to get
at his wife who didn't want him. As he talked, she touched her
bruised jaw, and when he saw her do that, he began to cry, letting
the few skimpy tears which accompanied his rasping sobs fall
on his big clenched fists.

She had not left, then. She had pitied him, and hated him
more because she felt pity for him than because he had hurt her.
She had known in some obscure way that his hurting her was
her own fault and he was not to be blamed for it.

She set down the coffee cup hard on the sink board. She
had finished her tortillas. And God knows, by now she should be

finished with Brady. But she had never completely exorcised him. The picture of him came back, forever and forever sitting on the bed crying, hurting her more each time she saw it than a blow on her jaw ever could. Always it made her feel sorry for him. In the few months she stayed married to him, before he too agreed that their marriage had been a mistake, for him as well as for her, she never managed to get another, different picture of him, more indifferent, less injured, to carry with her like a passport into other marriages, or like a locket—yes, that was better —like a locket heavy as a stone on a chain around her neck. This was the picture of Brady that stayed, grooved into her memory with the sharp stylus of shock.

She should start work. But her head ached, toxically, and her mind was full of tag-end ideas, like a dustpan full of broken glass. She looked out at the bright sunlight on the garden walls. Maybe if she took a walk first? Cleared her head . . . went down to the pier, the pointless anachronism of a pier, and looked out at the lake and the mountains, and, in that felicitous *ambiente*—Was there an English word *ambience*? That was a good word, sounding *lambent* and onomatopoetically suggesting *radiance*—in that *ambiente*, evoking the creative spirit . . . ?

She went quickly into the living room, picked up her shoulder bag and slipped the strap over her shoulder. She put on her dark glasses, and stepping briskly, walked out of the house into the bright hot day. Heat came up from the cobblestones and struck her in the face, and eddied like hot water around her bare ankles.

She walked carefully, not because she wasn't used to the uneven cobblestones, but because it was necessary to watch where you stepped with animals roaming the streets all the time. And not only animals . . . some Mexicans, like Europeans, regarded the street at night as an ideal bathroom. How hateful they were. Here was a beautiful country with the sky an unwinking bright blue, the air sweet with the scent of frangipani, the lake a glistening lavender jewel in its setting of green mountains . . . and they did ugly things to it. She could hate them for that. She had a well of hatred to draw upon anyway, so that she could hate them and hate Americans, Europeans, Asians, her father and mother and all human beings . . . The carpet slippers slapping across the sagging floor of the tene-

ment flat were not so different from the slapping of huaraches
across a dirt floor, and her mother's image could be seen in any
dark doorway of these adobe huts. . . . Just as it had stood behind Brady the night he hit her in the jaw. Her mother's image
had driven her to Brady, and as the days passed and she got so
she could not breathe with the smell and sound of him in the
room, and could not look at him, for seeing the shadow of her
mother behind him, so it had happened to her always in every
place . . . that she moved, moved! got married four times, and
always the suffocation would come, her writing would get bad,
choked off, and gradually she saw her mother everywhere and
felt her everywhere waiting like a shadow to envelop her, to
embrace her like death itself. And she moved, oh but she ran, oh
but she scrambled, out of the marriage, out of the love affair,
whatever it was, away from the shadow, the warm, humid-
smelling, not cool, spongy shadow, to a new place, where for a
while she could work and live and breathe, and words would
seem to write themselves on the paper. . . .

Now on the wide dry path beside the lake, look at what
your eyes see, don't involute your vision so that you see the past,
look instead at the scallopings of the fish nets strung up on
the poles to dry, look instead at the sharp black silhouettes of the
canoas, floating like paper cutouts on the wide lake. Fatigue
would be good. Walk far enough, get tired, and then go back
to the cool oasis of the house, out of this too bright world . . .
and then, work.

But soft! Who comes around yon corner? Tourists. There
was no missing the girdled American bodies, the high-heeled
short shoes with the plump ankles stemming up out of them,
the tourists' sombreros—bought in Mexico City or Acapulco
against the tropic sun—festive and childish, the American-cut
navy-blue-sheer dresses—drip-dry, you just rinse them out at
night wherever you are and hang them up in the bathroom and
in the morning there they are, neat as a pin. And there, there was
the father-tourist, pink and fat and bespectacled, wearing a
fancy silver Mexican belt—bought in Taxco—on his whipcord
trousers and a camera hung on a cord around his neck. Wasn't
he wearing the biggest sombrero of all, a nice wide one, and
wasn't he carrying the wallet, fat with traveler's checks, so that
the female Drip-Dries could buy all the crockery they could want
to send home . . . ? (But can you be sure they'll really ship

them? Supposing they break? My goodness, by the time you pay the duty, they cost more than the ones I got at Sears!) And in a minute they'd be facing her, trying to ask questions, mistaking her for a Mexican, saying, "Dispense me, seenora, but, how you say? Where is the hotel? Or habbla you-sted some Inglis?" She turned sharply onto a higher path, away from them.

The sun beat down hot now, and no breeze moved up from the water. The *chicharras* in the trees clacked and chattered, and there was an insane rooster somewhere crowing. In every Mexican village there was an insane rooster who couldn't tell time.

The clacking intensified and it wasn't only the *chicharras* in the trees. It was a typewriter. She paused and looked around. She was almost at Willie Chester's house. He was en- shrined there on his patio only half hidden among the *teléfono* vines, typing away. He wrote. Merciful God, how he wrote. A story every day he said, good, bad, indifferent, sensational, like a nondiscriminating machine, learning, he said, with each one he wrote, but writing them so fast, so terribly, frighteningly fast. And he sold some of them, not many. That he sold any was alarming. He had no reverence, no respect, no fear of his own possible or impossible talent. He wrote; it was the answer to everything for him. And there, in the patio behind him, was his wife . . . Sam. Of course Sam wasn't really her name— that is, her parents didn't name her Sam when she was born— but it was the name she had chosen for herself and which she requested everyone to use. It wasn't used very often, because nobody ever had anything to ask of her and if anybody did, he just called her "you." Sam was behind Willie, circling about in a stained and tattered leotard, steadily but badly practicing her ballet. Did she woo and win him with her twittering, soiled dancing? Oh, turn my eyes from the vision of their lives. . . .

Today there might be a letter at the post office from her agent, saying, that story you sent me was marvelous, although slick, immediately accepted by the *Journal*, and here is your check for fifteen hundred dollars. . . . Cushman was loath- some, a small-rectumed man who nursed his integrity and beat her with the small but unbreakable straws of his criticism whenever she tried to write something just for money . . . as he put it.

Just for money. If it hadn't been for money, she wouldn't

be here. She'd still be immured in Mexico City with Ramón, choking, unable to breathe again, suffocating on the unwritten words which raced through the shadowy passages of her brain all the long, sleepless nights, like inexhaustible gray rats romping in an empty attic . . . for want of the miserable five hundred dollars Martha's death bought her to bring her here where, alone, she could think . . . If it was the only sisterly thing Martha had ever done for her, in return for the endless gifts, lavish presents, eagerly offered loans, it meant more perhaps than all she had done for Martha . . . for she had been trying to buy Martha, trying to buy peace from Martha, who had as little chance of a supply as she herself . . . but who pretended peace, who wore the calm face of peace, and talked like a psychologist's pamphlet, saying sometimes, "I don't care, Vee, you have to face it . . . that's *life*. That's what life *is*." Is it? Oh is it? Is that *all*? "It's enough," Martha said.

And now, Martha, explain to me death, now that you're dead. Do you know no more of that than you did of life and do you think because you died that you know what death is, as you thought you knew what life was merely because you lived? Ah, damn you to hell, Martha, thank you for the money, but you owed me so much more than money . . . because I saved you, I made a life for you to live, drew it for you, pushed you into the frame, I got you out of there and paid your way so you could develop that ordinary, carefully mediocre sense of normality and then explain the profundities to me. As I ran, panic-stricken, stained with passion and gnawing with greed, you stood there holding a mediocre, middle-aged smile on your lips and told me what life was. So now, tell me death.

Standing still, getting a piece of cloth out of her purse, patting it against her suddenly wet forehead. Think now, is today one of the crazy Mexican fiestas or some stupid thing so that although the letter from Cushman will be at the post office, you can't get it? Better to think of that now and not count on it, not to be disappointed. It happened that way sometimes. The second-class bus from Jocotepec would jolt into town carrying the leather mail pouch, and the driver would hand it over to Don Eliséo, the postmaster, who took it then into the shady living room of his house which he had converted into a post office by fitting niches onto a wooden frame nailed up against one wall. If it were a fiesta day, then he would dump the pouch down on the worn brick floor and leave it till tomorrow, refusing, no matter what the urgency, to open it for anybody. It could be one of those days, the celebration of the martyrdom of some unheard-of saint. Or it could be that the letter from Cushman would be there all right but there would be no check in it. Of course Cushman wouldn't have liked the story, and the few lines he'd have written about it would manage to convey the New England-prissy disapprobation he felt if she were to get a check for a story he thought less than worthy of her. He disapproved of it. But then she disapproved of it herself. She had written it for money, not approval. So if there were a check, there would be a few tight, constipated Marquand lines in which he made it clear that he was glad to have sold the story, but sorry that she wrote it, and sorrier still that she had asked him to sell it for her. Cushman was not a realist; the times of his New England ancestry were more of a reality to him than the sharp world of present-day business; he gazed out his window, habitually scanning the horizon to see, she was sure, if the red-coats were coming, and he had her confused in his mind with Jane Austen, who was, beyond doubt, good company.

The path widened here, coming up on the rise, and there was the view of the scalloped black fish nets spread out to dry. Soon there would be, when she turned this next bend in the path, the place where the Mexican women of the village did their washing at the edge of the lake. They knelt on wide, flat stones, rubbing the clothes on big rocks in the water, their backs bent deeply, their bodies straining. On the low wall at the foot of an estate, the clothing they had already washed was strung out to dry in the sun, to make a banner of faded color and ragged cloth.

The sight of the women, like grotesque birds, ungainly, dark-clothed, slavishly bending in the hot sun stopped her . . . Look away from them. Look out over the ancient lake toward the green mountains, misty velvet beyond the saffron water, under the bright painted sky . . . One of them was singing, in a high sweet young voice.

She looked back, not wanting to, and saw behind them the almost real, misshapen shadow of her mother, and heard the voice strain on a high note, break, right itself and lift higher, true again as a bird song . . .

Turn quickly and go home. *Scuttle home.*

Back in the village and near enough to her house that she was already fishing in her purse for her door key, she met Harry and Charles. Harry approached her with his arms wide, as though he were playing a final scene in a movie.

"Is it you?" Harry cried in false, farcical disbelief. "Is it really you, my darling? Don't let me think it's you, if it isn't . . . I couldn't bear . . . that."

"Buck up, old man," Charles said in a loyal-friend voice, and put a brotherly hand on Harry's shoulder where his too-big jacket was slipping off. "I'm afraid it's just another one of your visions, old cock. It's not . . . your Vickie."

Harry turned on him a look of terrible dismay. "Not . . . Vickie?" he said, his voice breaking. "Oh, what am I to do, Carruthers? Every woman I see looks like Vickie to me . . ."

"Hallucinations," Charles said, medically. "Nothing to be alarmed about. Quite common among my patients. Oh, quite."

"Quite?"

"Quite."

"Then why is she smiling at me, Carruthers? In that . . . remembered way?"

"Hello, Harry," Victoria said through her nose.

Harry started, came to her, clasped her in his arms. He smelled musty. She pulled free of him.

She changed to her own voice. "I can't play movie today, Harry," she said. "My mother won't let me. I . . . have to go to work."

Harry raised his eyebrows at her, took her hand in his. "We're going over to Abel's. He's making some crazy food and we were just coming to get you. It's on the house, no charge." He thrust his arm through hers. "Though *I* may have a little charge," he said laughing. "Come on, chickie. You got food in your pad?"

She looked at him.

"You got juicy in your pad?"

Silently she shook her head.

"Your eyes are hungry, Vickie-chick."

But my soul is hungry . . . If I don't work today, after throwing yesterday away . . . But I *am* hungry and I can work later. I'll have the whole rest of the day and the night, the whole rest of my life . . . I, Victoria, being of sound mind and healthy body . . . Yes, health was important, food was important, and her head still ached. A little time could be stolen, couldn't it?

She put the key back in her purse, smiled broadly and wickedly, but already feeling the first twinge of anxiety in her middle.

The three of them began to walk along together, down the street and around the corner to the street which led to Abel's Bar.

"But I have to work, you know," Victoria said, not even meaning to say it but needing to hear the words spoken out loud. "I'll leave right after we eat. I'll just nip in for a few minutes with you and then I'll get home and back to the typewriter."

Neither Charles nor Harry made any sign that they heard her.

Abel's Bar was on the corner. On what the Mexicans called *la pura esquina*, meaning the exact corner, not next door. There was a grocery store across the street and beyond that a cantina and next to that a poolroom. There were a few Mexicans standing outside the pool hall and one of them squatted on the ground, making marks in the soft dirt with a stick. Over his head there was a chipped tin Coca-Cola sign and beside that another, which said MEJORAL, *Para la dolor en la cabeza.* The Mexicans watched the Americans coming toward them, with stolid interest, silently. From the tile roof of Abel's Bar, there was a scarlet fall of bougainvillaea, plunging down the plastered white wall and trailing onto the rounded cobblestones of the street. The shutters on the window were still closed.

Charles said, "Man, look how they watch us without looking like they're watching us. They bug me."

Harry said, "Oh, they dig us. They just stand around and dig us."

The patio door of Abel's Bar was open and they came through it and stood inside on the brick flooring of the patio, and waited to be welcomed.

3

Abel

ABEL had the only four-story house in the village. It was as narrow as a brownstone and rose up from the squat buildings around it, the stunted trees and flat land, like a questing, thin-necked vegetarian beast. Originally his plan was to have a two-story house, which would be a rarity in the town, but then he had decided to use the bottom floor, which made a narrow room about thirty feet by ten, for a darkroom. As such it was perfect. He built the stairs up to the next level, steep, thigh-pulling stairs, without banisters and with nothing to mark them off at the top. They simply opened up out of the floor. The second floor was the *sala* and his studio where he painted, and the bedroom. He kept the end with the big north

window for the painting section, the middle for entertaining—
although so far nobody had ever visited them since everybody
went to the bar instead—and the south end for the bedroom.
This held the two not too large beds and a pair of leather
equipalis and a chair he'd begun to design of leather straps
stretched on an iron frame, but it wasn't finished yet and
mostly he and Lucy piled their clothes on it. On the wall there
was a row of hooks, where one day he would have a wardrobe, for the rest of their clothes. In the middle of this room
rose another abrupt staircase to what would be, when he
managed to get hold of a stove and a real icebox, instead of the
carbón stove and the Coca-Cola cooler they now used, the
kitchen and dining area. Now it had a sink, a *pila*, where water
could be stored for use since there was no running water in the
house. It was a long way up for Chatta, the maid, to haul water
to fill the *pila*, and she grumbled from the instant she set out
for the well with her buckets until she came back, carrying only
one at a time. She increased the volume of her complaints every
time she saw Abel. He had not so far managed to build a flight
of stairs to the fourth floor and, in the meantime, a ladder
served, somewhat shakily, as a means to the fourth-floor roof
garden. This was a marvelous place for Lucy to lie naked in the
sun away from curious eyes in the daytime, and for the two
of them at night when the bar closed, before dawn, to sit together and look at the stars, the blackness of the Mexican night,
the deeper dark of the wide, rolling hills, the pooled dark of the
murmuring lake.

In the rainy season, no matter what ingenious but thrifty
arrangement he had tried, water gushed down the hole in the
kitchen ceiling, ran down the steep stairs and finally settled in
the cistern of the darkroom. It struck them as funny, except
when they had to go out at night in the storm, down the wet
stairs into the darkroom, slosh through the water there, and
out into the wet garden to the separate building where the bathroom was. But the rainy season was bad really only from July to
late October, and last year he had managed to take Lucy to
Acapulco through the worst of it. It was due to rain soon now,
and he found as he painted, that he often put down his brushes
and nervously walked to the south window to see if the tallest
mountain, García, was wearing a hat of cloud, because he felt
the rain in the air, even though there was no cloud there yet—

the cloud being the only sure sign of rain—and because he knew, looking at how the wind rose suddenly sometimes in a fitful excitement and swirled the dust up in spinning cones, and rustled the papery leaves of the bougainvillaea, that rain was coming, now, soon. The way the flies clustered too, in thick groups, and moved slowly, made him think of rain . . .

But such natural disasters were the least of his worries, and hardly counted in his emotional budget which, if not so planned, was certainly completely used up by a series of crises and panics, usually having to do with money and his health and his love for Lucy and his guilt toward the wife and the then un- born child he had deserted in the States. . . . He was al- ways in such a state of mania, so panic-stricken, so desperate, that the falling of water into his crazy house was a minor matter of faint amusement. He rushed through the days of his bor- rowed time, plugging up the holes in his economic life, trying to keep going until finally it all collapsed . . . until the States brought him back to the Army he had deserted, or until the brain tumor—which daily filled his cranium a little more tightly —finally exploded its cage, maddened him entirely, and put an end to his love of Lucy, his painting, and the life of his long, skinny body.

He did not think of it as a black body, although he was Negro and very dark. It seemed to him that he would have had to have a white body (or "gray" as he most often thought of the color of Caucasians) to think of his body as a black body instead of just his body. When life permitted, he had never thought of himself as a Negro. Among Negroes, he felt like a pretender, a phony, a white man who was trying to pass as Negro. Among white men, he had to remind himself (if they failed to do so) that he was not like them, but different. Some of them sensed this; some of them resented it; some of them, like Harry and Charles, were puzzled by it. Charles said to him one time, "I'm more spade than you are, man. Because you know for a spade you're so square, you're white . . . and for an ofay, I'm so hip, I'm spade."

He used to try to figure out why he didn't feel like what he was, but he never solved it. He wandered along the marginal land between the races, not knowing why he did. But he de- liberately took on the mantle of his color and defended himself, and his "adopted" race, as he supposed a real Negro would and should do naturally, but it was always an unnatural obligation imposed upon him, from outside himself.

But perhaps his very inability to feel whatever that special identification with Negro was supposed to be, was still a Negro feeling. Maybe the idea of feeling Negro was a white concept. There was the old blues which said . . . "I'm white inside, it don't help my case . . ." Maybe being hip, as Charles said it, meant the white concept, or misconcept, of what a Negro is. Ofays were often surprised to find a square Negro, saying in an amazed way, why he's middle-class . . . And *hip* ofays, imitating the Negro as an expression of their rebellion against a society they considered crushing, assumed that the Negro must necessarily rebel too, and conform to the ways of, and use the language of, rebellion.

Abel's rebellion was, he believed, a matter of his being an artist rather than of his color heritage. In fact, it seemed square to him that Charles automatically expected him to be hip because he was spade.

What is hip? Why, hip to what's happening, man. Conscious and aware of the struggle of life, and putting down the old rules and the old ways and finding new ones. Finding the answer within yourself, within the cool circle of yourself, reaching new heights and depths by blowing pot, or however you had to do it to get there . . . but digging life for yourself, your own way, and the hell with groups and responsibilities and trying to make the world work right, because you can't succeed anyway and because this is all there is for you, just this handful of time for you to poke through and use for yourself. . . .

Ah, the hell with it. He went up the ladder to the roof and stood there, conscious of his headache and the numbness traveling down his left arm—the left hand is the dreamer, the left hand belongs to the brain tumor, but the right hand belongs to me—and stood, skinny, scrawny, snaggle-toothed, or so he thought of himself, with a boy's callow face . . . an errand boy's face, a "Shine, mister?" face . . . a you-such-an-ugly-chile face . . . and looked along the narrow, rutted streets for Lucy. He didn't see her. He'd sent Lucy out to shop for the spaghetti things today instead of Chatta, because Chatta would be sure to come back with an empty basket. Chatta was really a lousy maid, afraid to ask for credit for him anymore, because she might be refused, and she was sure she would be, and this

would mean a loss of face, not only for Abel, but for her. Lucy
was different. There was something irresistible to the Mexicans
about the way she wandered into their markets with her basket
on her arm and a child's notebook in her hand. They couldn't
explain to her child-smiling face that Abel owed them too much
money and she couldn't charge any more. With exasperation
and love, they watched her carefully noting down the prices of
the things she charged, moistening the point of the stubby
pencil with her tongue, earnest and sweet and needing to be
protected from the hard facts of the grown-up world—and
they refused her nothing.

Lucy's eyes were pale placid blue, and although she laughed
often and easily, as certain children do, her eyes never lighted
but remained vacantly, widely blue. Her pale, perfect skin did
not flush with excitement or anger. Once in a great while she
was sullen, with a sullenness as inexplicable to her as it was
to Abel, which, without discernible cause, came on her suddenly,
lasted its time and, just as inexplicably and suddenly, disappeared. Aside from these April moods, she was pleasant, always agreeable, a little sad, and most often smiling.

She drove him mad. He loved her. He loved her with
grotesque devotion, and she maddened him because she was as
placid as he was frenetic, as slow to thought as he was fast.
There was something vegetable about her, he thought, as though
she lacked the indignities of animal life. She was as pale and
convoluted as an onion, with pale layer upon pale layer to the
lilac heart beneath it all, which sang a small, thin, childish song
. . . But her placidity was not peace, and Abel needed a
peaceful place very badly. If he could have accepted her totally,
as well as loved her, he might have found peace in the lilac
heart.

Lucy had a husband. He was a check forger serving a sentence at the Islas Marías and Lucy was waiting for him to come
out. She had told Abel how she and Johnny had grown up together in Canada, side by side, he in one house and she in another, and he had taken her for his own when she was ten and
he was eleven. They had drifted around the world together and
finally into Mexico, and there he had been arrested. She'd been
there waiting for him for three years now. When Abel met her,
she had no means of livelihood but she didn't even seem to
know it, or think she should have. Sometimes he wondered

how old she was. When he had first seen her—in spite of her long silver-white hair—he thought she was about sixteen; she had come to him and put her hand in his and looked up at him and waited, like a child. But she was not sixteen. He supposed she was about forty, older than he was by five or six years. But he was used to thinking of her as about sixteen. She was, he knew with his artist's eye, terribly white . . . probably the whitest woman in the world. But oddly enough, he always thought of her as the same as himself, and if that made him white or her dark, it didn't matter.

She didn't belong to him, the way his wife had belonged to him, but he loved her as he had never loved his wife, nor his mother, nor his father, nor anybody. He was in a constant state of shock to find himself loving her, because he could not imagine what it was about her which evoked this love in him. She got on his nerves, the pinks and blues and pale whites of her shocked him sometimes, irritated his skin, made his eyes itchy . . . but he did not really live until she came slouching through his doorway and let him cook for her, or fuss with her hair, or make her a crazy drink . . . which she would drink as long as it looked pink and innocent with grenadine in it, never thinking it could make her drunk, and so it didn't . . . He bought her what she needed, no matter what kind of plotting it involved, or what thievery, or what tricks and frantic adding up of figures in his head, and he talked to her when they were alone, and teased her when people were around, because strangers came to the town and the bar to see the White Woman Who Lived with the Negro. But Lucy didn't know that, never sensed it, and smiled at them; he teased her to distract her from seeing it, and gradually the prurient curiosity would dwindle into some kind of acceptance of her, which became in the end the deeper curiosity of what in the world was she like.

This was a bad day. Abel stood on the roof in the hot morning glare, absently rubbing the benumbed elbow of his left arm and at the same time pressing it in against his side to make it feel something, and swore at the way his head ached. It wouldn't be so bad, if only he could stay home and paint, or work in the darkroom on the photographs and not have to go to the bar until tonight. Or if he could just go to bed, and sleep. Sleep always seemed to push the idea of the tumor from his mind . . . jostling aside its separate pink, glistening, contoured universe . . . filling his mind with darkness instead.

He possessed almost demoniac energy, but today he was tired. Time would not wait. He must connect with Harry today, feed him good food, charge him with pot, pour alcohol on his inner festering wound . . . do whatever it was that would ready Harry for the touch. So that when Abel finally put it to him, Harry would reach into his pocket and pull out some sticky pesos. There was no one else now to whom he could turn for a loan. . . . He was sorry it had to be Harry, because underneath his apparent warmth and admiration for Harry, he disliked and feared him.

Harry was an erratic tyrant, and although he was adored by all the hipsters as a kind of hip-saint, Abel secretly thought him a weak and evil man of second-rate talent and bad influence. He blew a good horn, but Abel did not hear when Harry blew, what he had heard from Stan Getz and Lester Young and Dizzy, or any of the first-rate musicians . . . he did not hear what, in fact, he saw in his own paintings. Abel knew quite well that he had a lot to learn, and no time in which to learn it, but he was potentially a fine painter. Harry, he believed, had exploited his potential beyond its natural limits, and achieved mediocrity by an effort of will. It wasn't that Harry could do better if he would . . . he would, but he couldn't, so he pretended he wouldn't. All of Harry's publicized sufferings and reading into Baudelaire and Rimbaud and talking about existentialism, and about beating the world to his death and going out swinging, were just so much window dressing for a false talent. His stooges wouldn't know . . . Jim, for instance, was only a sick, tired boy who stood beside Harry, usually stoned out of his mind, his eyes staring obediently into the plaster eyes of Harry, his saint, and whose mouth moved only to echo Harry's in a compulsive, hysterical amen. Jim wouldn't know . . . Charles, the number one stooge . . . ah, but Charles was no Jim. He was far more worldly at heart and one day he would know Harry's measure, for he tracked him constantly, watching and smiling wisely, but listening . . .

But sainted or evil, Harry was the only one to whom Abel could turn for the money. Harry had it and held on to it, no matter how gone he was. Charles usually got rocky and acted like a protector to Harry at such times. Maybe if he told Harry the truth . . . "Ned's back in town today and when he finds out

I haven't been paying the rent to his maid every month like I promised, he'll bounce me. He's a cold mother, you know it! He'll get to the Mexicans, and I haven't been able to pay them the *mordida*, and man, do they want their graft! They'll have me in a squeeze. Think about it like the war, Harry. Remember that time you got the Purple Heart, Harry . . . those guys were caught in a squeeze and you got them out . . . Get me out, man."

If only there were someone else. Harry was hard. But there wasn't anyone else. He couldn't stall Ned. He'd managed to stall Fausto again, and Fausto, being the blacksmith, was *macho*, a rough stud who couldn't be pushed around by a *gringo*, and a black *gringo* at that. Mostly the Mexicans liked his being darker than they were; they called him "Negrito" with affection. But lately, when the officials came into the bar at night, they stood around, throwing down the free Tequila Sauza . . . the most expensive kind, although they drank the cheapest in their own cantina where they had to buy it. They were waiting for the pay-off and they were getting loud and they called him "Negrito" with a different tone, and swaggered and fixed their eyes upon him and waited . . . The heat was on with them; all they'd need was to hear that he owed Ned, too.

No, Harry was it. The last chance. Harry was Your Last Chance To Buy Gas for Miles.

He began to walk up and down agitatedly. He could just cut out and be long gone. He might as well be in Chicago as here because here he found himself suddenly, for Christ's sake, a goddamned householder worrying about bills, a businessman with a woman to take care of. He hadn't come here for that. He'd come here to paint. When you've only got a little time, you don't spend it maintaining a house and a business . . . you paint. When you're dead nobody will stand around and say you were a good provider or a good man. . . . They'll say, it's too bad his talent was wasted . . . he threw away his little bit of time . . .

Even Lucy. When he was dead, she'd be with Johnny again. She was only waiting for Johnny to get out of jail, that was all, and she might as well wait with Abel as wait alone. One day Johnny would come for her and she'd just wander off with him, with no regretful sigh to flutter those perfect pale lips,

without any pity or sympathy in the pale blue eyes . . . He
shook his head roughly to clear it of the picture of Lucy walking
away from him down a street, with her hand in the hand of a
shadowy stranger's . . . She was an idiot child who took whatever love he offered her . . . an amiable, beloved child . . .

He held his head in his hands and pressed in with his
fingers to equalize the pressure inside his skull. Blood pounded
up in his temples and bright cones of light revolved past his
eyes like slowly falling stars, and slowly sank into shadow . . .
The shadow of the headache was now moving down on his
head, fitting down on it like a helmet and he longed to run out
from under the helmet onto the deserted street of sleep.

He could offer Harry interest. That might appeal to him, if
he'd give him 6 percent, and any time he fell behind on a payment, he'd promise to pay double . . . Harry might like to
play the usurer. Giving Harry something to do, some evil game
to play about the money, was important. Of course it worsened
his own problem, but Harry liked to think of himself as a hard
guy, a villain, innocent of any virtues . . . He could play on
that . . .

He could see Harry's face, the mouth going a little tight
and petulant, like an aged spinster's, and the eyes behind the
smeary glasses going hard and small. Harry would try to brush
it off. "Don't bring me down, man," he'd say. "Don't spread your
evil woes all over me. Don't drag me." Buddy, can you spare a
dime? Harry would make him feel as though he'd held out a tin
cup.

He let go of his head. He wouldn't tell Harry about his head.
No matter what, he couldn't do that. He'd never told anyone
about the brain tumor, because in the beginning when he first
came here, he was still refusing to believe that it was real. In
those days, every so often he'd think of the Army doctor telling
him about it, showing him the electroencephalograms, shaking
his head, pointing his big wrinkled jointy finger and talking
about an operation. Then he'd get mad at the doctor. He'd take
the thought of the tumor and put it away . . . put the idea of
it, all growing pink and vivid in embryonic lobes, glistening
and opalescent, on a shelf in a corner of his mind. That ofay
quack had tried to bug him, saying the tumor would kill him
if he didn't let them drill a hole in his skull and get it out. . . .

He probably wanted to see the black boy roll his eyes and say
"Lawdy, Massa," lak he was goin' past de cemetery in de moonlight and skeered ob de goblins.

He had turned his back to the doctor and tried not to hear
what he was saying. He sifted out the frightening words, like
surgery, and listened hard only when the doctor said that
nobody could know about how much time he had. He said in
view of Abel's history he was reasonably certain that the
tumor was not malignant and that he'd had it going there quite
a while. But that was an educated guess, and a biopsy was
worth a thousand guesses. It was possible that Abel might be
able to go along for years as he was now but it was also possible
that he didn't have much time at all. It was his recommenda-
tion that Abel have the operation immediately, at the *Army's*
expense.

Abel heard all that, and under that he heard the doctor's
eagerness to do an operation and he thought he'd better get
the hell out of that consultation room and away from that eager
quack before he started trepanning right then and there. He
sure as hell didn't want the Army doing any more to him than
it already had. He got out of there, and once he was out of the
room and away from the doctor, and away from the Army, he
found that he did not think about the tumor at all—except that
he began to think about time in a new way because it had become very precious to him. He thought of time in terms of fixing
life so he could paint.

He pressed his hand against his eyes and discovered that
only his right eye was crying and that no tears came from his
left eye, and this was a new step. Every few weeks now he discovered where the tumor had silently advanced and taken over a
new area of himself. While he'd been busy with his painting or
scraping up money, he thought of these advances and invasions
with a spurt of terror because every one of them cut down on
his time. He kept telling himself he had a couple of years
anyway, didn't he?

He shouted out an obscenity at his own helplessness there
on the roof. Then he looked down and saw Lucy in the
street, with her basket on her arm, and he could see that the
basket was full of vegetables, and her eyes were looking up at
him and her mouth was smiling. . . .

"Abel!" she called to him in pleased surprise, as though

his being up there shouting at the wild blue sky were part of a nice new game and she was ready to play it with him.

He looked down, noticed how small she was, like a frail, sunny doll, and gradually his mouth twisted out of its grimace and he smiled.

"I got everything," she said and held up the full basket for him to see.

He nodded at her, smiling.

She said, "Shall I get Chatta and go to the bar and start cooking it?"

He said, "Wait for me."

She said, "But hurry, will you? I want to dust the lemon tree in the patio before everybody comes. It looks awfully dusty."

He shook his head in wonder at her mind which could think of dusting lemon trees. "Oh, you crazy Canadian," he said softly, laughing, and hurried down the ladder, leaping the bottom three rungs, in his eagerness to go to her.

4

Victoria

FROM WHERE Victoria was sitting in the lounge of Abel's Bar, she could look out through the open door at the golden sunlight on the red brick patio. The shutters were closed against the midday heat and Abel had lit candles for the table and stuck them into empty rum *garrafóns*, so that, in the flickering light and shadow, it was like a summer dusk in the room. While the talk flowed around her, rising and falling with little currents of enthusiasm, Victoria looked out at the glossy green leaves of the lemon tree making an oasis of deep shade in the midst of the glowing golden world outside the room. Occasionally a leaf stirred, danced, sent off little shining lights on the breeze, and when this happened, melancholy washed through her at the thought that she must get up, out of the chair, leave the place, go home to her dreary house, and work. It was quiet in the village, which still soaked in the warm siesta silence, and a silent time, rare here, was best for work. But her eyelids were heavy and her body—she looked down at how relaxedly it sat in its *equipali*—wanted to sag and sleep and rest, and she did not want to make it work. She wanted to keep looking at the cool lemon tree in the sun-steeped world outside.

The truth was, her body was engaged in the activity of digestion. It was as simple as that. She was inert, sitting inert in a chair, listlessly trying to prod herself up out of comfort and into work, while her stomach was pleased with what Abel had fed them . . . a hot, good meal with a rich sauce on the spaghetti, and a spiky salad bestirring the palate to appreciation.

Abel was a great cook. She was moved to tell him so and turned her head and looked at him, giving up the cool pleasure of the lemon tree for the moment, but even as her lips parted to speak, she stopped. Abel was watching Harry, and the expression on his face was one she had caught several times before, today. He was concentratedly studying Harry's face as he would study a painting except that there was an unmistakable desperation in his eyes and in the way he bit his lips as he watched Harry. She wondered, with a certain regret as her nerve endings came alive and told her this was something to pay attention to, what it was that bothered Abel, that had him so frantic.

Harry rubbed his hand over a worn place on his corduroy jacket. "Can I have some lush?" he asked Abel, and there was a whine in his voice.

Abel's face smoothed out. He made an effort to sound gracious. "Go, man," he said. "Get some for everybody, except Lucy. I'll make Lucy a drink."

"Why thank you, Abel," Lucy said.

Harry stood up, smiling happily at Victoria. "Going to get you some juicy, chick," he said.

"No, no," she said, meaning it and then as if she hadn't changed her mind at all, "just a little one and then I must go. Something to sip, Harry. A vermouth cassis, perhaps. In Paris that was all we ever drank, and today feels like Paris to me."

Charles looked at her. "Which husband was Paris?" he asked lazily.

"The second," she said.

Harry walked into the bar. Abel watched him go, then got up and followed him.

"Was that the sculptor?" Charles said.

But she was thinking of Abel, examining his desperation. He was always a little wild, a little frantic, and she believed that there was something physically wrong with him, but today his desperation was different and specific. She said impatiently to Charles, "My husband was an artist. He was trying to be a sculptor but it didn't work. That was not his talent. His talent was painting. If I told you his name, you'd recognize it. He's famous."

"How long were you married to him?"

Harry came back with her vermouth and gave it to her and waggled his fingers at her. "Been meaning to tell you, Vickie," he said. "You shouldn't go bugging everybody at a bash like last night. You can't flip over every sick square comes down here."

"I know, I know," she said. "But it would have been a tragedy."

"I don't believe in tampering with tragedies. They're too valuable. Tragedy makes the world go round. Can't you dig the tragedy and then write about it?"

"*I know*," she said, turning up her hands. "But it was because of what happened on the lake. I felt . . . Chinese about it. I saved the admiral's life. He was my responsibility."

Harry leaned forward and looked into her face. Then he straightened up, tore a strip of the white paper of his cigarette package and wet it with his tongue. He slapped it on his forehead at a careless angle, so it looked like a Band-Aid, and when it stuck, he began to walk around the room, leaning forward at a drunken angle, and saying in a good imitation of the admiral's voice, "Anybody seen my wife? Excuse me, will you, but is Annie in here?" He stared with unfocused eyes into Lucy's face. "Where's Annie?" he said. "Are you in there, Annie?" He executed a grotesque little shuffling dance step, paused on the up-beat, staggered, righted himself and bellowed, "Where's Annie?"

Victoria stared at him with her mouth slack. It was very disturbing how he had caught, perhaps because of his musician's sense of key, the exact buffalo note of the admiral's voice. She felt, even as she grew angry at the foolishness of her reaction, the same sort of fear she had felt last night. Her fists clenched together.

Charles laughed. "Wheah *is* Annie?" he said, sounding like Deetsy, with the same nasal Southern twang . . . "and wheah's that pretty Clay-boy . . . ?"

"That fly-boy, Clay-boy?" Abel said, laughing too.

Harry staggered around some more and the drying paper bandage loosened and flapped as he lurched. "Where's Annie?" he cried, more loudly and drunkenly.

"Where's home?" Charles said. "Where's the Navy?"

"Where's Mother? And Dad? Where's God?" Harry bumped into a wall and stared around at all of them theatrically. "Where did the world go? Where did the world go, Mother? Where did they all go? What's the matter with the lights? It's getting dark in here, Mother. . . . I'm dying! I meant to be a good boy, Mother, honest I did! I meant to be a good admiral until the minute I died. Annie! Where's Annie?"

"Oh Christ!" Victoria said. "That's disgusting, Harry."

Harry looked at her and smiled, took the paper off his forehead and settled again into his usual slouch. "Ain't I wild, sweetie?" he said.

She could not look at him. Anger had hold of her, the way it did sometimes, so that she felt like an old slipper a terrier had in his mouth, shaken and helpless, and she was too furious to look at him. Making mock, that's what he was doing, and all that he ever did; do not mock me, you foolish boy, do not mock; God will not be mocked, He said so. "Shut up, Harry!" she said out of her choking throat, standing up, glaring at him now, but not seeing him, seeing only the good, sweet admiral, not Harry playing a buffoon's game, playing a stupid child's game . . . what stupid child could not dangerously mock his betters? "Just shut up!" she said.

Slowly the pounding blood left her head, so that she was able to sit down again. She took a big swallow of her vermouth and it soothed her dry throat. Where there was all that anger, there must be fear. There was always fear; fear was anger's mother.

She said, into the room, not looking directly at Harry but now that she was admitting her fear, feeling it, "The admiral's gone, isn't he? I mean, the two of them left this morning, didn't they?"

Charles nodded. "Gone, long gone," he said.

Lucy said, "They left early. They went off in the Delegado's taxi at eight o'clock."

"Gone," Harry said. He looked over the tops of his glasses at them all, looking longest at Victoria. "But I ask you . . . I ask you profoundly, 'Where's Annie?' "

He shuffled off into the bar again. Victoria twisted the fork in her twitching fingers, staring at the bare, shining board of the table.

Lucy said, "Don't look worried, Vick. Abel is so worried these days." She glanced up at where he had been but now he was following Harry into the bar again. "What is there to worry about?"

Victoria could not answer. She could have bared her teeth wolfishly and sobbed, but she could not answer. How could you answer that kind of placidity? Whether it was stupid, or angelic, or feeble-minded, or clever, how did you answer such a question? She said, finally, because Lucy kept waiting for her to say something and Charles was smiling in a knowing way at her, but waiting too, "I'm nervous."

She got up quickly and went into the other room where Abel stood in the shadow behind the bar and Harry put his foot on the rail and leaned forward.

"I got a proposition to make you, Harry," Abel was saying and his voice was high with earnestness. "I got to talk to you alone."

Victoria stopped abruptly in the doorway. "Then I'll stay out," she said.

Harry turned quickly. "No, sweetie," he said. He came over to her and put his arm around her. He said, "Abel . . ." He paused and gave a patient sigh. "Later, man."

"I haven't *got* much time," Abel said quietly, "later could be too late," and she saw the desperate look naked on his face.

She said, "Talk to him now, Harry," and she pulled away from him and went back to the table. She could hear Abel's voice rise and fall in the other room, but not what it was saying. She stood there and drank down her vermouth. She was thirsty.

It was only a moment then and Harry came back into the room shaking his head, saying, "No, no," and she looked to him and from him to Abel coming in behind him. Abel's face was disappointed but still strained, so she knew he hadn't really been allowed to talk yet.

Harry said, "Abel says Ned's back in town." He grinned. "Big deal."

Charles said in a mildly dissenting way, "I've always liked Ned." He looked Harry up and down. "He's clean," he said pointedly.

"Except for the brimstone," Harry said like a ham actor. He lifted his arms. "Man, the smell of brimstone and sulphur that clings to his Brooks Brothers suits. Is that clean?"

Charles shrugged. "He's got *suits*, man. And he washes. I'd like to have a suit."

"And shirts and sweaters and neckties and shoes and closets and cupboards and hangers and bottles of cologne—wow, is he a user! *mop!* with the shaving lotions and the skin oils— and his maid makes hollandaise sauce, and when it rains she hands him a black umbrella with a gold-headed cane . . ." Harry smiled evilly and let his arms drop to his sides. "That's the outside. But the inside, you dig?"

Abel began to laugh and now, as he talked, his laugh trailed up and down through his words. "Oh the inside," he said. "Outside he's all angel-shit. That's what I call him, I call him Angel-shit." He kept laughing, talking fast. "That's how he looks, that's what he talks, that's what he paints . . . angel-shit!" He swallowed and although the smile stayed like a grimace on his face the laughter fell away under it. "That's what I'm trying to talk to you about, Harry," he said. "He's a mean mother and you know it and he's . . ."

Harry lifted his hand to stop him. He said warningly, "Just let old Harry have his juicy."

"Then will you talk to me alone, Harry?" Abel said.

"Sure, sweetie," Harry said and settled down in the chair again and closed his eyes behind his smeary glasses. "Right now I'm suffering from my world-pain. Ease my world-pain, Vickie."

She shook her head. "I don't feel Chinese about you, Harry," she said.

He opened his eyes. They were sharply blue, suddenly. "How *do* you feel about old Harry, Vick?" he said.

"I don't know," she said. She saw that Abel was staring at the floor with a look of helpless consternation. She was sure now he was trying to talk to Harry about money, and she hated that. The thought of money frightened her, all by itself, let alone associated with Abel's panicky look, and reminded her of the

letter which might be at the post office, which might have a
check in it and might not, and she knew that was why she
hadn't left here yet. She couldn't bear to leave until the post
office was closed and it would be too late for her to find out
Cushman hadn't sold the story yet. "I don't know, Harry," she
said. "Maybe I despise you."

"An honest broad," Harry said. "Tell me about your second
husband, Vickie. How did you feel about him?"

"My God," she said calmly, "I can't remember."

"He was the painter," Charles said. "Except in Paris
when he was trying to be a sculptor."

Harry said, "I'll bet you were tampering, chickie. I'll
bet you were telling him he should be a sculptor."

"Oh my, no," Victoria said, and her eyes rolled at the
thought of such impudence. "*Nobody* tampered with him." She
did not want to think about him, but he had sprung into her
mind, as though she had seen him just yesterday, and the image
of him was singularly vivid—colored by her lasting reverence for
his talent, even now—and began to form itself in her head. "I
don't want to talk about him," she said. "I don't want to
remember him."

"You are already remembering him," Harry said in a
soothing hypnotist's voice, suggesting, insisting. "If you wrote
him, what would you say . . . ?"

"Katherine Mansfield," she said. "Or maybe Virginia Woolf.
No, Mansfield. That was a good deal of his charm to me . . .
the first one was, oh you know, Hemingway or Dreiser . . .
but he was Mansfield."

"What did he look like?" Harry said, probingly.

"He was a big man," Victoria said, speaking slowly, "heavy-
featured. All the time we were in Paris—we got married there
—he'd been trying to be a sculptor, but it was no good and he
knew it was no good. When we ran out of money, he wrote to his
ex-wife—she was rich—and she sent us some money and we
came back to the States and took a house on the ocean. It was
her house, and maybe we didn't have to pay rent. I don't remember for sure about that. But I remember the house." She
paused. "The house," she said.

Extraordinary how important houses are. They aren't just
shelter for human beings; they become, once built, a form of
life; they make demands, they insist, they intrude themselves,

and always there is the knowledge that they will be there after you, so that you regard them with envy and fear, as you might sometimes secretly regard your children . . . they will out-live you, they will have another life after the life you have shared with them, they will dare to remember you. They take part of your life and keep it for their own, and you can never get it back.

"Go, Vick," Harry said.

"I can't." She could not smile. "I'm not in a Mansfield mood." But it wasn't true, for already her mind was writing the words . . . "Vermouth cassis," she said, absently swallowing some of her drink, "very reminiscent, you know, nostalgic, evocative . . ."

She told them . . .

The first time she saw the house, it seemed to her that she had just come upon a place which had been waiting for her; which, if not built for her, had at least expected her to come to it. With a sense of appointment, of adapting herself to an ar-rangement, she got out of the car and stood a moment at the edge of the narrowing road, saw how it seemed to dwindle, so that at the end where it rose over the low brow of a hill, it merged into what seemed a path, a poor skinny streak of tar and not big enough for a car to ride along. Standing there she could hear the sea pounding, just beyond the house. The sound did not come from either side of the house, but through it, as though the house contained the sea slightly beyond itself. The door opened, she stepped into the wide hall with such a sudden rush of anxiety within herself that she almost wrung her hands and cried out. So profound was the feeling that she realized with surprise that she was not doing that, but moving quite cer-tainly forward into the living room.

Isn't it beautiful?

Yes, yes, she cried.

And in the first days, she thought it was. She could scarcely wait in the mornings to arise, to come downstairs to look out, past the golden dunes, to see the sea churning under the bright blue sky, to feel the waiting wind, which kept the small hardy blossoms atop the dunes in a constant quivering.

In the morning the sun leapt into the sky and threw itself upon the left side of the house. It blazed through the windows and spread profligate on the floor; it dazed the eye and the senses with its brightness. At noon the sun rolled to the front of the house and beat with heat against the rattling windows. When the sun went down it left the sand, the house, the dunes and the sea streaked with vermilion.

In the night the house was cold but filled with noise, with rattlings and wind-howls, with creaks and shiftings and an occasional groan of wood and pilings sinking into wet sand. She tossed in her bed and awakened with a sense of being caught in a living hand which clenched about her.

There was a day when the sea was the color of pewter and the foam showed, not white but dirty, like soiled lace, and the wind flung itself against the house with redoubled intensity. She packed cloth around the sills of the windows but still they trembled and rattled and the sun shook its hot image on the worn rug. In the afternoon, dazed by the sun and the wind's buffetings, she went into the back room of the house where the sun never shone, and looked out at the bleak hills of the north. She felt a chill coming up from the floor, and breathed in the smell of damp wool, the never-quite-dry nap of rug. She went back into the living room, into the sun's sick blaze . . . Of course it was sick . . . the house, she felt, had a disease . . . racked by fever and chills, suffering and alive and fighting death's assault all day, coughing and shivering all night. . . .

There was no place in the house which she could make hers, which she could make a place for her work. The house stood between her and her work, and its conflict pulled at her, tugged at her, kept her choking, clogged with the words every day piling up, unwritten inside her. He painted. He went out to the studio in the back garden and locked himself in, and he painted, untroubled by the life of the house.

Whenever she drove into town, she was surprised to see the people walking up and down and smiling at each other and carrying bundles. She felt as she had felt when her mother was dying and she had been taking care of her . . . desperate to get away from the sweet smell of sickness and the confining room of the invalid and out to the flow of life, and yet misplaced as soon as she was away and attempted to move along the streets with the others. She did not belong there, and she must go back.

As she drove home to the house she went faster and faster, scarcely able to wait until the car would round the bend onto the scratchy little road and she would be able to see the house. She never failed to feel surprise when she saw it, as though she had really expected its destruction in her absence. When she got

*to the garage it was hard for her to drive in, after making the
turn against the sun. She groped the car into the dark garage,
knowing to stop only when the bumper nudged the far wall
and she had added another minute bruise to the battered walls
of the house.*

*One day . . . it rained and damp dark shadow came into
the house, and the new multitudes of sounds of rain, the
coursing of water along the gutters of the roof, the incessant
fall of the heavy drops over the tiles of the roof . . . like many
soldiers, scrambling and sliding and pounding . . . and she
went to the east windows and there was no morning sun fulmi-
nating, and no fever to the exhausted wood of the table; she sat
dazed in the world of sound. She thought, I am not living in the
house. The house draws the life out of me for its fight; it needs
all of it, the sun and the wind and my strength, too. She went
to the guttering fire and tried to get warm and told herself, I
must get away.*

*She drove a long way, acknowledging the packed suitcases
in the trunk as the equipage of defeat. She took a room in a small
hotel. The window looked out upon a tree which in the evening
was filled with thousands of small birds who shrilled and
tweeted with the noise of nervous breakdown. She put out the
light and went to bed and after a while the birds were quiet and
no wind blew. At four o'clock in the morning, she got up and
dressed and put her things back into the suitcases and got the
car. She drove home, through the morning darkness into the
sunburst of the dawn, and it seemed to her that she could hear
the great sigh of the house miles before she got there.*

"I went to the studio where he worked. I knew he was
there. He was one of those adjusted artists, routinized. He got
up at five o'clock every morning and went out along the sandy
path and stood in his studio drinking coffee and looking at the
canvas he'd worked on the day before. Then he began to paint.
He was painting when I got there and he stood with his back to
me while I talked to him. He painted flat, you know, not on an
easel but with the canvas flat on a counter, and he liked to paint
by electric light because he imagined the world looked at paintings only at night." She stopped, clogged suddenly with the
recollection of how it was when she stood there like that,
staring with hatred at his broad back, barely able to speak,
stifled by him and the sense of him and the house together so

that they were inextricable. "I told him the house was impossible for me. I told him I couldn't live in it and I couldn't leave it and come back to it, and I didn't know what I was going to do. I told him things choked me and I couldn't write. I told him the house choked me and knowing he was out here in this little building all the time, silently painting, was choking me, the sense of him was choking me and I couldn't write. I waited. He looked around at me, blinking, whistling through his teeth. He plucked ineffectually at the old gray sweater he wore when he worked . . . it was torn, there was a lacy fray of yarn hanging from his elbow, and I saw in his eyes that even while he looked at me he was forgetting I was there, I saw that it did not matter to him whether I stayed or went, choked or wrote. I got up and went into the house and got my things, the rest of them, and I drove away. I looked back at the house at each turn of the road until I could not see it any more."

There was a silence when she stopped talking and then Harry said, "Thank you, Vickie." He sat there nodding forgetfully like an approving old man.

She looked away from him and down at her hands twisting in her lap. "I'm not going to play this game with you any more Harry," she said. "You're draining off my material. You're decimating me."

Harry smiled. He said, "If you wrote it, the jerks who read it wouldn't know you were swinging, would they? I love you when you swing."

"You love me," she said, sounding dull, feeling empty.

Lucy said, "I would have liked the house." She stretched lazily. "I loved it when we stayed at that hotel at Manzanillo. It was right on the beach and the ceilings were made of cloth that hung down in the middle like rain clouds."

Abel said, "I stand up and paint flat, too."

Harry held up his glass to Abel. "Give Harry some lush," he said.

Abel took the glass and looked into it thoughtfully.

It was nice, Victoria thought, to have somebody like Harry appreciate you, but now it was over and they were back to where they had been before, and there was nothing left of what she had told them. It was lost because she had said it; the words were gone forever, for now she would never again have quite the same need to write it. Now it had limits, whereas, unwritten, it had no shape to confine it. She looked steadily at her hands lying in her lap, small and grubby like two shells a child had played with and gotten dirty. It was as though she had become a parlor actor, performing just for a pat on the head. It wasn't as if these people and their approval meant anything to her. The only quality they had was their immediacy; they were there, and that was all. And yet she had betrayed herself for them.

She slumped in the chair, and ah God, the chair was Mexico and the wasted day was Mexico and these people, whom she entertained only because they were here, these were Mexico; the real world, and real life, rushed past its borders. Look at flabby-faced Harry, the weary devotee of hedonism, and Lucy, the child-enigma . . . her child's voice piping imbecilely "I loved . . . that hotel at Manzanillo. It was right on the beach and the ceilings were made of cloth that hung down in the middle like rain clouds." And Charles, the watchbird, watching and listening, an old-young, nonliving cynic . . . and Abel. But looking at Abel staring for an eternity into Harry's glass, she felt the intuitive certainty come back, interrupting all the flow of her thinking as though she were a physician whose single task was diagnosis and nothing else: there is something seriously wrong with Abel. There was no way of her knowing what it was, since, in spite of her moment of dedication, she really knew very little about medicine and bodies and the illnesses to which bodies were heir. There was nothing more than the wave, like a radio wave, striking against some intuitive antenna; he was physically sick and not just, like the others, sick in his soul. Of course—how still he stood, waiting—he wanted to talk alone to Harry, and all of this had taken time, had taken the afternoon, and it was as though he had come to the very brink of screaming out in madness and now searched the bottom of the glass to see what words might be written there for him to shout.

She got up. It was time to walk out of the afternoon into some other place and be some other, nobler Victoria, and leave the shucked-off, sell-out Victoria behind her at the scene where she had performed her creative striptease and gotten her penny's worth of applause. A smattering of applause for that long time, those years in Paris, that time in the house by the sea, that marriage which had taken hold of her and cracked her into two, that husband whose disinterested gaze was with her still, making her feel invisible. . . .

She began to gather up the red-stained plates. Lucy looked surprised, but like an obedient daughter, rose too and began to help her. "Chatta should do this," she murmured, but Victoria pretended not to hear because this way she could carry the plates to the kitchen and then she could get away. Everything looked ugly to her . . . the messy table, the stained plates, the dust on the floor, the flies slowly circling in the stale room, the glimpse she had of Harry's feet, dirty in their huaraches.

As she started across the patio with Lucy, she heard Abel's voice beginning.

Chatta was in the kitchen, sitting on the three-legged stool in the corner, embroidering in the poor light. There was water boiling in a big *olla* on the stove for the dish-washing, and when she saw them come in with the plates, she got up and set her embroidery down on the stool. She smiled broadly at Victoria and took the plates from her hands.

"*Buenas tardes, señora,*" she said, pleased to see her. It would be nicer if she weren't pleased and didn't show quite so much of her teeth. There was a loose one in the front which had worked its way down so that it was lower than the rest, and touched her lower lip when she smiled, like a fang. "How does it go?" Chatta said, and the tooth moved a little more when she spoke, rabbitlike.

"*Regular,*" Victoria said, making the standard village reply to the idiomatic question. It could mean anything. Today it meant I'm sick of everything, I hate everybody and myself and you and your goddamned tooth and why don't you have it pulled out or pushed back up or something . . . it just won't disappear because you ignore it. She stood there, smoothing her braids, trying not to look at the tooth, and asked the polite, ritualized questions. "You are well, eh, Chatta? And your little mother?"

Ah, the *mamacitas* of Mexico, the adored, brown-nut-faced indomitable women who carried all of Mexico slung around their necks in their *rebozos*! The *rebozo* was the national umbilical cord and the cord was not cut as Mexico grew older.

"*Está bien,*" Chatta said. "She is beautiful although I am ugly. But she has pain in her heart for my brother Cirilo. He is not alleviated."

"No?" Victoria put the proper amount of surprise in the question, although how they expected him to get better was beyond comprehension. Their ways were beyond comprehension sometimes, their ancient stupid ways. Everybody knew about Cirilo and how they wouldn't take him to Dr. Obregón, but, with what little centavos they scraped together, took him instead to the witch doctor in Ixtlahuacán, who prescribed leaf poultices and the drinking of jamaica tea and, no doubt, incantations. With Obregón, Cirilo would have had penicillin or some other medicine which might help him, but that cost money, and they called Obregón a money-hungry quack, and gave their money instead to the scrofulous native medicine man. It was hopeless; they were hopeless and you couldn't tell them so or they just clammed up and disliked you. . . . "*Ay*," Victoria said. "I am sorry. It is sad, *verdad?*"

Chatta pressed her tongue against her tooth and pushed it forward.

Victoria patted her broad shoulder, trying not to let her impatience show. "Poor man," she said. "One day soon he will be better."

Chatta nodded, eager to agree, but there was no conviction in her eyes. "If God gives license," she said dutifully.

Lucy said in English, "I saw him the other day. He looked like death."

Victoria was looking at Chatta at the moment and she saw how, although her face stayed blank, her breathing quickened. In French, Victoria said quickly, "Don't say any more. She understands English."

Lucy looked amazed and shook her head and made as if to argue, so Victoria turned away from her and stood staring out the low window into the patio.

Now Lucy's voice was going on behind her, asking Chatta in a teasing way what were her plans for the fiesta next week, the *kermess* . . . *por exemplé*, what boy was she most eager to meet as they walked around and around the Plaza? Would she take a flower from one of them? Or give a flower? Chatta giggled. Victoria's eyeballs burned in their sockets. There must be a way to shut off the sound of their voices. She let the darkening lids come down over her eyes like cool cloths. She was mortally tired; no doubt that was the reason for her shortening temper. She'd go home. What difference did it make if she were impolite? Who here knew what "polite" meant? She opened her eyes.

A young man came into the patio and stood there a moment, looking around. She leaned forward, peering at him through the clouded glass of the window. He wore a dark suit with a round white collar; he was a young priest. He was very tall and thin, but broad-shouldered, well-built, very handsome for a priest. He did not look Mexican. He had high Slavic cheekbones.

"Is anybody here?" he called toward the open dark door of the lounge. "Abel?" He took a step forward into the bright sunlight and then it was apparent that he wore a dark suit with a turtle-necked dark sweater for a vest. His collar was round and white, edging over the dark wool of the sweater, but now she could see that it was not a clerical collar at all. She had been wrong. He was not a priest. How aristocratic he looked! If he were in the Church, he'd surely be a cardinal, marvelous in red with traces of the world clinging to his rich garments.

Behind her, Lucy said in a pleased voice, "Ned! Why, it's Ned!" and she hurried past Victoria and ran out to him, smiling. He opened his arms to her and, when she was close, hugged her lightly in a brotherly way, so that he held his body away from her, and kissed her silver-white hair.

"*Yá volvió!*" Chatta said, sounding pleased and excited too, and leaning forward to see him better. "Señor Saltamontes!"

"*How* does he call himself?" Victoria said sharply.

Chatta giggled. "It is a joke, señora. Excuse me," Chatta said. "He does not call himself that."

It was one of their jokes. They had names for everybody. Unimaginable what they might call her. But one day she would hear it; one day one of them, bursting with the richness of the joke, would feel compelled to share it with her. The names were usually unkind, with the unkindness of caricature, but accurate. Looking at the young man in the patio, who was not a priest, Victoria felt in this instance there was not the usual accuracy. He looked to her nothing like a grasshopper, but who knew? Maybe he leapt about and seemed to them to jump. Or maybe it was because he was so unusually tall, especially to them. But, even arguing with herself now, about the ineptness of the nickname, she could see something of it . . . in the long body, the eye-glassed eyes which looked large in his long thin

face, with more a praying mantis look than a grasshopper's. . . .

She said in a sharp voice to Chatta, "You do not like him,
this señor?"

"Oh, yes," Chatta said, "he is a true señor," which meant
probably that he was arrogant and demanding and a true
señor in the Spanish sense. This was one of the most irritating
things about Mexicans and Mexico, that instead of despising
their conquistadores, they were still proud of the shine of the
boot which long ago had rested on their necks.

"Then do not speak of him so. It makes harm."

"No, señora," Chatta said in a chastened voice, but she
turned her head so that the long tooth was in full view moving
on her breath, and she giggled again.

Lucy called back to Victoria to come and meet Ned. She
stood with him and they both looked toward the dark windows
of the kitchen, waiting. But when Victoria did not answer,
they turned together and strolled into the lounge. She should
join them but she was reluctant. She did not want to step into
a circle which she was now outside; she stood still again. The
afternoon had made its turn; the sun would soon be going down;
fatigue made its own dusk within her being, its own twilight
. . . She was a child standing outside the closed double doors
of a living room where a birthday party was going on, listening to the other children inside chattering and shrieking;
she stood there, reluctant, holding her present in its tissue
paper—It was old, wrinkled paper and her mother had ironed
it, trying to make it look new before she put the tacky little
ribbon bow on it, but it didn't have a new, tissue-paper smell—
and she glared at the closed doors, afraid.

Are you shy? they said to her in those days, teasing her,
and she would shake her head. Not shy then, not shy now. It was
clear to her very early, that life was full of rooms waiting for
you, and some of them waited for you as though by appointment; the instant you went into them, they changed you . . .
the self that you were outside the door would never again be the
same, once you had gone through and were inside the room.
Sometimes it was the outside self you wanted to keep on being,
and sometimes it wasn't that you wanted to continue being the
outside self as much as that you feared the unknown self you
would become inside the room. And sometimes you were un-

bearably curious, so that you told your outside self, go in, hurry, be part of it. And the outside self could hardly be heard saying, no, wait, stay here, keep on being me.

Chatta edged past her. "*Con permiso, señora,*" she said. "I go to get the rest of the plates."

Chatta was in a great hurry. She grabbed up a tray and wiped it off with a smeary cloth. Her excitement was palpable. There was no ambivalence in Chatta about the outside self and the inside self, no fear of the rooms of destiny. She went, her huaraches slapping quickly across the patio floor.

Now while they were all in the lounge busy with Ned, she would go home. They wouldn't notice . . . But then just as she started out, Abel and Harry came out of the lounge with Charles right behind them. Abel was moving fast, trying to pull Harry along with electric urgency, but Harry lagged like an unwilling child, ready to balk. "Slower, man," Harry said, but Abel tugged at him, bringing him toward the kitchen. She backed into the room, out of sight again, and looked around, but there was no other way out of there.

"Don't come in here," she said when they were at the door. "I'm tired of you."

They came in anyway with Harry saying, "Here's Vickie," with a pleased smile. He put his hand heavily on her arm. "Stay," he said.

Abel said, "*Alone*, Harry."

"I'm always alone," Harry said, whining. "It's easy."

"Let me go," Victoria said and tried to pull away but Harry's grip tightened and she was surprised at the strength of it and looked at his flaccid, pale face; the hand and the face did not go together. She looked to Charles slouching there in the door-way.

"How about it, Harry?" Charles said. "Let Vickie go. I'll go to the *excusado* and blast a joint while Abel talks to you."

Harry said, "Don't leave me, mother. I ever tell you about my mother?"

Charles sighed. "You know it," he said. But he made no further attempt to go away.

Abel said, "Six percent. I'll pay you 6 percent a month and if I'm late with a payment I'll double the interest, okay? Like business. I mean, we'll write it down, man."

Victoria said, "I cannot *stand* this conversation. Harry, let me go. Let me out of here. Why should I go through this?"

"On how much?" Harry said to Abel.

"Five hundred."

Harry stared at him, body going slack, eyes suddenly sharp-pointed, blue behind the glasses.

"Angel-shit's *here*, Harry. I got to have five hundred."

"You warp me, man," Harry drawled. He shook his head. "I got no amount of bread like that."

Abel put his hand to his forehead, pulled hard at it, getting the sweat off. "You dig Ned will take the bar away from me?"

Victoria said, "Let me go, Harry." She tried to jerk her arm away.

"Let her go, will you, for God's sake?" Abel said.

Harry didn't even look at her. He said, "I haven't got five bills, man."

"Why do you con your friends, Abel?" Charles said gently. "There must be a sucker in town. Can't you find yourself a John . . . ? Harry, let the broad go."

Abel said, "You think I'd ask you if I had any place else?"

Victoria said, "I absolutely cannot endure this another minute and I'm going to scream, Harry, if you don't let go of me and let me out of here."

He turned his head and looked at her, his attention caught by the way her voice rose, and he loosened his hold and looked at her arm as though he hadn't known he was holding it. "Yeah, yeah," he breathed.

Victoria dug into her purse, scratched around against the worn leather lining and found a crumpled bill. It was the only one, unless there was a check at the post office, but you couldn't see somebody beg and beg. She pressed the bill into Abel's hand. "That's all I have," she said. It was a hundred pesos. "If I had more, I'd give you more." The look she turned on Harry was scorchingly contemptuous. "Now, let me *out* of here." There was a silence and she walked through it, out the door.

Her heels jarred down hard on the bricks of the patio as she stamped along. No dignity, no damnable dignity for anybody. Nobody was allowed to have it. Lack of money stripped it from them, or fear, or failure, or lovelessness, or stupidity. They stripped it from each other, that was part of it; oh yes, when you've lost it yourself, tear the shreds, the raveled edges of somebody else's from him and then we can all be Look-Alikes.

Lucy caught up with her and took her hand. Arrested, she turned her angry face to Lucy, trying to warn her without speaking because now was not the time, you know, for Lucy to be feeble-mindedly insistent about something. Lucy insisted. "Not now," she said through her teeth, but then she saw that the stranger was standing beside her, looking down at her and waiting. Was that what Lucy had said? Yes. "I want you to meet Ned," she'd said.

"You're in a hurry," Ned said. But Lucy made the introduction, and Victoria thrust her hand out violently for him to shake, but instead of taking it as normal people could be expected to do, this fool held it, looked at it and bowed over it. She snatched her hand away from him. "How do you do," she said, not looking at him, but knowing that he was smiling, not so much at her as at the occasion of meeting someone. He probably thought he was charming. But she didn't have the time for this bowing-formality and smiling-formality and what kind of pretension was it anyway, to bow over a woman's hand? He was not a European, his accent was American. But everything about him was pretentious . . . his perfect grooming, the lemony smell of toiletries which came from him . . .

"I was telling Ned about the beautiful party he missed last night," Lucy said. "It was lovely, wasn't it? Abel and I didn't go, but it sounded lovely."

"It was *vile*," she said. "A vile party. *Another* vile party." Lucy looked bewildered. Victoria groped in her purse for cigarettes and found none. "I left my cigarettes in the lounge," she said, and started for the door.

"May I get them for you?" Ned said.

"I'll get them." She went into the lounge, hoping that they would not follow her but they did, and then Charles appeared in the doorway after them and said, "Abel said to tell you he had to cut out, Ned. The—ah—the Delegado sent for him. He said he'd see you later."

"I see," Ned said but he looked puzzled; Charles was an unconvincing liar. But then Harry came slouching into the room after Charles, and Ned's face changed when he saw him. The puzzled look left him; his back stiffened, his neck lengthened; his head tilted back a little so that he looked down on Harry. He turned away and picked up the new bottle of rum from the table, and then Victoria's cigarettes, which he handed to her. "I'll be going along then," he said. "Lucy, you must come have tea with me some afternoon."

Lucy said delightedly, "Oh how nice!"

Ned turned to Victoria. She was pushing the cigarettes into her purse, knowing they were getting crushed in the process but not caring. "Where are you staying, Miss Beacon?" he said.

"The López house."

"I'll send you a note. Maybe you and Lucy would come together."

"I don't make dates," Victoria said. "I'm not here for the social life. I'm here to work."

He smiled winsomely. "I'm working too, but we can take time out for a visit one day, can't we?" He continued to smile imperturbably. "I'd like to say I've read your books, Miss Beacon, but I haven't. I read almost no contemporary literature."

She grunted. "It doesn't matter," she said. Who cares what you read?

"But I shall read at least one of them before I invite you over. Then we can talk about your work as well as mine."

She glared at him. "I don't like to talk about my work. I detest writers and painters who talk about their work," she said.

Inexorably courteous, he said, "I seldom like them myself." His gaze traveled over her, assessing her, and she got the feeling she was being measured against a set of standards strange to her. He probably thought her ugly and shabby, as well as ill-mannered. "Then we won't talk about your work," he said. "But I *will* send you a note."

"Don't," she said flatly. "I don't want a note. I don't want you to read me. I do not defend my books. I wrote them when I was young, you know . . . *young*, and now I deny them."

Harry cut in. "Oh they're not bad, Vick. They're really not bad . . . They have a Rimbaud feel, a little Joyce . . ."

She wheeled on him, and her hand on the purse stiffened into a claw which could rake his face with its nails. "You," she said. "Don't *dare*, you sniveling, infantile boob, to reassure *me*. You nursling!" At bay, she swung around like the madman of New Jersey who suddenly machine-guns fifteen innocent people, and said to Ned, hearing her own theatricality and hating it, but unable to hold it back anyway, "And you. I looked at you once and I knew you. I don't care what you think about my books. Because *you are easily known*, did you know that?"

Ned stared at her as though she were an articulate part of a bad dream, and even as she saw him look at her so, she was composing in her mind the note of apology she'd have to write him, because, really, he had, after all, only walked in where other things were happening and had tried to be nice. She was ashamed but her anger was stronger than her shame, and she met his look with a hard stare now, and ignored the way Harry had begun to mumble a protest . . .

Ned froze, drew himself up again, looked around at the others and in a subdued voice he said, "I'll be going." He nodded to Victoria again. "I apologize, madame," he said, which was infuriating . . . another European grandiloquence. "I seem somehow to have offended you. I'm sorry." Oh, get your damned coals of fire off my head, she thought, and then he was lifting a hand in a wave to everybody at once, impersonal and friendly, so that the big ring on his little finger flashed with bishoplike forgiveness, and he said in a cold voice, "*Adios'n*, everybody," which was the colloquial good-bye, and then without haste, with dignity, he was gone.

Victoria stood there. Harry said, "Angel-shit," and laughed.

Charles said, "He's not a bad guy." He looked at Harry, shaking his head disapprovingly. "When are you ever going to take a bath, Harry, for Christ's sake?"

"Your interest in me becomes more overtly homosexual every day, sweetheart," Harry said. "Not to mention your touching devotion to Prince Darling."

Abel came in.

"I thought you went to see the Delegado," Lucy said.

"I was hiding in the *excusado*," Abel told her.

Harry said to Charles, "Are you having a nice Sunday afternoon visit with the family, mother?"

Victoria walked out the door and into the patio, as Harry said, "Old Vickie's sick of us nurslings," but she did not pause. In the patio she fumbled in her purse with shaking hands and found her dark glasses and pushed them on.

As she walked through the patio, Harry's voice, like a

thorny twig dragging over her brain, went on in the lounge . . .
"You want a bill and I offer you a bill to get me some junk
and you won't even do me that simple favor and I'm supposed to
lay loot on you . . ."

"It's no favor," Abel's high voice said, rising hysterically.
"I told you, I won't push. Lucy, get out of here." He was yelling.
"You ever see a junkie die, Harry? You want to die, Harry . . . ?
That what you want?"

There was a crash of breaking glass, and she turned and
looked in the open window as Charles said commandingly, "Put
that bottle down, man. Abel, give it to me. Lucy, stay
here . . ."

Abel stood there, wearing a strange smile, the jagged bottle
in his hand, ready to lunge. Lucy gave a little whimper of fright,
but Harry did not look afraid. His voice was relaxed, and he
stood there as though he did not see the broken bottle in Abel's
hand. "Is there a good way to die? Can you tell me you'll be sad
when I die? Tell me you'll grieve. There's no argument against
my death. I want death. But I want to go out swinging." There
was a pause. "Put the bottle down, Abel. Here's a bill. Get me
some C for it and I'll match it with another. With Vickie's hundred, that makes three. Baby makes three . . ."

Abel's hand holding the bottle dropped lower; his shoulders relaxed, slumped, and he settled down on his heels again,
and then he put the bottle down on the table. "No, man," he said,
shaking his head. "No."

It was over. She went away from the window, down the
two steps into the street. Now forget it. Now put the fear
away. Look at the world. Put your fear away, put away your
rage. Forget these strangers you've been with, look at the world,
see how the shadows along the wall are darker now, more moist;
night is coming. There's a breeze, hear it sighing up from the
lake, see how it stirs the tops of the mango trees, rustles
there, rhythmically. . . .

Look at things, make the world back into its old shape, see
there on the distant highway to Guadalajara how a plume of
white dust rises in a geyser toward the foothills from the small
shape of a truck traveling the road, disappearing now beyond
the papaya grove, passing the cemetery.

Along with the anger burning in her and her sense of
betrayal, and deeper sense of self-betrayal, there came on her

a feeling of vagrant sexuality. It seemed to have no object, no beginning, but simply to be there. Harry? Charles? No, no. Something someone said? Ned? The memory of her old house at the sea, her old husband? The release of rage? Or was it, humiliatingly enough, just possibly the result of having eaten a meal for a change instead of grabbing up whatever cold crust the *niña* left for her? Probably. Disgusting, but true. A full meal could do that after months of deprivation.

Look at the arching cumulus clouds making pillars in the lilac sky . . . white, deific, grand. Feeling sexual was also part of the approach of the tropical night. You knew it affected tourists but you forgot that it could affect you, too. Look at the clouds.

Beside her, the white wall, going pink in this light, had a crumbling surface where the dark mud of adobe showed through in ugly patches. There was not a whole wall in all of Mexico untouched by the moving finger of decay.

Nor a whole soul. Dismiss the Mexicans for a minute, because right now they seem like another species, healthy, sometimes stupid and sometimes magnificent, but mostly strange. Strange to the strange Americans. For we are the real strangers, always strange, doomed to feel out of place, even at home . . . and here, clustering on this shelf of land by a lake in another country, with the finger of decay pointing at us, too . . . we work our strangeness upon each other. We are all refugees, having run here from something, out of one reality into another, out of the burning building which was life in America, to this displaced persons' utopia . . . where a full meal of spaghetti was a celebration.

If only she hadn't come here and found these old-new demons to plague her, if only she hadn't come here to make a last desperate try! She was full of anger, held in thrall, her own prisoner, her own encaged, wretched madwoman-prisoner. . . .

She walked rapidly, even though the day's heat struck up at her from the cobblestones. She could see the group of men standing near the pool hall, their big hats tilted forward like shields against the vermilion sky. The sunset light gave them grandeur, and the smoky smell of corn cooking, coming from the houses a little burned, was exotic, and surrounded them like a musky perfume. She knew of two American women who had taken lovers from among the villagers . . . It was said that Jesús, the *mariachi*, was one . . . Their faces were mysterious and beautiful now, with an ancient beauty, and they stood silent, watching her come toward them.

Night is coming, she yelled silently at them, trying to summon revulsion against them. At night they would turn into their dark, dirt-floor houses and lie down on their mats with their exhausted, misshapen women—like her mother, oh yes! like her mother—and the weight of the dark Mexican night would be upon them, while outside the finger of decay would scrape two more tiles off that roof, gouge out a wall and expose the dirty brown adobe beneath . . . Mangoes which had fallen during the day and lain rotting in the tropic sun, filled the smoky blue air with a rank sweet stench. Chickens ran erratically across the road, and the twin-towered church gleamed with pink light.

She turned the corner at her own street, fishing in her shoulder bag for the door key, which was as big as a pistol, finding it among the wads of tissue and the empty wallet and the powder box with the rubber band holding it together. She opened the door, locked it again from the inside, walked quickly up the shadowed *zaguán* and, standing at the edge of her small, ragged patio, let her purse drop onto the leather table by the living-room door. "All right, you're home," she said. Beyond the patio wall there were jacaranda trees, beyond the flowering trees the mountains, and down from the mountains, night coming, and small, inefficient trains stringing like beads through the dark hills . . .

So what? So the dark Mexican night is coming, and the subhuman apes may not turn the lights on and there you'll be sitting at your typewriter unable to see. She walked into the cool living room and sat herself at her typewriter, making herself sit there and wait for the lights to come on, sitting with her hands folded in her lap and her face lifted to the purpling sky, as she would look up at the teacher. Waiting, she tried to brush off the last clinging bits of rage, and pull together the forces within her so that she could now—*if* the cretins put the lights on!—without the usual blocs, inhibitions, tortured self-pokings, explorations, journeys through tangential meadows of emotion, write what she wanted to write, instead of dying slowly and amiably in the company of wastrels and assassins.

Darkness came slowly until the instant it was suddenly there, impenetrable. Make them turn it on, she said, and at last the lights came on and the room around her sprang into being. All over the village, radios burst into raucous sound, and the adobe walls took up the cacophony and trembled with it. She put her earplugs in place, and took up a first blank page and put it in the typewriter.

She began to write, and then paused and picked up the last page she had written before. As she read, her eyes seemed to run off at the corners, so as not to read it, but she forced them to track. Then she came back to the page in the type-writer and lifted her hands over the keys. Suddenly her truant mind showed her an image of her last husband. If it had been the husband she'd been talking about at Abel's, that would have been easy to understand. But it wasn't. It was quite clearly Ramón, standing in the *sala* of their apartment in Mexico City, reading the note she had propped up against the little stone idol on the mantel, when she left him months before. Did the memory of one ghost evoke another? She continued to write. The phrases at first came slowly, so that she wrote in little explosive bursts, gradually in this way managing to put many phrases between herself and Ramón, who still stood there on some ill-lit stage in her mind, forever reading the note, until it was as though the phrases strung up and down into the kind of bamboo curtain which hung in the doorways of the house in Yucatán, and she could scarcely see him.

As she wrote, she tried to slow the plunge of her thinking . . . and look how the afternoon's mood was working in here, even the sight of Lucy's pale face and paler hair . . . and Harry, talking, scratching at her nerves steadily through the whole afternoon, every word etched into her mind, so that he talked and hooted with laughter and was Harry, but Harry car-ried forward to another degree of mania, refusing with vulgar craftiness Abel's sick and desperate plea. The whining, shame-ful dialogues between them, which in the beginning became like worms in her blood, now swelled like cobras; and Ned, with an aura of gold pretension, stepped out from between the cobras, with a hand on each side pushing them apart as though they were no more than a curtain, a drape to be so handled. He had existed behind that drape for some time now, and the conversa-tion came back, word for word. There was his astonishment again and now, discordant, herself in her rage with her eyes popping.

She must have looked ridiculous to such a stranger, and

how could he have been worth the investment of this rage? And worse still, now he appeared to reproach her. She was a wretch who wasted her substance on poltroons, who delusionally considered herself the vessel of a great and honest talent. Who ever used the word "great"? Modesty, said Ned, was not only a virtue, it was the *Good Housekeeping* accepted seal of sanity in the world, but now Ned was beginning to sound like one of her selves, one who appeared in many costumes when she wrote, but also played the same skinny role of the dominie with the drop of wet at the end of its pointed nose, wagged its blue-white bony finger at her, chiding her with its eyes and telling her, regretfully, that she was simply insane, but not divinely so like Dostoevski, not with a defined, circumscribed insanity like epilepsy, but insane from a deep flaw in her being, born there, put there by her father's seed and her mother's—oh Christ, re-volting—egg . . . What rancor, what rage, what acidulous fury that life was not the way she infantilely demanded that it be, and all this while she began to separate into many selves, like an amoeba, while the story rolled out, finally, as though she were not now creating it but had had it all the time in a solid piece within herself and the first pages were just a way of breaking open a passage so the whole story could get out . . .

She even rocked as she wrote, rocked on the chair like a grieving old woman, brought down on the side of the road, grieving in shapeless age through the centuries of time, and like a child, who sings to itself and contains itself and as it croons itself its own lullaby, enchants itself by rocking and rocking into a half-numbed state of elation.

She reached up and untied the drawstring neck on her blouse, vaguely unable any longer to endure the tight-pressing cloth. She worked as steadily as a machine, with all the selves within her quietly watching what was happening. But then, nightmarishly, the words began to ring in her head with a false sound and somebody in the distance laughed at her. It was as if she were a child who was living in a tree house which was beautiful and then people jeered at it and she learned it was only two old boards stretched on a branch with a dirty, ragged blanket draped over another branch and not, to anybody else in the world, a tree house, and on no account beautiful, and the doubt grew strong as her breath came shallow and weak, and it was abruptly not any good at all, any of it.

She was buried alive in Mexico like those men in the

Eisenstein movie years ago, buried alive to their necks and then having their heads trampled by galloping horses. Her sister Martha threw off her shroud and rose from the grave, saying coarsely: I didn't die and give you money so you could write that trash. Her father, putting down the pages, drawing on his cigarette, looked at her with bestial, narrow-eyed disappointment.

Abruptly the lights went out. Her arms cramped; her fingers went rigid. She made a tremendous effort of will, sitting in the drowning dark, joining all her selves together to rout the enemy, and she fought it back, fought the darkness around her and the darkness of rage within her, dueling it back with the broom of her childhood with which her slatternly mother chased and beat at the cockroaches in the kitchen, and she kept writing, clearing her mind by writing, holding in it now only the words she was writing, until the page was done. The work was done. She leaned back limply.

No flicker of light showed under the shutter, so the darkness had come over the whole town and was not just a fuse blown in her house. But she'd beaten them. She'd gotten it done. Some cretin somewhere had tampered with the wires, or some *borracho* straggling home from the cantina had probably climbed the ladder and turned the switch which controlled the village power. . . .

She got up stiffly and went into the *zaguán*. She found her purse and got matches out of it and lit the kerosene lamp on the table there and then got cigarettes out of her purse and lit one. She gulped the sharp smoke into her lungs. Her mouth was dry and her fingers were shaking. She took up the lamp and the cigarettes and came back into the living room and scooped up the pages and crouched down on the corner of the couch in the light. She shrugged off her clothing so that, except for her shoes, she was naked. She removed her earplugs. With the power off, the radios of the town were silent. The streets were quiet. There was someone laughing somewhere, that was all, and an animal in the street, brushing against the wall of the house as it cropped the sparse grass between the cobblestones. She smoked and, feeling a little sick with fear, nauseated, with the taste of old metal in her mouth, read what she had written.

She finished, rubbed out a cigarette on the floor, lit another one, let the pages fall on the floor in a chunk and lay back on the couch. She ached. Her shoulders ached. She stretched her cramped muscles, listening to the way her heart knocked in her chest, listened to the dishpan church bell, being hand-rung now that the power was off, and learned that it was midnight.

She had worked for six and a half hours. She had written twenty-two pages. She thought they were marvelous, and instantly reminded herself that she couldn't know that now; tomorrow they'd look different. But right this minute, they were marvelous. She thanked God. "Your daughter thanks You." Her voice was dry and harsh.

Exhaustion came at her from different parts of her body in various aches and numbnesses. Her skin was cold, tightening up against the cold air, but it was better than the feeling of tight clothes on it. She was starving. She got up and went with the lamp into the kitchen, her heart brimming with love, loving the night and the feel of the cool night air on her skin, even loving the animal bumping now against her door. "There! There!" she called to it soothingly in the special husky voice Mexicans used for talking to animals. "Run along!" she called. "*Andale!*" And her voice was amiable and deep. She found in the Coca-Cola bin she used for an icebox a papaya resting against the small cake of ice, and a couple of limes. She took the fruit, cut it down the middle, scraped out the seeds, squeezed the lime juice over it and ate it while she searched for more to eat. There was an egg and there was a fresh roll.

She was cooking the egg when she heard the music and paused. The lights had not come on so it couldn't be coming from a radio or phonograph. It was outside in the street and she came into the *zaguán* to listen. *Mariachis* were singing "*Las Mananitas*" and she heard a clarinet playing with them, but a different song, it seemed, and someone was bowing the bass. She moved the egg pan off the flame and went out to the door and peeked through the wide crack in the upper panel.

There was a group standing in a semicircle before her shuttered window. The white sombreros of the *mariachis* and the glittering trim on their jackets picked up the faint moonlight and they were easy to see. In the dark like that in the street, they did not look like just ridiculous Jesús and Nicolás, but like troubadours put there by the custom of centuries. There was Charles, playing the bass, bowing it; she could see the flash of his white hand going from side to side, and she knew it was he because he was so tall and besides he laughed once and she recognized the rich sound of his laughter. Harry was there, very drunk, so that he swayed, even though he stood still with his feet braced wide apart to hold himself up, playing a melancholy clarinet, thin and flutelike. Harry played another melody against the *mariachis'* "*Las Manañitas*," and after a minute or two she recognized it as "If You Were the Only Girl in the World," and it was amazing how he could put the two songs together with his variations and make them one.

Jesús stopped singing and began to blow the cornet and soon Harry pulled the clarinet out of his mouth to argue with him the way he always did, interrupting his own music to say, "Jeez, man, no Clyde McCoy . . . Jeez . . . oh you square . . . oh you mother . . ." Charles laughed again and suddenly she heard Abel's high voice—what was he doing with them?—singing, "Doing the ricky-tick for Harry's Vickie-chick . . ." in a kind of chant, and then they all began to do a new rhythm to that and Jesús came to a full stop and there was only Harry's clarinet now, climbing high up the rich steps of Charles' bowed bass and overriding the homely chording of Nicolás' fumbling guitar . . .

She leaned against the door and let her cheek rest against its rough grain and felt its coolness down the whole side of her, and gnawed on the butterless roll while she listened. She felt wonderful and foolish but she was tired and when one was tired one was easily touched, sentimental, vulnerable. In this moment she loved being serenaded, loved Harry and Charles and Abel and Jesús and Nicolás, loved Mexico, loved the world.

5

Ned

NED'S mornings which began when he awak-
ened, usually after ten, were an exceedingly pleasant part of the
day. He had taken considerable trouble to train Jovita to an
approximation of good service, so that the coffee brought to
his bedside when he rang was fresh and hot, and his breakfast
table in the patio was invitingly set, with one flower in a delicate vase beside his water goblet. The meal was served with
silent attention, so that he was able to read, uninterruptedly,
with none of the chitchat, the *plática*, of which all Mexican
maids seemed so ingenuously fond, until after he had eaten
and read, and was equal, if one is ever equal, to facing the day
before him.

The cat, Hassan, a handsome, cocoa-tinted Siamese, was kept out in the *corral* until then and, if Ned asked to see him, released to stroll in an admirable affectation of indifference to his chair, to sit down beside him, with no noxious leg-rubbing or hoarse pesterings for food or attention. Ned respected the cat's princely manner; he had done his best to inculcate it. Sometimes, when he was in an especially good mood, he vouchsafed it a great swooping, hugging embrace which both he and Hassan enjoyed very much; when the cat twitched his tail or sat with his ears back and low, Ned understood that it wanted no demonstrations of affection and ignored it until finally it strolled to an open corner of the patio and lay there, incredibly beautiful, receiving the sun.

The cat was a remarkable companion, neither demanding nor insensitive, and always beautiful. Ned found when he had house guests . . . when Manuél stayed overnight, or Chloë visited him . . . that he became more appreciative of the cat. Chloë was a beautiful girl and Manuél was a beautiful man, but in its own way the cat was more consistently beautiful than either one, made fewer demands and gave him greater pleasure.

He enjoyed Chloë, especially early in her visits. She was informed and cultivated, if foolish, and she had a lovely, trilling laugh, long slim hands, and almond-shaped eyes. But the laugh could trill at him mockingly, the eyes could narrow in criticism and widen with disappointment, and the hands made no contribution to the household. Chloë's arrival not only demoralized his servants, but the entire village. The Mexicans became positively demented around Chloë; the cook did not cook but ran in and out of Chloë's room, helping Jovita, who was helping the laundress with Chloë's tissuey, expensive negligees and lingerie . . . acquiring for herself—Chloë was generous with her toys— things she would never use . . . a jeweled comb, a jar of Elizabeth Arden's Eight Hour Cream, a couple of nearly black, unmatched, web-sheer evening stockings. The gardener was busy choosing nosegays for Chloë, and delivering them all over town along with little folded squares of creamy thick paper which contained invitations in Chloë's elaborate handwriting and which were sealed with sealing wax and indented with her crested ring, as though they were precious documents indeed. God knew the notes and nosegays were effective; they brought a flurry of answering notes upon his house in a way which re-

minded Ned of the pigeons of St. Mark's, flying up all together
with a great wing-rustling and settling down all at once on his
doorstep. Chloë invited people to cocktails and supper, and then
forgot to tell the cook, or tell him; usually he found out about
imminent guests only when she consulted him about what she
should wear for the evening. She was young of course, but not
that young . . . nobody was *that* young. It made him cross at
the moment, but then he forgave her because she pleaded with
him charmingly and they were soon engaged in the business of
trying on this dress or that; the cook alerted, on her mettle
now, came through; the evening would be delightful, and
through it all, no matter who came, Chloë would parade her
love for Ned.

She loved him completely, even if he did not love her, and
he wasn't certain that he didn't love her. In a way it often
seemed to him that he did, even to the point of his showing
jealousy when she flirted in front of him, although he always
put it on the basis not of love but of disgust with her current
choice. "Him?" he would say. "He's a cretin. He's the milk-
delivery boy." Or "Good God, what do you mean Ignacio is coming over here on his horse to serenade you? He drives a bus all
day. He's a bus driver, Chlo . . . How could you?" Or "Diony-
sius? The muscled one who works for the gardener? He plays
with a yo-yo on the street corner at night. He's about six years
old mentally . . ." And sometimes she laughed with him and
sometimes she didn't. Sometimes she pouted and said something
inconsequential—"He's got marvelous cheekbones. Haven't you
noticed?"—as though that were an answer. The point about
Chloë was that she adored Ned whether or not he loved her;
he was the love of her life and she never doubted that one day
he would marry her when all of "this" was done. She never
seemed jealous of the other people who adored him, not even
the ones for whom he admitted desire. Her attitude was that
life was for living and he must have what he wanted as she
must have what she wanted, so that when at the end they came
together, it would not be ruefully with old hungers to keep
them apart, but with the knowledge that they'd had it all and
now could be content with each other.

She and Manuél were friends; the day she met him at
Ned's and understood, with one of those light quick glances, all
there was to be understood, she simply adopted him as another

cavalier, strolled along between the two of them, putting a
hand on Ned's arm, and the other hand on Manuél's. Manuél
was a brooder, sullen, heavy-browed and selfish, but he liked
Chloë. There was no other acquaintance of Ned's whom he accepted; he resented them all. When he was alone with Ned,
he demanded an inordinate amount of attention; all of Ned's
time was devoted to reassuring Manuél, appeasing Manuél, and
trying in innumerable ways to alleviate the mysterious pain of
soul from which Manuél suffered.

Manuél was a fine artist, very talented, highly skilled,
wonderfully developed; had he not been, no matter how much
involved emotionally Ned became with him, he would not have
been willing to play spiritual valet for him, giving up even
briefly his own aristocratic pretensions. Manuél was Spanish,
and his family's blood, remarkably enough, was not mixed with
the Indio blood of the adopted country; Manuél faced life in
Mexico and elsewhere with the arrogance of the conquistador.
But he was not, even distantly, of noble ancestry, and his family, although rich, was not listed in the Almanach de Gotha. As
an artist, however, Manuél had every claim, by Ned's standards,
to nobility, and therefore his hauteur was reasonable and justi-
fiable.

Ned believed that talent was knighthood enough; he
shared with Manuél his own self-attribution of aristocracy, re-
gretting the lack of a birth claim to nobility only because that
would have made everything easier. In actual fact, Ned's background was far, far beneath Manuél's. He had come from a
family of poor Slavic immigrants and was only a second-
generation American, reared in stringent economy and a poverty of education, cultivation or even ordinary lower-middle-
class wholesomeness. His childhood had been horrible and he
had lived through it with his teeth clenched, at the fitful mercy
of his madwoman mother, and victimized by an irresponsible,
begrudging, slow-witted father who could neither read nor
write, in an environment of deprivation and ugliness. His father's farm was on poor land in an area where other farms
flourished in rich wheat and his father stupidly and doggedly
toiled to gouge out a sickly crop from unyielding soil. Because
he was slow, Ned's father did not grow impatient with the land
and move off to take a chance elsewhere; he himself was begrudging and he did not expect the earth to be any different.

Because he was irresponsible and unobservant, he did not see
that his family lived in frightful want and that his wife's mind
had become deranged and she was torturing his child; what he
could not avoid seeing, he saw with a shrug—this was women
for you. Ned hated him, and even more hated his mother and
the place where they lived; the farm was unsightly, the weather
was treacherous and ugly, and he spent his early years searching for something to like—a dog, a bug, a moth—anything. He
began to live the day he first saw something he thought beautiful. The painting was, he now knew, not beautiful at all. But
he had found it himself—it was set in the window of an empty
store in a nearby town, presumably just to fill up space—away
from home, away from the snickering torments of his school
life. He stood in the street by himself and looked at it; he *saw*
it; he saw color and design; there was a sharp knife of exquisite
pain in his chest and he drew in the first long, sweet breath of
his life.

Now he began to grow. Until that day, he'd been a sickly,
spindly child who sat hunched over like a turtle with his long
neck stuck skinnily forward, looking palely out at the world.
The sight of him had always baffled his father—for Ned had
come from a family of strong-backed, thick-legged peasants,
emotionally volatile, erupting into laughter or tears at any
slight provocation, Slavic and wild; they lived on and with
the land, ate and drank and lusted until too much work stiffened
them into hard beings, stupefied and petrified by exhaustion. It
was difficult to believe that Ned was their descendant. But now
at least, after a childhood of apathy and weakness, he became very busy. He studied. He went to the library. He read,
almost constantly. A light burned in his pale eyes. He began to
carve perfect little figures out of soap; grasshoppers and crickets,
hens and geese, horses, cows, dogs, and a remarkable fox which
he carried for a long time in his shirt pocket and, when he was
alone, looked at, running his fingers over the carving. These
were no mere whittlings, but each one a flawless miniature being, superior to the models he used from life. One day he got a
broken easel somewhere, carted it home and fixed it, and drew
and painted until all the paper he could get was used on both
sides. He made friends with a teacher, a scrawny fellow with
frightened eyes and loose, silky hair which fell over a pale forehead, and he spent every possible moment with him.

On the morning of Ned's fifteenth birthday, his father came running into the house to him, shouting that his mother had killed herself. The father said, repeating it over and over with a look of mystification and disbelief on his face, that he had gone into the barn and found her there, swinging from a rafter. Ned went with his father to the barn and looked up at the figure moving slightly in the cold shadows and he said, "We must cut her down." His father was sobbing. "My God, my God," he said in the language of the old country, "what a terrible thing!" Ned, setting up the little stepladder which his mother had kicked over, looked at him with loathing. "Can't you speak English?" he said. It was he who cut the body down. He came down off the ladder and looked at it on the barn floor, at the outflung hand on the straw, the matted hair sliding over the blue face.

His father, in the midst of gulping great sobs, finally looked into his son's eyes and saw no sign of feeling there; his sobs lessened and he said in horror, "My boy . . . that's your mother on the floor there!"

"I know who it is," Ned said softly.

And then he was gone, in the quiet way he had learned of moving noiselessly in his old, torn sneakers, out of the barn and then out of the house, letting the sagging door whisper shut behind him.

One day the door shut and stayed shut. Ned was gone, and the schoolteacher with the silky hair was gone, too. People said they'd gone off together. But that had no meaning for Ned's father, except that after a while he realized that neither Ned's mother nor Ned himself had been of any real help to him on the farm and that, in fact, he now did better without them.

Years later, after college and his first one-man show, when he was in Venice, Ned realized that beauty was a hard mistress. He read "The Hound of Heaven," and identified with the voice saying, "I fled him down the labyrinthine ways," and thought not of Christ coming after a soul with relentless love, but of himself pursuing beauty in just that way. His pursuit had become a drive so strong that nothing else mattered to him, nothing else and no one else. The schoolteacher had had to be escaped in time, and the subsequent relationships seemed to end much the same way—in an outraged cry from the rejected one, with reproach, with rage, with always the same sentence of terrible recognition, "You never cared for me at all! You're not human! You love only yourself!" He never failed to be surprised by the inaccuracy of the charge, the more so when the speaker was intelligent, or schooled by the world. Of course he had cared for the other one—in his way. Of course he was human, but he learned early that by "human," people meant "like me." This was a lesson tiresomely repeated over and over in each relationship as though by cosmic design, as though some God-figure doubted that he had learned it yet. Of course he did not love himself. He loved only those things in and about himself which were beautiful.

But "beautiful" was no longer an undefined idea. Beauty contained—must contain—order, perfection (or only a perfect flaw), exactitude, precision, plan, design, control, completion. Beauty was habit-forming. He was deeply addicted to it.

When he was twenty-six and back in the States, he had a nervous breakdown. He was put into an ugly hospital room, with walls painted institutional-green, and fed unattractive food; when he refused it, a tube was shoved up his nose and set to travel down his throat; he was force-fed. He knew he was now necessarily a functioning integer in the world's conspiracy to make ugliness. To avoid that crime, he ate. To avoid the sight of the walls, he lay with his eyes closed and listened in his mind to Mozart, or Hindemith, or Haydn. He looked, in his mind, at beautiful places in France and Spain, in Denmark and Italy, carefully expunging from his recollection any attendant ugliness in the scene. He erased a thousand pictures, dwelt lovingly upon five or six he considered perfect.

A friend sent him Henry James. He read him, and when he went to sleep at night with the rank taste of paraldehyde in his mouth, he took one of James' titles, *The Golden Bowl,* and ritualized a statement of his own about it, thinking to himself, There are roses in the golden bowl, there are white roses in the golden bowl, the golden bowl is flawless, a perfect shape, the roses it contains are flawless, with no thorns near the bloom, with thorns beginning only near the middle of the stem, with each rose at the same stage of bloom, and they shall live, bloom and fade together, and when they are faded, their color will be beautiful, a pale green yellow curling the edges of the petals.

When a cry rang raucous and terrifying from down the hall, he made a stupendous effort, shut out the sound and began it all again.

But that did not cure him. Nothing the doctors did for him cured him either. But one day they took him into the Occupational Therapy Building and told him that he must begin to make things. The bird-bright face of the little woman-therapist lighted as she proudly showed him what her patients had made. Tears came into his eyes as she showed him one execrable ash tray after another; one hideous bowl after another; one clumsy plate after another. He had never seen such ugly colors and poor shapes in his life. He began to tremble all over, but he was too wise in the ways of the hospital to scream now, or smash these atrocities on the floor. The therapist held up a crooked, badly conceived vase. "One of our patients made this just last week," she said pridefully. "You'll see . . . you'll soon be doing as well yourself."

He stared at her with terrible lucidity; he had made far better things than these when he was seven; if he tried he could not produce anything so ugly. He must get out of here, at any cost, by any means. This realization, he thought afterward, was the moment he began to cure himself; nothing they could have done to him, no shock therapy could shock him as much as the sight of these "accomplishments" and this horrible little woman's pride in them.

That night, trying vainly and desperately to summon the golden bowl, he knew he must get out of the hospital if he was to get well. He would not swing from the rafter like his mother —ugly, swollen, purplish face, clothes awry from the struggle, making a dreadful sound when the body is cut down and lumps heavily upon the floor . . . terrible, terrible, terrible—and he would not let them persuade him that they, with their disgusting food and ugly buildings and dreary, oversimplified conceptions of life and normality, could help *him*. They could no more help him than his father might. They were doing him injury and what he must do was get away from them, work in a garden, listen to music, spend an entire night looking at a Paul Klee, gaze for hours at an arched doorway, a Greek colonnade . . .

The friend who had sent the Henry James was persuaded to bring him several rather elementary psychiatric textbooks.

He skimmed through them, with one eye so to speak, in order
to learn what it was the doctors expected him to do to appear
sane, and properly progressing. His closed eye protected him
from the case histories of dullards but in the Rosanoff text,
the drawings of patients, which he saw before he got that other
eye closed, set him back for days, so that they threatened him
with the force-feeding tube again. He hated them. But a childhood of hatred had taught him how to hide his feelings. He ate.
He knew that even if they had been told what it was which
had caused his relapse, they, with their lesser knowledge of art
and their ignorance of beauty, and their presumptuous knowledge of that greater mystique, the *norm*, would consider his
reaction symptomatic. Anyway, his books were found and con-
fiscated and he was reproached for attempting, as they thought,
to diagnose and cure himself. He listened patiently, for each
time they talked he learned a little more of their standards. By
their standards, he was mad, and in order to meet their standards of normality and get out of this ugly place, he had to know
what those standards were.

He lay awake at night, thinking and planning, feigning
sleep only when an attendant came near him. The old man in
the bed nearby, a senile dementia case, traveling on a dark internal river of destruction toward the greater darkness of death,
snuffled in his sleep like a vaporizer.

One night there was a violent excitement in the ward, an
unruly patient tried to kill somebody, and was subdued with a
good deal of cuffing and the soft socking sound of head-beating.
Ned heard afterward with a little alarm the guilty jocularity of
the three attendants; they stayed close together now, their
blood streams still spiked with adrenalin from fright, and the
excitement of having crushed a danger to mankind. They were
guilty heroes. He lay there listening to them joking with each
other in shamed camaraderie, and knew that this could be a
dangerous moment for him. Right enough, for two of them,
traveling in a pair like nuns, came to the sides of his bed and
looked down at him, playing the blazing flashlight hard on his
eyes; he kept his eyes closed, and his face relaxedly still, letting
his mouth hang open a little, slackly, unattractively, to prove
that he slept.

He knew who they were. The sadistic one said, "This fairy's
a tricky bastard, too, you know. Jeez, I hate faggots!"

Behind his sleeping face, he smiled, in his cynical, amused mind, and kept his breathing even. He wondered how the other one, the fat one, liked that remark, because he *knew* about the fat one, had known about him from the first soft glance the fat one gave him. Now the fat one said nothing but he leaned closer to the bed than he needed to, resting his hand on Ned's leg. Careful, George, Ned thought.

When they were gone, he reminded himself to be extra careful with the fat one in the future. It wasn't that he couldn't cope with a homosexual advance . . . it was simply that at this point he could afford neither a friend nor an enemy, and an outright no would certainly make an emeny of the fat one. He must just manage to avoid him.

They thought he was paranoid, the young, badly dressed doctors who saw him from time to time, he knew. He had to get them off his back, and once that was done, get some money with which to build walls and a moat around himself so that never again could he fall into the hands of people like these. He was not rich; he was rather poor, for all that he managed to maintain an elegant appearance. The schoolteacher, when he'd finally died of the damned t.b. he'd been so proud of (Camille), had left him a small sum of money, but that was nearly gone. He'd been thrifty and clever with it, but he couldn't make it grow into a respectable fortune while he had to live on capital. He needed a large sum of money to put between him and the world which threatened him now, and would, he recognized, threaten him all his life.

The discipline which he evolved and embarked upon was exceedingly difficult and demanded a patience not natural for him even in optimum health. But, if the discipline was difficult, it was also therapeutic. It was his own, and if arduous for his temperament, at the same time acceptable to his temperament. He managed to seem to recover slowly, to build a façade and maintain it with such strength and shrewdness that the attendants and doctors, who were too busy to do much more than be grateful now that he was less trouble, finally, after six months, began to believe in him. He learned the trick of a big warm easy smile, no matter how he felt; he learned to sound normal, to say in answer to a greeting, "How are *you* this morning? How was your date last night?" He learned to be helpful, to hide his revulsion at what he saw and, more important than anything else, to hide his enormous contempt for dogma-ridden doctors . . .

In a surprisingly short time, he was released. One physician, an earnest young man, dedicated and perceptive, was not deceived by Ned's apparent recovery. He said so. "I didn't argue against your release," he said in a troubled way. "Not because I believe you are well but because I don't think you will get well here. You need private treatment. You're a brilliant young man and a talented artist. Let me give you the names of a couple of doctors who could help you in private treatment."

There was more that he said, but Ned, listening to him with the false respect he'd learned to affect, ceased to listen. I am an artist, he told himself, not ordinary like other men. I shall cure myself, with my own medicine. What dreadful shoes this slob is wearing . . . and that necktie, with the Windsor knot . . . too bad I can't tell him. How could he imagine that anyone like him could cure me? No . . . one lives alone in the world, suffers alone, dies alone . . . and thank God for it! I must simply flatter this tiresome meddler and get away. At other times in my life if I fall into a depression, or a disturbance, I'll cry and storm behind thick walls, where no one can hear, for I must never let myself fall into their hands again. . . .

When he was outside, the discipline he'd learned was invaluable to him in a subsequent relationship with an artist and his wife; the artist loved him, and the artist's wife loved him. He let them, learning technical skills from the artist and, he sincerely believed, helping the artist in return to an honest admission of what had been a dormant homosexuality; he accepted from the wife—a little more difficult for him, but she was the strong one of the union—and rewarded her with instruction about how to dress, behave, think, and generally become a more attractive human being. If she could not be beautiful physically—and the unfortunate woman had a poor body, wispy hair and a large doughy face—she could be chic, interesting, a personality. He helped her hatch the egg of herself into a fascinating ugly duckling. Frieda, like most human beings, had never really had any attention paid to her in her whole life. She fastened upon it, and did not notice that Richard was similarly absorbed and no longer behaving as a husband toward her at all. She was soon surrounded by young men who were, although effeminate, devoted; if she no longer had a bedroom, at least she had a salon where she was more successful than any daydream had ever promised. It was nice that she was rich; the sum of money she finally settled upon Ned was a large one and gave her pleasure since it meant so much to him. And, too, it took him away from her, and she found when he was gone, that it was nice not to be daily confronted by a mentor who was so strict and who remembered how she was "before." When, very soon after Ned's departure, her husband took an overdose of Seconal, there was a dim stab of grief and loss, but quickly the young men were there with flowers, with tender words, with the infinite consolation of shopping for nice mourning clothes, gossip, cups of tea laced with rum or brandy, and plans for distracting her mind. She went to sleep at night, alone, a little drunk, smiling, and passed out before she could realize that she was, for the first time in her life, quite happy.

With the money, not as large an amount to him as Frieda had supposed, and which he adjudged a little less than his due, Ned considered the building of his moat to protect himself from the hostile world. He invested most of the money, lived frugally, buying only the best, simply doing without what he could not afford to buy the best of, and painted. His next show was successful; the write-ups he got were good, although one or two of the sloppier critics hinted at a lack of "humanity" and "compassion" in his work. He sold most of his paintings . . . not for enough, because in his perfectionistic pursuit of beauty he labored over a single painting for as long as four months. But he was becoming a name. Everyone, sloppy critics included, marveled at his technique; if little else, Richard had been an excellent teacher.

Ned himself was pleased with his progress, and understood that now, artistically, the chips were down; the next show must be a dazzler. Analyzing his needs for the time ahead in which he must work harder than ever before, he realized that most important to him was a beautiful place to live and work, a house which was both tonic to his soul and which could give him a feeling of splendor, without too great a cost. What he really needed was slaves . . . to maintain the house he would build, to cook and care for him. He also needed to get away from the young men of the sort who now sat in Frieda's salon. He, personally, did not like them. He hated to be seen with them, that is to see himself with them . . . to identify himself with what he considered an unnecessary, unbeautiful, playful imitation of femininity. He hated their high, girlish laughter, their turned-up soft blue eyes, their delicate white hands, the way they walked, the sibilance of their talk, their interminable, slight, malicious gossip. Finding himself desiring one of them was depressing; he succumbed, of course, and as quickly as possible, by this indulgence, immunized himself against such experiences. When desire became disgust, he was free for flight and he fled, to Mexico.

In Mexico, after he decided that here he could build his splendid house and have his "slaves," for domestic labor was wonderfully cheap, he went to the Old Poet.

The big soft smiling poet lived in a house in San Juan. He was very elegant and he gave many parties, but for the most part, now that he was old and fat, he went about in a brocade dressing gown, with thonged sandals on his purpling feet, holding a slim volume between his swollen white fingers. He was like an old god, compassionate and forgetful, and when Ned came upon him sitting in the drawing room of his house the first day, it was like coming into a cluttered garden where a brooding hen sat upon her nest, with her feathers puffed up fluffy around her very small head. It was necessary to search to find the eyes, and a shock to find them at last in the softness, sharp as a bird's and watching.

"How perfectly marvelous," the Old Poet said, "to have you here! You have come to the right place for painting. They've all been here, you know, the great ones. Writers, too. D. H. Lawrence was one of the first, but they say he was impossible . . . a difficult man. They called him Red-Beard. Red-haired people are always brooding, aren't they? I much prefer life here, writing here, that is, to anywhere . . . the Lido, Paris, Egypt. No place compares with it . . ." His voice dimmed and from the other room there came a spattering of laughter, at once masculine and feminine, sportive and malicious . . . the teasing laughter Ned had heard in Frieda's salon, and from which he was still running.

He looked at the poet.

"They leave me out of their games now," the poet said with an indulgent smile, "but I like to listen to them, even so. It makes me feel like Pericles."

"I liked the last sonnets, better than anything you've ever done," Ned said. "The one called 'Rain in the Street' . . . Masterful!"

There was a silence in which the sharp eyes of the poet estimated him and what he'd said, and then he gave a clucking little hen's sigh, as though he'd just endured insult rather than compliment. There was another flash of laughter from the other room, shrill in the quiet. "Sit down, dear boy," the Old Poet said. "I'll ring for a gin and tonic. Your arrival is a good excuse . . . I shan't wait for sundown. You may have the gray room . . . or is Waldo staying there? . . . I'll ask Fernando. He's the houseboy, knows everything. You'd love that room . . . marvelous carved doors. I had them brought from Italy . . . coals to Newcastle, but I had to have them. And an *armoire* you could die for. Oh yes, and a small Venetian chair. (I like the French better usually, but this is exceptional.) Yes, wherever Fernando puts you, you must have the chair." The sharp eyes glittered under their puffy, folded eyelids. "I don't expect to live long, did you know?" He sighed again. "I suppose, God help you, you're a genius. Ah well, a gin and tonic doesn't solve anything, but it does make it remarkably easier to bear."

The boys trooped in after a time and grouped themselves around the Old Poet, two or three at his feet, several beside his chair, all of them as ritualistically well behaved as upper-class English children permitted a brief visit to the drawing room. They drank, too, and made soft jokes with each other and laughed lightly, but when the Old Poet spoke, they fell silent, and rolled up their eyes at him reverently and called him "Maestro" and "Patrón." Only one boy was naughty, pinching another one until he cried out so that Bert, who acted like the governess of them all, fussed at them and shook his finger as though they were in their early teens and not in their twenties, and tweaked the ear of the pincher until, when he took his fingers away, the ear was red as coral. The Old Poet, observing this, reached out a tremulous hand to stroke the soft downy blond hair of the pincher, smiling a tolerant, reminiscent smile.

Bert said, "Well, really . . . !"

Ned drank the gin and tonic quickly. The sight of the Old Poet in his ratty old satin dressing gown dismayed him so, he could have wept. This, this mountain of feathery, puffy fat had written the beautiful poems . . . He looked at the parasitic "boys," their pink or dark or pale faces, their taut, muscle-conscious bodies, as he would have looked at a bottle of leeches. But, as his stomach retched, his mind said, "The poems. Don't forget the beauty of the poems," and he reminded himself that age is harder on the homosexual than other people. This was not a rationalization; he never thought of himself as a homosexual; a couple of homosexual affairs did not make a man less a man, so the poet's condition need not apply to him, nor frighten him. He accepted another gin and tonic and drank it more easily, already thinking of the *armoire* and eager to see it and the Venetian chair . . . some of these could stab your heart they were so light and lovely . . . and there was one boy— Rudolfo, his name was—among the parasites, who turned a look on him out of eyes so beautiful that his lungs constricted and he could hardly breathe . . . El Greco eyes they were, melancholy, slant-dark, liquidly black. He was astonishingly handsome and he had the long El Greco nose, the tapering church-steeple fingers. . . .

Having a later gin and tonic—the fourth, the fifth?—he decided the chattering of the boys was too annoying to endure. The church bell was clanging hideously and the room was almost dark. He was impatient for the sight of the Venetian chair, and he wanted very much to be out of there . . . He stood up and surprised himself enormously by turning to the El Greco boy.

"Come here, *chiquito*," he said, snapping his fingers. "Show me to my room."

Three weeks later Ned went to the Old Poet and told him that he had decided to stay in Mexico, and he wanted to buy land and build a house. The poet remembered the land he owned in a nearby village on the lake. It was a sizable lot with a two-room dwelling on it now, which was fit only for destruction. He would be happy to sell it to Ned, and hold the ownership papers on it, since he was a citizen of Mexico and Ned was not and could not own land. Ned said he would apply for papers of his own—*rentista* papers which allowed him to own land without citizenship—and meanwhile this was a good arrangement. He liked the land and the deal was made.

When he moved, the Old Poet gave him a note which said,

"Let this be the cornerstone of a beautiful house," and presented him with the Venetian chair. Ned was deeply grateful. He left, happy to leave everything in the Old Poet's house, except Rudolfo. Rudolfo stayed.

While his house was being built, Ned forced himself to continue to visit the Old Poet, reminding himself that this was a good friend and a very talented man, fighting down his loathing for the life the Old Poet lived. For himself, the Old Poet, who was called upon by every creative personality of importance who came to that part of Mexico, was proud of Ned and liked to show him off to his visitors. He took pride in Ned's dignity, his lack of girlish affectations, his refusal to be sibilant. Once he complimented Ned on his bearing, and Ned was able to tell him that the other way was offensive to him. . . .

"There's no reason for it," he said. "These boys indulge their effeminacies . . . flying around like that!"

"Yes," the Old Poet said. "I know. I used to feel the way you do about it when I was younger. But age brings compromise . . . among its other rewards. I used to be quite happy alone with Bert, and I think I could be so now. It was he who got restless, bored with me, you know, running off all the time . . . worrying me. So, I let him fill the house with . . . these others." He smiled. "But they're harmless, don't you think? Pretty children."

"They are a plague," Ned said.

"Ah," the Old Poet said, small eyes bright. He nodded. "It's true what they say about you. You're not quite human, are you? I can see it. You hate what you are."

Ned glared at him. "What do you mean . . . what I am?" he said.

"Only a fool would ask that question," the Old Poet said. And then, like a doctor searching out the source of a pain, "Tell me, how are you getting along with Rudolfo?"

"Without him," Ned said.

The poet smiled. "I'll ring for a gin, I think," he said.

When his house was completed, Ned found that he worried greatly about his dependence on the Old Poet. Legally, the whim-ridden old fool *owned* Ned's house. Who could guess when an impulse might lead him to take the house back as casually as he had sold him the land? Or, since he had said

to Ned himself that he was not going to live long, it was possible at any moment that he might die and the house then be
owned by Bert, who would be his heir, and Bert had no love
for Ned. Getting *rentista* papers was a long, complex, inefficient
business . . . in the meantime he had no protection. He found
Hanschen. Hanschen was a boy born in Mexico, of German
parents, who had lived all his life in the village, and who
needed money . . . habitually. At first, with shining good
humor, he agreed to holding the ownership papers of Ned's
house in his name, with no charge made. But as time went on,
he explained to Ned that he needed money desperately and he
would greatly appreciate it if Ned would buy from him at the
same time—while he continued to hold the papers on it—a
piece of property down the street from Ned's house. Ned understood, although Hanschen never made such a bald statement,
that he would have refused to take ownership of Ned's house
without this purchase of the other land. It was a corner on
which a Mexican cantina now stood, in a fine location. Hanschen asked a good price and Ned paid it, and Hanschen gave
him in exchange for his money a written statement of the
transaction.

But Hanschen had no legal right to sell. The land belonged
to his old parents, although it would be his when they died.
Hanschen lied to them, lulling their suspicions by doling out to
them a fraction of the money he got from Ned, saying it was a
rent payment. They believed him; Hanschen was their jewel,
a blond, handsome, Nordic young man. When they looked up at
him standing there, tall and blue-eyed, he was more comfort-
ing than memory, as clear and refreshing as a breeze off the
Rhine . . . Teutonic, Gothic, an assuagement of their lifelong
homesickness in a land of dark eyes and dark skin.

Hanschen saw his parents only in the mornings, or at noon
when he came home to eat one of his mother's rich *comidas*.
By afternoon he was drunk and he stayed away from them.
When he was drunk, he muttered about selling his birthright,
imagined himself injured, persecuted, gulled. Anger burned in
his eyes; as the money Ned paid him dwindled, his anger grew.
He drank harder to alleviate his burgeoning guilt, but it took
more all the time until finally, it seemed, no amount of liquor
could ease his spirit.

Ned observed this development, and urged the Mexican

Government, with various bribes and rewards, to deliver from its untidy womb the *rentista* papers. And at last, when he had given up—it was always necessary to give up before anything was granted in this country—there was a burst of activity, more money was demanded, and the papers were delivered.

The papers meant that he was no longer at the mercy of Hanschen, whom he disliked thoroughly by now. Not only did Hanschen paint badly—great slobbery canvases of self-pity, turgid, torpid scenes of blackened, violent bodies in struggle— but he was stupid. He managed to be illiterate in three languages, since he did not know any one of them well; although he'd known creative people all his life in the village, associating with artists and writers who knew the world and who were cultivated, he'd gotten only a glaze from them, and underneath the cracking glaze he was a farm boy who did not farm but felt that to be the equal of the travelers he met, he must paint. When he was sober, he had a hangover. He did not admit it, usually, but it was evident. There was only one thing he was sure he could do as well as anyone who came along, and that was drink.

When he was drunk he was full of guilt; his eyes would glitter, his lips take on a thick pout, his skin would grow greasy with perspiration. At such times he talked wildly about borrowing the money to buy back the corner property from Ned, hinting that he had powerful friends in the government, rich friends who would lend him money without asking a question. Would Ned then be willing to sell him back the property? He doubted it. Ned did not trouble to answer . . . he was collecting a tidy rent from Abel, who ran the cantina for Americans. It was this fact which rankled deep in Hanschen, and filled him with festering envy and resentment. Ned had taken his land, tricked him into selling the property of his parents, and now would not sell it back to him.

The day the final papers came from Mexico City, Ned invited Hanschen to come for cocktails. He was drunk when he arrived, full of maudlin reproach and steeped in self-pity. After several drinks, Ned explained that he no longer needed the use of Hanschen's name. He showed him the papers, thanked him and presented him with a small gift for his trouble. Rising, he said he must excuse himself; he had a date for supper and he must dress. Hanschen's eyes filled with tears and he broke into

noisy, childlike weeping. He stormed and pleaded, sensing
that banishment was about to come, while Ned stood utterly
still and watched him and listened to him. When, after fifteen
minutes of a truly dreadful scene, he subsided temporarily,
Ned turned on his heel and left the room.

He paused on his way past the kitchen to tell Jovita and
the cook that Hanschen was in the *sala* and he was to be permitted to remain there now as long as he wished, but that in
the future they must never let him into the house, never, under any circumstances. Then he went on to his bedroom and
locked the door behind him.

Hanschen told his troubles in the next days to everyone
in the village who would listen . . . and everyone listened at
least once because everyone was curious about Ned. But everyone knew how Hanschen got overfriendly with newcomers and
then soon ran around shouting that he'd been betrayed by them.
It was only another chapter of an old story, with which his lis-
teners pretended to sympathize, and hastened away.

During the night when Hanschen would come to Ned's
beautiful orange and gold door, to shout recriminations, pleas
for admittance and promises of good behavior, Ned himself
would come out and order him away. So cold was he, so without emotion, that Hanschen would go. Soon if Hanschen were
at a party when Ned arrived, it was Hanschen who would
slink guiltily away, unable to bear Ned's cold eyes looking at
him as though he were not there. Ned never permitted himself
to make any defense when Hanschen's story was repeated to
him. He only smiled, shrugged, and changed the subject.

Gradually everyone in the village believed it was another
one of Hanschen's lies. Hanschen went to an old friend in
Guadalajara, Manuél, with whom he'd gone to the French school
for two years. Manuél listened, and because he was devoted to
Hanschen's parents, came to the village to investigate. It was
his intention to buy back the land from Ned if possible, later
to make trouble for Ned if Hanschen's story was substantiated.
Manuél had never met Ned, but he'd heard about him from the
Old Poet, and he'd heard of his painting; Ned was a name.
The Old Poet had another name for him, however; he called
him, chuckling, Machiavelli. This lent credence to Hanschen's
story.

Manuél called on Ned after the siesta hour one day. He

looked at Ned's paintings and then, having looked at them, sat down to study them. They talked and at six o'clock they had martinis. Manuél was persuaded to stay for more cocktails and supper, and to listen to some of Ned's excellent records.

At two-thirty in the morning when Hanschen came to Ned's house to pay one of his drunken calls, full of rum and tears, ready to beat his big red fists on the orange and gold door, he fell against Manuél's white Cadillac and slid down into the street among the rotting mangoes and dung, and lay there, staring up at the Jalisco license plate, and knew that this car belonged to his friend Manuél. He yelled and shouted, flat on his back, the worst words he knew in three languages.

Ned came to the door in his black silk kimono and looked down at him.

"Who is it?" Manuél called from within the house.

"Just a *borracho*," Ned answered. "Nobody."

"No!" Hanschen yelled.

Ned said to him, "Do you want Manuél to see you like this?"

Dumbly, Hanschen shook his head, and Ned closed and bolted the door.

Hanschen stayed all night in the street beside the Cadillac, thinking—although he was never to remember what it was he had thought nor what decision he'd made. In the morning when the milk boy came, on his horse, with the two cans of milk slung over the saddle, and the maids came out carrying pitchers to get the milk, he stayed still although he was awake, and he heard their whispered, laughing jokes about him. When they were gone, he sat up in the terrible glare of the sun and held his head; the reeking mangoes were stuck to him; there was dung on his trousers; he was very sick. He got hold of the car and pulled himself to his feet, swallowing the sour vomit which gushed up in his throat, and staggered away. He went along the path at the lake's edge toward his parents' house, blind with the flashing light, longing for a cool bed and drawn shutters.

In his room, he closed his eyes. His mind told him relentlessly, Now you have lost Manuél. Ned has taken not only your land, but your best friend, your last friend. Now you have found hell.

Then he plunged down the roaring *barranca* of sleep.

The day Victoria came to apologize, Ned was still at the breakfast table although it was afternoon. His sleep had been disturbed in the night, not by cries and shouts and poundings on the door from Hanschen as usual but, preposterously, by the lack of them. The silence was disturbing. He awakened with a sense in his half-sleep that Hanschen was there. He rose, put on a robe and then, because he did not want Hanschen to see him pull aside a curtain and peer out like a frightened burgher, he climbed the steep stairs to the *mirador* on the roof. He walked quietly to the edge and looked down into the street. As he did so, Hanschen, who was standing there, swaying slightly, looked up. In the cold moonlight, their eyes engaged and held, like the *épées* of two fencers, with a chill flash of steel. Then Ned drew back, walked down the stairs and returned to his bedroom and lay down on his hard bed. He smoked a cigarette, and because he was not at all sleepy now, he began to read. Usually that summoned sleep, especially if the book was dull. But not now. It wasn't that he was afraid; he was annoyed that Hanschen could think he would care that Hanschen stood there in his rum-fumed stupor watching the house. Ned felt no fear . . . if violence burst its flimsy dam in Hanschen's brain . . . Ned was more than a match for him physically, and a thousand times smarter. He did not even fear his own inner violence; it was controlled by a series of locks and gates and canals and dams, and most important of all, he knew it was there and he knew its measure. He did not imagine Hanschen's rage to be of comparable quality or quantity. He did not fear him; he did not fear himself. But he could not sleep.

Now, at the breakfast table, he lingered over a cup of Nescafé, which had grown tepid and tasteless. When Jovita asked him if he wanted the cat to be released for a little visit, he simply shook his head. He had planned to have an early talk with Pablito the gardener about taking out the cannas along the back wall and putting in something less untidy, but Pablito had already gone off to the *granja* on the outskirts of Guadalajara to buy new plants. Pablito was a fine gardener but a poor designer; doubtless he would come home with something hideously *florido*.

It was getting on toward one o'clock and he had thought to paint today, but now he felt listless and strange, without energy. He stared at the *New Yorker* magazine, all of which he had already read, and it was as though he hadn't read it; the marvelous story by Mavis Gallant which, when he read the first lines of it, he knew was something to send off at once to Chloë, for it was exquisite, now seemed to him still unread. He thought, with a rise of ill temper, that this was Hanschen's doing. His eyes stung with lack of sleep and his teeth bit together wrong, and he even felt the prodromal stirrings of dysentery.

The feeling reminded him of something . . . echoed some experience of his childhood, clamored for recognition.

It had been the thing with Hanschen last night, of course. Hanschen had recalled the very thing he had worked so long and hard to forget, and which he could not now remember without physical and mental agony. It had been the most horrible experience of his whole life.

One morning—it was still dark, about five o'clock it must have been, because his father was already up and at the milking —his mother had come to his bed and shaken him awake. She said, "You must go for the priest." Her voice was sepulchral and her eyes wild as a wolf's. "I have a demon in me," she said, rocking from side to side so the lantern swung in her hands as though it were on a ship in a storm. "A demon! I must be exorcized! Tell him!" He scrambled out of bed as she began to shriek, and got shakily into his clothes, unable to look at her as she moaned and tore at her hair, and ran off on his terrible errand. The children at school said she was a witch. He'd heard the teachers say with a certain tone in their voices, "Well, his *mother*, you know, is . . ." But, however bewildering she'd been, she'd been his mother, and he hadn't believed them for a minute. Now, it was as if she herself had told him, "It's true . . . I am what they say." He wanted to beg her not to admit it, but instead he ran out into a morning as cold and still as steel . . . to find the fat German priest and deliver his terrible message.

He shook his head now, thinking bitterly what a charming errand for an eight-year-old boy . . .

The priest agreed to come. They set off for the farm, the two of them, on the priest's horse, he riding behind the fat man, hidden from the wind and enjoying a rare sense of protection. When they rounded the turn of the road and turned off onto the crusty-frozen path to the old house, there was the single crack of a shot fired, and almost simultaneously a whistling

noise brushed past them, bumping the sleeve of the priest's coat
and making the horse swerve. The priest whispered something
that began with *"Gott!"* and wheeled the horse into a stand of
trees. "Show yourself," the priest said to him. "Get down. She
won't shoot at you." Ned doubted that, but he let the priest help
him down and he stood there beside the horse, feeling small,
and looked up at the house with dread.

He saw her right away, there on the roof in the snow, in
her old nightgown which she had torn in many places, with her
hair wild, holding the rifle in one hand, dementedly thumbing
her nose with the other.

The moment of shock never left him . . . never would
leave him . . . the sight of her thumbing her nose seemed far
worse to him and frightened him more than her shooting at
them. His brain went empty and he did not know what to think.
His father came to the stable door and waved for them to come
toward him, and they did, clinging to the cover of the trees,
while the woman danced and cavorted and brandished the rifle
and thumbed her nose, there on the slippery snow-caked
roof . . .

In the stable his father and the priest talked. He listened
to them, full of inner dismay because they did not seem to make
any sense, and he watched until his mother went in through
the little attic window; but they did not pause in their conversation so he could tell them it was all right now. After a while,
alone, he went back into the house. As he passed the kitchen
door, he saw her, working in there at the sink as though it were
any ordinary day, and he went upstairs. She was quiet all day.
She did not speak once that he noticed, but she hummed to herself in a toneless, endless way.

That night, just as he was about to go to sleep, she came
into his room and gave him a long, cold look. She said she had
come to thank him for running the errand. She seemed to
preen, there in the lamplight, gaunt and ill-smelling. "It was too
late, you see," she said to him resignedly. "Too late. Now the
demon possesses me. I belong to the Devil. He is me." She
laughed, turned her head with its tangled, graying locks co-
quettishly, gave him another strange look, and was gone.

He did not cry, although when he was alone in the dark his
face twisted up for crying. He was ashamed. He was awake almost all night, trying to understand and to anticipate how life

would be different now that the demon had won; he knew it
was going to hurt him and he wanted to be ready for it, so it
wouldn't hurt him too much, when it came. . . .

Too much, he thought now; only a child would try to
measure how much of a hurt was too much. But last night was
a little like that time. He didn't think Hanschen was possessed,
nor did he for that matter, now that he was a grown man, believe that his mother had been possessed of a devil which could
have been exorcized with prayer and incense and candlelight.
It was just that last night, looking down into Hanschen's face
and meeting his eyes, he knew that Hanschen's demon now
possessed him, whatever psychopathological demon that might
be. How strange of him really to have awakened from a sound
sleep and gone looking for Hanschen, and how very strange
to have gone up on the *mirador* at night like that! He never
went there except for a sunbath; he did not trust the narrow
banisterless steps even in sharp daylight; why hadn't he looked
from a window or gone to the door boldly as he had other times?
The difference was, that it had been *he* himself on the roof,
quite sane, looking down at a silent madman in the street. A
reversal . . .

There came a griping pain in his abdomen, so sharp that as
he began to stand, his knees gave way and he sat down abruptly
again and felt the cold sweat break out on his face. His head
ached . . . and he rarely had headaches . . . but this one
was like a cloud just over his eyes . . . The cramp ended and
he began to shiver. Was it cold? He glanced at the thermometer
. . . Ninety-six. No, it was he who was cold. It was a hot day.
His teeth began to chatter. I really am ill, he thought with
surprise, and another cramp brought his knees to his chest. He
writhed.

"I will not be sick," he said out loud, and as if in obedience
the cramp faded to a tolerable, steady pain. He slammed the
New Yorker down on the table and stood up in the bright sun.
He resolved then and there to forget that German boor and his
pretensions to honor. What had he done to Hanschen after all
except buy property from him?

He was freezing. He stood there shaking, discovering that
as he trembled, his joints gave out agonizing, sharp pains; sweat
poured from his hair onto his ashen forehead; he was dizzy
and clouded and sick, and another cramp struck him . . .

Dysentery, he thought, doubling over, and heard distantly the knocking at his front door.

Jovita, hurrying to answer the knock, called out to him, without looking at him, "Are you at home, señor?"

And he answered through his teeth, the only salient reply in his mind, "Not to Señor Hans."

He could not straighten up. The cramp was incredible. He reached out and took from the table his silver lighter—seeing the etching on it in the glaring light, ever so sharply, "To Ned, *como siempre*, from Hanschen"—and a pack of Delicados. The bathroom, my God, he thought, I've got to get to the bathroom, *now*, with alarm bells clanging in his ears, and the doubt that he could move with this cramp holding him bent double like this and the shooting pains in his hips, and saw Victoria coming up the *zaguán* with Jovita. He recognized her, but he could not wait to greet her or dismiss her. He looked at her, straightened up a little, and spun about and ran, actually ran, for the bathroom.

6

Victoria

THE MAID was holding open a tall, wide door. "Will you wait in the *sala*, señora?" the girl said.

Victoria turned obediently and came to the open door and paused on the threshold. The room was very beautiful . . . but much too still, much too shadowed for her today. She had come here to apologize, not to be comfortable; this was a day of atonement and attrition. She had no right to enter the room. She backed out of the doorway and walked into the patio.

"I shall wait here," Victoria said and went to the table where Ned had been sitting. She sat down, facing the white closed door where Ned had gone. When the maid let the door of the *sala* swing shut and hastened to the table to begin clearing away the magazines and papers on it, she waved her hand. "No, no," she said. "I shall be here only a moment. That doesn't matter. Don't disturb anything. I don't want to disturb anything."

"Shall I bring you coffee, señora?" the girl said, still loading the things onto a tray. "Iced, perhaps?"

"Yes," Victoria said. "Or no. I don't know. It doesn't matter."

"*Bueno*," the girl said as though she had received a perfectly lucid, civil answer. "*Con permiso, señora . . .*" she said, and waited to be dismissed.

"How do you call yourself?" Victoria asked.

"Jovita," the girl said.

"Then, *ándale*, Jovita," Victoria said with a gesture of weary benevolence, and the girl went away.

She put her hand over her eyes. It was very tropical today, very hot. The sun's glare shimmered off the white wall of the kitchen and made the patio seem to jerk in and out of focus. But that was good; it intensified her discomfort. She knew she should have worn a hat but she had not permitted herself to do that because she had let herself wear the dark glasses to hide behind. After three days of being immured in her house —*in herself* really more than the house—the fear of coming out, of exposing one's self was very strong, and it was necessary, no matter how unwillingly or how fearfully, to force oneself out into the street and into the world. Harry, passing her on the street, had said, "You wearing shades, Vickie?" and she'd nodded, hurrying past him, saying, "You can't see me. I'm invisible." He'd smiled and shuffled along, not bothering her . . . Harry would always play a game.

Should she take off the glasses and face Ned when she apologized to him? No, eyes weren't necessary for an apology . . . only words, formal, humble words. It wasn't only her rudeness to him at Abel's she had to explain either. Once, sometime in the last three days, he'd come and knocked on her door and she'd peeked through the deep crack in the wood panel and seen him out there, looking foolish, a dressed-up dandy with a bouquet of flowers in his hand. She had screamed at him, especially inflamed at the sight of the flowers, "Away! Get away!" He had dropped back a step and stared at the door as though he'd been struck through it, and then he went away.

She sat straighter. No comfort. No ease. Pain is your portion. Ashes and dust, thorns and nails.

What a night it had been . . . full of frightening dreams, so that she'd awakened before dawn, stiff with cold and at the same time so thirsty she could not stand it. She'd wrapped the blanket around herself and gone to the kitchen for the bottle of Delaware Punch she'd seen the *niña* put on the ice yesterday . . . just what she wanted, cold, sweet, innocent as the punch at a children's party . . . the perfect antidote to horror. She'd opened the bottle and was bringing it back to drink in bed, when she stepped on the damned cricket in the *corredor* and screamed because her foot was bare, and dropped the bottle which spun when it hit the floor, spinning out a stream of the cold drink all over her bare legs, all over the tiles, and there was the broken body of the cricket which had been under her foot, wet, crushed and ugly. She ran from the sight while the bottle was still spraying its syrupy purple, and hid in the bed. But she had to jump up in a minute because she knew the cricket's blood or life-juice or whatever disgusting thing had been inside it, was on her foot and she must wash it off. She went into the kitchen and got cold water from the *pila* and scrubbed the foot. She came back to the bed and was about to get into it when she thought, with a start that perhaps . . . no, *certainly*, the sheet must be stained with the cricket's blood. She couldn't get in there and let it touch her. Finally she went over to the other end of the living room and wrapped herself in the couch cover and lay down on the couch.

When it was light she awakened to a dull feeling of apprehension; dread moved in her veins with her blood, although she could not yet know what it was at the base of this feeling, but seeing the pages on the typing stand, she went and got them and brought them back to the couch and began to read them. Oh, she knew well enough it was a mistake, when you woke up feeling like this, to read them, but she kept thinking she might find some strength in them, some kind of rock on which she could build the day to come, continuing to read them even after it seemed to her that the pages were lifeless . . . saying, "It's your mood. They'll look better to you by tonight . . ." but hearing, at the same time, hope and faith crash to the floor at her feet.

She lay down again. How long had she been in here, working and reworking these pages? Three days or four—whatever the number was—it had been too long, so that night and day were mixed. Had the thing about the dead cricket really happened last night? Perhaps when it happened she had not been fully awake; it had had the horror of a dream. Such an extreme reaction to the experience, which to anybody else would be just a matter of stepping on a bug in the dark, was a warning. She was going to pieces.

Of course she could just go to pieces; it would probably be more restful all around; if the pages were dreadful, what was there to live for? She forced herself to walk out of the room toward the kitchen, demanding of herself that she glance over casually, as any sensible person would do, at the cricket on the tile. But her head stayed rigidly turned toward it. There was a string of big black shiny ants as thick as a rope on the floor, running urgently back and forth from what was left of the cricket's corpse, hastening along in an excited way that was somehow reminiscent of a carnival, touching each other, in triumph. . . .

She gagged, put her hand over her mouth, and hurried away.

She must dress; she must get out into the world; she must go *now*.

She did not think of where she was going until she had locked her door behind her and the decision had to be made to turn left or right. If she went toward the lake . . . but there were animals there, drowsing along the shore, cows and burros. Nature itself was frightening, and she did not want to come upon some animal gnawing on another animal's foot, or some ugly sight of death. Then she remembered Ned, the way the tongue remembers a canker in the mouth, a small thing, neglected and painful. Apologizing to him would be correcting one small evil in a world of evils; it was something "right" which she must do.

The white door opened and Ned walked slowly and carefully toward her. He was still a little bent over and he looked pale. It was obvious to her at once what the trouble was; dysentery was the common cold of Mexico. He stood behind a chair, leaning against the back of it as though it were a lectern.

"Yes?" he said coldly.

"I came to apologize," she said.

He waited, looking at her without curiosity.

"I didn't mean to be rude," she said. "That is to say, it *happened* that I was rude to you, but you had nothing to do with it. It was not a reaction to you. At Abel's that day I was very upset, you know; the world was distorted, everything was awry." She made a shape in the air with her hand to show him how the world had been awry. He said nothing; his face held a look of disinterested, formal politeness . . . nothing more. "When you came to my house," she said, "I was working. I am like that when I'm working. It wasn't personal. I apologize."

"I see."

She made her mouth smile even though her cheeks were stiff and wooden. "When I was a child they told me an apology was worthless unless you said you would never do the bad thing again. But I can't honestly say that, can't promise that, do you know. I might, you see. How can I prophesy? My emotions . . ." Her voice choked in her throat and she lifted her hands in a gesture of helplessness.

"You don't really mean to apologize at all, do you?" he said. He did not smile and his eyes held a light as cold as snow. But he leaned more heavily on the back of the chair and she saw that his forehead glistened with sweat and that he was growing pale. "You'll have to excuse me," he said, "for a moment. I'll have Jovita bring you something . . ."

He turned abruptly and walked rapidly toward the white door. As he passed the kitchen, he shouted at the maid, and then he ran again and slammed the white door behind him.

She smiled. It was quite an achievement to maintain dignity and suffer from *turistas* at the same time . . . very few people could manage it. There were many jokes about it, many funny names the Americans had for it, but of course when you had it, it wasn't funny at all.

She shut her eyes against the pulsating heat, drummed her fingers on the table and waited.

Jovita said, "Your coffee, señora," and set a tray on the table. There was a tall, handsome glass of iced coffee with cream curling down through it, and a pretty little dish with two macaroons.

"Thank you," she said. "That looks very good."

In the street outside, the peddler called, *"Ropa barata!"* and Jovita's head turned toward the sound and her eyes shone.

On her way here Victoria had seen the man walking through the village with the yards of cloth folded into rectangles stacked on each shoulder, and the young girls hurrying out of the houses, with their pesos in their hands, eager to take advantage of the man's bargains. They weren't bargains, of course; the *ropa* was no more *barata* than in any store, but the cloth looked better than it was, shining and colorful in the sun, and buying from the man was great fun, because he knew how to joke with the girls and tease them.

"You do not buy cloth from that man?" she asked Jovita.

"The Señor buys cloth for me himself. Like this," Jovita said, plucking at the strong cotton of her dress.

The cloth was good, correct, a quiet, sturdy gray. But probably the girl craved something a little shiny, with some flash to it . . . a piece of bright rayon.

"That is very nice," Victoria said.

Jovita nodded and went back to the kitchen, walking softly over the glistening tiles. The maid had been taught to be quiet; most of the local girls made as much clatter as possible, for noise meant gaiety and youth to them. Victoria drank the refreshing cold sweet coffee, and when the memory of the dead cricket came back into her mind to plague her, she forced it away. She looked at the pattern of shadow and sun in the patio, because it was also necessary, once you had come out of your house and out of yourself, to look at the world around you, to make an effort to perceive everything and receive it into yourself . . . Otherwise, although your body sat in the world, you were not there.

She ate the macaroons and finished the coffee and sat waiting for some time. At last, thinking that Ned must be very conscious of her out here waiting for him and possibly embarrassed by it, she rose, adjusted the strap of her shoulder bag, stood straight and marched to the *zaguán*.

Jovita appeared quickly in the doorway of the kitchen.

Did the Señora require something?

No, the Señora required nothing. "Tell the Señor I am sorry he is ill," she said. "Tell him I could not wait any longer. And thank him for the coffee. I hope he will feel better soon."

In the street, the heat was intense. She walked around the

great bulk of a sow who lay panting on her side near Ned's gold and orange door, in the shade of the building. It watched her without turning its head, its ugly little eyes flickering maliciously after her. It was too bad pigs were smart; once you knew they were smart, you didn't feel safe showing them that you despised them.

The houses were all shuttered and still. The church bell rang and farther up the hill she could see the cloth peddler resting against a shady wall under a jacaranda tree. The stores were shuttering now for the two-hour siesta. There was nothing to eat in her house and with the stores closed she would not be able to buy anything until the siesta hours were over, at four. That wouldn't do. If she went home, she probably wouldn't be able to force herself to come out again. Perhaps she should go to the Posada of the Tres Marías where Harry lived. The Doña María would always serve another *comida* . . . on the cuff, or Harry could stake her. She would go there. It was better right now not to be alone.

She heard the voice calling her name, thin and high. She stopped and looked around and saw Jovita running up the hill toward her, pulling on her *rebozo* as she ran. Such haste could only mean trouble; maids adjusted their *rebozos* before they left the house, like Moorish women donning their face veils. Trouble it must be . . . the girl's eyes looked big and frightened. Briskly she began to walk back toward her.

"Please," Jovita said breathlessly. "Come back. The Señor . . ." She shook her head, swallowing with a dry throat, anxiously trying to get the words out. "Sick," she said. "Maybe dead."

"Not dead," Victoria said automatically. She began to walk along beside her. "Don't be silly."

Jovita made a dry, sobbing sound. "On the floor," she said. "Dead."

They hurried down the street together. Victoria said, "The Señor is not like a bug, a cricket or something. People don't die so easily." But of course they did. "A man is a different thing," she said firmly. "A man does not die so fast."

They hurried up the *zaguán* together and along the *corredor*. Jovita made the sign of the cross when they came to the white door and then, taking a great breath and holding it, timidly she pushed the door open. It was difficult to see into the darkness of the room, after the blinding sunlight, but then, she saw Ned's body lying on the floor, very still. His arms were flung out before him; he lay face down and he did not move. It was necessary to go in there whether you wanted to or not; the girl beside her was making a whimpering sound of fright.

She tiptoed forward as though, absurdly, if she made any sound she might disturb his sleep. She dropped to her knees beside him and took his hot wrist into her hand and felt for the pulse. The arm was a dead weight . . . but yes, there was the pulse, bounding, erratic, going like a bongo drum.

She was instantly angry, with Jovita for frightening her, with Ned for being unconscious and looking dead, and with herself because she had been frightened, too. "He lives," she said.

"Thanks to God," Jovita said shakily, staying outside.

"Come in here. Help me to turn him over." It wasn't right for his face to be down on the tiles like that somehow; that more than anything had made him look dead. She looked up and saw that Jovita had not moved but stayed out there, frightened. Pretending she had not seen, she called quickly in a sharp voice, "Jovita! Come here. I need you to help me."

Together they moved his body. His face was dull-red with fever, and she could feel the heat coming through the thin stuff of his shirt. His glasses had fallen away from his face and lay on the floor beside him. She picked them up and handed them to Jovita who took them and held them and looked at them, not knowing what to do with them.

"Put them there . . . on the table. Then get someone to help us to lift him into bed," she said. She looked up. The girl did not move but stood there, swaying, dreamily shocked, staring. "On the table!" she said in a loud voice. Jovita gave a jerk and put the glasses down. "Now *ándale* . . . get somebody!"

She went. Victoria got up and ripped the quilts and blankets off the bed and covered him quickly. Then she brought the pillow and put it under his hot, heavy head. She looked at him. He was not broken like a cricket, not dead. She had not stepped on him, he was not crushed.

The girl brought Pablito, the gardener, a nice-eyed, not-too-bright young man who clucked at the sight of the Señor on the floor and announced, as though it had some bearing on what had happened, "But look, I have been in Guadalajara. Only just now I have come home . . . *entonces*, on the two o'clock bus and it was late, *verdad?* Only just now I . . ."

Victoria cut in on him, glaring at him. "You must help us lift him to the bed," she said.

"*Pues*, what has he?" Pablito asked, not stirring from the doorway.

She saw his fear. She said, "He has *paludismo*. Only malaria. He has just fainted from the fever. You can't get it from him. You can get it only from a mosquito. Help me first. Then you must go to telephone the doctor."

He sidled unwillingly into the room, pushing back his sombrero so that it hung on his shoulders from the black strap around his neck. He said, "Maybe we shouldn't move him."

She ignored that, and the three of them got Ned into bed. Soon he regained some degree of consciousness, beginning to moan, and, as a chill began, shuddering. She opened the cupboards and got all the blankets she could find and piled them on him. She sent Jovita to get money from the kitchen so that Pablito could telephone Dr. Obregón in San Juan. "Tell him to come at once, Pablito. The doctor knows me . . . tell him I think it is malaria. Tell him I have had it and I know."

She didn't know for sure, but it was a good guess, and intended to reassure Pablito and Jovita. When Pablito was gone she sent Jovita to get a *brasero* so that they could set it, with coals burning, on the tile floor. The air in the cool room must be warmed.

She sat on a white marble bench against the wall and looked at the man in the bed. His face was flushed with fever, his skin overwhite next to the flush. Strange to look at a man you neither knew nor liked, when he was unconscious . . . Even now she was not drawn to him by his helplessness. He had good bones in his face and a strong mouth . . . but the mouth could be petulant, selfish. But then, whose could not? It was not a nice face . . . handsome but not nice. In spite of a certain nobility to his features he had the face of . . . of a poisoner. Exactly. He would look perfect in the garments of another time, leaning over a body, dropping poison into an ear from a jeweled vial . . .

She looked at the floor, nervously. There was something shameful about looking at him when he was helpless, thinking of him as a murderer. She got up and moved through the room, came to one of his paintings on the wall—it was signed—and stood absolutely still. She took off her dark glasses, and it was like taking off a pair of too-tight, pinching earrings. She stood, rubbing the bridge of her nose where the glasses had cut into her flesh, and stared at the painting. She stepped closer, moved back, never taking her eyes from it. There was a sensation of shock as she realized that the painting was marvelous; there was no other word for it.

Jovita brought the *brasero* and set about getting the fire going, and still she could not stop looking at the painting. It was an abstract, done with infinite care in perfect color, so that it was as cold, finally, and as pure, an an icicle. Having looked long at it, she came back to the bed and looked into Ned's face again.

Ned's eyes opened, he looked blindly up at her, groaning, and his head began to roll from side to side. Another chill seized him and his teeth chattered. There was another sound in the room and she realized that it was Jovita, kneeling by the *brasero* but no longer fanning the coals or blowing on them, praying—a prayer with many Indio words in it, so that it could have been as well directed to Quetzalcoatl, the feathered serpent god of the Aztecs, as to the Christian god of later racial experience.

"Hush, Jovita," she said briskly. "The Señor is not dying. He just has a chill. Is there a hot-water bottle? Good. Heat water till it almost boils, fill the bottle with the water, wrap it in a towel and bring it to me."

When she was gone, Ned said, "Are you sure?"

She looked at him.

"That I'm not dying?"

"What nonsense!" she said.

"I had dysentery this morning. Amoebic, you think?"

"No," she said. "I think malaria . . . but I don't know. I've sent for Dr. Obregón."

He bit his lips. "I don't like doctors."

She said, "You don't have to like him."

"I don't want him," he said.

The next chill caught him. "Cold," he said desperately. "My God. Cold!"

"Yes," she said.

He lapsed into unconsciousness again, and now he was delirious, muttering unintelligibly in English and Spanish, with an occasional word in some Slavic language. She heard names —Manuél, Chloë—but most of it was incoherent, with some fragments about a moat and not letting the doctor cross the moat. He thrashed about on the bed and, repeatedly, she replaced the covers he threw aside. She stayed beside him. When Jovita came with the hot-water bottle, she sent her off again, this time to fix something to eat, because she was hungry. Then she went back to look at the painting again.

When she saw Ned looking at her, and knew that consciousness had returned, she said, "Is there anyone, some close friend, you would like me to send for? To take care of you, I mean."

"I have no friends," he said, and his eyes were self-pitying.

"In Guadalajara?"

"No friends," he said. "Oh God, my head! I have such terrible sharp pains everywhere . . . in all my bones."

"Yes," she said.

His eyes were rolling up out of focus. "Don't go!" he cried desperately. "Don't leave me!"

"All right," she said. "I won't leave you."

His eyes closed and he lost consciousness.

Dr. Obregón came into the room with Pablito. He was not a tall man, but he stood erect so that he seemed taller than he was, and he looked like the distinguished doctors or lawyers of Mexico City. Like them, he affected blue-tinted sunglasses, wore black suits, and shoes with sharply pointed toes, polished to a high gloss. The only way to tell a doctor from a lawyer in Mexico City was to look at the bag he carried; if it was a brief case he was a lawyer, otherwise he'd be carrying a worn satchel, a medical distinction as unmistakable as a caduceus. Dr. Obregón's skin was good, dark and creamy, and his teeth were very white; his eyes, without the sunglasses, were dog-brown, with much of the same sad, thoughtful look dogs have, big-eyed and soft. He was stockily built and now that he was in his forties, white had appeared in his rich black hair, streaking like swallows' wings back from his temples. He was, altogether, a good-looking man.

He looked at Ned and turned back to Victoria. "Señora," he said, "how are you?"

She wanted to cut the amenities short, not only because of Ned, but because she knew, since Dr. Obregón had made it quite clear on social occasions, that he was a little too charmed with her. They had a standing joke; he refused to believe that she was not Mexican, saying that he had never met a *gringa* who could speak Spanish so well. She always answered him by saying formally, "I am not Mexican . . . except in my heart."

Now she held out her hand toward the bed, saying, "I am concerned, Doctor."

He went immediately to Ned, set down his bag, drew up a chair and began his examination. He joggled him awake and then kept him awake with little jostlings long enough to get a temperature reading. He looked at the thermometer and then handed it to her. Like the doctor she steadied it on her finger, rolling it to get the red line. It stood at 105.2.

"Does he speak Spanish?" he asked her.

"Yes."

"Señor," he said, "how do you feel?"

Ned said, "Very bad," and seemed to be sliding away again.

But the doctor kept him awake with questions, while he took his pulse, checked his respiration, listened to his heart.

Then he leaned back, thinking. "I think you are right, señora," he said. "Malaria. But we do not see much malaria at this altitude. Malta fever, yes. Brucellosis . . . *Aftosa*, we have beaten, thanks to your country, señora, and here we do not have the dengue."

She explained that Ned had been traveling.

Dr. Obregón prodded Ned awake again. "Where?" he said. "Were you in Yucatán?"

Ned groaned, weakly tugging at the covers, getting them closer about his neck. "Yes, yes," Ned said through his clenched teeth.

"Then, malaria," Dr. Obregón said. "We make tests to be sure, but I am sure now. I shall go to the kitchen and fix an injection for your pain. Then we begin treatment. Can you take the quinines, do you know?"

"Yes. In Italy I took them."

Dr. Obregón frowned. "An unhealthy country," he said. "Do you remember the name of what you took? *Atabrina?* Yellow pills?"

But Ned had passed into unconsciousness again. Dr. Obregón leaned forward and looked at him fixedly. Then he stood up. "Pablito?"

"*Sí*, Señor Doctor?" Pablito stood in the doorway.

"Come in here and stay with the Señor while the Señora and I go to the kitchen to prepare the medicine. See that he does not uncover himself, nor try to get up, nor shake himself out of the bed."

In the kitchen Dr. Obregón set his syringe to boiling. "The artificial quinines are better now. There are less side effects. In some cases, none at all. But I do not know the patient. He is very sick. Is he your fiancé?"

"No, Doctor. I scarcely know him."

He looked at her. "He is *very* sick, you understand?"

"I know. I have had malaria. This same kind, I think . . . in the jungles in the south. But . . . after two weeks, I was better. I have never had a serious relapse. Aching, sometimes, or the headache."

"Ah but you have the dark skin, the dark eyes and—as we have said—the Mexican heart. He is fair, this *gringo*, and it has been my observation that the light-skinned ones who come here, the blue-eyed *güeros* are the ones who get sick. Get sick and *die*," he said emphatically. He turned and looked hard at her, his eyes heavy with thought. "I ask myself, what is the element? Chemically, what happens? It is a hard question for me. We Mexicans are so poor, we have so little of everything—sanitation, medicine, nutrition—we expect to die. But the *gringos* . . . why do they leave a land of plenty? Why do they come here?" He smiled as though to say, "I am casual about this; it is not important to me," but his face was heavy with the seriousness of his question. "Tell me, do they bring death with them? Do they come here seeking death?"

He waited for her answer, and although she had been going to answer him facetiously, now she saw that this would be insulting. The doctor was not naturally a thinker, but he was troubled, laboring along an unfamiliar path. She said, "No doubt

some of us bring death with us, carrying it on our backs while
we think we run from it. And others come here to find death.
Who knows? Let me ask you, when the *torero* goes into the
arena, does he bring death with him? Or does he go to meet
death, and possibly to defeat it?"

"*Ay,*" he said, shaking his head, "bullfighters! They have
no motive except to make money. But *gringos* leave the country
where money is, and come here to our poverty."

"I cannot explain it to you," she said. "Everyone who comes
here has a reason, whether he knows it or not. But the reasons
are different."

"But so many!" he said, musing. "I have been watching
them for years. One sets his bed on fire with his cigarette and
dies. Another one paralyzes himself with peyote and dies . . .
and he is only twenty-one years old . . . a poet, they say. Many
drink their way into eternity, taking a slow time about it, destroying themselves cell by cell. Like children they escape their
governesses and come here to play with the poisons of the
spirit." He sighed deeply. "I think often of this childlike quality
in them. So they seem to me . . . like runaway children. You
know the blond one called Harry, the musician? I am told by the
Doña María that in his room he plays with toy soldiers. He has
them set up all the time on a table. Is that an occupation for a
grown man?"

Victoria could not help smiling. "It hurts no one," she said,
"so perhaps it isn't. But, Doctor, are there no Mexican drunkards, self-poisoners, self-destroyers, and no childlike men and
women?"

"Of course. But Mexican drunkards are poor men, uneducated. Most of them have no beds to burn; but they do not
burn their mats." His face darkened and he frowned. "I used to
believe that to become educated, to have—not happiness because that is an affair of the soul—to have knowledge and understanding, would bring health. It does not."

"No, it does not. But understanding and health are affairs
of the soul, too."

He said, "You are not sick. I am not sick. *They* get sick
. . . the *güeros* . . . the wicked, spoiled, runaway children.
Why do I not get sick? Why are you not sick?"

"But I am. And you are, too. Your questions are those of a

guilty man. You have great guilt. I have seen it in your face and
in your eyes . . . in your hands which tremble when I say this
to you. Guilt is a sickness."

"We are all guilty," he interposed hastily. "It is the human
condition. I believe in the doctrine of original sin."

"It is not original sin which makes you tremble. It is the sin
of cupidity." His eyes flashed and the heavy lids lowered pro-
tectively over them, as though he were sleepy, but his body was
taut with attention. "This is why you ask your questions. You
treat the *gringos*, when there are sick, neglected Mexicans, because the *gringos* can pay more. A *gringo* will pay you twenty
pesos for a house call . . . a Mexican will give you five, and do
without eating to pay you that, and not buy medicine from you
either. You love your country, Doctor. It was for your own people that you studied medicine . . . yet it is the *gringos* who are
able to pay for your knowledge. So it is they who get it. You re-
sent what you are doing. It makes you ashamed of yourself . . .
you blame the *gringos* for your sin."

He stood very still with the syringe in his hands, looking at
her from under his lowered lids. "*Eso es*," he said. "Perhaps.
My wife is young and pretty, and she likes the pretty things of
life. My two sons must live, and have money to buy education
and position. We are not simple *Indios*. What would you have? A
sick man is a sick man." He leaned closer to her, looking into
her eyes. "You are very interesting, señora. My wife is pretty
. . . but we cannot have together a talk like this. I should like
to talk with you sometimes."

She met his look, slowly shaking her head, understanding
him.

He shrugged and drew back, smiling again, his face mask-
like.

"And you then, señora, what is your guilt?"

"I have wasted much of my life, much of my talent. That
gives me guilt."

"You have not had children?"

"No, but that is not the talent I mean. I am a writer."

"I know, and also a woman. No one is all mind." His smile
broadened and warmed his face, erased the shadow which had
been there before. "Now you will waste more time, nursing the
young man."

"No."

"People do not change in basic ways. They try but they do not change."

"People *do* change," she said passionately. "If you do not know that, believe that, your education was wasted."

"We shall see," he said. "It is not the value of my education we are discussing." He turned to the door, beckoning for her to follow him. "You will take care of him," he said, "because you know that if you do not, the *güero* may die." He watched her. "I wonder will he die, this one?" he said.

While the doctor gave Ned the injection, she went and found Jovita. The girl explained that she had prepared a cold lunch for the Señora and put it on a tray in the studio . . . this was where the Señor usually ate his midday meal.

"*Bueno*," she said. The girl wore a bright green leaf plastered to her forehead. Victoria pointed at it contemptuously. "What is *that* for?"

"It is the old way, señora. I have a headache. My mother put it on."

"To protect you from the Señor's sickness, I suppose?" Victoria said.

Jovita looked down, ashamed. But she did not take off the leaf. "Is there anything else?"

"No, but do not go away, Jovita. The Señor will need you."

The girl did not look up. She jerked her head toward the closed bedroom door. "My mother does not want me to go in there."

"I am not afraid to go in there. Dr. Obregón goes in there." Jovita shook her bowed head stubbornly. "You will not leave the house."

"*Sí, señora.*" The obedience was immediate, but Victoria did not believe her.

"You may go to the kitchen."

"*Sí, señora.*"

When Dr. Obregón came out, she asked him to talk to the maid before he left, to be sure that she would not just "disappear." "*Sí*," he said, nodding. "*Adios, señora*," he said. "Send for me if there is any change in the night. I shall come tomorrow."

It was not until he had gone that she realized that he had assumed, in spite of what she had said, that she would be there tonight and tomorrow.

Pablito was persuaded to stay with the Señor while she ate. Pablito, too, wore a green leaf stuck to his forehead, muttered about his little children at home, other lives dependent upon him. She swore all the way into the studio and then, forgetting her anger, ate ravenously, rapidly, grateful that no one could see her. She was very hungry, and the food was good. Afterward she found some of Ned's cigarettes . . . Delicados . . . her favorite. Smoking, she leaned back in the big chair and relaxed.

It was a beautiful room with an enormous skylight tilting up to catch the best painting light, other wide windows looking into the marvelously neat shrubbery of the patio. There were high, wide counters with the paints lined up, regimented into colorful order; a single bed covered with a handsome Guatemalan throw rug of rich orange-red; a fireplace; the floor shining deep red tile; and in here too, plants, leathery green, with healthy, glossy leaves. She stood up, gazing at the patio; she had not really seen it before; how disciplined it was, with the vines evenly pruned, how the white flowers bloomed ingenuous and meticulous at arranged intervals, so that the whole square area was ordered into geometric serenity and gazing at it filled one with peace. She went into the *sala*, free to look at it now, and saw the floor-to-ceiling curtains billowing white in the soft sweet breeze, and the light filtering through fine louvres with cool beauty; there were wonderful cupboards going along one wall in flowing lines of orange-red; there was a perfect fireplace set flush into the wall; there was an enormous flat coffee table almost as big as a room, with couches along three sides of it, and on one side a great slab of marble, and on the marble, luxuries of a kind she had not seen for a long time and had forgotten existed in the world . . . almonds in a beautiful milk-glass dish, macadamia nuts on an opaline plate, decanters which were laboratory-clean and labeled in old-fashioned, beautiful hand-lettering: GIN, SCOTCH, RUM, VERMOUTH, SPANISH SHERRY, DRY SHERRY, and an exquisite Steuben pitcher for stirring martinis . . . There was white everywhere, many shades of white in shadow and sunlight with different depths, as though the white itself must capture and muffle sound, giving stillness and peace to the whole house. She turned slowly, looking at it all, thinking that never at any time in her life had she seen a room which so approximated perfection. She found more of Ned's paintings and looked long upon them, getting lost in

looking at them, and these, too, seemed to her to be perfect.
What talent! What discipline!

She came out into the *corredor* and saw with a stab of fright
that Pablito was standing in the open doorway of the bedroom;
he had probably been afraid to go any closer to the sick man.

She strode over to him. "Coward!" she said. "Judas! Is this
how you care for your Señor?"

He twisted his big hat in his grubby hands. "I am a gardener, señora, not a nurse."

"But to be a coward is not to be a man! Get out of my way,
coward," she said.

He bent his head before the judgment in her eyes, and
shuffled away. She went into the room. Ned was uncovered, raving, tossing in the bed. She went to him at once and settled the
covers around him, searched in the built-in dresser drawers until she found big safety pins, then pinned the covers to the
bottom edge of the mattress. The fever had not yet broken. She
looked at his face. His raving mouth was cracked with fever.
She went into the bathroom and moistened a small linen towel
with water from a silver carafe labeled Boiled Water Only,
brought it back and wiped his mouth with it.

Then she stood there, counting the little hammer beats of
the pulse in his neck which she could see. Very fast and bounding. His fever must be up a little more. *I wonder will he die,
this one?* the doctor had said.

In the next days, Jovita and Pablito watched Death hover
like a bird over Ned's house, heard the sound of its wings in the
night; in the dawn its small, delicately boned feet scratched
on the tile roof. Death appeared in many guises: a huge butter-
fly, bigger than a bat, with a bigger wingspread, threw itself for
an hour against the screen of his bedroom window; a thin black
dog slunk through the garden, passed through to the front door,
and then in the street, sat with its head drooping, its bony back
to the house, waiting. The *chicharras* hummed and clacked in
the mango tree, inexplicably falling silent in the intense heat of
one afternoon—heat was what they sang—when Ned's fever
reached its highest point.

After observing these signs, Jovita and Pablito disappeared.
There were no declarations; they did not leave, separately or together, in a single moment. They did not flee the house—they

trickled away, like a stream going dry, so that when they were gone, it was, finally, hardly noticeable. Before they left, knowing they would go, Victoria arranged for a laundress, for when the fevers broke into drenching sweats, sheets and blankets were soaked through in moments and must be changed constantly. The laundress came to the house but she would not come in; she stood outside the door, muffled in her *rebozo* against the plague, with her baskets full of freshly washed and ironed sheets, taking away huge white mountains of soiled linen. Dr. Obregón came every day and sometimes twice a day, with dust on his face from the hurried drive over the dirt road; this was the dry season and the air was choking dry with dust; it got on everything, even the white swallow-wings of Dr. Obregón's hair. He frowned when he looked at Ned, saying *"Pobre hombre!"*, making no effort to conceal from Ned or from her his dwindling hope of recovery. He talked to her, or tried to, on a variety of subjects, but he was businesslike, dignified, showing his admiration only in his steady, dog-brown gaze.

The schoolteacher, who was also a nurse, came twice a day to give Ned injections. Her facial expression was naturally lugubrious; but the sorrow deepened in her eyes when she saw him, and could be heard in her voice when she said to Victoria, "Now it is with God, *verdad?* to see if the *güero* lives. *Pobrecito!*" But she was brisk, setting her syringe into its metal case on the stove, lighting the alcohol into a blue flame to sterilize it. Always, as she watched it, Victoria thought of Paris, the blue flame of cognac on *Crêpes à l'Alsacienne*, and remembered that elsewhere there was another life, another world. But the memory was short, as quickly snuffed out as the blue flame, by the needs of the moment.

Victoria's *niña*, being brave and steadfast, came constantly to the house, appearing unafraid of Death's mark on the portal, to make coffee, to bring live chickens to show Victoria before she bought them, holding them up for inspection in their feathers with their frightened eyes rolling, so that Victoria said, "Oh my God, just buy them and pluck them. How do I know? I know nothing about them. I don't want to see their eyes, you understand. Don't show me their eyes!" The *niña* could not help grinning at the Señora's panic, but then she pulled her face into what must have been an imitation of her mother's, so that she looked old and shrewd and calculating, saying, "I think this one is not very tender. She looks old, señora. I shall not buy her if I can't get her for less than nine pesos." Then when Victoria, looking fixedly away from the chicken, refused to answer, the *niña* patted her arm kindly like a tolerant parent, and went forth to bargain. After the chickens were plucked, she kept the feet for her own family, because these made the best broth of all—full of *vitaminas*.

Without being asked, the *niña* brought the typewriter, getting a small brother to help her carry it. She also brought paper, all she found on either side of the typewriter, that which had writing on it and that which was blank.

She brought clothing and took away soiled clothing when she left. She never asked about Ned, but then she was busy and Victoria was her responsibility; Ned was not. One luxury she always took time for on her way out of the house; she opened the door to the *sala* and stood a moment, on one foot, looking like a small crow in her black *rebozo*, and gazed into the room. "*Qué milagro!*" she exclaimed and her eyes widened with the awe and reverence she experienced otherwise only in church, at the beauty of it.

Watching her, it seemed to Victoria that she and the *niña* were much alike . . . poor, gamin, impressionable. But she was dazed most of the time now, with exhaustion and strain, unable to think clearly. Would that happen to the *niña*, too? And the other wise-old-young children of Mexico . . . the tireless, ambitious, clever, conscientious ones? Would life blunt and daze them, befuddle their minds, exhaust their bodies? Would the *niña* one day join the bent women of Mexico, tired and superstitious, nursing one child while pregnant with another, with older ones playing in the dirt at their feet? Would she be one of these? Where then would go the bright-burning intelligence, in this fertile grind of poverty? Would she always live in a dark hut, someday plaster a green leaf on her forehead to ward off pain, stand one day in a low doorway at dusk, sucking on a strong cigarette with a toothless mouth?

Sometimes it was light and sometimes it was dark, but the days had no other meaning. Victoria looked at the dusk sky and was not sure whether it might not be dawn, until she found the sun, flaming red, either in the east or the west. Otherwise time was marked by the four-hour medicine, the spongings, changings of the bed, Dr. Obregón's visits, the schoolteacher's.

She bent over the bed, sponging Ned's fevered body, wishing there was someone else to do it. She did not like touching skin and hair, scrubbing it, sponging it, drying it. Most of her life she had tried loftily to ignore her body, and all she knew really was how to punish it, how to make it work on minimal feeding, how to find sexual ecstasy through the mind, and, the instant it was done, forget that it had ever been . . . deny it with all of herself, so that if it did break through the window she closed on it, she declared it belonged to someone else, was needed by someone else, or that it simply was not there. Did Dr. Obregón attract her? *Never.* If she attracted him, that was a weakness in him. Yet, she had sexual feelings, obtruding themselves in dreams, in her work, and suddenly on a day standing in the patio in the almost liquid shadow, looking out at the fierce sunlight, for no reason . . . and that was the most frequent way, so that she never knew what caused it but thought only of chasing it away. You are not there, she said to it, and set herself to the disgusting work of stripping off Ned's soaking pajamas, swathing him in towels while she changed the sheets, rolling him from one side to the other of the bed he could now scarcely leave.

He was, as much as any profoundly sick human being can be, dignified. But he had become physically very weak. When the fever was not raging, and he was not groaning with the pains in his bones, he lay in a pool of sweat; between attacks, in the periods of remission, he was exhausted, sleeping profoundly, snoring, breathing stertorously, or awakening with a cry like a baby's, thirsty, always thirsty. At first he insisted on going into the bathroom and she helped him in there, supporting his tall, thin, shaking weight, saying, "No, we must leave the door open. No, you must talk to me so I know you are not fainting in there . . ." But then there came the time that, on quivering, rubbery legs, he did not make it. He cried out in shame, beginning to faint as he became incontinent, and she dragged him back onto the bed and dropped him there, where he did faint; she looked away from him, lifted her eyes from the wretched sight of him and her mind from the contemplation of what she must do now, and gazed steadily at the painting, The Icicle she called it, and reminded herself that there was a reason for her to be here. If she had doubts of her own talents—and she did now—doubts which ran around in the henyard of her brain, scratching up bits of evidence to prove that hers was no talent at all, but a precocious facility which she had overvalued all these years, she had no doubt of his talent. The man who could paint The Icicle was a genius; he must not die.

When he was clean again and conscious, he looked at her pitifully and weak tears came flooding into his eyes. "I am so ashamed," he said in a whisper. "So ashamed."

"You can't afford it," she said briskly; because of the nausea at the back of her teeth, trying to sound unaffected by the experience she had just had. She lit a cigarette, thinking the smoke preferable to the vile odor in the room.

"What would I have done if you had not come that day? I'd have died. I know. And it may be for nothing, what you are doing . . . I may die."

"Please," she said. "No threats. And no gratitude. I'd rather deal with your excrement than your gratitude."

To her absolute surprise he laughed . . . weakly, but he laughed.

She had moved a cot into his bedroom and here she spent the night, and sometimes a few moments in the afternoon.

One night he said, "Are you there?"

"Yes."

"Were you asleep? Did I wake you?"

"No," she said. "It's almost time for your medicine."

"What time is it?"

"Almost three . . . in the morning."

"What day is it?" he said.

"Wednesday."

He was silent again and she thought he was drifting off to sleep, but then he said, "I'm afraid. Could you put the light on?"

She sat up on the cot and got her slippers and pulled her robe around herself. The room was full of the diffused light of the moon. "What are you afraid of?" she asked him.

"There's a dark shape over there in the corner. I'm afraid of it. It moves toward me."

She looked toward the corner and she saw the shadow. It was large and, yes, it looked like the hooded figure of Death. She said, "It's good for you to be afraid. Fear is important, terribly important."

She gave him his medicine in the moon-lightened dark and he took it, lying back with a sigh, and turned his head toward the black shape again. He caught at her hand.

"Nonsense," she said and pulled away from him. "Don't clutch at me. Be afraid. Stay afraid."

When she was back in her cot and its springs had stopped squeaking, he said, "You're a tough one, aren't you? Don't you know what that shape is?"

"Yes, I know."

"Don't you care?" His voice was small, like a child's, thin with fright.

"Yes, I care," she said. "But it's your battle. Fear will make you fight."

After a while she could tell by his deep breathing that he was asleep. She waited a few moments, and then got up quietly and came over to him. His face seemed sanctified by sickness, so that sensuality and petulance and selfishness were stripped away and all there was was purity. She fastened the covers around him.

One morning she brought him the breakfast the *niña* had cooked for him. He looked at the tray, hopelessly.

"The food looks ugly," he said. "Couldn't Jovita have put a flower on it or something?"

"Do you eat flowers?"

He grinned. "The ancient Chinese dipped lilies in honey and ate them."

She said nothing, merely sitting down beside him and beginning, after laying the linen napkin on his chest, to spoon the gruel into his mouth.

"I heard your typewriter last night."

"I couldn't sleep."

He held up his hand. "Please, no more . . ."

She pushed his unresisting hand to one side, lifted another spoonful to his mouth. "Eat it, *niño*," she said, "or the shadow in the corner will get you."

"It's there in the daytime, too," he said wearily. "When I turn my head, I see it fading out."

"When it begins to talk to you, tell me," she said.

"I can't eat any more," he said. "What will you do when I tell you?"

"I'll drive a stake through its heart," she said, "*if* you eat all of this."

He swallowed more, gagging a little, and feebly wiped his mouth with his napkin. His hands shook. "I can't," he said. "If I had the strength, I could hate you for making me eat it."

"You'll have the strength to hate me one day," she said. "How could you avoid hating me? Look how much I've helped you!"

He looked at her questioningly and wearily shook his head and closed his eyes.

One afternoon he asked to be propped into a sitting position. She piled pillows behind him. He wanted his eyeglasses. She brought them. His head wobbled on his neck and he had to lean back. He was breathing hard from the effort of sitting up.

"Now, I've done these things for you, I want you to do something for me."

"What?"

"Drink this eggnog."

He took it without a word and drank it down. "Where the hell is Jovita?" he said.

She told him about the maid's defection and Pablito's disappearance, and was astonished at how angry he became. His hands shook badly; sweat came out on his forehead and his mouth went mean. He told her furiously to see Jovita's mother.

"Demand, don't reason with her. I want Jovita back here today. My God, how maddening! I've educated that child, spent hours training her! When Jovita gets here, send her in to me. Get Pablito. He's probably working for that goddamned English sneak thief, Hogarth . . . He's always tried to get Pablito away from me. The garden must be in terrible shape . . ."

"It looks all right . . ." she began, soothingly.

His eyes flashed behind the glasses and impatiently he swiped at his wet forehead with his shaking hand. "I won't have it! I won't have the garden destroyed because of that superstitious baboon . . ." He stopped abruptly, licking his lips, close, she thought, to a faint. "When the schoolteacher comes this evening, make her stay with me while you go and tend to these things. Will you?"

She began to say thoughtfully, yes, she would try, but then his head lolled and he began to slide off the mountain of pillows and she went to him because, as she had expected, he had fainted.

When the knocking came on the front door at one-thirty in the morning, Victoria was in Ned's studio, typing. Now that Jovita was back, she had arranged for her to sleep on the cot near Ned, so that she could get on with the rewrite of her pages in the quiet night hours.

Finally the pounding, which continued, annoyed her so that she stamped out to the *zaguán* and opened the door.

Hanschen Friedhofer stood there, feet spread wide apart, clutching the lintel with one hand, swaying drunkenly in the moonlight.

"What do you want?" she said angrily.

"How is he?" His watery eyes found her face and clung to it. "Will he live? It is said he won't live."

She said, "I don't know. Get away from here! This is no time to call on the sick."

"Oh I can't come in," he said, shaking his head and staggering as he did so. "I don't expect to come in . . . he told the maids never to let me." He gave a great belch, and tears ran down his face. "Will he live?" he demanded.

"Yes," she said shortly. "Go home."

"Tell him I called, will you?" Another freshet of tears caused him to wipe vaguely at his cheeks with the back of his hand. "Tell him . . . Hanschen called . . . and that I love him . . ."

He staggered around in the street and lurched against the wall.

"Oh for God's sake," she said and slammed the door shut and bolted it. She came back into the studio and lit a cigarette and listened to the further shouts and sobs in the street. How ridiculous he was! But Germans—she had never understood any German she had ever known. They were sentimental. They wept as they pushed the emaciated Jews into the gas ovens. They murdered millions of people, but they retained their cuckoo-clock sentimentality. Out of many Hanschens the Nazis had been made. "Shut up, you Nazi boob!" she yelled at him through the wall and, when silence came, she went back to her typewriter, but all the while she worked, she had the feeling that he was still there, silently, stuporously keeping his tequila-vigil outside Ned's house.

On a morning when Ned was feeling stronger, she told him about his nocturnal caller. He listened expressionlessly, lying on his side and staring at the wall. When she finished, he turned over on his back.

"Next time, don't answer the door," he said.

"He made a lot of noise."

He frowned. "He made just as much noise after you talked with him, didn't he?"

She nodded and went to the door but before she left the room she said, "He told me to tell you that he loves you."

"That's sweet," he said. "He hates me." He put his hand over his eyes. "My head aches very badly this morning."

She came back and looked at him and saw the yellow tint to his skin. "I think Dr. Obregón should look in on you today."

He groaned. "I don't want him." He took his hand away from his eyes and looked at her. "Are you thinking of leaving me?"

"Yes," she said. "Soon now you'll be better." She paced up and down twisting her hands together. "I'm getting nervous . . . being here. I want to go home."

"Not yet," he said. "Please. Don't make me beg you. I *know* I'm not really better yet. I feel . . . cloudy."

"Your temperature is down," she said. "Now it's only a matter of getting your strength back."

He did not argue. He continued to look at her in that way, wide-eyed, as though he could see into her mind. "Please," he said.

She shrugged and went out into the patio. The garden looked better now that Pablito was back. She looked around at it, at the freshly watered plants shining in the bright sun, and then she went into the *sala*, a little the way the *niña* went there, to look at it because it was beautiful, and to think. She stood in the middle of the room, turning slowly, looking at everything. It was beautiful . . . but it was not hers. She had not made it, nor contributed to it, and she did not belong in it; she was not beautiful; she was the only thing in the room which was not beautiful.

That night Ned had a relapse. Jovita came running for her, frightened at how sick the Señor was, unwilling to stay on the cot in the dressing room, so near to anyone that sick. It was too late for Jovita to go home alone in the dark and there was no one to escort her, so she put a mat down in a corner of the kitchen.

"I will fix medicine or cook, señora," she said, lying down on the mat. "But I cannot be in that dark room with the Señor. I am frightened in there. But I will do whatever is needed in here."

Ned was conscious, but dimly so, tossing in the bed, shivering with chills and groaning with pain. She piled the blankets on him, all she could find, and some heavy coats from the closet.

"I told you, I told you," he muttered at her wildly. "The dark shape is back. I see it with the lights on. Just as I turn my head, it's there, and then it's gone. Do you see it?" He clasped her hand in his, so that his flesh seemed to burn into hers.

She touched his forehead tenderly, smoothing back the black tousled hair, saying the first affectionate thing she had ever said to him. "There, there," she said. "It will break soon. You'll see. I'll get the towels and fresh sheets ready. Let me go."

He caught at her hand and pressed it against his fevered cheek and saying, "So cool, so cool," turned it over and pressed his burning lips to it.

When she went to the linen closet, along with her feeling of astonishment she could feel the kiss on the back of her hand, still scorching her skin like a brand.

Ned was better. Once the relapse was over, his strength returned quickly; he was young and naturally vigorous and impatient with illness. As he grew steadily stronger, he became more and more irritable, and any evidence of physical weakness exasperated him. He made a disciplined, consistent effort to hurry his convalescence, eating what he should and resting when he should. But his mouth was tense with annoyance; little things rasped his nerves. He glared for two days at the equipment which had been used for his intravenous feeding; the sight of the unsightly stand, like an old-fashioned hatrack, with its bottles and loops of rubber tubing, inflamed him, and he demanded that it be put in some other room for the time being since it wasn't being used, until Dr. Obregón took it away permanently.

Victoria became more and more impatient to leave, and after two weeks of coddling him and nursing him carefully to prevent another relapse, she came to the end of her endurance.

She marched into his room and, not looking at his wan, handsome, weary face on the pillow, but staring fixedly instead at
the neutral territory of the wall above him, announced that the
time had come.

"Today," she said. "Not one more minute here. I have no
more time for you."

When he made no answer, and she had stood there a moment, with the impetus to action draining away from her by the
second, she looked at him to see if he might have drifted off to
sleep and not heard her.

But he had heard; he was watching her, unsmilingly, with
no emotion at all, with a look of curiosity which she had seen
lately several times in his eyes, and which she resented. Every
day, as he got stronger, he devoted more time to studying her
in this silent, appraising way; she had reminded herself that
it was not necessarily critical, but the reminder did little good;
she had an immediate impulse to tug at her collar or smooth her
skirt; she became aware of her clothing and her physical being
in a way that was foreign to her nature.

"Well?" she demanded.

He smiled. He said, "Jovita can help your *niña* move you
back to your house this afternoon. Pablito can carry the typewriter, and then, after you have settled yourself into your
house, I want you to come back here for the evening. You will
be my guest for dinner. . . ."

"No, no," she said.

"Oh yes," he said, overriding her. "When you've put everything away, take a nice shower, dress up in your prettiest dress
and come back. I'll plan it all . . . the shopping, the menu,
everything . . ."

"You can't do all that," she said impatiently. "You're not
strong enough yet even to get dressed by yourself."

"I am," he said. He set his brown silk marker in the book
he'd been reading. "You come back at seven o'clock, *en punto*
because I'll time everything."

She stood there shaking her head, looking annoyed. "Oh,
do as I say!" he said crossly. "Seven o'clock. It's an occasion.
Let's celebrate it."

It was a curious day. The air was dry as paper, and a hot
wind blew down from the mountains. As she went back and forth

carrying things from his house to hers, she saw how the wind flattened the little waves on the lake and seemed to push them back, out to the deeps; the waves fell away, rallied and came back, only to be pushed back again. The dry wind pulled and tugged at the trees and finding the brown, sere leaves, pulled them loose so that they fell, spinning down in little showers of dust. Twisters of brown dust, like the cores of small tornadoes, spun up at the street corners; a brown leaf skated across the street, flattened against her ankles, and when she bent down and pulled it away, crumbled in her fingers. Across the lake, the mountain García was wearing his sombrero, a black cloud which settled low on him; the air was sharp and hot, like crystal-dust; flies rode the wind, clung to doorways and cloth and the burros, any rough surface at all, and stayed where they could stay, dazed and buffeted and stupid.

The *niña* said, "The Little Waters are coming." She nodded wisely. "After that, *pues*, comes the true rain."

Her house was much hotter than Ned's, and where it was cool, the air was stale and old. The house had gotten ugly while she was away. Where she had thought of it before as rather empty, a temporary perching place, a roost no more hers than any other, now it was evident to her that there was every sign here of her occupancy. Everywhere there was chaos, because her meager belongings were strewn about; each thing she had used, or worn, she had dropped as though she never expected to need it again, and now, picking the things up with the *niña* to help her . . . she had to shake them out and scold the *niña* and, once, jump quickly away from the scorpion she knocked out of an old slipper.

"There you are, my girl," she said angrily; "that's the result of poor housekeeping," as if it were solely the *niña's* fault. "An *alacrán* in my shoe."

He had said, "Put on your prettiest dress." She stared into her closet in dismay; there was nothing pretty there; there wasn't even a dress. She always wore blouses and skirts; her dresses were probably still in the trunk in the apartment in Mexico City, growing moldy and beginning to get the Mexico smell, the old-wood-corn-damp smell which came out of the soil and the doorways and the walls of Mexico. She took the best-looking of the blouses and handed it to the *niña*, along with the full red skirt, and asked her to press these. The child

bustled away, and she looked into the cracked, distorting mirror in her bathroom and saw her own face for the first time in
weeks.

At the orange and gold door she fought down her reluctance.
She knocked and Jovita opened the door to her, and just as the
church clock rang out seven notes, she strode up the *zaguán* and
was led into the *sala*. He was not there yet, and she went across
the room and sat in the low chair by the fireplace, and smoothed
her braids . . . her hair was glossy with oil, and she had rubbed
oil into her skin so her face shone cleanly, and the only make-
up she wore was lipstick. She knew she was not elegantly dressed,
but those things had never mattered to her. Were they to matter to her now?

There were lighted candles in the French wrought-iron
sconces on the walls so that the room was warmed and tinted
golden with their soft light, and where the light fell down
through the carved black iron flowers, the walls repeated in
shadow their dark lacy pattern. A eucalyptus log burned high in
the grate; a lamp glowed softly in the distant alcove.

Quite suddenly, Ned was there. He came in and stood by the
huge window a moment, and she looked at him. He was wonderfully groomed, and he looked tall and handsome in a black
silk suit and snowy white shirt with a narrow black tie; small,
unobtrusive jet cuff links flashed at his wrists and light came
back from the glossy leather of his polished black shoes. He
smiled at her, a smile of rueful triumph and embarrassment.

He said, "Good evening." He came to the low chair where
she sat and took her hand and bowed over it, kissing it lightly
with cool lips, and she realized that this, which had seemed absurd to her in Abel's Bar the day she met him, and melodramatic
and delirious the last night he had been so very ill, now seemed
quite natural to her.

She said, "Good evening."

He put the Mozart quartets on the record player and wonderful sound flowed from the cabinet. He made martinis, stirring them carefully in the beautiful Steuben pitcher.

He lifted his glass to her, smiling over it. "To you," he
said. "I thank you."

"No, no," she said.

He took a swallow of his drink and leaned back in the

chair. "My damned legs are shaking," he said, "but it's wonderful to be back in the world again." He looked around at everything, at the appointments of the room, at the fire burning in the
grate, and then at her. "Stop scowling at me and drink your
martini," he said, "so I can make another. You look marvelous,
all glossy and refreshed, but your expression is terrible. Relax
. . . life *can* be attractive."

She did not answer him because there was no reply; he
was probably euphoric as one got sometimes after a serious illness was done, and one came back from a world of grim con-
tours, of fear and pain, to realize that death had been successfully postponed one more time. Good for him, and she would
drink her martini; none of her problems was solved, and life
looked exactly the same to her as it had weeks ago . . .

"Seriously," he said, "how am I going to thank you?"

"You aren't," she said.

The music flowed between them and he took their two
glasses and filled them. He said, "God, what a dreary time we've
been through together!"

"Yes," she said, "but it's over."

He lifted his glass to her in salute and she glared at him
again. Was he going to toast her with every drop of fluid he put
in his mouth?

"What's done is done," she said.

He shook his head. "No, it isn't. Because you won't let it
be. It can't be done until you have let me thank you."

"I can't," she said.

"But that's very ungenerous of you."

"I can't help it," she said.

"Why not?" he asked. He was looking at her that way
again, with that same almost scientific curiosity; it was unnerv-
ing to her and she moved restlessly in her chair under his gaze,
and then began to grope in her purse for a cigarette. He handed
her the thick crystal jar which held his Delicados, but she refused him with a shake of her head and took out the pack she
had of cheap Tigres. She meant it as a declaration of a sort, to
emphasize their now different footing, but he smiled at her
and when she was fingering in the purse for matches, she heard
the click of a lighter and found that he was holding the flame
before her. She leaned forward to put her cigarette into it,
realizing that no one had lit her cigarette since Ramón in

Mexico City in the beginning when she first came there with him; he had given up such little gallantries in the last six months of their marriage. They were easily given up; usually the men who did this kind of thing—opened doors, and kissed hands, and lit cigarettes—were the sort who, later on in a relationship, would just as casually break your heart, or let you die of neglect when you were sick and lonely, or knock you down in a fit of temper . . .

"Why?" he asked.

"I don't know, I don't know," she said rapidly. "I just shouldn't be here. I didn't want to do this. I have my work to do, and . . . as I told you before, I'm not social."

"That's only part of it," he said. He handed her her glass with a little down-the-hatch gesture and she took it. "I want to know the rest. Come on," he said. "Don't mince words with me. Out with it. We know each other very well."

"We know each other very little. We've simply been through a disaster together. We have the unfounded intimacy of two people who've shared a famine, or a flood, or something. Comrades against a common enemy . . . but when the enemy is gone, you see, and this is very simple, but true, the reason for our temporary intimacy is gone. I don't know you. And you, my boy, don't know me at all."

"You're wrong," he said. He got up with the glasses and began to fix a new set of drinks. . . .

"I don't want any more," she interpolated hastily, but he went on anyway as though she hadn't spoken. "I'll only have a headache later and not be able to work. . . ."

"We have more than one common enemy. Death is only one of them . . . or let's say Death is our common enemy but it wears different faces, comes at us different ways . . ." He looked at her. "This is ridiculous," he said. "Do you know it? Why won't you let me say thank you for saving my life and then we can get on with knowing each other on different levels?"

"I don't want that drink you're making."

"It won't make you drunk. I just want you to ease up a little, for God's sake, and then we'll have dinner and we'll talk . . ."

She stood up, clutched her purse in tight fingers. "I want to go home," she said. "I'm going."

He looked at her. The record came to an end and another one dropped down on the changer. He stirred the martinis in the pitcher and speared two olives with toothpicks and put them in the glasses. "You're behaving very badly," he said.

"Yes," she said. "I suppose . . ."

"No 'suppose' about it," he said. "You *are*. Sit down." He stood before her, towering over her, and she turned her eyes up and saw the disapproving set of his mouth. He held out her drink. She could not reasonably, without making a scene, get away. Very well then, make a scene. Do what you have to do and escape, because you know, although you don't know why, that there is some subtle but profound danger to you in this atmosphere, in yielding to this young man's wishes.

Deciding then to go, she observed with astonishment that her hand was taking the glass and that she was, really was, sitting down again, smiling, saying she was sorry about her moodiness.

He sat on the floor at her feet, gazing earnestly up at her. He said, "If you left now, you'd only be coming around tomorrow, looking wild-eyed, to apologize in some cryptic, nonapologetic way. Anyway, I've planned a wonderful dinner. And damn it, since I've gone to so much trouble I have no intention of letting you run out on me and leave me with it all, like the child each of us has been once at least, all alone with the party favors because nobody came . . . No, you *don't*." He smiled. "You stay here and behave."

She laughed at how he shook his finger at her, and she knew that her eyes looked at him softly.

"So," he said, "tell me first why you act like somebody in a silent film when I try to say thank you, and shake your head and act like Theda Bara. What's so bad about 'thank you'?"

She smiled. "Don't press me for an answer, my boy," she said. "I *didn't* do it because I liked you, I can tell you that."

"I know that," he said and sipped his drink. "But why did you do it? Were you being mystical about it, saving your own soul in some Buddhistic way so that now you feel guilty when I say thank you?"

He waited and she smiled at him and shook her head.

"Were you being your brother's keeper?" he asked.

"You *are* persistent," she said. "Very well, I shall give you an answer, and it is the truth. I did it because of that painting."

"What painting?"

"The one in your bedroom. The Icicle. Remarkable! When I think of all the paintings in my life, the ones I've stared and stared at and tried to like, or at least to understand, you know, so that I could know what the *intention* was . . . Because when the painting's bad, and it usually is, then I think you've got to go looking for the artist's intention, if you see what I mean, so that you can find what he saw hanging on the wall of his mind; and then if you can forgive him for making a botch of it, for not knowing his techniques and developing his skills, at least you know that he meant well." She closed her eyes. "Oh the crimes that have been painted by the ones who *meant well,* you know! But what I am saying is, that painting of yours is one in which the *intention* has been fully realized . . . fully. That is, you know, an enormous achievement. To have intended well in the conception . . . to have done well in the creation . . . Marvelous! Marvelous and—I am a good judge of painting— unique."

He stared at her and then he laughed. "Well then," he said, laughing, "everything is solved! I'll give you the painting. That's the way to say thank you." He paused, and his eyes widened with surprise. "I just realized . . . I've never *given* anyone a painting of mine before in my life."

She smiled at his ingenuous candor. "No, no . . . I could not take it," she said. "But how charming you are to think of it!" When he looked at her questioningly, she said, "Don't think I don't appreciate it. But I do not have possessions, you see. I don't want them. No, I do not want *things,* especially not something as fine as your painting." She lifted her hands as though to hold back the gift, as though he were actively forcing it upon her now. "All that I own, I own in my mind. I consider that true ownership; I believe that the mind can truly possess a concept. But when the concept becomes a *thing,* with a physical shape and form, it threatens to possess the mind. I cannot afford, you understand, to own anything."

He shrugged. "As you like," he said. "But really . . . I think it's only a bankrupt mind which cannot afford to own anything . . ."

"Bankrupt?" she said, interrupting him, staring closely into his eyes. "Bankrupt? Is that what I am?"

He looked a little startled. He drew back, saying, "Well, I

was only theorizing, you know, abstractly . . . making an impersonal remark . . ."

"Bankrupt!" she said again, frowning with great concentration, and got up and strode to the door and came back, not as if she were wandering at all, but marching. "No," she said. "Not *quite* bankrupt. But you have come close to the mark, my boy . . . dangerously close to the mark." She paused in her pacing to stand in front of him and look into his face, nodding to herself. "What sharp eyes you have! I must remember that. No, I am in that place which is just *before* bankruptcy, intellectually, creatively, emotionally and—although it hardly matters —financially. But of course, you can see it, because bankruptcy is very close. I anticipate it. Most lives are entirely bankrupt. In most lives, there is no second chance, did you know that? But I have been given a second chance; I have given it to myself. But, it is also, as I well know, the last chance."

His expression gradually shifted from dismay to amusement. "I'm going to have to change the music if you talk like that. Mozart doesn't do for this sort of thing. Anyway, every expatriate in the village is living on a second chance. Who's to decide it's the last one? That's just a way of frightening yourself."

"Is it?" she said.

He tipped the pitcher over their glasses and added the last drops of the martini. He said, "I should play drippy Chopin for you, or some melancholy Tschaikovsky, or Kodály . . . We Slavs . . . we have to emote so about everything . . ."

She said, "Being Slavic has nothing to do with it. I am, to put it simply, half-mad."

"Half-mad . . . Slavic . . . That's just redundant. They mean the same things." He smiled. "I know," he said. "I am only one generation away from Czechoslovakia."

She shook her head. "It's an amusing attitude," she said. "But I take responsibility for what I am. I do not blame my parents."

"Why not?" he said. "It simplifies everything. Why not blame them for the heritage they gave you, the environment they gave you? At least that way you don't have to hate yourself. I don't believe in self-hatred," he said. "It's corrosive."

He got up and went to the record player and she watched him, thinking how pleasant it must be if this oversimplification worked for him, and apparently it did. He seemed to accept himself.

He glanced at his watch. He said, "We'll have some Edith Piaf now. She'll go well with dinner." He adjusted the stack of records, then turned around and leaned back against the cabinet and looked at her. "I understand you better than you think I do. I'm going to help you, because you have helped me and because . . . you do everything all wrong, don't you? You don't know how to live, do you? And you make yourself unhappy. . . ."

She stared at him. Jovita came in quietly and said that dinner was served. Ned nodded. "*Bueno,*" he said.

Now he was looking at her and Jovita was gone and there were many things which should be said, even to a face as young as his, to eyes as coldly intent as his at this moment . . . warnings to be sounded; she should tell him not to tamper with her, to leave her systems of dealing with reality alone, because everyone developed what he must for his own survival, however disorganized it might appear to be to a stranger. He *was* a stranger, in the truest sense of the word; he would always be a stranger to her, and her ways, and everything which had made her what she was, whether what she was had value or not. That was the real reason she could not accept his gratitude. . . .

"Are you hungry?" he asked, smiling, coming over to where she sat.

She said, "Yes." She looked up into his handsome face, at the way he held his body, and she began to feel frightened. She could not separate him from the environment he had created, an environment which was, like him, somehow threatening to her.

"Shall we go in to dinner?" he said. He bent down and offered his arm.

She stood up. "Let me walk alone," she said.

7

The Beautiful People

IT WAS RAINING torrentially. This was the third day of the rain, and the village on the lake's edge wallowed where it lay, half-drowned under the mountains, ready to be swept into the boiling brown waters of the lake itself. Water gushed and gurgled down the hilly streets of the town, and at the bottom, close to the lake, it was impractical to try to cross a street, and no one tried, except for some young Mexican girls who built a temporary bridge of chairs. This was unnecessary and not entirely effectual; the chairs, although tied together, were often sucked down into the swirling water. But that only added to the fun, and the fun was attested to by shrieks of laughter and simulated fright. Any one of them might have crossed the street higher up on the hill and run no risk at all. But they were celebrating the rain; the rainy season was late this year; the lake had drawn back from its banks and shrunk shallow at its edges, suffering from attrition, and the wild green tropical growth of the plants and flowers had been curbed, in a way more suited to an unfamiliar temperate climate than a tropical one.

Above the water-stained adobe walls there were lowering leaden clouds, and over the mountains, rapid, successive flashes of lightning, bright and blue as moonlight, which came very close to the land and, once, struck a tree into a brief, blazing torch. Thunder—not polite, drum-beat thunder—but deafening crashes of sound rocked the village. Water gushed through holes in new roofs where the tiles were unevenly locked together, and spilled more gently through older roofs where the tiles were swollen with more water than they could hold. Scorpions came down from the wet *bambú* ceilings and took up an oddly permanent position and stayed, with their tails curved up and back and at the ready, halfway down the walls.

Jerry Ramsay sat in Jackson Garth's house, with his thin legs crossed, one bony knee loosely hinged over the other, and swung his foot. He was seated in an *equipali* in a dry place in the *corredor* watching the rain plummet into the puddled patio. He did not shudder when the thunder cracked, because he was almost entirely deaf, but the lightning flashes lit up his aged pink face and glistened on the shine of his edematous, finely wrinkled skin. Each time he looked at his watch, as though he planned and supervised these flashes, like trains, and was checking them against the celestial schedule in his head. He would nod with satisfaction, and once in a while glance around at Jackson and Elinor Garth to see if they appreciated the punctualities of his storm. They were busy unpacking boxes and suitcases, which were strewn around the living room, and they hardly looked at him. He smiled anyhow, a careful smile so as not to show that he hadn't worn his false teeth today, and sipped on the tequila they had given him, with the manner of a man who has earned a reward whether anyone else knows it or not.

The Garth's child was a nuisance, and although Jerry smiled dutifully at him too, Ricky Garth did not add to Jerry Ramsay's air of well-being. Ricky was mean. He looked like an angel, a four-year-old one, with blue eyes and a halo of blond curls, pink cheeks and a beautiful, sturdy little body. There wasn't a trace in his peach-blossom, seraphic face of the consistent cruelty with which he busied his days and from which education, it was to be assumed, he would grow into adulthood. He stared enigmatically at Jerry, and his steady gaze made Jerry uncomfortably conscious of how he looked, so that he put his hand over the shiny elbow of the sleeve of his blue serge double-breasted suit, and then attempted futilely to tuck back the hanging threads of his frayed cuffs. All the while he propitiatingly included the child in his cosmic smile, although he knew the child did not like him and would hurt him if he could; he tried not to seem to observe how Ricky continued angelically to torture the cat.

Ricky had hold of it by its legs, grasping two legs in each perfect small hand, and was assiduously trying to drown it by dipping it for longer and longer periods in the deep brown puddle of water at the corner of the garden. The cat struggled convulsively, tried insanely to bite the inexorable hands which held him, and beat the water with its long thin tail.

Jackson Garth called over to his son in a sharp voice, "Ricky! That's enough! Let the cat go!" but Ricky pretended not to hear.

Elinor limped over to the boy and stood looking down at him. "You heard your father," she said. She took a long swallow of the drink she carried with her. "Ricky!" she said, echoing his father's tone.

But Ricky waited, with expert timing, for the second when his father looked around again with anger in his face and took a step toward him; then he lifted the cat from its moist deathbed and released it.

"It likes its bath," Ricky said cherubically. "It was dirty."

Erratically the cat scraped to its feet and ran, eyes wild in its wet face, ears back and flat to its head. Its ribs showed in its frighteningly thin body, and it careened, hardly able to run, into a distant room.

Elinor looked down at Ricky with a faint suspicion flickering in her glassy blue eyes, but she spoke softly. "No, Ricky," she said gently, chiding, "cats don't like water. You know that."

"Don't they?" Ricky said with false wonder.

The suspicion left his mother's eyes and she smiled at him. "No, darling," she said.

"He knew that," Jackson said. He picked up a stack of

blankets and now he walked with them past his wife and son, out of the living room, past Jerry Ramsay along the open *corredor,* carrying them to one of the bedrooms which opened darkly off the long, open passage.

Elinor went to the table which made a bar in the living room and poured tequila into both glasses. The tequila was warm, but the kitchen was in a separate building, across the patio, and it wasn't worth going out in the rain to get ice.

She brought Jerry his drink and touched his shoulder lightly so that he'd know she was there beside him. He jumped up quickly and gave her a courtly bow.

"A beautiful drink from beautiful hands," he said, but his diction was blurred with drink and the lack of teeth. Elinor smiled at him, not having understood him, and limped off after her husband.

The child was watching him contemptuously. Jerry beamed on him, lifted his glass to him in false bonhomie, and drank.

Experimentally, Ricky said an obscenity in Spanish to Jerry and when he saw no reaction, tried it in English. The old man's expression did not change. Ricky turned vacantly away, bored with failure.

Jackson was packing the blankets away in the big Spanish chest when Elinor came to the doorway. She said, "Jerry doesn't show any signs of leaving."

Jackson did not turn around. "So what?" he said.

She looked down, twisting the glass in her hands. "Harry and the others will be here any minute."

"You're not going to be very *lista*," Jackson said, "if you keep juicing."

"I want you to tell Jerry to go," she said. "He makes me nervous sitting there nodding at the lightning."

"Tell him yourself. He isn't bothering me."

"I mean it, Jackson," she said, but she did not sound very assertive now.

"So it makes you nervous. Big deal."

She laughed. But she always laughed when something hurt because she didn't know what else to do but hide it in laughter.

"*Do* something," he said. "Make sure there are enough beans and tortillas in the kitchen for supper." He sighed. "Don't just hang *around*," he said.

She laughed again, more softly, and limped away. Listening

to the scrape of her limp on the tiles, his face swelled with frustration.

The power was turned on at dusk. It was not strong, and even as it came on, it flickered. There weren't many lights in the Garth house, which was, in size at least, a mansion. The goat in the *corral*, tethered in the open, began to bleat insistently. Jackson paused in the *zaguán*, a few feet away from where old Jerry sat in the corner of the *corredor* sipping his tequila, and stood with his hands in his pockets, not yet willing to go into the living room where his wife was. Jackson was a handsome young man, short, stocky, broad-shouldered, with an erectness of bearing which was evidence of the number of military schools he had attended in his life, and the fact that his father was a West Point man. He had a silken gold mustache, and golden hair which he wore long and which fell in a careless wave back from his high, even forehead. His head was large, perhaps larger than it should be for his body, but he was physically beautiful, and so was his wife. Elinor was Boston Irish, with blue eyes and full upper lids which hinted at a remote Oriental background. With her symmetrical black brows and her black hair parted in the middle, she somehow looked Egyptian. Her teeth were square and white and her mouth was wide and well-shaped. The thick creamy column of her throat trembled a little when it contained laughter, like the strong stalk of a flower in a breeze.

The Garth house, which for centuries had been called the "Murillo house," and was still so called by the Mexicans, stood on the corner at the top of the hill near the highway. Its carved, age-pocked doors were fifteen feet high. The high ceilings were made of *bambú* and its unglassed windows were deeply set into the thick adobe walls. When it rained, as now, the wooden shutters were closed and latched. They banged and pulled with the wind, shutting out most of the rain, and with it, most of the light.

There was a legend that stolen gold had been buried in the Murillo house and men had died trying to find it—not only Mexicans, but *gringos*, too, who had heard the story and come here greedy for money, to find only death. At another time in its history the house had been a convent for a set of pseudo-nuns —six Mexican lesbians who had worn nuns' habits and carried prayer books—Was it Boccaccio behind the innocent, often-thumbed bindings?—who had opened an academy and accepted several pious young girls of good and rich family as students. These had learned to cook, definitely; what else they learned was never to be told. But the hoax was discovered and the eldest son of the richest family in town had rounded up a group of his class—*macho* brothers all of them—and they had mounted their horses one night and ridden to the convent, and when the doors were not opened to them, they charged the doors and rescued their tainted virgin sisters, carrying them off on their horses through the night and returning them to the sanctuary of their families. The self-styled "nuns" had fled in the night and only one was found, lying dead near the waterfall in the hills, with her throat cut and her starched white coif now no more than a bloody bandage.

Jackson imagined the scene with its trampling, whinnying horses and the hoarsely screaming nuns, and here and there a whimpering, cowering novice. He had attempted to do a water-color of it the first week he lived in the house, but it never got quite the urgency he had in his mind, and he stopped trying.

Along with the house, which they rented on a long lease, the Garths had to endure old Señora Murillo Rojas, who lived in one of the small outbuildings in the *corral* with the old ill-smelling goat tethered near her door. She wandered through the great house at will, with or without the goat, watching the pretty *gringa* and her so handsome husband and the *diablito* of a child. When they told her the house teemed with scorpions, she pretended she could not understand them—although Jackson's Spanish was flawless—and drew her black ragged *rebozo* over her face and tottered away. Her presence became increasingly troublesome to Elinor and she insisted that several moonlight nights she had seen the old woman standing motionless at their bedroom door, watching their conjugal embrace; she had even smelled the cigarette the old crone smoked. But when Jackson, naked and angry, went to the door, the empty patio lay still and silent in the fish-silver light of the moon. Once, although he did not admit it to Elinor, he saw the black flapping skirt whisk around the corner of the gate to the *corral* and he, too, smelled the smoke. But whether or not she watched them in their sexual engagements, Elinor became very oppressed by the concept of the old woman's presence, although Jackson continued to deny it, and she imagined that she was there all the time, watching them.

The electric power flickered and Jackson got matches out of his pocket and lit the kerosene lamp in the hallway in the *zaguán*, pretty sure now that at any moment in this storm the electricity would go off and stay off. He set the lamp on a pile of bricks which served as a table and took occasion, in this new light, to look at his paintings, which were hung along the walls all the way to the patio. It puzzled him that his paintings gave him so little pleasure, and he often tried to see them anew, as though someone else had painted them and he had never seen them before. They were all watercolors, representational, and as such, quite good. At first glance, they looked like two lines of bright tropical birds moving toward the patio, splashing reds and greens and blues, with thin streamers of yellow and occasional studies of rolling tan hills, curving upon each other like full mulatto breasts. But there was no progression in them, no improvement, no lessening—no *change*. His uneasy suspicion that he had gone as far as he could go in this form, was one of the reasons he had not painted anything in the last months, as though there was nothing new for him to paint. Harry had looked at his work and said, "Man, why doesn't this stud buy himself a color camera and save time?"

Just as he expected, the power clicked off and he could hear Elinor talking loudly now to Jerry Ramsay, or, since Jerry couldn't hear her, to herself. The important thing to her was to talk, whether anyone listened or not; it was a physical activity with her, in a way he could not understand. She didn't care what she said, or whether anybody answered her really, although that was preferable; it was just that she could stand silence only so long. He tried to remember if she had been that way before the thing with her leg, and he couldn't be sure. But certainly she was worse now than she had ever been. On the trip she'd been worse than he'd ever known her to be, and the steady, dry drone of her voice as they traveled was maddening to him. One hot, steamy afternoon as the truck labored through jungle country he was startled to discover that as she talked he was drifting into a dream of having killed her, of having thrown her body into a thick clump of jungle undergrowth and driven on.

As he walked now toward the voice which clamored for him in the unlighted *sala*—Why hadn't *she* lighted a lamp? How exasperating of her not to have guessed earlier, as he had, that the power was sure to go off!—the idea of having killed her was less of a shock to him, but seemed a good deal more impractical than it had in the sleepy, sweaty boredom of the jungle. Anyway, it must have been a dream. He was half asleep in the heat. He would never have gotten away with it. Someone would certainly have found the body. And the corpse of a *gringa* with only one leg, being so rare a thing to find and gossip over, would have served as a large arrow of guilt aiming at him.

He was used to living with guilt; he didn't even see it any more. It had been there since the accident, and since they had finally had to amputate her leg. The accident was his fault, but it was maddening because nobody else was really hurt. Just Elinor. The guy driving the other car was hollering so and there was so much blood, he was sure the guy must have a fractured skull. It was all he could think of then, and that it was his fault. He hadn't even seen Elinor, lying there silent and unconscious. The ambulance got there and the doctor said the guy was all right, just cut, and he'd sagged down, crazy with relief, and it was then they discovered her and the leg.

Marrying her, he swore it was because he loved her and not because he felt he had to, not because he felt guilty.

He came directly to the table in the living room where the lamps stood, struck a match, lit two lamps, turned the wicks down, and looked at Elinor there in the flickering warm lamplight . . . surely the most beautiful warden in the world. She was smiling at him and the light caught and swung in the gold hoops of her earrings. "Jackson," she said, "I tried, but I can't get him to go. You tell him to go. It isn't raining so hard now."

He looked from her face to the glass in her hand and down at the tequila bottle on the table. Even counting Jerry's drinks, she'd had plenty. But what was lost? Was the precious sharp edge of her intelligence dulled?

She said, "Every time I tell him to go, he thinks I'm offering him another drink." She looked away from her husband's cold face and set the glass down.

He went to the duffel bag where they had the marijuana and lifted it out. It was in two brown bags, two kilos in each.

"I'll put one of these away," he said. "Take a lamp with you and go into the bedroom. I'll bring the other one to you with the sieve and you can start sorting. Where's Richard?"

"Outside," she said. She rose awkwardly, straightened up, pushed her hair back with her hands.

"In the rain?"

"He went to Pedro's house. About Jerry"—she looked at him pleadingly—"he's driving me crazy."

He took the two bags and went out and when he came to where old Jerry sat in the half-dark, still watching the patio and the steadily falling rain, he said, "You've got to go home, old boy."

"Thanks awfully," Jerry said in a blurred way, and gulped down the rest of his tequila. He lifted his empty glass for a refill. "Warms me," he said.

Jackson leaned down close to Jerry and, smiling a little cruelly, he said loudly into the big, almost useless ear, "No."

"No?" Jerry turned and looked up into Jackson's hard smile and beamed at him, but his reddened eyes looked a little frightened all the same.

"Go home," Jackson said.

The meaning seemed to travel to him slowly from the sound. He sat there listening as the meaning came to him, and then he said, "Oh." He jumped quickly to his feet, put one hand in the pocket of his coat, executed a rickety but jaunty bow. "Can't thank you enough, dear boy," he said. "Great pleasure visiting with you and your dear wife. *Beautiful* people. Pleasure just to look at you. My pleasure. You must call on me." He gave a great swinging wave of his hand and turned and plunged down the *corredor* as though it were steep, and pulled at the big door. A wet gust of wind swept the rain in against him. He turned up the collar of the double-breasted jacket and stepped out into it.

"Get lost," Jackson said behind him, knowing he wasn't heard. Then he walked off with the marijuana.

When Harry and Charles and Jim came, they went directly into the bedroom where Elinor was sifting the pot. She sat on a low bench and used the bed as a table. There was a big white cloth laid out over the *serape*, which was their bedspread, and on this white island, in little mounds of about a quarter of a pound each, was the marijuana. Elinor sifted it by the handful, laboriously, picking out the seeds and twigs which were mixed in with the stuff itself, and put the sifted marijuana into a *cazuela*.

Jim sat down at the table in the lamplight, and took the

marijuana from the *cazuela* and rolled it in the cigarette papers. He'd brought a stack of London *Times Literary Supplements* with him and he cut and smoothed the thin, tissuey pages very exactly and rolled the marijuana in them to make the joints. He concentrated very hard, with his mouth a little open, because his hands shook, and he had never had very much manual dexterity anyway. It took concentration and coördination, and Harry and Charles watched him respectfully for the way he did it. It was the one thing he could do, besides blowing pot and getting stoned, that anybody knew about, and he was the best of all of them at making the sticks.

Sifting was hard for Elinor because she was drunk, and once she dropped the sieve and laughed and Jackson looked at her knowingly, but he was always looking at her knowingly anyway. She was sure the others didn't know she was drunk at all.

The rain, coming down hard again, scrambled and clattered over the tiles of the roof, and the warm, wet wind whined in the trees. Harry leaned against the wall holding a glass of tequila and watched Elinor. Jackson walked around the room, straightening things, physically restless, looking out at the storm sometimes, responsive to it, boring everybody telling them about their trip. She knew they weren't interested, but he kept on anyway and they pretended to listen.

Charles slouched in the fan-back bamboo chair and studied how Harry looked at Elinor. He recognized Harry's expression of closed-in, salacious concentration for what it was, and maybe it had been that way before with Harry but he hadn't known that was what it was, if it was. He tried to understand, while Jackson droned on, turned and watched Elinor himself, tried to see what Harry saw. Her plump arms moving whitely as she worked were beautiful, he supposed, and her eyes had a smoky, sultry look and her mouth was full. . . . But it didn't work. As far as he was concerned, whatever beauty she had, had been given to the wrong broad. When you really looked at her and knew how dumb she was, you couldn't keep on thinking she was beautiful. She was just a sodden, lushed-up, dumb broad.

Jackson said, "And then we had to wait on the river bank for two hours because the river was so flooded they wouldn't pole out the auto ferry. Christ." He turned around and walked to the open door and looked out at the falling rain. "The other river had a bridge. We hit it at night, and you could feel it sag under the weight of the truck . . . rotten wood."

"Was it a formidable bridge, Roberto?" Harry said in a Spanish accent. "Did you blow up the formidable bridge?" His eyes swiveled back to Elinor. His face was pale and his eyes glittered pale-gray. "And did the earth move . . . under the sleeping bag?"

Elinor looked up at him and her hands went still. She managed a little smile and kept looking steadily up at Harry, until her vision blurred and there began to be two Harrys. Sometimes she liked it like that, liked the world to be blurred and misty. But not now. She closed her eyes again, and swallowed, because her throat had gotten dry, and when she opened her eyes she could see straight again. But she couldn't keep closing them like that or she'd pass out.

"Let's light up," Jim said. "I got lots of good joints here. Enough for a bash. These over here are the best ones . . . the others are a little loose, but good enough."

"Shall we?" Elinor said.

"You are the goddess of pleasure," Harry said, "and I am a hedonist."

Jackson said, "Let's go. But you better clear this stuff away first, Ellie."

Jim gave the cigarettes he'd made into Jackson's open hands. Jim had a passive good-child way of doing what he was told; it didn't occur to him to do anything else. He stood there now, swaying slightly, staring astigmatically out at the rain, waiting for the command to go.

"Come on, Jim," Harry said, and he and Jackson and Jim went out into the *corredor*. Elinor picked up the cloth by its corners, so the marijuana rolled into the middle of it, making a bundle. She got up stiffly, moving carefully, leaning her hand against her leg, and took the bundle to her small, nearly empty dresser. She did that all right and she didn't think that Charles, sitting there with his hand over his eyes like a shelf, knew she was drunk. But under his hand his eyes were watching her; she could feel it.

"Quit watching me," she said. "Old Jerry sat around here all day and watched me until he about drove me crazy."

"I'm not watching you," Charles said.

She stood in front of him. "You watched Harry and me and now you're watching me." Her speech was a little thick and it annoyed her. "Well?" she said.

He smiled pleasantly, teasingly. "It's bad when you think everybody's watching you."

"You're not fooling me," she said. "You got ideas about me and Harry and you don't like it."

"Like what?"

She leaned forward and stared into his face. "That he's got eyes for me, that's what."

"Jesus," Charles said. "What are you talking about?"

"Oh *I* know." She smiled at him knowingly. "*I* know."

"Harry's only got eyes for Harry," Charles said.

She held her head a little to one side like a bird. Then she said carefully, "No, I can feel it. He's got eyes."

Charles laughed. "Broads!" he said. "Especially juiced broads . . . wow. Crazeee." But she didn't smile. She continued to look at him in that listening way, and suddenly he felt sorry for her. He said quickly, "I know Harry better than anyone. You don't want to get mixed up with Harry. You got a husband."

"Jackson doesn't like me," she said. Her eyes were filling with easy tears. "He only stays with me because I'm a cripple and he feels sorry for me." She gave her pained little laugh now, soft and helpless. "You feel sorry for me, too. You wouldn't be saying this to me if I weren't a cripple. Okay. Okay. I'm a cripple. Feel sorry for me. But Harry doesn't. Harry's the only one doesn't make me feel that way." She smiled wisely. "That's how I know," she said.

Charles moved uncomfortably in the chair. "Look," he said, "you're bugged on this cripple thing. I'd warn any chick off Harry."

She continued to look very sorry for herself. She put her hand against the leg. "Harry *likes* me," she said like a child in a singsong voice.

"*Likes* you!" he said. "Because he stares at you and makes cracks about did the earth move? That old crappy line . . . Harry doesn't *like* anybody, not even himself." He shook his head. "Wise up," he said.

"Did you ever live with pity, Charles?"

He looked at her in disbelief. What corn, for Christ's sake. She was wallowing in self-pity, lush-pity, sold on the idea of herself as a sad, crippled girl who got only pity from her husband, and was offered passion by another man. He said, "Did you ever try to live without it?"

"Harry likes you," she said with her lips trembling. "You're friends. If he likes you, why can't he like me?"

He got out of the chair and stretched. "Forget it," he said. He looked at the dumb, trusting way she lifted her face to him, waiting for him to say more. He said, "Harry doesn't like me, or Jim, or you or anybody. So forget it."

Elinor said, "You're trying to shut me out, that's all. It's okay if Jackson and I make the run for the pot but we're not really one of you. I mean, I'm not really one of you, am I? You think I'm a square. If you didn't think I was a square, you wouldn't be telling me to stay away from Harry."

"Okay," he said in a bored way. "You've conned yourself. I'm warning you off for two reasons . . . because you're a cripple and because you're a square. I told you, I'd warn any broad."

Her eyes shone with satisfaction. "You don't say it isn't true. You do think I'm a square, don't you?"

"Well, you blow some pot but you're not a real head."

"Why not?" she said, looking more hurt again.

"You don't even know what a real head is, baby." It was time, he thought wearily, that somebody laid the truth on her. He said, "I'm what you call a head. I've been a hophead . . . smoking opium since I was seventeen. I got busted once, and I kicked it once before. That's why I'm here. They say . . ." He laughed abruptly, suddenly, because it seemed absurd to be saying this to her or anybody, or even for it to be true, which it was, because it was telling so little of it all . . . "The Chinese say you can kick hop three times in your life and that's it. This is my second time. I was going to get busted again so I had to get out of Manhattan. I came down here to kick and I kicked. I still keep dreaming every night about getting busted. I can't go back to New York yet—not yet, not for a while—because I'd be flat on my back in the first fifteen minutes with a pipe in my hands. I'm a head. Jim's a head. He used to be the biggest junkie in town. He shot everything. He couldn't get across Forty-eighth Street one time for five hours because he couldn't stand up and walk straight enough when the light changed. They took him to Bellevue. When they asked him what he was on, he told them and they wouldn't believe him. He should have been dead. When he got out he came down here like me, to kick. Now he stays stoned on pot—and like, you know, all he wants is a fix but he knows this is case—he'll never kick again once he starts. You know Jim. I don't know all about Harry, except he talks more like a head than anybody but he's getting virgin kicks on C right now. I don't know where he got it. Abel wouldn't get it for him. Harry knows I hate junkies . . . he won't tell me who his connection is." He laughed. "All hopheads hate junkies. Like, it's a caste system. But when I was kicking this time I had to shoot something, like a junkie kicking will smoke a toy if he can get it. I'm a good chef . . . I've made it for enough of them. But they're two different types, junkies and hopheads. Harry's on his way. Sniffing isn't bad, but he'll go from that to joy-popping and from there to Route 66 . . . the mainline, baby. And it won't take long. There's no place else to go, dig? *Cocaine* is what Harry *likes*. Not me. Not Jim. Not you. No junkie wants a broad, unless she can make money for his habit. No junkie is anybody's friend. No hophead is anybody's friend. No head is a friend. Kicks are all that count."

She hadn't moved all the time he talked, and her face hadn't changed while she listened. It was as drunk and dumb as before. He thought about the first time he'd seen Jackson and her and the kid in the green panel truck when they drove into town. The truck had Washington, D. C., license plates and he'd figured for sure that Jackson was a narcotics man come down here to bust him. But Harry found out Jackson was a teahead and persuaded him that he'd been wrong, crazy with kicking. But now looking at her again, the thought came back to him. There was something very square about these two and maybe Jackson *was* a narco man, and here he'd been very uncool. He listened with the old fear flickering through him, for the whirr of a tape-recorder, but all he heard was rain. He sighed. There was no recorder. Just crazy again, getting wigged by the sound of his own voice. His nerves were bad. He said, "Let's go light up."

He turned to the door. She limped beside him, carrying the lantern, and they went out and along the *corredor*. The lantern light made the raindrops yellow as they fell in the patio, brightening the shining wet of the red tiles under their feet. The warm, wet wind blew hard against the lantern and

sent rolling shadows and smoke out of it against the white adobe
wall. He had an impulse to put his hand on her shoulder, com-
fortingly, and to restrain her from thinking anything which
might threaten them all, but he was careful. She'd probably
think he had eyes for her, too. Had he betrayed Harry? Himself?
Had he betrayed them all? The sound her wooden leg made
on the tile was different from the other one, and that was a
stupid thing to be noticing, he thought. I don't even *like* this
broad, for God's sake. . . . I don't care if I save her from Harry.
It's just I have to keep trying to save everybody from Harry,
even Harry.

They went into the living room and closed the doors after
them. The marijuana smoke in the room smelled good and acrid
and Charles had a little of the feeling he used to get when he
was a kid and he first smoked gauge, of recognition, of . . .
yes, this is what I want, what I've been wanting all day. But
it was a very small feeling and, even with the close memory
of the horrors and torment of kicking this last time still vivid
in his mind . . . he couldn't forget, and would never forget,
that other greater recognition, that other greater surrender . . .
yes, yes, this is what I want. This small recognition only reminded him of that one. It was true what he had said to her
about New York. Last week in Guadalajara when he had seen
an old Chinese shuffling along the street, his eyes began to
water, and his stomach went hollow, and, long after the old
man had passed him and disappeared, he had stayed there,
wiping his streaming eyes, sick with longing, fighting the knowledge that he could get opium in Mexico, just the way Harry got
C. All he had to do was go hang around the bus station at the
Calzada for a minute and there would be a connection . . .
He felt as though he were on fire and he wished that he could
perspire, but he couldn't, and he clutched at the rough uneven
bricks of the wall and talked to himself steadily, and finally
there were no more tears in his eyes. But he had taken a cab
home to the village, even though he couldn't afford it. He knew
better than to go near the bus station that day. Thinking of that
now, he went toward the marijuana determinedly; this time
he was really going to get smashed, get high and eerie and cold
like on a mountaintop. . . .

Time, like a rubber band, stretched long and snapped
short and no one of them in the Garth living room had any

lasting impression of how much of it went by; time was not measurable and it did not flow. In between the marijuana cigarettes, they smoked other cigarettes and the room was blue in spite of the height of the ceiling. In the lamplight, and the soft candlelight, with the sound of rain in the street, all of them sat around, heavy-eyed and quiet. When the maid knocked on the living-room door, the sound came sharp and sudden, becoming dim and remote almost at once. Elinor rose and slowly wandered over to the door and opened it and looked at the maid who stood there holding Ricky by the hand, saying she had fed him his supper and she was going to put him to bed now and then go to her own house. And if there was some other thing needed, would the Señora be so kind as to call upon her in her house across the way? Thank you. May the Señores pass a good evening. Elinor leaned against the open door listening to her, thinking of an answer to this in good Spanish, but rigid-faced and unable to say anything. She could have been standing there a long time like that, she didn't know, for even as she perceived this possibility, or seemed to perceive it, the perception raced away from her, like a piece of debris on a flooding river, and she watched it go, and knew again that more time might have passed. Ricky looked at her reproachfully and said, "Are you cross, Mummy? You look cross."

She made her lips smile, concentrating hugely to do this, feeling stony and immobile. She made herself say good night to him, almost in a whisper, and to add, "No, no, darling. Not cross." She closed the door on them and turned back into the *sala*, away from the two of them, gratefully coming back into the safe room where it was silent. Not really silent, but at least there was no talk, and nobody would demand anything of her or ask her questions. There were notes sounding, rich, deeply plucked guitar notes, slow and intricate. Jackson sat on the floor with his legs crossed under him and, squinting against the smoke, played the guitar.

Harry drank. He was the only one who drank when he smoked tea. "I have to, man, or nothing happens. You know, like nothing's happening, man," he said in the whining, muttering way he talked when he was high. . . . But that must have been a long time ago, wasn't it? Days, months, hours, minutes. Time was fluid, immeasurable. But this was living The Life. Fences fell down; time built no bars; there was no compelling need to speak; unspoken things were understood and

enjoyed, but there was no need to laugh at them . . . they
floated away too fast anyway, just as the answer to a question—ready before the question was asked—was forgotten when
the question was finished, because the question was forgotten
when the last syllable of itself died away. But for each moment
the question lived in its syllables, it was intensely alive, unlike
any other question ever asked . . . There was no need to communicate anything, there was neither demand nor command;
they were like statues, stony-faced, marbleized and beautiful.
Jackson's hair was more golden in the lamplight, his mustache
looked silken, like corn silk, soft, as she knew it was silken and
soft on a naked shoulder, and his big rough hands, which
could be so cruel, seemed now to curl over the strings of the
guitar like those of a huge stone baby. The copper ash tray held
warmth, glittered, danced, made another light of itself like fire-
light, and black shadows romped slowly like big sleepy panthers
in the corners.

When the knocking came on the outside door of the house
—loud, imperious, importunate—they all sat up, eyes alert,
looking at each other.

"Cool, now," Harry said, suddenly sharp. "Is the maid
gone?"

Elinor was surprised to hear her own voice, husky and
hoarse, but brisk. "Long ago," it said.

"We have to answer," Jackson said, reasoning slowly,
"because of the rain. Whoever it is won't go away . . ."

"You think it's a bust?" Charles said, his eyes going wide,
staring at Harry. "One to ten years in Mexico."

"It's probably Jerry again," Jackson said as though no
one had spoken. "Or whoever it is could knock the window in.
We have to answer." He got up and put the guitar down on the
table, swayed a little and then stepped out, high as though he
were climbing stairs, and Elinor heard herself laughing
softly. There was another cannonade of knocking.

"You're not climbing, man," Harry said. "Walk easy. Relax."

Jackson tried, and he did better, but he still looked odd, and
even as she laughed at him, Elinor turned to Harry to be told
what to do. He was the man in command. He was the head.
That was funny too, but she'd keep it to herself; it was her joke
and she wouldn't share it with anybody.

"Open the window," Harry said to Jim, who did not move, and to her, "Where's the Air-wick?"

"Too far away," she said. "In the bedroom. But there's cologne in that." She made a sweeping, pointing gesture to her open, half-unpacked suitcase near the door.

"Sprinkle it around, chick," Harry said urgently.

She walked over the tilting floor to the valise, hearing now a high music whining in her ears. There was a sore place where the wooden leg rubbed. It had been bothering her for two days. Now it bothered her very much, so it was hard to remember the cologne, as though some dentist had found the nerve on the leg and was drilling on it. Her hands reaching into the suitcase were dulled, her fingers bumped into things, and wasn't this taking an awfully long time? Or was it only a minute? As if to answer her, Harry whispered urgently, "Hurry it up, sweetie," and she hurried. She heard him talking while she found the bottle.

"Charles, you're stoned," Harry said.

"I'm hip," Charles said and chuckled.

"I'll talk," Harry said. "I'm straight."

Then he was beside her, taking the top off the cologne bottle for her. She began to sprinkle it around.

Harry went to the window. He opened it now and let the wind and rain into the room and looked out. He shut it again, picked up the big ash tray on his way across the room, and emptied it into the ashes in the fireplace.

"It's Victoria," he told them. "But I think someone's with her. Vickie's george, anyway—square but george, but you never know how a square will flip."

Jim said, "Look at that," laughing, and Elinor realized he was laughing at her, because she was dashing around sprinkling the cologne, like a clumsy dancer doing *The Rite of Spring* or *Swan Lake*, and immediately knowing the picture she made, she would not let herself be hurt or cry, and told herself to laugh and imagined herself laughing with her lips pulled back, a big throaty, the-joke's-on-me laugh, but no sound came out of her mouth.

Harry was beside her, taking the bottle away. "That's enough now, chickie," he said. He stood in front of her with the handful of unsmoked joints they had left, and he said, "I'm going to lay these on you. Okay?" She nodded, and looking into her eyes, he opened the front of her dress, and pulled her brassière forward and then, lowering his head, looked at her exposed breasts. Gently and tenderly, he lifted each one, and placed the cigarettes in the cup of cloth beneath. Her mind told her that this was really very clever, a clever place to hide them and that was all, but he was handling her, intimately and amorously, and her heart pounded and she swayed toward him and the eyes with which she looked up at him were limpid and surrendering. He smoothed the cloth over her breasts again, taking unnecessary pains with it, letting his hands curve over the swell of them. He smiled with sheer pleasure, and then he buttoned the bodice of her dress as though she could not possibly do this for herself, and put his hand under her chin and, lifting her face to him, bent his head and kissed her mouth.

Charles stared at them and then, muttering, slid down in his chair and closed his eyes on the sight of them, just as Victoria came into the room.

8

Victoria

VICTORIA burst into the room without waiting for Ned or Jackson to come in from the *zaguán* because all she wanted was to get inside, into a room with walls to protect her from the damned rain and wind. It had been going on so long, the rain flying in her face and the wind pushing her around, that she couldn't really see yet. She was angry and her jaws ached from the tightness with which her teeth were clamped together. She set down her purse and plucked at the wet cloth of her blouse and skirt, pulling it away from her skin. She smoothed back her hair, pressing the water out of it. She sat on the nearest chair and got her shoes off, and saw how water stained the tile floor where she had stood. She would ask for a towel. Why didn't people think of such things?

Looking up she saw how Elinor stood in the middle of the room, not saying anything, with her beautiful eyes glassy, and her body leaning, curiously rigid, at an angle, on nothing. There was a statue look to her as though she were part of a tableau and not allowed to move or speak. It was peculiarly silent here . . . Harry stood in front of Elinor, gazing at her, gazing *into* her, as though his eyes were saying something to her; he was as motionless as she. The room was utterly still. Charles slouched in a chair, his body long and thin in repose; he seemed to be asleep. Jim sat cross-legged on the floor, not looking at anybody, looking down, and there was the same absence of expression on his face as on the others except—and she leaned over and peered at him to make sure—that his mouth was set in a smile; but Jim had that kind of mouth, which seemed to be smiling when it wasn't.

The room reeked of cologne and over that, stronger now when she stood up again, was the acrid, mordant smell of marijuana. That was what made them so still and strange. It was as if the marijuana was a separate presence in the room, as if each one of them had somehow left himself, left his body, and in the place of each individual personality there was a common personality. No, because each one was empty, there was no union in the common personality. But they all acted together like an audience, listening to something she could not hear, seeing something she could not see. There was no noisy atmosphere of drunkenness; there were no voices; there was no joy. The atmosphere was melancholy, thoughtful, grave. No wonder they said they were "gone" when they smoked marijuana, because, in a sense, they were. But what was the place they went to, with so little apparent pleasure?

They did not see her. If she banged two cymbals together, they would not turn their heads and look at her. She watched them. Ned wasn't going to understand this, or like it. He was still out in the *zaguán* with Jackson. He was afraid to come in and, no doubt, still angry with her because she had refused to go all the way down the hill to his house, a distance of at least seven blocks. He didn't care how long he kept her out there in that Wagnerian downpour just because, snobbishly, he did not want to come into the Garths' house. "Do you know them?" she'd yelled at him and when he'd shaken his head, "Then how do you know they're so damned dreadful?" "I know," he'd said.

But she was exhausted. She'd been tired even before the flat tire and having to walk all this way in the dark. He'd said, "I don't believe in any port in a storm."

"Too bad!" she'd said, very angry by then, because he had no consideration for her at all. "I'm going in." That was when she'd begun pounding on the door. He'd even started a few steps on his way, but he couldn't go on. Gentlemanliness demanded that he come in with her . . .

He was in the *zaguán* now, looking around surreptitiously at Jackson Garth's watercolors hanging there, while he opened his umbrella and leaned it against the wall to dry out. He wasn't going to like Jackson's work, and he wasn't going to like the atmosphere here even if he didn't recognize the smell of marijuana. He hesitated in the doorway now, peering into the room . . .

Harry said, turning his eyes slowly on her, "Where you been, Vickie McVick?"

"I need a towel," she said. "Guadalajara. We had a flat tire just outside of San Juan. We walked all the way here . . ."

"Who's 'we'?" Harry said.

She pointed toward Ned, and Harry turned and looked at him.

"Well, well," Harry said. "Visiting toffs."

Jackson was coming into the room just behind Ned, walking stiffly, and he grinned. He said, "Yeah. Rain must be the great leveler."

"I'm soaking wet," Victoria said. She looked at Elinor. The girl had not moved a jot. "Could you let me use a towel, Elinor?"

Elinor moved her head very slowly and gazed at her, blankly, beautifully, and said nothing.

"We got a towel in the suitcase," Jackson said. He raised his voice. "Ellie, look in the suitcase."

Elinor went, in a rubbery way, over to the suitcase and stared into it. After a moment she found a towel and brought it to Jackson.

"For Vickie," he said to her.

"Oh." She turned, and in that same walking-through-water way, brought the towel to Victoria.

"*Qu' hubo lé*, Ned?" Harry said, genially.

Ned tried to smile, but he looked uneasy. "All right, thanks. *Regular*. You?"

"Magnificent," Harry said, beaming. "'I am the king of a rainy country,'" he said. "'*Je suis comme le roi d'un pays pluvieux.*' Very *pluvieux.*"

"I am 'like' the king," Victoria said. "That 'like' is the difference between royalty and delusion. Will somebody give us a drink? Ned's got a chill and I feel miserable."

"Tequila is all we got," Harry said.

"Fine," she said.

"Not for me," Ned said, "but thanks."

Harry smiled. "Jackson," he said, "ain't you got some champagne to lay on this cat to cure his chill?" Jackson shook his head. "You don't know what's nice," Harry said. "I'm ashamed of you. You is crude."

"Okay," Jackson said. "I is crude." He slid down along the wall and sat on the floor with the guitar on his knees and began to tune it.

Victoria unplaited her braids and shook out her wet hair and began to rub it with the towel. Ned was staring at her in dismay, probably that she would do such a thing in public, sit there with her feet bare and her hair down. She went on vigorously rubbing her scalp. He made it very hard for you to like him. He was full of criticism. He stood there now in his trench coat, apart, keeping himself out of the room and away from the people in it while he was in it. He was always like that except in his own house where the environment was suitably elegant . . . In her house he sat gingerly on the chair and did not glance about him. She shut her eyes and rubbed the towel over them too, as much to rub away the sight of him as anything else. It wouldn't be so bad if he isolated himself unobtrusively; there was something very aggressive about the way he did it, as though he were saying, Look at me being apart from you.

She could use a little of that *apartheid,* as far as he was concerned. It was a disservice to herself that she had gotten so accustomed to being with him, spending so much time with him, spoiling him and putting up with his demands and trying to please him for the sake of a little peace . . .

Harry handed her a drink. "We're all juiced," he said. "You got to catch up, Vick. We've been having a Hi-jinks."

"Well, *we* haven't," she said. "We've been out there like Liza crossing the ice for an eternity." She lifted the glass to her lips but the rank smell of the liquor stopped her. "I hate the *tufo* of tequila," she said. "It smells like gasoline."

"It smells like gasoline but it's a gas," Harry said. He sang in his husky, whispery voice:

". . . The bloodhounds that once chased Liza
Chase the poor C.I.O. organizer
It's the same old South."

She drank it down quickly and took a bite of lime afterward. "Have a drink, Ned," she said.

"Yeah, sport-o," Harry said.

"No, thanks," Ned said. He came over to where she sat, drying her hair. He said, "I think we should go. We're intruding."

She looked at him. "It is raining," she said precisely. "I am tired of walking around in the rain. I am getting dry, do you understand?"

She saw how he compressed his lips and glared at her, and she pointedly ignored how he stood there stiffly, waiting, grim-faced.

Elinor said in a dry, thin voice, "Jackson buys our tequila at the *mercado* in Guadalajara. It's cheaper there. Everything is cheaper there. I don't go in. I stay outside in the truck and wait while Jackson shops, on account of the woman who sits at the front door with the frogs' legs on a tray in her lap. She sells them. You ever see her? It makes me sick. The frogs' legs look like the bottom halves of people. I can't go in." She swung around somnambulistically and her eyes were almost closed. She looked, when you thought about it, much more than drunk, or whatever it was they got on marijuana. She seemed to be almost catatonic. She spoke in a singsong child's rhythm. "Jackson is very good with money. He knows how to make it last. Once we lived a whole year in the States on five hundred dollars. Jackson knows how. He even knows what kind of rice to buy. He buys it by the barrel." She brought her forefingers together and then forced them apart in a V. "The rice grains go like this when they're cooked."

Ned stared with evident embarrassment at the wall. Hadn't he ever seen anybody drunk before? Why did he act as though the girl had done something inexcusable? He got drunk; Victoria had seen him. But he never admitted it at the time, nor afterward. Hanschen had said once, "He never gets drunk, did you know? He may lose his balance and fall down, but he never gets drunk. I get drunk . . . oh yes. But not Ned." However, it was true that nobody got as drunk as Hanschen. Nor, now that she looked at Elinor, had she even seen Ned get as drunk as that. How odd it was the way she stood there with her eyes closed, saying those subterranean things . . . but probably that was the marijuana and not liquor at all.

"You sure sound *borracha*, Ellie," Jackson said. "Go to bed."

"Oh," she said sadly. "I thought I sounded fine." She tilted her head to one side like a bird, still keeping her eyes closed but smiling. "I was just being a hostess, Jackson."

"Go to bed, Ellie," Jackson said.

"I'm sorry," Elinor said. She smiled waveringly and started to the door. Her limp was more pronounced than usual, so that her body went down a little with each step, and her head dropped lower on her neck; she looked like a flower ready to break high on its stem. She paused and shook back her black hair and the light sprang from her earrings. "Come with me, Jack," she said. "The tile is wet. I'm afraid I'll fall."

"No," Jackson said.

"Oh wow," Harry said miserably. "I'll walk her to the bedroom . . ."

Jackson turned and looked at him, in a measuring way. "No, Maestro," Jackson said in a hard voice.

"You insecure?" Harry said. "You putting me on?"

"Nobody walks my chick into any bedroom but me, Harry," Jackson said. He turned back to Elinor. "Go alone, Ellie," he said.

She went out and the door closed and there was the hollow-sounding footfall, the drag of the leg along the *corredor*.

What was she doing, sitting here immobilized, actually waiting for the cry and the sound of the fall? She jumped up and threw down the towel and started for the door, saying, "Mexico has brutalized you, Jackson. How can you treat that poor girl this way?"

Jackson said, "Stay here, Vickie. And don't 'poor girl' my wife."

She glared at him and went out, slamming the door behind her. She could see Elinor slowly staggering along the *corredor*, clinging to each pillar she passed.

"Wait, Elinor," she called and the girl obediently, swayingly, stood still.

It wasn't till she got to her and took her hand and led her

along that she realized she had come out here in her bare feet. The wind blew violently against them. In just that space of time, Elinor had gotten very wet and Victoria was wet, too. The girl let go of her hand and clung to her, leaning on her heavily.

"It takes a woman to understand," Elinor said laboriously. Her voice was thick and dry.

In the bedroom, Victoria pushed her toward the bed. The girl was a dead weight, and her hands gripped her shoulders so tightly that they felt like pincers. Reflex alone demanded that she tear them loose. "You're all right," she said, pushing Elinor down. "Just don't talk. Go to bed."

Elinor snatched at her hand, clung to it. "I don't know any women, you know that? I didn't even have a mother. I mean, I had one but she died when I was born. There were just my sisters but they were cold and they thought I was dumb, and they wouldn't talk to me. No women ever talked to me." The tears welled up, sliding drearily down her cheeks. "My father was Irish. He liked to sit on the front porch. He had blue eyes and he drank lots of tea all the time and he ate bread and cheese for breakfast. Tea filled him up, made him sweat, he said. He said it kept his skin clear. He had fine skin. But oh my God, my mother was dead an hour after I was born." She hiccupped. "Somebody's got to help me undress," she said.

Victoria stepped back, away from the clutching hands. The girl lay loose on the bed like a bundle of rags. Her eyes opened, slid wildly and deliriously around, and she sobbed through her open, pitiable mouth.

"I am not your mother. I won't help you undress. Go to sleep," she said.

"I'm so rotten drunk," Elinor said.

Victoria left the lantern burning on the dresser and turned away, out into the passage again. The voice in the room behind her babbled and cried as though she were still there, listening.

She stood a moment in the dark, letting the wet wind blow against her. The first time she saw the Garths, when they arrived here six months ago, she thought that they were unbelievably beautiful, like stars of an operetta. Jackson had golden skin and blond silky hair and blue eyes, and he wore a faded denim shirt the color of his eyes, so that he was all light blue and gold, with white, white teeth. Elinor was like an operetta princess, slim-waisted and flower-faced, with even teeth and wide blue eyes, light blue like a shallow pool of water on pale sand. Even Ricky was beautiful, an operetta child. They were fictional, totally fictional, but because fiction was often a way of arriving at truth—that is, adding up to a new element which was truth— it would be better to say that they were fraudulent. Mexico had disproven them. Perhaps the light here was too strong for their kind of beauty and like old photographs left in the sun, they had lost color in the months they'd been here, so that now all three of them had a graying look, as though volcanic ash had sifted down on them. Mexico could do that; it could heighten your color and sharpen your wits, or it could cloud you and turn you to ashes.

When Victoria was back in the *sala* again, she sat down and dried her feet on the towel and put her wet shoes back on. Harry leaned down and said to her quietly, "Is the chick all right?"

She nodded. His face close to hers seemed very pale and his eyes were red-rimmed, inflamed around the blue of the iris. His hair fell forward, long and lank. She looked at him with distaste. "Did you ever lend Abel that money?"

"No," Harry said, straightening up.

"He must be frantic," she said.

"That poor spade was born frantic," Harry said, shrugging. "He worries like an ofay about his damned bills." He looked at Ned sitting stiffly in the chair, politely eyeing Jackson as Jackson began to play the guitar. "You got a new friend, Vickie," he said. "You dig your new friend?" He laughed, a whispery laugh. " 'Where are the snows of yester-year,' Vick?" he said.

She said, "Oh get me another drink, Harry."

He said, "Sure, sweetie," and took her glass.

She got the comb out of her purse and dragged it through her damp hair and then began to braid it. Harry was jealous of all relationships which excluded him. But, Ned *was* her friend, and her anger at him out on the road was really anger at herself. When they'd realized they'd have to walk back, because Carl Rogers had forgotten to give him the trunk key and he couldn't get at the spare tire, Ned had been astonished to discover that she had brought neither raincoat nor umbrella. He had shaken his head in exasperation; he'd looked at the sky this morning and seen the storm coming, why hadn't she? She told him she didn't own an umbrella or a raincoat and that never in her life in any country had she ever had an umbrella in her

hand when rain fell on her. Such disorganized living was in-
conceivable to him and he was quick to point out that now, as a
result of it, they must struggle along under his umbrella together
and that both of them would get wet. She'd exploded then, saying she wouldn't share his umbrella and marched away from
him into the gale. He'd caught up with her and taken her arm,
but she pulled away as soon as he started to nag again. He'd
been infuriated and dragged her back, but by then she was
thoroughly soaked anyway. Ned didn't realize that the way he
arranged his life was unusual. It was awesome how he went
about shopping in Guadalajara, not hurrying but judiciously consulting his exact lists and planning what shop to visit next on
their route so that they could have a nice leisurely lunch during
the siesta hours and conclude their shopping so as to arrive at
the Alameda just when the movie began. If the car had a flat
tire, if she had no umbrella . . . these mistakes were not his
responsibility. There was no logical reason for her to have
been so angry with him . . .

But he stood there now, with an unpleasant look on his face,
never thinking that perhaps he should pay Jackson a compliment for his good playing; for that matter, he was probably unaware of just how good Jackson was; he stood there, in the
wings, so to speak, not part of the performance but not part of
the audience either, just watching what happened on the stage.

Harry handed Victoria a glass and a slice of lime. His eyes
on Ned were inimical, and he moved toward him in the
silence. "You got on all your togs, ain't you, man?" he said.
He fingered the fine gabardine of Ned's trench coat. "Got on
your spycoat and all. Very *nice* spycoat, too. *Very* nice. And
you got your gold-handled black silk umbrella." He leaned down,
lifted Ned's trouser leg. "Even got your rubbers on? Sure,
bought rubbers in that toggery . . ."

Ned said evenly, "Get your hands off me, Harry."

Harry fell back a step or so and bowed low, ludicrously
humble, rubbing his hands together, talking in an Uncle Tom
voice. "Yas*suh*, Young Marse," he said. " 'Scuse me, boss-man.
Jack-of-diamonds gets all his nice togs on, uses his deodorant
and all, he jest nacherly doan want some bum like me filthying
him all up."

Jackson was laughing. Ned said to her, "Let's go," in a controlled voice.

" 'Let us go then, you and I . . .' " Harry intoned.

"I'm not ready," she said.

There was a flash of anger in his eyes, and he said, "I said let's go."

"No," she said.

"What's the line about 'etherized upon the table'?" Jackson asked Harry. "The evening or something."

Ned stood in front of her implacably. Perhaps it was a betrayal of their friendship or relationship or whatever you could call it, but she did not want to go. She did not want to be *told* to go. She didn't blame him for being offended by Harry, by all of them really, but then, they were offended by him; he should know that. Anyway, she was sick of him. He was in every crack and corner of her life, demanding things, criticizing things. She wanted to stay here.

She looked up at him. "Then go," she said. She was tying the strings of wet yarn into her braids and watching how cold his eyes became. It was, oddly, satisfying to see that. She was a bad child, in company with a group of other bad children, defying the teacher, bolder than all the rest of them.

He turned abruptly, not saying good night or thank you or anything, and walked rigidly to the door and went out and took his umbrella. They heard the wooden bar of the big door scrape back, and his voice calling over the loud wind, "Somebody'd better bolt this after me," and that was all.

Good. He was gone.

Harry said, "I'll get the door."

She went on fixing her hair. When Harry came back, Jackson said, "You got your axe here, Harry? I'm going to blow."

"No," Harry said.

Jackson began to play again, Bach now, compellingly, with vigor. He seemed to have come out of his lethargy and although he still looked gray, the music was not gray but all golden sound. The music gradually enmeshed her in its pattern, its filigree of shining gold, and sipping her tequila she began to feel relief. It was as simple as that. Ned was gone. These boys, whatever was the matter with them, however badly they lived, however wretched they were, were more her kind than Ned could ever be. To hell with organization, and well-timed pleasure and umbrellas . . . Tequila, music and emotion . . . that was life to her, the very breath of it.

When the music was done, she set down her glass and

clapped her hands loudly and cried, "Marvelous! Marvelous!"

"I want some jazz," Jim said. "The square's gone. Let's have some jazz, baby."

"Yeah," Charles said, opening his eyes dreamily. "Music for mountaintops." He stretched, and smiled at her. "Hey, Vickie," he said, "you sure cooled the prince."

Jackson began to play a blues and to sing. His voice was excellent, true, trained. But his throat was tighter than it used to be, the sound not so rich, more strained. It was a bad sign when a singer's throat began to go tight, but maybe he was tired. The tension was going out of her; she felt less hobbled, less corseted. The last month of seeing so much of Ned had not been good for her; that was quite clear now. Every day there was something; he had planned a trip into Guadalajara or a visit to San Juan, or supper at his house or she had to prepare for a visit from him.

Harry said, "Jackson, you're blowing square. Take eight and tell me Where's Annie?"

"Get your axe, man," Jackson said amiably, but he began to make up a blues then, with that theme, picking it out, working it over, muttering sometimes that he was losing his high, but working, and it was good. That was something else Ned couldn't understand. He didn't know that this was creative, too; he made a fetish of creativity, altarized it, ritualized it, turned it into something pompous. He did not see that these people, in their way, were artists; they were creative, too.

She realized it had been quiet for a while, and she had been sitting here in a distraction not noticing that the music was over. She looked up and Harry was gazing at her, his eyes heavy-lidded. "And was that marvelous! Marvelous! Vickie? Clappy-handy, coo-coo, marvelous, ovoutaroony?"

"I'm sorry," she said. "I was thinking. Music does that."

"My square lady," Harry said. "A square wants music for just one thing . . . background music for his inner cacophony. You forget it sometimes when the square claps his hands, but that's what the square's clapping for—not the sound but the role he's just played in the inner movie of his life. He wants a score for the movie of his love story with himself. The attention-span of the mole-mind of the square is very small. You got to remember that. It can hardly last the three minutes it takes to play a record. That's why they cut them down all the time, so now it's two minutes and thirty-five seconds. There's one I know that's one minute and forty-five seconds. That's just about how long a square can get off the kick of himself."

He put his drink down and straightened up, no longer slouching, but stiff, sullen and frowning. "You know, man, you ever play one-night stands? I used to see the square come in with his stupid broad, and I could see in his face that she's all he's got eyes for. He's after that one little pleasure, that one meager spurt of orgasm before he falls back into his coma of self-love again. That's *it* for him. He'll fight wars for it, he'll kill for it, he'll kill himself for it . . . because it's the only thing that ever happened to him. That's when he knows he's living, man. Nothing happens to him with music; he's a tin ear, baby. He talks to his broad in a big voice, right through the music, about all the important things, news bulletins from the Mas-turbators Garden Club, and really worthwhile groups like the Royal Order of Mother Lovers, or the Chamber of Commerce, or the P.T.A., or the Let's-Try-It-In-The-Bathtub-Tonight Junior League. The money-jerks and the work-jerks, the ones who want to get ahead . . . the squares. They're running the god-damned world. They're busy. They got responsibilities. They want lullabies they don't have to listen to . . . songs Mom could sing. They been busy, man, you know, with hatching up their stink bombs, and hanging people, and electrocuting peo-ple, and they plan. Yeah, how they plan! They plan while you play." He stopped, sagged against the table, and his head drooped. "Jesus," he said, "I'm all alone."

Charles said, "You talk better with your axe, Harry."

"Yeah," Harry said. He smiled sadly at Charles. "You'd have made a great den-mother, sweetie," he said. "You want to chair the meeting?"

Charles laughed. "You got a mother-thing," he said. "And I always thought till now you had a father-thing."

"A man of stature can have both," Harry said. He shuffled to the door. "I'm gonna walk out back to the can and let the big fat raindrops just fall all over me," he said. "Ain't I wild?"

He went out, slamming the big door and a shower of red dust fell from the old lintel.

"What childishness," Victoria said. "He bangs his spoon on the tray of his high chair because the world doesn't always listen to music when he thinks it should . . . the world doesn't do anything it should, read the books it should, treat people the way it should. But it's the world. That's all there is. You have to do what you do within it. That's the *deal*."

From the echoing *corredor*, Harry's voice came back to them, howling through the night. "Annie?" his voice called. "Where's Annie?"

Charles looked at her. His smile was vacuous. They listened, all of them, while the cry grew fainter and fainter as Harry got farther away, coming back to them thin and eerie . . . "Where's Annie?"

Jackson played again, not singing now, but absorbed in the sound. She looked at his gray face bent over the guitar. He made music . . . but for no one. Jim's skin was purplish; his mouth hung open a little, and his eyes were dull as grapes. Charles smiled emptily . . . a child's smile, without a child's kindness in it.

She had not seen other people for a long time . . . too long a time, which was why she had wanted to find this group charming and enchanting. She had gotten away from the teacher for a minute . . . and she forgot to notice that these were not "nice" children to play with. Her relationship with Ned was all dependence, all her yielding, his dominating, his demanding, her succumbing . . . what wonder that she should run from him when she could! Once she had quoted Emerson to him about friends—"Who are you? Unhand me: I will be dependent no more." But after the quotation she had not run. And now, when she chose to run, it was into the arms of these destructive children, shouting, I am free! This is where I belong.

But it wasn't true. She did not belong here, either. She got up and took up her purse.

She went out. Jackson's music, plangent and plaintive, came after her through the thick walls of adobe into the night and mingled with the sounds of rain. The notes he played were like snowflakes, each one multishaped and beautiful.

She stood at the edge of the patio. Rain rustled in the leaves of the bougainvillaea and splashed from the waterspout. The patio was flooded; the wind gusted in the mango trees and thunder rolled, but the storm was lessening. She would go home. The bed would feel wet after this long rain. Maybe tonight, miraculously, she could sleep. Sleep had been difficult lately. In a whole night she would sleep only an hour here and there; it was light sleep, like lying on the top shelf of sleep, not sinking deeply into it . . . and the dawn came after her own unrefreshed awakening.

Some movement off to the side caught her attention, and she saw Harry standing in the *corredor*, motionless. In the yellow lamplight there was a look on his face of intense concentration as he gazed fixedly into the Garths' bedroom. His expression was goatish, as though he had deliberately summoned up the lust in himself. He lifted the cigarette cupped in his hand and dragged on it with a sucking, gasping sound; his hand and lips went red with the glow and she could smell the marijuana smoke. He held the smoke in his lungs until his face swelled like a gargoyle's, his gaze staying steady on the open door of the room . . .

She saw, looking where he looked, slightly to the side of the door but illumined by the lantern burning in there, a disembodied leg—no, a wooden leg, standing by itself on its foot, with a stocking wrinkling down from its hinged knee, with the silver buckle on the Mary Jane shoe, winking silver there in the light. This was what Harry stared at lustfully and fixedly.

She did not like the look on his face, nor the leg standing there waiting, a part of somebody, but not whole . . . it was fetishistic, perverse.

She turned and hurried back up the *zaguán*, grabbed at the street door and pulled it open, stepped out into the street, letting the door swing shut behind her, feeling as though she had swallowed the world and now must throw it up. It rained hard now, but she ignored the rain blowing against her. Water gurgled urgently in the gutters beside her as she hurried down the hill over the cobblestones. Lightning flashed and she saw, by its blue light, the blacker shape of a burro standing stupid and still in the rain and she hastened around it. Without the lightning she would have walked into it. No matter. What mattered?

But then a few moments later, she slowed and stopped. "Oh, look here!" she said out loud. The lightning had been distorting and deranging, and the storm and her fatigue and depression might have made her behold a different Harry than the one he really was in truth. He might have been wearing a

look of sympathy instead of perverted lust. Maybe it all was in
her interpretation of his look . . .

She discovered that she was staring steadily into the black
pyramid of a tree. It was the vulture tree, the one in which, for
reasons known only to the birds themselves, all the vultures
roosted. Now she could distinguish the big bird bodies on the
bare branches in ragged shapes, darker than the darkness around
them, so that their eyes shone out evilly and they brooded baldly
in the rain, looking at her . . .

She began to walk along again, but slowly now, ignoring
the rain. There was a memory of her father taking her home
from a dance hall in Manhattan when she was thirteen. She had
sneaked out of the flat to go to it, wearing her old oxfords and
her school skirt. In the alley outside her house she stopped and
smeared the ten-cent-store lipstick on her mouth, thinking that
would make her look grown-up, as though she belonged there.
She stood at the edge of the dancers, twitching her shoulders
to the beat of the music, staring hypnotized at the big, pink-
lighted bass drum until suddenly a man stepped between her
and the sight of it and her eyes were staring straight into her
father's shiny vest, and then moving slowly up into his cold,
angry face. Her father reached out and wiped the lipstick off
her mouth with his hand. He led her away through the bright
pastels of dancing dresses and the little cloudy smells of perfume and sweat and cigarette smoke . . . her father had led
her out of there as though she were a horse, holding onto her
tight braid as though it were a bridle. There had been laughter
as they passed, kindly laughter, tolerantly soul-destroying.

Lightning forked in the sky again, blue, and thunder
cracked instantly after it. Closer now. Her father's taking her
out of that obvious danger was far more dangerous to her than
being left in it. His arm around her in the street later, his bringing her home, making cocoa for her, sitting with her while she
drank it, telling her how he loved her, begging her to wait until
she grew up before she did these living things . . . these
dangers were the most seductive of all.

She was at the door of Ned's house. Light showed in the
window of his living room. There was the house, serenely beautiful, a temple of grace. But she had not realized that she was
walking in this direction. If someone had said where are you

going, she'd have said I'm going home. She'd thought she was
going home. She must have been impelled to come to him,
even as she realized how dangerous to her he was, how seductive
his affection, how treacherous his domination. She lifted her
hand to knock at the door, and hesitated.

Because she had come here did not mean that now she
had to go in and see him. But she felt that she must undo
whatever hurt she might have done him, explain to him somehow, why it was that she had felt that she belonged with Charles
and Harry and Jim and the Garths, and sent him off alone.
She had behaved very badly, but the important point was that
it was his fault, and he must be told that it was his fault.

She stepped back from the door. This was ridiculous; she
seemed ridiculous to herself. He would despise her irrationality.
And, aside from what he thought, she had perceived tonight how
profoundly hemmed in by him she was and had resolved to
put an end to their morbid closeness. But after her first relief at
his departure, she had felt lost among strangers. Was she going
to go in there and blame him for what she had done?

She turned, walked a few steps away from his house wondering if he'd heard her and would open the door. She stopped.
He wouldn't. He'd think it was Hanschen. Or, if he thought it
was she, he might still be so angry he would not open the door
and invite her in. They had had so many quarrels . . . He
was alone. Anything she did seemed irrational and childish.
Going in was unreasonable; going home seemed wrong; she did
not want to go home. Perhaps the most foolish of all alternatives
was standing here, undecided, doing neither one. . . .

In an explosion of confusion, she turned back and
pounded on the door. When Ned came and opened it to her, she
pushed her way past him, saying, "Let me in, boy. Just let me in."

9

Dr. Obregón

USUALLY WHEN Dolorosa had to send for him,
she sent a message by Nacho, the driver of the bus. This time
she had telephoned, so he could be certain that it was a more
severe emergency than usual. She had said only, "It is time
for you to come to the Señora Biddy, Doctor. Death is near," and
she had hung up. Dolorosa had a good eye for the condition of
her Señora, and he had always been struck by the exactness
with which she timed her summons to him . . . never too soon
and, so far, never too late.

He could not drive fast because the road from San Juan was
deeply rutted since the last storm, and the ruts were full of slick
mud under the brown water. The car skidded at thirty miles

an hour, and the wheels spun when they slid off the decomposed granite of the higher ground.

In the last two weeks, ever since the big storm, there had been emergency after emergency in the village and he had had to make the trip at least once a day, and sometimes oftener. It was not surprising. He had noticed in years past that, after the first big rains, the weather affected the *gringos* peculiarly. It was beautiful now, and it rained every day for an hour or so, enough to wash the air clean and make the green leaves glisten; plants grew and the hills were opulent with foliage. He breathed deeply. The air was like silk, subtly exciting even to him; sunsets in this month were unbelievable, like not quite good paintings. Banked rain clouds stood like dark marble columns high in the vaulted blue of the sky, and flowers bloomed everywhere, filling both San Juan and the village with the sweet scents of jasmine, masking the ugly odors of ordure.

"Death is near," Dolorosa's voice said in his mind again. *Ay,* he knew well enough that one of these emergencies of Biddy's would be the terminal one; he had explained it to Dolorosa. But the fact that she had not said more, not specified the indications of death, made him uneasy. He felt his usual reluctance to make a call on Biddy. Watching her destroy herself over the years was a painful thing to him, and difficult to understand. There had been many times when he had not known whether she would survive . . . She reached the crisis about every two months. Once he had thought that if he could get to her *before* she drank up half of her eight-week check, he might be able to prevent the physical holocaust which was the consequence of each spree. But that was foolish. She was not to be stayed from her appointment with the bottle. It might have been different if she would admit that she drank, but she would not, and he had come to believe that she did not admit it to herself; she was not deliberately lying, trying to deceive the world; it was herself she deceived, and she demanded that he be a party to that self-deception. "I don't drink," she had said to him with the bottle in her hand when she was too drunk to stand; when she could not speak but lay there stuporous and he suggested that tequila might be the cause of her misery, she denied it with her eyes. She would not hear him.

She was not one of the fortunate alcoholics with a resilient constitution who could, after sedation, regular injections of

Vitamin B, fluid replacement and a high protein diet, arise from
her bed apparently unmarked by the experience. It was true, of
course, that the resilient ones also eventually failed to recover
. . . Death took them, too, slowly but surely. But to her particular metabolism liquor was a poison; Biddy arrived almost
immediately at a state of toxicity which was terrifying. Five
years ago when he had first examined her and palpated that enlarged hard-edged liver, he knew there was damage. Her blood
pressure shot up to dangerous heights; her spleen was enlarged,
and there was evidence of arterial thickening, a cardiac ar-
rhythmia with the promise of fibrillation to come, and occasional moist râles at the base of the lungs. There were
vasculatory "spiders" on the abdomen . . . He shook his head.
She said she was fifty-five, but her body, organically, was the
body of a woman much older than that, as though, during her
sprees, she used up whole years of time, burned up middle age
and moved, in the space of a few months, into the ashen hope-
lessness of sickly old age.

The car skidded coming up out of a rut, so that the back
wheels spun the car sideways on the road. He righted it, cautiously. Without realizing it, he had been pressing forward,
trying to hurry. Perhaps Dolorosa was wrong. The weather
could have affected her judgment, as well as the *gringos'*; it was
like a big spoon stirring up *gringos* to excesses of every kind.
Drinkers drank more; sick people got sicker. Those tourists who
were not sick were overexcited, behaved as though they were
somehow electrified. The permanent foreigners got amoebic
dysentery, bacillary dysentery, typhoid and paratyphoid. There
were, inexplicably, three cases of malaria; these people had
not been out of the village, and malaria was not endemic to this
part of the country. There was one case of brucellosis, which
made him expect more, since undulant fever did not come
by ones, and two cases of hepatitis. What he really dreaded, but
nonetheless expected, was an epidemic.

But the new tourists, the ones who spilled into the Posada
every day in greater numbers, struck him as peculiarly disturbed.
They came to his drug store in San Juan asking for sleeping pills
and tranquilizers; they were not the sort of people who
habitually sought analgesia from the conflicts of life; they were
not chasing sensations, nor the kind who usually complained
of insomnia and nervousness. These were lawyers, schoolteach-

ers, housewives on vacation . . . the sort of people, even among
gringos, who disapproved of "taking things." They looked surprised to hear themselves asking him to give them something to
help them sleep. When the weather was like this, it had always
been so, but never, as long as he could remember, quite to this
degree.

He smiled, thinking of how the Embezzler, who owned
the Posada, had come to him and tried to buy a quantity of
sleeping pills to have on hand for his guests. What a stupid that
gringo was! He could do nothing honest, everything he said
sounded somehow crooked. It was impossible not to be suspi-
cious of him, difficult to smile at him. He'd answered mildly
that such an action would constitute the Embezzler's practicing
medicine without a license and he could not be a party to it.
The Embezzler assumed at once that he did not want a private
citizen cutting in on his drug-store business, and hastened to
assure him that he would pay more than the full price, for the
convenience to his hotel guests. Looking at his watery, reddened eyes, Dr. Obregón had felt a momentary pity; the man
could not help what he was. He considered warning the Embezzler that the Federales were already investigating him for
running a business in Mexico without proper papers and that
selling drugs would be only adding to his guilt, but just then
the Embezzler said something derogatory about "uneducated
Indians," and he gave up the idea. If Lola, the Embezzler's
secretary, and mistress, did not warn him—and she knew he
was under investigation since her brother was the Mayor
of San Juan—why should he? The Embezzler was not liked by
any Mexicans and there was no one to tell him what was about
to happen to him. It was old news, very stale; any foreigner who
went into business in the village, sooner or later fell afoul of the
law, made enemies and insulted the natives, and either fled,
died or was deported.

He turned down the hill road into the village. Two men,
their faces hidden by their huge sombreros, stood on a corner
scratching themselves and watched his car come hurtling over
the cobblestones. They did not wave at his mud-spattered car as
they used to do, because these days they resented him more than
ever because of his *gringo* affiliations. It had been a mistake to
give the lecture, but he hadn't realized it at the time, so concerned was he with the medical problems he faced. The lecture

had been well attended by the villagers. They sat in rows, cross-legged on the tile floor of the big Ramirez living room, looking up at him while he talked, and politely listened while he explained why it was that there were so many people sick in the village now. When the men went up into the hills to work their *milpas*, granted them after the revolution, and fertilized the soil of their plots of land with their own excrement, they caused the deadly bugs of disease to be put into the warm cradles of the earth. When the rains came and washed the topsoil down into the village, and the waters ran into the wells, the deadly bugs were then in the water and the vegetables, and even if precautions were taken, one fly, a single fly, carrying such a germ, could start an epidemic of dysentery. They listened, seeming to understand, but then they asked him, what was a man to do? The *gringos* built elaborate rooms in their houses as shrines to the unattractive evacuative function, which any well-bred Indio ignored . . . but if a single fly could undo the work of man, of what use their indoor bathrooms? Further, did the doctor think they should walk five miles back to the village every time nature demanded? Did the doctor imagine that they were wealthy men and could build *gringo* shrines to their own dejecta in the hills? They were not as well paid by the *gringos*, they said, as he was; had he become so Americanized that he had forgotten what it was to be poor? He answered the questions, ignoring their provocative manner. Lime pits, cheap and simple, would solve the problem. No man need come all the way home, nor build a lavatory with plumbing on his land . . . This was, he said, a simple thing. But Don Eliséo rose. Who would pay for the lime pits? he demanded. Was the doctor prepared to dig such pits, bending his back in the hot sun, handling the lime which could burn the hands, hauling it, raking it . . . ? Or was he too busy caring for the corrupt *gringos*, who were themselves weak, drunkards, drug addicts, unable, because of their wicked lives, to resist disease? Did he by chance own some lime, and was this a way of selling it, a new form of *mordida*, to take more of the poor peasants' few *centavitos* of income?

He looked around at them, thanking God in his heart that so far he was getting only reproach, complaint and ignorance. He was watching the Delegado in particular—Gordo was considered a very witty fellow, fat and funny . . . If Gordo

ridiculed him, the room would rock with mirth and he would
become a figure of fun who would have to live down the comical
aspects of his pleading with them. Casimir, and a few of
the Masonic brotherhood who were opposed to the Church,
bridled when the Padre shook his head and frowned, and were
ready to form into a group behind the doctor. Casimir even
came and stood beside his chair, and while Casimir was disliked because he was rich, he was also, grudgingly, respected
for the same reason.

The Padre rose and the room fell silent. The Padre was an
educated man, comparatively, and his response to Casimir's
gesture of allegiance to the doctor was immediate and the
worst thing, aside from ridicule, which could have happened to
his proposal. The Padre spoke solemnly and at length. He said
that he perceived before him now an alliance of godless men,
probably Communist-directed, working to turn the people away
from a Christian, Catholic concept of illness as one of the
trials used by God to bring sinful men to the Church, to a state
of grace, for the benefit of their immortal souls; life and death
were God's gifts to men; the will of God must be obeyed; he was
not sure yet, he said, but that this was not an attempt of the
members of a secret brotherhood to wrest control of the village
from God and to take it into human hands.

The next move Dr. Obregón made was disastrous. Instead of answering the Padre, he called upon the schoolteacher,
María Jesús, to speak before the Junta—the first time in anyone's memory that a woman had been asked to address this
masculine assemblage which ran the town—and to report
what her experiences were in nursing the sick, since she went
from house to house giving injections, both to *gringos* and
Mexicanos alike. María Jesús, who would be, if she dared, a
feminist, did speak, did plead for sanitation in the hills, and
added a desperate request of her own for the establishment of a
public dispensary in the village itself, so that medicine would
be available at all times, day and night.

At this point the Padre asked to be excused from the meeting, since it did not seem appropriate to him that he should listen
to a woman discuss these indelicate matters, a woman whose
every impulse, in his opinion, was not toward the natural ones
of wifehood and motherhood, but toward an inhuman identification with the state, who was employed by a federally sup-

ported school which did not teach the True Religion to the unfortunate children who attended it. Now, he said, this woman
who had identified herself with the state was turning toward
witchcraft. There was a gasp as he used this word—and he was
silent for moments afterward, letting it sink deep into the room.
Was it not witchcraft, he asked, which declared that it could by
the use of roots and herbs, which was all that medicine was,
after all, cure human beings where God failed to do so? He was
not saying that when a man was sick he should not be assisted
toward health; he was saying that the first means to helping
the sick become well must be, for true Mexican Catholics,
prayer. In godless communism, where the state was the only
god, a federal agency dispensing medicine was all the citizens
had to turn to—*pobrecitos*! But in this village, poor by ma-
terialistic standards perhaps, there was a wealth of faith and
religion on which to draw in times of need. "Thou shalt not put
false gods before Me," he quoted and left the meeting.

The cause was lost then. Had the Padre stayed, his ex-
pedient arguments could have been disproven. But he did
not stay. The people were bewildered and divided. Everyone
considered the priest a poor priest, and everyone knew that he
was neither infallible nor impeccable; but he *was* the priest,
representing the power of the Church, with the power to excommunicate and refuse absolution. Even the ones who knew
that his arguments were ridiculous, shook their heads, looking
away from the schoolteacher, for clearly she had incited the
wrath of Rome. She was not popular anyway; she was too
lugubrious for that, and too rigidly insistent upon having the
children attend school faithfully, no matter what needed to be
done at home or on the land. A painful woman, it was said,
awkward, without grace, without a husband, without *corazón*.

The word "witchcraft" was enough to frighten the least
sophisticated, and these looked at her fearfully, already con-
sidering the possibility that she was a witch. The idea was at-
tractively dramatic. Because she was gentle and nervous, like
a homely but delicate old horse, she wept into her *rebozo* and
sat down as far back in the room as possible, trying not to be
seen any more.

At the time, seeing how it had gone, Dr. Obregón hoped
that it would be possible to salvage a good deal from all of this
at a later date, when reasonable people could be reasoned

with, when the priest was not there to confuse them with propaganda. But a day or so later the first case of infantile paralysis occurred in the village. A young couple came from the States with their baby and the baby became sick. The maid who worked in the house reported that the baby's legs would not move, but hung down cold and useless when it was picked up. It suffered from what was called "the American sickness." The anti-*gringo* newspapers in Guadalajara published editorials reproaching the *Norteamericanos* for bringing their plague with them into the beautiful Mexican *campo,* and advised them distinctly: Go home, Yank. Mexican opinion solidified behind the Padre; he employed his advantage to the full, and heightened the anti-*gringo* feeling by pointing out that while flowers bloomed extravagantly through God's grace and filled the days and nights with exquisite perfume, the *gringos* were drinking and laughing and bedding with each other, marrying and divorcing each other in civil ceremonies which the Church did not recognize. That God punished such people with dreadful illnesses was not to be considered an injustice; it was God's way of trying to show them that they could not live godless lives. Look at them, the Padre said: The poor one-legged Señora Garth goes every day alone to Harry's room at the Posada of the Tres Marías. Señor Jim is always drunk; he is a *borracho* who gives nothing to Mexico. El Negrito does not pay his rent, nor any of his bills, and he lives with the blond white girl and this is unnatural. The Embezzler who owns the Posada is in trouble with the Federales.

The list was long. He took his time, named names and denounced the *gringos* for their sins. The Padre was an implacable, conscienceless enemy, a talented gossip. It must have been he who saw to it somehow that the schoolteacher's check did not arrive from the government, so that, having no money, she was forced to go to the Padre's sister, who was the village moneylender, to borrow money for food. The Padre's sister, whose interest rates were always exorbitant, as high as 40 and 50 percent, added an extra penalty to the schoolteacher's loan—a penalty worded by the Padre himself. She was not to enter any *gringo* household for any reason whatsoever, not to give them injections, unless she was willing to give up her job as schoolteacher. For, said the Padre, she ran the risk of getting one of the frightful American diseases, like polio, and passing it on to Mexican children. More, he honestly believed, he told her, that she endangered the salvation of her own soul by having contact with these atheist enemies of Christianity, and that without their influence she would never by herself have thought of the witchcraft idea of dispensing medicines at her own discretion, setting herself up against the will of God. If she failed to heed his warning, he would be forced to excommunicate her.

María Jesús capitulated, getting down onto her knees before the Padre, weeping, to plead with him for mercy, promising absolute obedience.

Now there was no one in the village who could give injections. Aside from that, nothing was being done about the amoebic dysentery problems and sanitation; the anti-*gringo* feeling was rising all the time, and a good deal of it was directed against Dr. Obregón. If his wife, Ysat, had not been born in the village, and if she were not a faithful churchgoer and a friend of the Padre's, it was quite possible that he'd have been forbidden the village himself.

But it had not come to that yet. It was now only a matter of a turned back, of no hand lifted in greeting. The doctor sighed. Biddy's house was just before him. In the past, Dolorosa, who was sensitive and ashamed of her Señora's weakness, had asked him to park his car a distance away so that no one would know where he went. The precaution was foolish, and she knew it as well as he. Everybody knew where he went, watched without seeming to, and no doubt knew just how sick Biddy was. But it did no harm to yield to Dolorosa's silly little deception, except that he must walk farther. Lately he had been tired, without energy, without his former optimism. Perhaps he had been working too hard, he thought, but even as he thought it, he knew perfectly well that this was not the reason for his heavy-heartedness. There was another thing . . .

When he finished with Biddy, he got up stiffly, wearily, and walked out into the patio of her house. He was grateful for the sweet air after the steaming discomfort of Biddy's bedroom, with its assorted unsightlinesses, its hovering smell of decay. He stood there, breathing deeply, looking at the ground, watching a lizard dart with marvelous swiftness into a crack between the worn bricks. He looked at the crack, thinking he would like that, to run swiftly into a cool, dark, safe place.

Dolorosa was coming toward him, walking like a nun
with stiff shoulders and no motion of her body, in a sexless glide,
with eyes downcast and mouth tight, and hands folded under
her apron.

"Doctor," she said. "Are you going?"

"*Sí,*" he said. "I shall come back tomorrow."

"She lives, then?"

"*Sí,*" he said.

"Will she live?" Dolorosa asked him.

"*Entonces,*" he said, "it is with God. *Pobre mujer.*"

Dolorosa sniffed. She did not show pity and disapproved of
fools who did. Her voice was harder now. "She will live?"

He glanced at her. She must have been very frightened
to demand an answer to that question twice. "*Créo qué sí,*" he
said gravely. "But who knows?"

Walking to the door with him, she told him how, at the
height of her spree, Biddy had staggered to the wooden shutters
which opened onto the street from her bedroom, and flung
them wide. There, with her gray hair tangled and matted, and
her eyes wild with love and alcohol, she had thrown handfuls
of pesos into the street so that any Mexican passing by could
find and take them. Greedy children had come running. Dolorosa had gotten the Señora away from the window—a dreadful
sight, she was, symbolizing what the Padre called the wanton
American derangement—and then she had hastened out and
gathered up as much of the money as remained. She stuffed
the bodice of her dress with the bills, and made a basket of
her apron, and brought it all back, and hid it in a box in the
kitchen. But it was a worry to her that some of the money was
gone before she got to it, because when the Señora was better,
if she got better, she would not remember that she threw the
money away and she would accuse Dolorosa of having
stolen it. She had not taken even one peso, but how was it to be
proven?

He patted her thin shoulder. The shoulder twitched away
from his hand—oh very nunlike, this one. He promised to
discuss it with Biddy when she was well enough to give him her
attention.

Dolorosa nodded brusquely. She did not thank him, and
he was startled to see as her thick, blunt lashes swept up and
her eyes turned on him, that they were bright with bitterness.

She bade him good afternoon in a cold voice and opened the
door just enough so that he could get through to the street;
then she closed the door instantly upon him.

He walked heavily to his car. One of the unpleasant-
nesses in visiting Biddy was Dolorosa. She regarded him with
open disapproval, out of some mystical certainty, sourceless
as far as he could guess, that he was a base scoundrel, to be
summoned and talked to only when it was a matter of life and
death, as though there were times when one had to shop at the
Devil's store . . .

He got into the car and turned on the motor and sat there.
He lit a cigarette. Far down the street he could see Josefina, the
blond one who owned the store, toiling up the hill, heavy with
child. She would, he knew, pause at his car, with one hand
pressed against the lumbar-sacral region of her back, and try to
get some free medical advice from him. Two men in front of the
cantina, old ones, the huarache maker and Tomasino from
Jocotepec, squatted in the shade, and the huarache maker
was holding a stick, making marks in the moist dirt in front of
him, while the other watched.

He should go home. But thinking that, he realized that he
had already decided to make another stop. He did not remember
when that had happened unless it was when the call had
come in from Dolorosa and he had known he would be here. He
tossed his cigarette away. His fingers, loosely gripping the
steering wheel, trembled slightly. He drove to Victoria's house.

The *niña* opened the big door and looked up at him,
curtsied and gravely waited to hear what he wanted.

When he told her, she shook her head. "The Señora is
working," she said. "It is the thinking part of her work, you understand."

"Yes," he said. "But tell her I am here, *chula*, please."

He waited on the sidewalk, and then the *niña* came back
and pulled the door wide for him. "She will see you," she said,
and there was disapproval in her voice.

He smiled at her and as they walked up the *zaguán* together,
he put his hand on her head and rumpled her hair. She flashed a
smile at him then, flirtatious as a woman, and he smiled back at
her.

The room was so dark after the brightness of the street that
at first he could not see Victoria sitting in the chair by the fire-

place. But he came in and his eyes adjusted by the time she greeted him and he bowed to her. She gestured for him to sit down, her hand moving white in the shadow with what he thought of as regal grace. He saw that there was a hood of some kind over the typewriter. He observed that she sat like a queen, erect and idle, that though the room was thick with shadow, she wore huge dark glasses and that she was pale. He sat down.

The *niña* stood at the door and asked if she should bring something, serve something. "Rum?" the *niña* said. "A pitcher of boiled water?"

Victoria nodded. "And clean glasses," she said.

When the child was gone, he said, "I have come to talk to you. I have . . . There is a problem. I should like to ask your advice. But perhaps I have come at the wrong time?"

"You are here," she said. "What is the problem?"

He sighed. Her voice sounded as though it came from a throat choked with tears and she looked, now that he could see better, in spite of her dignity, extremely unhappy. He had heard a great deal of gossip about her and Ned, speculation about their growing relationship, how often they were together, how they fought, shouting at each other, and then later were seen laughing together, showing every indication of profound affection; now all of it came into his mind, and he stared at her as though to read in her face—to him, her beautiful face—a denial, a statement that all of it was untrue. Even now, rigid as she was, with her large, wonderful eyes hidden from him, the sight of her filled him with pleasure and peace, as though he had come home.

He said, "*Señora*, are you well?"

"Yes, yes," she said. "I am never sick. I am—" She lifted her hand again and let it fall like a petal through the dark. "I am only troubled about my work, you see. I am trying to write a great book." She laughed and the laugh had a bitter sound. "Or, I should say, a good book. The time for modesty is upon me." The *niña* came in with the tray and set it on the table at her side. She thanked her and the child went away, closing the double doors of the *sala* after her, so that he found he kept thinking in an astonished way: I am alone with her. Alone. She was fixing a drink for him, pouring a polite amount of rum into the other glass for herself. How beautiful were her hands,

like two ballet dancers moving close to each other! He rose
and came to her to get the drink she fixed. "No ice," she said.
"There is too much dysentery now to take a chance. You agree,
Doctor?"

"Yes," he said. "Very wise." He took the glass from her.
"To your book," he said, lifting the glass. "It will be the great
book you wish it to be."

She made a face, and said something in English, which
was too fast for him to understand. "Do sit down," she said in
Spanish.

He went back and sat down. "I just left the Señora Biddy.
That far," he said, holding his fingers closely together, "from
death."

She said, "Doctor, you did not come here to gossip with
me . . ."

"No, señora," he said. "I came because I need the help of
someone with an American mind and a Mexican heart. There is
strong anti-*gringo* feeling in the village and in San Juan right
now. The Padre for his own reasons fans the flames. But perhaps you know about this?"

"No," she said. She sipped her drink. "I neither know nor
care."

"The Padre enumerates all the wickedness going on. The
list is endless. You understand, I am a man of the world. I
don't care. But I tell you because there is bad feeling now, and I
want to warn you to protect yourself."

"I have not been threatened," she said. "I have not been
wicked." He thought he saw her lips flicker in a faint smile.
"Also, I have the good fortune to be a Mexican citizen."

"But you are alone," he said. "A woman, and alone."

She gazed at him steadily, enigmatically, through the dark
glasses.

"Unless your friendship with Señor Saltamontes amounts to
a protection. *Se dice*," he said, making a point of his lack of responsibility for the gossip, "that you are together a great deal."

Now her smile was more direct. She said, "Each one of us
is alone in life." She leaned back in the chair, resting her head
against the curving fan of leather. "What do you want to say?"

He shook his head. "Now, I am not certain," he said, and it
was true. "I do not understand the Mexicans now, and I do not

understand the Americans. I am troubled, señora." He went on, and he heard his own voice in his ears, droning, dull, he thought . . . boring her, explaining all that had happened, while she sat silent, unmoving. At the end of his chronicle his voice died away and he thought she might have gone to sleep. I am a very dull man, he said to himself; I do not interest her.

She said, "You want lime pits in the hills . . . then you must get them. I cannot help you do that. I have no interest in these things. I am interested in my book. In answer to your oblique insult to the Americans, I must say to you only—and perhaps you can sometime point this out to the Padre and the other anti-*gringo* people of the village—that if the list of American wickedness is endless, so is the list of American virtue in this small part of the world and small part of time . . . a backwater, you understand, a minute place. Even Biddy, who is an alcoholic, is also a kindly woman, good to the Mexicans; she has fed and clothed the Pérez family for years, yes? And she has done other good things. I don't want to name everybody but you know as well as I do that the Americans have given love, money and help to your people. The Mexicans have worked hard and been hospitable. Where is the problem? If we have brought infantile paralysis, the Mexicans have quite an array of weapons in the medical field as you yourself point out . . . how many of the Americans are sick, not of sin, but of Mexican bugs?"

He said, leaning forward, "Mexicans die at an average age of thirty-two. You die at an average age of sixty-five."

"Not here," she said. "Here Americans do not live long, under your conditions, do they?"

He thought that she had not so much an American mind as a man's mind; it was amazing to him how she could answer him, and in that bored way, distractedly as though she weren't even thinking of what he said. He said, "I do not quarrel with the United States of America, a small man like me, alone in a village. This is a small part of the world as you say . . . minute. But in another way, it is the world, the whole world. I think, I dare to think that the Americans who come here exploit Mexicans; you give examples of patronage and charity. Is this the American answer?"

"Oh my God," she said. "I'm not a diplomat or an econo-

mist. Ask your questions of the American Consulate in Guadalajara . . ."

He laughed. "The Consulate!" he said. "They have no
answers. They would not even hear my questions."

She shrugged. "But why come to me with this absurd
harangue about scandals in this village? I have no interest in
these things. You say the village is the world. It is not my
world. It is nobody's world. It's the other side of a cloud."

He stood up. He looked at the floor. "I apologize. Yours
is an artist's mind and I have intruded upon it with my worldly
worries." The drink must have bemused him; he felt as though
fumes rose into his brain, making it warm and smoky. "It is
only that I am alone with these things," he said, "that I turn
to you."

"First, you say you are here because I am alone," she said.
"Now you say it is because you are alone. Which is it?"

"But it is true," he said, stammering. "When I talk with
you, I know that I am alone the rest of the time."

Everything he said seemed to annoy her. It would be best
to go. He bowed to her and started to the door, but then he
paused and came back, because in that moment, he got the
feeling that he was never going to see her again. He was pulling
at the lapel of his jacket. He took his hand away, put it in his
pocket. "Something has been happening to me," he said.
"I have tried to think what it is but I don't understand it. I
cross from one world to another, all day, going from the *gringo*
world to the Mexican world. I am always traversing a boundary.
Yes. I think this is true of you, too. In the night when I cannot
sleep, and I hear the bell toll the hours—it is careless with the
hours of my life, that bell!—I think of you, as though we
journey together across the boundaries, as though we walk side
by side. But do you know . . . ? You are the only one. In the
night when I am lonely, I think, 'She is the only one I have.' "
His mouth trembled and he put his hand to it and pinched it
tight to hold it still. "When I think of how I shall die, how one
day a sudden pain will come, or in my head I will hear the log-
jam of a stroke . . . I think of you. I do not think of the pain
of leaving my wife, nor my sons, God forgive me. I do not even
think of the pain of leaving life and going into nothing, do you
know? To me death is death, the end of everything. I do not

believe in any church-made fiction of paradise. No. But I don't
know why it is that at such a time the thought of you comforts
me. It is very strange. Is it not strange, señora?"

He stared at her; she was probably no more surprised by
what he had just said than he was. He had not known he was
going to say that . . . he had not known that it was even
true. But now he could see that he had been occupied with the
thought of her for a long time. At night when he closed the
farmacia, or came home from a call, and sat down in his little
dining room, with its ugly tan-yellow tiled floors, and ate his
evening meal of beans and tortillas and fruits, and lit a cigarette,
and then, with his arm around his wife—she was plump and
pretty—went with her into the stuffy little bedroom, Victoria
was in his mind. While the bell tolled his hours away, while he
lay wide-eyed on the hard bed, he was troubled by this un-
expected feeling, and at these times, in his mind, he talked to
Victoria. He was brilliant then—not a bore, as he was now
—and quite handsome; his own face, as he imagined it, was
not so heavy, not so jowled, but dark, intense, its darkness
heightened by the white swallow-wings of hair at his temples.
Then he was not dressed in his shabby clothes, not wearing poor-
quality shiny shoes; then he was not poor, not dull, not ugly, not
a married man, middle-aged with the duties of middle age . . .
but a fantasy creature whom Victoria's eyes admired, whose
words filled her with awe and reverence.

She got up and came to him and put her pale hand on his
arm. "My friend," she said in a kindly voice, "you are troubled
by an American thing, a *gringo* thing. You think of me as your
friend, and that is hard for a Mexican man because I am a
woman. The feeling you describe is friendship."

"Friendship?" he said, frowning, feeling a little blinded
by the stupendous effort it cost him to concentrate when she
stood so close to him.

"*Sí,* friendship." She smiled persuasively. "Is it not natural
when you think of yourself as alone and dying, that you should
remember that I was with Señor Ned when he was alone and
dying, and that he did not die, Doctor? Together we saved his
life. So now you say to yourself, 'Together we can save my life.'"

He could not speak now. There was nothing to say. She
removed her hand from his arm and stepped back a little.

"This little thing, this *cosita,* of the Mexicans and the North

Americans, it is nothing . . . an evolvement of the weather
only. It will blow away on the next wind. You need not concern
yourself with it, Doctor."

"*Bueno,*" he managed to say. "*Entonces,* now I go."

"Yes," she said.

He bowed to her and before he started for the door, he
suddenly heard himself say, "Señor Ned . . . it is something
between you? Of the heart, I mean?"

She did not answer.

He withstood her silence as long as he could. His mouth was
trembling and he put his hand to it and pressed hard on his
lips to quiet them. "Why do I ask you such a thing? Why do I
offend you?" he said in a hollow voice. He felt as though he
were talking about someone other than himself. He felt
dazed as though he had had too much sun.

He turned quickly and hurried out. In the *zaguán* he said,
"No. I am mad. I must have gone mad," and he hurried to the
door and out into the street.

The *niña* stood in the kitchen, smiling to herself about
what she had just heard, but then the Señora called out to
her that the doctor had not closed the door after himself and to
shut it and lock it. She did so, and she heard his car start up and
the engine race and his tires squeal on the wet cobblestones as
he drove away.

Coming back up the *zaguán*, she saw that the Señora stood
in the doorway of the *sala* frowning. She said to her, "Señora,
why does the doctor say he is mad?"

"Because he is," the Señora said shortly. But then she
turned and looked at her and shook her head. "No, in truth,"
she said. "No, he is not mad. It was a joke, *niña*. He is a brilliant
doctor. He saved the life of Señor Ned, *verdad?*"

"*Sí,*" she answered. "With your help. My mother says it
was you who saved him. That is what Jovita has told everybody."

"Jovita is a fool and a coward," the Señora said. "Why
would anyone listen to her?"

"Because she is one of us," she explained. "The doctor is
from San Juan."

"What nonsense!" the Señora said crossly. "San Juan is
only seven miles away. The Padre is from farther away than

that, but you listen to him, don't you? You say he is one of you."

"He is one of us in Christ," she answered. "That is what my mother says. But I do not like him. I know that's bad, but it is my feeling. Anyway he wouldn't notice because he notices only the boys." She stood there rubbing the pottery cup with the towel, watching the Señora. The Señora was looking at her.

She told her, "Even though he is a priest, he likes boys better than girls. Like Señor Ned." The Señora turned away into the *sala* to sit and think, the thinking part of her work. "But he *is* mad, the doctor," she said to the Señora's back. "He has a madness of the *corazón*. It would be better if you cared for him than for the other one."

The Señora stopped and turned around. "What other one?" she said.

"Señor Saltamontes," she said. "Señor Ned has no madness in his heart for you." She saw how the Señora's face darkened and how she frowned. She must say something quickly, because she had made her too angry now, said too much. The Señora did not think anybody knew about her; she imagined the world did not observe how she behaved. There were many *gringos* with this belief, she had discovered, but it was surprising in her Señora, who was a true Mexican Señora in many ways. She said, "There are nice soft rolls from the baker's. I have butter for them, too, and I can make you a cup of *chocolate* because I have gotten some of that. That would be a nice supper for you, señora."

"I don't want it," the Señora said sharply. Her eyes went over the *niña*. "You eat it, little skinny," she said. "Put food in your mouth instead of gossip. And before you go home, heat water and take a bath. Look at your knees . . ."

"I have already eaten. I have eaten much of our butter and rolls. I am ashamed." The Señora was turning away from her again. "But I shall bathe," she said.

"*Andale*," the Señora said and closed the door on her.

It was over. It had been a nice conversation but now it was done. The *niña* went into the kitchen and set the cup on its shelf and then went into the bathroom to heat the water for her bath.

She stuffed pieces of paper into the *calentador* and lit it. There was very little wood and she wanted to save that for the

Señora in case the Señora wanted a hot bath before old Reyes
came through the streets with his burroload of wood from the
mountains. Most of the time the Señora used cold water, gasping and shuddering like a fish under the cascade of it, but as
though she enjoyed it, coming out to the kitchen with her face
pink and her eyes shining, afterwards. Clearly, she believed it
did her good to suffer the cold water, and after one of those
she let herself eat with good appetite.

The *niña* got the three-legged stool from the corner and set
it in front of the mirror and climbed up on it and gazed at herself. It was interesting to look at one's self; she understood why
the Señora did that sometimes, stared at herself as though she
had never seen herself before. Because, it was true, one spent
most of one's life looking at other people, and got to know very
well how they looked and knew little of how one looked to other
people. She tilted her head back and lowered her eyelids, like
the girl on the calendar in Prima's store. She flashed her white
teeth. She flirted and coquetted, and then she leaned forward
and made a whole series of faces like the Señora's . . . angry
ones, and dazed ones, and smiling ones, and the working face.
The working face was the most difficult; she had to puff her lips
forward in a little pout, and widen her nostrils and frown and
at the same time keep her eyes big. She could do it, but it did not
look right until she pushed her fingers into her hair and held on
to her head as though she feared to let go; then it was perfect.

She tried to do the Señora's waking-up face, before she
put the plugs in her ears to shut out the music, but she had to
push the flesh of her face together to make it soft-looking the
way the Señora's was then. And she could not do the Señora's
laughing face at all well, because she could never think of anything that funny; there was nothing which made her laugh
that hard. It was wonderful when the Señora laughed . . . little lights shot out of her eyes and she made wonderful sounds
and her mouth was beautiful with white teeth.

There was a sound in the *sala*, and hastily she got down
from the stool and pushed it back into its corner. She put her
hand on the metal cylinder of the *calentador* to see if the water
was hot yet, but it wasn't. So she stood, looking out at the blue-
dark sky, and thought about the puzzle.

It was important that she work out the puzzle and find an
answer, because if she could do that she could really be like

the Señora and be young all her life, and people would admire her and she would not be like the people of her village, getting dull and old without any dreams. If her life was to be different, then she must be like the Señora, and to be like the Señora was to understand the mystery, to find the answer about what was true and why it was true.

This was the puzzle: There was a kind of bird in the trees of the village, an owl—just as she had told the Señora—which called people to their deaths. The owl sounded only in the night, saying, "Hssst!" in so compelling a way that when one heard it, one must answer, must go to the tree where the owl was, because it sounded like a person, and it was impossible not to believe one was called. It was not an owl at all; it was the tree witch who had taken the form of an owl. It was responsible for the recent death of Aurelia, a girl not much older than the *niña*, who lived at the junction of the Six Pure Corners.

One evening after darkness had fallen, Aurelia had gone alone far out to the end of the *corral* to draw up a pail of water for her night's bathing. The tree witch had called to her, saying, "Hsst! Hsst!" and she had leaned far forward until she could see the eyes of the owl in the tree and then she had fallen to her death in the well, and lain there in the water all night, dead. The Señora had listened, as she listened to all such stories, with patient attentiveness, and then she had said to the *niña*, "Was she dead when they found her?"

The *niña* nodded frantically. "Entirely dead," she said. "Totally dead. She had been dead all night."

Victoria leaned forward and looked into her face. "Then tell me, little stupid, how you know about the owl hssting at her? Who knew it?"

She opened her mouth to answer, and then she fell silent. She cracked all her knuckles one after another. She said, "*Pues* . . . it is said . . . it says itself . . ." and she was silent again. She said, "But it has happened before, just like that, to other people. That is how I know. I have heard many stories of the tree witch. I have even heard the 'Hsst!' myself!"

The Señora smiled at her. "If Aurelia was found dead, and if she talked to nobody as she fell down into the well, who could know that the owl hssted at her?"

The *niña* put her finger in her mouth and rubbed a back tooth with it. "I do not know," she said.

Since then she had thought up several explanations, and gotten others from her mother and other wise adults in the village, but there was no answer which would serve as an answer. Finally one day she had said to the Señora, "It is true, simply because it is true. I believe it."

"The answer to that," the Señora said, "is: You cannot make it true by believing it."

But the *niña* hated to give up the drama of the story which, when she thought of it in the night, lying on her *petate* on the dirt floor of her mother's house, made her shiver deliciously. She walked with Aurelia in her mind, all the long, shadowy way to the back of the *corral*; now she leaned over the well, lowering the bucket for the water, hearing the wooden winch creak in the night; now the tree witch made the "Hssst! Hssst!" sound; now she told herself to ignore the sound, and it came again; now she leaned farther forward, finding the glowing eyes of the owl in the tree, red and shining—for owls ate meat, and that alone was proof of the tree witch inside the owl's feathers —farther and farther forward, until, imagining herself falling, she got too frightened and opened her eyes and sat up, and looked around, being herself again and not poor dead Aurelia. It was a very hard thing to give up. She lay back down again, searching for reasons to give the Señora to prove that it was true, but every morning she awakened with no better explanation than she'd had when she fell asleep.

There were other things which the Señora had shown her might not be true, but which everybody knew and believed and understood, as they understood how the sun rose and sank. ("How *does* the sun rise and sink?" the Señora had said to her when she'd said that.) But, even though the Señora was smart enough to ask questions for which there were no answers, there were many simple things which the Señora did not know. The Señora forgot to eat unless she was reminded; there were times when she would wear one shoe of one pair and one of another, unless it was shown to her; she gave away money to El Negrito—a hundred pesos, Chatta had said!—at a time when she did not have money enough to buy food herself and El Negrito owed everybody . . . She did not sleep many nights but worked at the writing machine and then tore up all the night's pages into little pieces of paper and threw them away, and went to bed crying, at noon . . . The Señora did not know she looked

at Señor Ned in a certain way, with her heart in her eyes, as
the saying went, and that he looked back at her with his mind
only, with his eyes only, even though she had made him well
. . . The Señora did not know many things about Señor Ned
which everybody knew, things about Manuél, and about Chloë
and . . . of all the obvious things which everybody knew, the
most incredible was that she did not know about Dr. Obregón
and did not see how he regarded her with passion, even though
his wife was young and pretty. It was true what she had once
said to the Señora, "You think you take care of me, but I take
care of you." It was as though the Señora were her child and
she tended her.

She put her hand to the *calentador* and it sprang back, of
itself, from the hot metal. She got her *rebozo* wrapped around
her hand and turned the key. Hot water plunged from it into
the pail, like a horse down a *barranca*, making a fine galloping sound. She had not heated much, and the bucket was no
more than half full. She poured cold water from the other
bucket into it until she could hold her hand in it. Then she took
off her clothing and began to bathe, not singing although she
wanted to, because she knew it was not the time for her to make
noise. The Señora was thinking; she could clearly see her in her
mind, making the working face, and she smiled. When she had
bathed, she would perhaps go across the street and see if her
aunt had extra beans tonight and she would get some and a few
hot tortillas wrapped in a cloth and she would leave them for
the Señora to find. There were two fresh eggs for the Señora's
breakfast, papaya and a bowl of mangoes, and two of the soft
rolls. Tomorrow, when she got out of school, she would go
down to the fishermen on the beach and see if they had caught
any *vaigre*; it was cheap, and the Señora would eat catfish stew
if it was all made; it was good for her.

Drying herself, she looked down and saw that she had forgotten to wash her legs . . . but, no matter . . . She would
get some parsley for the stew, too, and maybe an egg to thicken
it, which, with a little garlic, would make it taste like *sopa de
ajos*. The Señora would like that. As long as she did not know
about it ahead of time so that she could object to it, she would
eat it, and it was very important that she eat.

Dressing, she saw that her knees were not any cleaner and
that there were streaks where the water had trickled down her

legs, making trail marks in the dust. That would annoy the Señora if she saw it. She would go out very quietly so as not to upset her. The Señora was very good to her, although nobody knew about that except herself and her family. She did not act nice to her in front of people the way some Señoras did, and then be cruel when there was no one around. She did the opposite, sounding cross when someone was there, being nice when they were alone. The Señora did not like her feelings to show and she did this to hide them.

She had talked that way to Dr. Obregón, in that hard voice, the way she sometimes talked to her, but probably not because there were feelings she wanted to hide. The Señora did not love the doctor, did not encourage his madness, did not even know it was there, until today.

She ran her fingers through her hair to comb it, and then put on her *rebozo*. If the Señora was so smart about the tree witch, why was she not smart about Señor Ned? *Pues*, now she had said something and maybe the Señora would begin to think about it. That would be better, because it was not good that there was gossip about her, that even the Padre spoke about her in the church. It made one very disgusted.

Perhaps she could get her mother to talk to him. She would try that, this very day. If her mother was not too jealous of how she cared for her Señora, she might do it. But it was hard to explain to her mother how it was she loved her Señora; her mother laughed when she said that she did not give her Señora love that belonged to her own *mamacita*, but gave her the kind of love *mamacita* gave her children. She would tell her again. She would say, "She is my doll, *Mamá*. I take care of her. I pretend she is my child."

She tiptoed out of the bathroom and along the *corredor*. It had started to rain again. Any minute it would come down hard. She went noiselessly along the *zaguán* and carefully slid the wooden bar back so it would not make a noise. When she was safely outside she called out that she was going, so the Señora could lock the door after her, and then, in the sudden pelting rain, ran to her own house.

10

Victoria

WHEN THE *niña* was gone, Victoria locked the
street door. The village was full of the sounds of sudden rain.
Coming back along the *zaguán*, looking at the patio and beyond
it, she saw how the rain fell between the village and the mountain, so that the mountain and the sky above it were still
streaked with the sunset's pink and gold. The rain fell in a
shining, rosy shower into the patio. She turned her back on
the beauty of it, came into the *sala* and shut the door after her.
The room was shadowed and quiet. She sat down. The memory
of Dr. Obregón lingered in the room, compelling attention. He
had been pitiable and simultaneously ennobled, as though his
ridiculous feelings lent him a special dignity. He could become,

with a little more self-knowledge, a brain-splitting nuisance to her. Like Ramón. It had been like a playback of the scene with Ramón, the way he stood there dismayed, discovering his wayward passion for a *gringa*. Like Dr. Obregón, Ramón had accused himself of madness. But Ramón had not been married at the time, and he was not a simple country doctor whose world was no larger than two villages in which he practiced. His world included New York, and while he stood out as a foreign being among the pink-and-gray-faced gentlemen of his profession, with his look of arrogance and melancholy, nonetheless he was in his transient way a part of the New York scene. That would never be true of Dr. Obregón.

The lamps came on abruptly and with the arrival of electricity, the first record, spinning slightly slow, on the plaza phonograph, proclaimed in a growling voice in Spanish that love is wonderful, beautiful . . . cha-cha-cha . . . In a moment it would pick up speed and then she would be able to ignore the automaticized fallacy, cha-cha-cha. Rain fell, records played, doctors announced their ill-placed love . . . and love was not . . . won-der-ful, beau-ti-ful. It was hideous, an experience which might better be described as the crumbling of the soul. Who could distinguish love from madness by any definition? Love was a severe disorder of the endocrine glands, to be treated as an illness and a disfunction.

Dr. Obregón thought that she and Ned were having a love affair. Actually, he was expressing his own fears and waiting for her to tell him that what he suspected was not true; this was only his clumsy way of bringing up the subject. She had not told him that she hated Ned, that she had not seen him for two weeks and that she never intended to see him, speak to him or listen to him again as long as she lived. The thought of Ned, even now, brought an angry flush burning across her cheekbones and turned her mouth as dry as paper.

She got up and began to pace the floor. Her legs trembled, and her hands went together twisting and twisting, and she stopped and looked at them, and pulled them apart. When she reached the table with the hooded typewriter on it, she paused and reached out toward the hood which had covered the machine for so long now and then her hand fell away from the thing. It wasn't alive. It was only her typewriter, covered up as a protection from dust and dirt and rust and mold, not a bird

starving there in a cage beneath its curtain. Protection? For
whom? She had not covered it up to protect it. She had covered
up the reproach of it at first, and then after the fight with Ned,
she found she could not uncover it and perhaps would not uncover it ever again.

It was painful to be in the room with the typewriter. It had
been covered for four weeks. Four. Not to remember the date
would be like not remembering the day the world ended, because her world had ground to a halt the day she had realized
that there was something very wrong with her novel. It wasn't
just the old self-doubt which came with fatigue, or a bad mood.
This was despair. One does not accept such a thing. She decided to ask Cushman in New York to airmail copies of her four
published books immediately. What she must find out was
whether she had ever had any talent, because she did not believe it was possible to have had it and lost it, and if she could
find proof of her having had talent once, then the question
would be of this specific book, and not of her entire being.

When the books came, she sat down and read them in
order, one after the other, not with a consciously critical mind
but as though she were reading the accumulated work of some
other writer . . . rapidly and steadily. But reading the four
books had not really helped her to judge her work on this one.
Because now that she decided that she had had talent once,
she discovered that this information was not germane to the
question of whether she was doing a good job on this book, and
whether she was using that talent now. At last she was forced
to the conclusion that the trouble lay in the fact that she was
alone with the chapters, and she did not know whether to go
forward or go back and start over. She needed to hear what
someone else thought of her work before she could move.

Ned had asked her many times to let him read her pages.
He said he knew a lot about writing, that one art was much
like another and that she could rely on him.

"Don't try to get your hands on my work," she'd told him.
"I warn you. Keep your bloody hands off my work."

There was no one else but Ned, really, to whom she could
turn. When you lose faith in the rightness of what you think
and feel, you begin to place rightness outside yourself in someone else. You cannot exist without a sense of rightness somewhere. He was well organized, a disciplined, successful artist,

and she respected him. When she was wrong, he usually proved to be right. She had decided to go to Ned.

He had sat on his couch with the manuscript spread out on the big coffee table in front of him, and damned every single thing she had done in the first two pages.

He damned the whole concept of the story, the style in which it was written, the construction. He poked at the pages as he talked, as people do in a restaurant when they don't like what they have been served and lack the courage to send it back to the kitchen, but still, to show their dissatisfaction in a passive way, push the food around on the plate. She watched his finger poke at her manuscript that way, spilling the pages on the floor . . . and although she had promised herself that she would stay silent and listen to his criticism no matter what it was, she had leapt to her feet screaming a denunciation of him which she could not now remember but which, even at the climax of her fury, appalled her, as though she were listening to someone else saying these dreadful things. She ran out of the house.

In the street, alone, clutching the manuscript to her like an ailing child, she screamed at him still as though he were still beside her, "Keep your thick fingers off my work, you talentless boob!" She could not remember gathering up the spilled pages, nor going to his door. When she got to her house and bolted the door and shut the *niña* out of the *sala*, she raced up and down the room sobbing, shouting insults, villifying Ned until finally, like a murderer, she fell onto her couch, still cradling the tattered pages to her bosom, and dropped heavily into an angry, toxic sleep. He continued to be with her through the sleep, which was as deep as a coma and which lasted for hours.

Awakening from that sleep was like awakening to find yourself buried alive. The weight of the earth was on her being; she gasped, certain she could not move, knowing that if she tried to move one finger it would not obey; the airless box in which her soul was confined pressed in; she did not try to move her finger, but lay there buried, unable to cry, staring up into blackness, the enclosed, limited blackness of a coffin. . . . Slowly and laboriously she pushed up the crushing black stone on her chest, rose, sat on the edge of the couch, still holding the pages of her chapters . . .

The rain stopped now, as suddenly as it had begun. She got up and opened the *sala* door and let the sweet, moist air into the room. It smelled of corn and smoke and marijuana, new green growth in the wet earth. There was a smell to Mexico after a rain, unlike that in any other country, a sweetness and cleanliness which belied the existence of disease. Yesterday she had noticed mold growing on the soles of her shoes, but tonight she could smell the jasmine making the air languorous, filling the breast with pain and nostalgia. Mexico was both . . . the mold on the shoes, the perfumed night air . . .

She went and lay on the couch, with the door open and the night-blooming jasmine coming like a ghost into the room, to stand whitely in corners and breathe its sweet, frosty breath upon the air. It was necessary to remind one's self of the mold on one's shoes and the dampness of the walls; to recall, if one was to be protected against the treachery of the tropic night, the danger of a man like Dr. Obregón, who could twist one's heart . . . But that should be easy for her; she had only to remember Ramón. She had smelled night-blooming jasmine before, seen dark Spanish eyes ablaze with passion before . . . If she met Ramón now, she would not feel as she had felt the first time she met him. Oh no, she was different now. Ramón and Dr. Obregón were alike, but she was different . . .

She married Ramón in Durango one week after her divorce from Jack became final. After the ceremony, her first Catholic wedding, she and Ramón drove to Mexico City together. He was a lazy, skilled driver who seemed to avoid the rough places in the road instinctually, without looking at them. He drove with one hand on her knee. She felt close to him, tremulous with hope and passion; this marriage would be different from the others, those failures of the past. Ramón had explained to her when he confessed his love that he wanted an old-fashioned marriage; he was to be the man and she was to be the woman; she was to rest in the protecting curve of his arm while he made decisions for both of them. It was enormously attractive and entirely new and because her intellectualism and what one husband called her "attempts to dominate the union" had led her to divorce, she was eager to give this a try. To be an old-fashioned wife, something she had never been, would be to begin to love and live as a woman, simply, without complication . . . how marvelous!

She gave herself over now to the idea of being married, as though for the first time, and being in love for the first time, and she turned her head and looked at Ramón's profile . . . the narrow nose with quite a bit of the Spanish beak about it, the liquid melancholy eyes—like Manolete's—the curving, sensual, aristocratic mouth. His profile, as it was at this moment silhouetted against the wild mountains of the Durango country, was like a cameo, recalling the conquistadores, that ragged, skinny band of greedy Spaniards clanking along in their ill-fitting armor, crossing this stretching plain to charge that hot green fertile mountain which must have seemed to steam with rage as it looked down upon their straggling advance.

This was how, her vision blurred with passion and new hope, she saw Ramón and not at all as what he was, a Mexican lawyer, one of a large lower-middle-class family, devoted to his dumpy, careless, dirty mother, and profoundly committed to the macho system. Since he was a man—however small-boned, sickly and slight—he felt himself superior to women, who were constructed for his pleasure and abuse. Because he was a man, automatically he was a little king and self-indulgence was his license and cruelty his right. Now he did not turn and favor her with his glance, but he tolerated her admiration, and his hand on her knee tightened perceptibly. Beyond his profile she saw a group of women in dark clothing like brown birds clustering at the edge of the road, and because she wanted to be one of them and, to add herself to his country, she waved at them.

Not one of the brown-bird women returned her salute, but all of them in the same, seemingly synchronized movement, drew their rebozos up and covered their faces so that only the blank, oblique dark eyes remained looking out at her as the car flashed past them. Immediately she felt shut out, ridiculous, the alien. The women were passed; the moment was gone, as though a shutter had clicked on a camera, immortalizing the tableau.

Ramón's hand did not stir from her knee and she kept silent. She did not want to call his attention to their difference, so uncertain was she on the shifting terrain of new love . . . It was, she learned later, a foolish fear; not mentioning their difference did not in any way vitiate it for him; but she did not know then that her difference, her Americanism, was important to him. Later she was also to understand that the women were only protecting their noses from the dust which flew up from the wheels of their car, and not in any way shutting her out.

Mexico was not, as she imagined, rejecting her; it was swallow-ing her whole, as through the centuries it had swallowed those other ragged, skinny conquistadores *in their foolish armor.*

Woe to him who looks upon the green mountain. Woe.

The car rolled fast along the road and then roared down onto a tiny, narrow bridge and over its mumbling planks and up onto the cobbled, rough streets of a town, never slowing when something was in the way, but urged forward by Ramón like a thing meant to kill, past women holding children stand-ing in doorways of houses, past the men grouped around at the corners where the dim light bulbs burned in the deepening dusk and diffused a lilac light on their dark faces and broad white hats; the car swung left into the square and lurched to a stop at a cantina where music, tinny and sour, flowed like thin beer into the purpling twilight.

Ramón had told her he was meeting an old friend here, that this was business and important, otherwise he would not leave her alone on this occasion. Would she be all right? Sweetly she assured him that she would, and he promised that he would try to be quickly done. He shut off the motor, pocketed the key and went into the cantina, leaving her to wait in the car, contentedly, like the brown-bird women on the edge of the road.

Time passed and he did not come back. The streets grew dark and a burro cropped at the tough grass growing between cobblestones. After a while she felt chilled and restless, and got out of the car and walked toward the flowering plaza, past the Sitio, where the cabs waited and the drivers called to her in Eng-lish, "Cab, seester?" and one dark, squat man wiping down his taxi with a dirty rag, gave her a knowing lecherous smile and whispered a lewd proposal as she passed him. A meager band began to play on the toy bandstand in the plaza and she went toward the music and stood among the flowers—the hibiscus and Grand Duqué and cannas and lirios—and listened to the din of the musicians while small children ran along the tiled walks, shrieking in their games, and little boys wrestled on the grass near the dry fountain.

She watched an old woman, withered, toothless, with a face like a walnut, who stood over a brazier and cooked sopés and sold them, holding them out to customers with her fingers dripping hot grease. Watching her, she sought some sign of grandeur, nobility, pride . . . and saw only stupidity, cupidity and vacuity. She turned away and looked at the flowers instead.

Two American boys came along in soiled white sneakers,

their fair hair cut short, broad-shouldered, lean-hipped, walking with a gait so American that it was unmistakable. She looked at them with recognition, thinking that she could never be assimilated in this country into anonymity, any more than they could. As they came near her, one of them was saying, "Did you see that beat-up, hairy old guy with the dirty feet? I mean, Christ! Did you see those feet? I'm telling you, he hasn't washed his feet in his whole goddamned life!" The other boy laughed and she thought, smiling down at the flowering bush, with a pinprick of homesickness, Americans are wonderful; there's nobody like them. Then the other one said, "She's really stacked. She's American, isn't she?" and she could feel the first one staring at her hard, although she did not look up. She was pleased that they admired her figure, but when the first one said, "Hey . . . you alone?" she turned guiltily away and pretended not to understand English.

Time passed slowly and she decided to join Ramón in the cantina but then paused at the door, hearing only male voices in there, and she realized that women were probably not welcome. She was hungry. She did not want to pester him, but neither was she willing to wait indefinitely. The least reproachful thing she could do would be to find a restaurant and order food for herself. She scribbled a note to him and put it on the steering wheel of the car and then went into the hotel dining room. It was warm and pleasant, and as she ate she was filled with an intoxicating sense of her own forbearance. How marvelously simple it was, just to forgive him, say no word of blame, feel no resentment.

Ramón appeared and before she could say a first, forgiving word, excoriated her for leaving the car and wandering around the streets in the dark . . . Only a whore did that in Mexico, he said, breathing rum and outrage upon her, and in the future she would behave like a Mexican wife or he would beat her into submission. She was amazed. At last when she did not answer, he became sullen and silent; the blood drained from his face and ceased to pulse visibly in the swollen artery of his neck. She sat at the table with him, unwilling and unable to eat any more and waited through his gloomy silence. He did not speak again until they were in their room and just when she was about to tell him that this was absurd, an absurd mistake, and they should put an end to this farce, he began to talk, to apologize. He explained his fear that something had happened to her, his fury at finding the note on the steering wheel because it made

*him realize how long the meeting had taken, how long he had
left her alone, and he was afraid, he said, that she had gotten
into a dangerous situation. He repeated his earlier speech about
how no nice woman walks on the street alone after dark. He
had felt that if something had happened to her, it would have
been his fault. He had not meant to be gone so long; the meeting was complicated; he hadn't noticed the passage of time. He
apologized. Watching him, in the ghastly blue fluorescent light
of the bedroom, she saw the play of fear and guilt on his face
and knew them for what they were.*

*"It is like when the mother thinks her child is lost and she
fears for it, you know? And then she comes upon it, having a
good time someplace and she is furious with it and hits it because it has made her suffer such fear." She nodded, accepting
not only that but what she had seen of his guilt toward her and
his fear. These things did not make him any more likable, but
they kept her from leaving him then. She was not used to the
volatile Latin temperament, perhaps . . . as he was not used to
an independent American woman.*

*When he was asleep, abruptly so, she got up and looked at
him in the moonlight lying there, thinking he looked like an
animal, spent and stupid, and covered him, and then went into
the bathroom. The bathroom door locked and she had a pack of
cigarettes, and she thought. She sat up on the counter which
ran under the frosted ill-set windows, and she was alone. She
thought of the two American boys ("Hey . . . you alone?")
and Jack, her ex-husband. He was a producer of plays, a director
and a boy-genius who had become a man-genius. He was famous,
intermittently successful and rich, articulate—a loud-mouth
was another way of putting it—and demanding. How he would
roar with laughter if she called him up and told him about
Ramón! She knew exactly what he would say . . . "Where are
you? What's the name of the town? Okay, I'll be waiting at the
crossroads with a couple of horses all saddled . . . Break out,
kid, and make it fast. Listen, I'll take tango lessons . . . come
home."*

*Sitting there in the chill night, with the smell of not quite
dry concrete walls around her—everything in Mexico was either
old and crumbling or new and still wet—she grinned. It was
tempting. True, he had been the most difficult human being on
earth . . . but he was familiar and he was a human being.
At this moment her only image of Ramón was one of animality,
and of herself as a lost imbecile. Jack was voraciously ambitious,*

a Cassius of the theater, lean and saturnine. He looked hungrily at theater marquees, envied the success of any competitor, tormented the actors and directors who worked for him, got himself thoroughly hated, and antagonized backers. He was not above vicious, screaming fights in which he displayed his cowardice unashamedly, and after these, for many weeks on end, lay in bed evoking an imaginary ulcer in his duodenum. He had fits of hypochondria in which he convinced himself and her that he had a serious disease, and even success did not soothe and ease him but seemed to prod him into further unhappiness. He was never content, never appeased. He could be charming to the world, when it was opportunistically suitable, a facility which always enthralled her and gradually blistered over the hideous picture of him burned into her brain. There were many occasions when he was charming to her, but the longer he was in her company the less charming he became. At a first meeting when he'd been in England and she'd stayed in New York, she would find him delightful. No one could be more charming, more brilliant. But the cab had not reached her hotel before trouble was beginning . . . over some trifle, as usual, and his face changed, gargoylized by splenic rage, until finally he spat bile and gall and they were engaged in their minuet of murder. In the midst of the death-dance, if the phone rang and he answered it, his voice was dulcet, quick, warm. She would stand, breathing hard, listening to him, thinking invariably, now it's over, now it must be over, he's out of the damned black mood, and then he'd put down the phone and turn his angry face toward her, and they would grapple again like two slow-motion wrestlers. She used to look long at him, when other people were around so that they diverted him from noticing. He had a predatory mouth which looked good only when it laughed . . . sharp, overbright eyes . . . a flush of ruddy color on his sallow cheekbones . . . his long, narrow, nervous feet were always tapping in their handmade English boots, tapping, tapping, like rain in a tin gutter, and behind his high forehead . . . too high, domelike . . . the brain went on at the same nervous double-time, mercurial, frighteningly swift and cruel. He was elegant, restless and creative; the theater was his life, ethos and creed. He was a brilliant man, and talk was more than talk to him; it was a physical expression . . . his voice going fast, staccato, machine-gun sharp, filled every moment with him, mowed her down finally until she was silent, with less and less to say, unable to think. When he was away—and he was away a great

*deal—it took weeks for her to get the sound of his voice out of
her head; it chattered there, spraying bullet-ideas, resentments,
fears, scoldings, pleas . . . ceaselessly. He had no patience. He
could scarcely bear to read the plays submitted to him, whether
they were good or bad, nor listen to her tell him what she had
read of them. He pulled at the pages, tapping his foot, sighing,
tossing his head, saying mygod, every few minutes, mygod-
whatadolt, mygod.*

*He had no patience with her, and none with himself. He
respected her, and sometimes begrudgingly said so, and he
found her always attractive to him sexually, so there was that,
and at those times everything was all right, and he was absolutely silent, saying no word, not making one sound. Afterward
he compulsively ridiculed and belittled her until the restoration
of sex was undone. He insisted that he was faithful to her, and
that she must be faithful to him. "Can't let these bastards in,
Vick," he'd say. "Not that close. They're all enemies . . . climb-
ers, hungry. No one but you for me, me for you." But then their
marriage could not survive on fidelity alone, and when she
asked him where are we going, he kept saying it didn't matter.
"Going up," he said. "What do you want? I'll get it." "Not material things," she said. "Go write," he said. "Will you just go
write and stop trying to make believe this is a tract-house marriage? This is a hotel-New York marriage, Vick. I never wanted
anything to do with the American home. I don't want a breed-
cow wife who rolls her Elsie Borden cow eyes and asks, why
aren't you true to me? If that's what you are, kid, get back on
the train . . . you got off at the wrong stop."*

*It might have gone on—because, hateful as he was, he was
her own kind, her equal, her peer—if she hadn't gotten sick.
But she got t.b. and their equality was undone. Her illness struck
him first as hilariously anachronistic, a kind of old-fashioned
female tantrum. She went to a hospital and he came to see her
twice and brought flowers. (They had to be taken away . . .
the other girl in the room had an allergy—rose fever, she said.)
The third time he came, it was to glower at her and tell her it
was time to stop this foolishness; he didn't have the money to
pay the bill and he was sick himself. He tapped his epigastrium.
"Here," he said. The new show needed a lot of work and he'd
counted on her to rewrite some lines because the playwright was
a dolt, and was she going to lie here for the rest of their lives?
Because if she was, he was getting off the train . . . He tapped
his foot and made fun of the nurses, and despised the green*

walls, and said the place smelled and he was afraid he'd get t.b. himself, and all anybody did in this place was cough and spit. There should have been money to pay for her care, but there wasn't. When he made it, he spread it—mink coats and butlers one time, limousines and an interior decorator another— and did not repay the people who had lent him money when he was hard up. He had no money now and no one would lend him any; he would never have any money, really; there would never be anything for the years of work and fury, but more work and fury . . .

She turned her head on the pillow and would not look at him. He lived at a different rhythm and his rhythm exhausted her, drained her so there was nothing left in her with which to think and to write and, now that she was sick, even to breathe. He filled the room, took the air meant for her nostrils. He never gave her anything. "All you want is a pat on the back," he'd said once, "but you won't get it from me." Even his love was not a gift, but something she pried out of him when she wanted it. She knew that day that he wouldn't come back to see her again; even though he didn't say it, this was the last time. The hospital did not belong in the hotel-New York marriage. And, she decided after two months of not hearing from him and no money, neither did she.

He fought the divorce action, shouted his outrage to the courts and the newspapers, lied, slandered her and called her up night after night when he was at home and alone, between two and four in the morning when he could not sleep, to demand, cajole, denounce, scream and threaten and, finally, when she would not come back, to use every trick and goad he knew. He was almost successful because she knew that in his way he loved her. Almost successful. It was so close she had to get out of range where he could not get at her, and then begin the work of healing herself, physically and creatively.

Now, in the damp, concrete-smelling bathroom, she looked at herself in the distorting Mexican mirror. She had started three short stories and one poem in the years she was married to Jack, and never finished one. Looking into her eyes in the glass, she agreed solemnly, even though it had started out so badly, to try this new kind of marriage to this new kind of man, and try to be this new kind of woman, and write, too. She missed Jack . . . she would miss him all her life. He had loved her in his miserable, fractional way . . . but that didn't make what they'd had together a marriage, nor what she'd been the thing she was

*supposed to be and must be. She went back to the marital bed,
glad that Ramón, unlike Jack, remained asleep.*

*A few days later in their journey, Ramón came upon her in
the hotel room shaving her legs—a chore as automatic and un-
considered to her as brushing her teeth—and flew into a rage.
"How could you do such a thing!" he demanded. He told her to
let the hair grow . . . that no Spanish woman would shave off
the hair that proved she had no Indio blood! He said, "And keep
your skin light. You're always walking in the sun with no hat
. . . do you want to look like a peasant?" She said nothing, only
stared at him, holding the razor, and then when he was gone,
she regarded her legs unseeingly and told herself that she had
married a snob . . . to put it nicely . . . The image of him
shrank as she thought about it, so that he was small inside the
coat of mail. Oh meager soul, she said, oh little man hiding in
your grandiose armor! The green mountain has defeated you,
and you are less the conqueror than the bloodied Indian you fear
and tyrannize!*

*His snobbery went deeper than she guessed at first. He de-
spised Mexico and Mexicans, and because through him she had
chosen to be one, he despised her; he worshiped the Spanish tra-
dition and identified with it, and grew ambivalent only when his
Anglophilia was stronger than that, but never in any way did
he accept himself as what he was, of mixed heritage, Spanish
and Indio. As he was uncomfortable with himself, in the small,
dingy room of his soul, so was he uncomfortable with her. He
could not rest with her. He was capable, in the beginning, of
rushing across a room to her and accusing her of despising him,
but he was not capable of understanding the real reasons she
might have for contempt. On the contrary, he assumed that
she must share his fallacies of thought and feeling—the very
ones which made her distrust and dislike him—and, on that
assumption, believed that she held him in contempt only for the
same reasons he had for holding himself in contempt. He was
exceedingly unhappy, and the reasons he gave himself for his
unhappiness were ignoble ones.*

*He began to go away from her. As he had gone away from
her on their wedding journey into the cantina, so now he went
away from her in Mexico City into the masculine macho life,
into the Turkish baths with his friends, into restaurants where
he sat with the other lawyers through long, ill-cooked comidas,
to bullfights and cockfights, to cantinas, and from cantinas into
whorehouses. He turned all of his life into an infidelity to her*

*and then stared into her face seeking the reward of her disap-
pointment and disapproval. When he did not get the reward, he
became unable to assert himself with her except in front of other
people.*

*In front of his family, he referred to her contemptuously as
"my gringa," and his family enjoyed, for reasons similar to his,
his mistreatment of her. They snickered with pleasure when she
would not fight back. He lavished devotion upon his little shop-
keeper mother, who held her children in her fat fingers, permitted no struggling against her control, no variance with her
bigoted opinions, no questioning of her superstition, which was
the main body of her thought. She smiled in invincible, biologi-
cal triumph at her daughter-in-law.*

*Because Victoria believed her other marriages had failed as
a consequence of her intellectualism, she kept herself in the
position he gave her. She was writing, but she kept that a secret
and pretended very often even to herself that she was not and
that all she was doing was being a woman in the basic, primitive
sense. This was her portion and she must not protest; she would
say to herself every day, "He is the man, the male. I am only
the woman." Saying this, with the secret knowledge that she
was writing although he did not know it, she would meet all of
his brutalities with love. (But what a poor male, her heart
would say, sighing, sorrowing; isn't it too bad? She would try
to hush it, for he seemed, with strange cunning, always to
hear that regretful whisper, and her seeming docilities were undone, and he was stung to further outrage against her. She
could not, in her guilty heart, blame him.)*

*He emphasized her Americanism, and when his business
required him to deal with Americans, he always arranged a social occasion in which he could show her off as his property,
having first told them carefully who she was—a famous American writer, a college graduate* summa cum laude. *At such times
he paid particular attention to her clothing . . . she must dress
in the old Mexican way—although his mother bought high-
fashion French imports and squeezed herself into them—and
behave like a submissive, lower-class Mexican wife. He enjoyed
parading her before the Americans, especially the gentle, powerful American husbands, who thought he was one of those little
Latin whippersnappers and who grudgingly at first granted him
a little respect—who did not want an adoring, obedient wife?*

*When she did not protest, he turned sullen, knowing he
had failed somehow, that she had made him fail, and his resent-*

ment grew and drove him farther away from her, so that he left her more and more alone, and he lived in the house with her as though she was not there, using her as a servant, not as a wife.

   Then he hired a new maid, a young girl with plump arms and a voluptuous body, who lolled in the kitchen with her feet up on a pulled-out cupboard drawer in the mornings while the cook served her coffee, and who stared in amazement, but not stirring, when Victoria came into the kitchen. The Señora was not supposed to come into the kitchen; clearly it was on her own head then, what she saw there. The girl wore crepe de Chine tea gowns with flat brown oxfords, or cheap shiny-leathered sandals; she was too busy taking care of herself to do any work; in the afternoons she washed her coarse black hair and dried it in the sun, pinned flowers in it and eyed herself in the small cracked mirror in her room. The room itself, a slapped-together tarpaper shack on the roof of the house, was littered with comic books, pornographic and otherwise, sticky pastel sweets and half-empty tequila bottles. There was a hand-wind record player too, on which she repeatedly played one record, webbed with surface noise, of a ranchero song called "Oh, Second-Class Bus, You Have Taken My Lover Away!" And in the evenings she stood in the doorway on the roof wearing a sleazy wrapper, chewing on a stalk of sugar cane, and looked out over the blue dusk of the city.

   At night when he came home, Ramón made enough noise and disturbance that he could be sure Victoria was awake, and then he put on his flowered-silk dressing gown and, leaving the door open that she might be sure to hear, walked with his heels striking hard on the tile floor and then ringing on the iron stairs up to the roof and across it to the filthy little room where the maid awaited him . . . presumably eager and open-armed. Victoria lay alone in their bed and listened as the ancient rhythm was begun. He came back in the gray dawn and sometimes he stood and looked down at her sleeping face, but always he sighed getting into bed, and he moved heavily and slept with deep exhaustion. She lay there wondering how it could be that she was indifferent. Now that she was unable to write—and since the new maid came she had not written so much as a word —her mind, unused at its chosen work during the day, punished her with wakefulness in the night. Her mind wrote compulsively, describing everything to itself, reworking reality, editing life out of life and onto the pages of her brain. It was no use now to tell her mind that he was the male and she was the female. The

*mind would not listen, would not hear, and went on with ac-
celerated energy in its purposeless night-writing.*

But then there came the morning when he awakened her
without getting into bed at all, to tell her that the maid was
pregnant—by him, he said—and then he waited expectantly for
her reaction because he felt, apparently, that now he had done
something so monstrous even she could not ignore it.

He was right. The whole masquerade was destroyed then;
the piñata was broken and its cheap, foolish toys spilled on the
floor. Enough, she thought, of this idiocy; enough of primitive
values and playing the stupid female in subjugation; enough of
getting stones instead of love. Through her mind went a tag of
an old song, "Don't bring me posies, when it's shoesies that I
need . . ." and she began abruptly to laugh. Having begun to
laugh, she discovered that laughter had been choking her for a
long time and that now she could not stop laughing, particu-
larly at the knowledge that she had done it all to herself and
he had been simply an employee acting in accord with her
tacit orders as she tried to become a "real woman" and "in love"
. . . It was ineffably comic to her, heightened by the sight of
his astonishment . . .

He gathered himself together and hit her in the face. She
saw that he was amazed when she hit him back a blow which
carried five times the strength of the one he had given her. She
never ceased laughing as she struck, and she stood over him
where he lay looking surprised on the floor now, in the dust, and
laughed some more.

"You're fired, Cortés," she said.

When she went to the armoire and began to pack her clothing, he got up and dusted himself off and tried to act threatening. But it was morning; the sun shone in the room. Everything
had gone wrong for him. He turned his back on her and stared
blindly out the window, mortally hurt by her continuing, bub-
bling laughter, and tried to think of a way to save face. There
was no way; he went to bed and shut his eyes.

When her two tin suitcases were packed, she took them
into the sala and sat there to write him a note of farewell—I
always write them notes, she thought, setting paper in the typewriter, I'm sentimental—and she was surprised as she wrote
the note to find that the laughter which still murmured within
her turned without warning into tears of humiliation and self-
hatred; for it was, no matter how you looked at it, another
failure. And although she knew she had used him as the whip

with which to flagellate herself, and that she could not blame
him since he was no more than a tool of her self-destruction,
she resented now whatever niggardly joy he'd gotten out of it,
whatever reward there was for his nasty little inferiority complex
in playing her superior . . . More than anything, she resented
the loss of another dream, an old one, in which she had believed,
and could now never believe again, that if she tried she could
be a woman and find fulfillment in the female role. Out of her
resentment and the tears of despair, she wrote him that while it
was true that the girl might be pregnant by him, she might pos-
sibly be pregnant by someone else. For the girl was, she wrote,
the recipient of other favors . . . favors from the man who
brought the water, the mozo *who ran his house so badly and*
expensively, the gardener who came three days a week, and even
the dirty old night watchman who came every *evening. "The*
one," she added with a sudden shaft of remembrance of the two
American boys who had outspokenly admired her . . . "the one
who hasn't washed his feet in his whole goddamned life!"

She sat up on the side of the couch. The air coming through
the open door had grown less perfumed and sharper with the
night's cold. She lit a cigarette, thinking how many different
ways she had been a fool in her life. A fool and a failure. She
was a failure as a woman, more than as a writer. Dr. Obregón
wanted her as a woman and that was momentarily gratifying,
but essentially it was an irrelevance, something happening in
the wings, not to her, and not on stage. It was when she walked
off stage to the wings and embraced the man who waited for
the woman, not the writer, that she got lost in a strange world
with no values . . . or without her values anyway. No
amount of examining the values of that strange world made
them familiar to her, and she could turn them over in her hands
forever and never find out what it was which made them satis-
factory to other people. She did not belong in that world, and
whenever she wandered into it she got lost and had to run
away again, back to her own world in which she worked, alone,
doing the one thing in life she knew how to do.

She must take her pages and examine them in the light of
Ned's criticism. It was more than that, his criticism . . . it
was an attack upon her life. But no matter, finally, now. She
must look, focus her attention on what he had said. Finding
the answers to his complaints would strengthen her, enable

her to go on. She must now begin to fight back, to cease being hurt and bitter with the knowledge of her injury at Ned's hands.

She could not quite do that. His cruelty stung her still, filled her with fear. But she must get to work. Because she would survive. She would endure.

She went over to the typing stand and took the hood off the machine and looked at it, grunting a little with the peculiar pain which came into her when she saw it. She took up the pages and brought them to the lamp, and there in the light set them in order again.

Her hands shook a little, holding them, remembering Ned's eyes, narrowed and mean, and his big poking finger, and the careless way he let the pages slide to the floor in a jumble. He, who was so precise with his paints and his canvases! That, more than any single thing he said, told her his disrespect for her work.

The hell with his disrespect and with him. She would never trust him again. She had no intention of ever seeing him again. You trust only yourself. Because while you may be mistaken sometimes, you are loyal, you are on your own side against the world . . . and no one else is. No one.

She settled herself to reading and when Ned's voice came into her ears, saying the vicious things he had said that terrible night, she listened to it angrily, but she listened to it and sought in herself for the answers to his dissatisfactions. Why had she written this? And it wouldn't do to say, "Because I wanted to . . ." for now she must justify every single word, every aspect . . .

When the knocking came at the door, she listened to that, too, thoughtfully. It would not be the *niña,* she would not knock so hard. It might be Dr. Obregón . . . It might be Harry or Charles . . . She got up and went to the shuttered window and peeked through the wide crack. Ned stood there, alone, looking handsome and beautifully dressed, and knocked imperiously upon her front door.

She watched him, seeing him become impatient, suspecting that she was in there and not answering the door. He turned away, starting down the street. As he came abreast of her window, she put her mouth to the shutter and blew smoke through it so that he could be sure she was in there and not receiving him. He paused, but he did not turn his head toward the shutter. Then he went on down the hill.

It was a mean pleasure, but she took it into herself and enjoyed it, small as it was. Then slightly strengthened, she went back to work.

11

Charles

CHARLES woke up with the horrors. It took half an hour to persuade himself that the old getting-busted dream was only a dream. He kept slipping back into it and dreaming more of it. Finally he sat up on the side of the bed, telling himself he was in Mexico, that he'd had a nightmare, turning his head from side to side to shake the blues away. He took one of the clean, folded handkerchiefs from the top of the chest next to his bed and opened it and rubbed his cold wet forehead with it.

"It's a mean old world," he said.

He fell back onto the bed, shuddering. It wasn't like kicking, nothing that crazy, but it was a bad, bad time. Because even knowing he was in Mexico and not about to be busted and that he had kicked and it was over, it was all waiting for him, waiting to be done again. When you got done kicking it, what did you do? What had he thought life was going to be after this besides no more opium? Just nothing? Had he supposed he was going back to Manhattan like a jerk and sell shoes, work at a square job, live like a square?

He sat up again, rolled his head on his neck to loosen up his neck muscles, hunched his taut shoulders and rolled them forward and back. He kept doing it. Maybe he was sick; there were sharp pains in his eyes. He said to himself, "You're sick all right, hophead. You woke up with the yens and that's sick."

He came out into the *corredor* into the bright, hot sun and said good morning to Josefina. He avoided looking at the explosion of her smile, told her to clean up the bedroom while he had coffee and shaved, and then to take the bus to San Juan because it was Thursday and the butcher in San Juan usually killed a pig on Thursday. He gave her ten pesos to buy the meat, so she'd buy enough, and extra for her bus fare. This meant a day's holiday for her and she was happy and grateful; she kept bobbing her head around so that he could see her incandescent smile. He slitted his eyes smaller and smaller and finally turned away from her altogether.

Most Mexicans had beautiful skin; Josefina's bad complexion was something of a distinction. She was fat and knock-kneed and she had a quick, foolish giggle. He would never have chosen her for a maid. But she came with the house, and her services were automatically included in the eighteen American dollars rent he paid a month. She scrubbed everything clean but she was a lousy cook; she served mashed potatoes flat on a plate, gray, with islands of goat cheese humping the shining, evil mess to a point here and there. He told her she'd missed her calling; she should make the adobe bricks for building in the village. This struck her, like most of the things he said, as hilariously funny. She threw her apron over her head and giggled behind it like a fool . . . A-sharp to A-flat to F was the phrase of her giggle, and it rasped over his nerves like a hill-billy harmonica. He tried not to say anything funny, and he did most of the cooking himself.

The coffee she made was indescribable, but today he was too low to throw out what she had made and grind new coffee

beans and boil water himself; it cost him all the energy he had
to wash and shave. He poured some of the black murderous
brew into a big pottery cup and carried it over to a bright corner
of the *corredor*. Maybe after he sat here soaking up some sun
and drinking the coffee, he'd be able to fry himself three or
four eggs, because, next to opium, solitude and cleanliness,
eating was the most important thing in the world to him.

He sipped the coffee.

It wasn't so much that he wanted solitude as that he considered it his natural condition. When he was twelve years
old, he ran away from the orphanage, which was the only home
he'd ever known, and went on the bum. He soon learned that
he was better off by himself than pairing up with any other
bum, and he got used to being lonesome. He learned that the
only people who would ever help him were the poor, the sick
and the beaten . . . but you couldn't always be sure of them;
they weren't *all* marks. Cadillacs roared past him; but some
loser driving a muddy, falling-apart truck, or a lonesome jerk
driving a car with a motor knock that had him scared, somebody in trouble needing company . . . these would pick him
up. Only losers had time for losers.

He lied about his age and joined the Marine Corps. He
looked older than sixteen. He was six foot two then, lank and
rangy, with stringy muscles as hard as wires, a large head,
orientally slanted brown eyes, good teeth . . . and an appetite
that drove him crazy. Hunger was what impelled him into the
Marines. He was sick of scratching for food . . . it took all
his time, because it took more to feed him than other people.
He was tired. He was still growing—his hands and feet showed
him that—and the draft was waiting for him someday, anyway. He thought of it as a time to pull up, eat, grow, and think.

The Marine Corps was full of hungry guys, but even there
his appetite became legendary. After a full meal, when the
others were groaning with discomfort from overeating, he was
still hungry. Maybe there was something chemical about it.
Later when he'd been turned on opium, he thought that there
must be a chemical connection between his habit and his hunger . . . because only when he was on O, good and hooked,
was he free from hunger pains. But they told him at Lexington
this was just an excuse . . . Anyway, whether it was chemical
or not, somehow his appetite got to be talked about enough

that it got to the Marine brass. He was selected to be a member of an experimental group. He knew he was in danger the moment he was singled out from the mass, because you didn't get singled out for presents and passes, that was for sure.

The experimental group of men was mostly from Kentucky, Texas and Arkansas. Charles was the only one from New York, the only one from a big city. With this set of hicks, he was to go to the frozen North, as the brass ominously put it. They wanted to know the minimal food requirement for optimum effectiveness; they were going to see how long it took for these boys to starve, to get to such a point of starvation that they couldn't be bullied into working any more.

They didn't know how young he was and that he was still growing. He was big-framed and skinny. He needed an enormous amount of food to maintain the little bit of weight he had. That whistling, howling cold up there was not just lack of heat, which most cold was, but an actual presence. The cold was all around you, and it went into you, through your clothes and your skin and into your bones.

They began with the rationing. He starved. He heisted and connived and boosted everything edible and on five times what the other men ate, he starved. One night he was so crazy with the gnawing hunger in his middle that he began to chew on a piece of paper to get himself to sleep, telling himself it was just a piece of tough chicken. It worked enough that he finally swallowed it and he knew he had *something* inside him. He began to do this all the time, and he got so he could eat a lot of paper. It didn't satisfy him but it eased the ache a little.

Chilblains put him in the infirmary, and lying there he decided the whole mothering thing was too much for him. The snow, the cold, the hayseeds he lived with, every one of them clyde as a cube, plus the hunger, had hung him up too long. The only thing for him to do, he decided in the logic of delirium, was to "psycho" out. So he lay there and let himself yield to a constant day and night fantasy of going into restaurants and ordering food. Sometimes it got so real, he'd just reach out and scoop something off a waiter's tray . . .

He didn't make a Section Eight, but he did get shipped back to the States because, much to his surprise since he thought he was pulling a phony, he was really sick. It was more than just malnutrition, although the doctors wouldn't say ex-

actly what it was, to him anyway; the next thing he knew he
was out of the Marines and back in New York making those
food fantasies come true. The Corps gave him a small pension
which would be coming in every month for the rest of his life,
which was great; by that time he was willing to pay *them*
every month just to stay out . . .

The first time he walked into Lindy's he was so moved he
wanted to kiss the floor. He was six foot four by then, lankier
than before, and although he moved as slowly and as seldom
as possible, he burned food the way a racing car burns fuel.
Lindy's was the fantasy come true.

He got a jerk job and he began to hang around Harlem
and Birdland and listen to jazz and some of the Latin stuff . . .
Later he put that down, but at first he liked it . . . and he met
a musician or two and they liked his hero worship—everybody
likes to be worshiped, even by a nowhere kid—and they let
him fall up to a joint when they were going to cut a session, and
run errands for them. They even let him fool with the drums
sometimes when they were taking breaks, and they were encouraging in an offhand way. One drummer passed him a stick
of tea one night and he took a big drag on it, and he began to
feel wonderful; the world got still and slow in his head, and his
hands on the sticks went twice as fast. The musicians laughed
at him, kidded him about it, but from then on when they sent
him to get marijuana, they'd give him a stick or two. Through
one musician, a nice junkie, which was a rare thing for
anybody to be, he got a job on a small radio station doing a
record show. He didn't think of himself as a disk jockey because
he didn't know enough about jazz yet, but he was learning all
the time and he knew more about it than the square jocks pulling down the big salaries for playing rotten roll. He was on late
at night when the hippies were the only ones still listening,
and he'd get a lot of phone calls from them and a lot of requests.
The station tolerated him, but it did not pay him munificently,
and he began to push a little marijuana now and then for
some extra loot. It was easy; he had the contacts, both buyers
and sellers, and there was plenty of marijuana around right
then. That was how he met Irene.

She was a beautiful chick and the Johns who checked
their hats with her at the club and handed her five-dollar bills
for packages of cigarettes, flipped for her. Charles didn't flip. It

never occurred to him this was anything for him, because he had nothing, but then Irene began to say how cool he was, and how she respected him for not making a square play for her. She called him at the station just before she got off work, and sometimes they'd meet, with her saying how hip he was not to flip like a square. She kept on saying it while *she* made the square play for *him*, and pretty soon she was around a lot. First she brought a negligee and a pair of mules to his place and left them, and then she began to bring clothes for the next day—her place was out in Flushing, so it only made sense —and then there began to be old candy boxes crammed with cosmetics in his bathroom, and her clothes all around the joint and jamming the closet so he couldn't get the door closed on it or hang up anything of his own. She hadn't moved in . . . she'd "seeped" in, and she was there, goofing off, buffing her nails, asking him what he was going to go out and get for them to eat.

"Chow mein?" she always said, like it was an absolutely flash idea nobody'd ever had before.

She turned him on opium. He was eighteen. He'd always been nicey-nicey about pushing any hard stuff, just sticking and nothing more, figuring junk was a jerk's game, a sure way of getting to be a loser. But she told him how O was different from junk, and the second time he tried it that was *it*, man, like something else . . . The routines of padding cloth around the window sills and doors became as familiar as sleep; she taught him the rudiments of chefing, and he picked up on the rest of it fast. He had a natural talent for it, and hopheads liked the reverence with which he handled the stuff—they were a fussy kind anyway, he noticed, different from other hypes—and he began to live The Life. He found the peaks of mountains he'd only sensed in the distance before, fooling around with pot . . . crystal-and-gold mountaintops, where it snowed warm white velvet and a gauzy blue sky rolled up and away from him into a balmy infinity. In his opium dream, he traveled mystical distances, lightly moving through a gentle, quiet world, feeling like a wise man, knowing he was wise. "Man, I'm a prophet," he said one day, and gave up the jerk selling job, and after a while the radio job, too, because who listened? And besides he made more loot the other way.

His only trouble was Irene. She looked clean, shiny-skinned, clear-eyed, clean-fingered, but he began to be afraid that she wasn't. At first when he asked her, like an inspector, "Did you take a shower?" she only laughed and rolled over closer and pulled him to her. She didn't understand why it got to be that unless she said yes, he shook and could not take her in his arms.

When she washed the dishes, he waited until she went out of the kitchen—it wasn't big enough for two people at the same time anyway—and as soon as she was asleep, or in the bathroom, or gone, he rewashed them all with scalding water. Irene just swished a dishcloth over them, the way she flicked a dust-cloth around when he asked her to clean up the place. He did the housework. Irene didn't know that washbowls could be white, that bathrooms had to be scrubbed, that floors could shine. Twice a week he took the linen to the laundromat and goofed around there until everything was washed and dried, and then he brought it back, put the clean sheets and pillowcases on the bed. She never noticed. He guessed she must just think they *stayed* clean.

One time when he was idly trailing his hand over her bare back—it was beautiful, like her arms and legs, naturally beautiful, like something sculptured out of ivory-colored marble —he felt a series of little bumps on her skin. His fingers stayed there, feeling the roughness.

"What's that?" he said.

She stretched around and poked carelessly at the place and yawned. "Bath powder . . . dried there, I guess," she said sleepily.

He controlled the shudder that went through him, but she saw the revulsion in his eyes because she pouted and told him he was getting too flippy, dragging her soul.

"What are you . . . crazy-clean?" she said. "Who told you to inspect me?"

"Baby," he said. "I just thought something was wrong . . . like a rash or something, that's all."

Another time when she wanted him to make love to her— all she ever wanted to do was ball—he said why didn't they take showers first because she'd been walking around the apartment all afternoon in her bare feet and it was hot.

She pulled away from him, frowning.

But the idea that her feet weren't clean drove him crazy. He said some more.

"You know," she said, "you make me feel like I'm dirty all the time."

"Yeah, well . . ." he said, and to his amazement, she belted him and burst into tears.

But she didn't get any cleaner. And it got so after she'd gone to sleep, even when he was good and high, he'd lie on the edge of his side of the bed, staring at the window where the dawn came pale and blue in a rectangle, unable to go to sleep because he didn't want her to roll over against him. She always did come close to him in her sleep, snuggling like an animal, making little sounds . . .

Irene's attitude about sex baffled him anyway. He liked her, she belonged to him, crummy or not, but balling never transported him, never did for him what opium did, never increased his pleasure, never made him feel more alive. On the contrary, it was a dim and distant sensation, minor, not important, vague, cloudy and troublesome, and he always grew lonely when the time came, felt alone and melancholy and depressed. The insipidity of his sensations brought him down.

Clearly, to Irene, sex was a different matter. No matter how high she got—and she smoked two toys to his one—and long after he had forgotten that she was even there, when the white velvet snow was falling and he was hearing Bird in his mind, or remembering a solo note for note of Monk's or Tristano's, she was asking him to ball.

For a while he thought maybe it was a bigger thing with chicks, but he'd heard a lot, not just from bums or the hicks in the Marine Corps, but from studs. He ruled out the hypes; they had to say it so nobody would think the junk had gotten to them yet. But, having listened, he was forced to the conclusion that Irene was wrong for him, or there was something the matter with him.

There was a call girl they knew who'd always had eyes for him. The next time he saw Mary Lou he didn't brush her off the way he did other times. She was knocked out with him, calling him "a cool-natured daddy"—but she thought she was a hipster anyway and said old-time things like "ool-ya-coo." She begged him to move in with her afterward, let her support him *and* his habit . . . anything, anything, if she could only have him. She was out of her stupid mind.

He hid his astonishment. He'd just barely made it . . . it had taken him a very long time—which was what she thought was so great—and a lot of concentration, while she went frantic, very uncool and unthoughtful, and he seriously doubted that he could ever make that scene with her again. He thought about Irene. Irene was sweet; she had a lazy, even disposition; she was never frantic like this . . . She was easy-go.

He finally said he was sorry but he was hung up on Irene. Mary Lou cried but she accepted what he said and told him any time, any time at all, if he ever had eyes, to come back . . . and he said thanks.

Walking home along the snowy streets that night, he decided that as far as he was concerned, sex was the biggest single piece of square conformity that had ever hit the world . . . worse than religion and all the other conformities; you had to dig sex or be considered a freak. You couldn't say you'd rather get high. You couldn't say you'd as soon have a well-cooked thick steak, or a big juicy melon, or a nice fat sleep. You could do any crazy thing, believe any crazy thing, explain any crazy thing . . . except the lack of feeling. Nobody could stand that. Nobody would accept the idea that maybe you really didn't feel much. But he'd never felt much about anything. Just when he was supposed to feel something, a blankness came and he was dragged and empty.

Irene didn't move out altogether . . . she "seeped" out the way she had come in, a little bit at a time, not saying anything about it or making an announcement or anything . . . just not saying "Chow mein?" but getting up and getting dressed and leaving. Gradually she took most of her clothes away and after a while he noticed it. He followed her and when he saw her new place—the building on Central Park West with a canopy over the front door and a liveried doorman and a luxuriously furnished apartment—he knew she'd picked up a John to pay her bills. She admitted it calmly enough. She had no eyes for the John, she said, so that should make it all right. She had eyes only for Charles. This was just for the loot, which she'd split with him and which they needed; Charles got paid for chefing opium, in opium instead of money, enough for both of them, which was getting to be more every week. They needed money. The John was square all the way; she didn't mind him and he wasn't around too much and she'd have lots of time to spend with Charles, balling and getting high.

It surprised him how much he minded. He dug Irene, and now he forgot the things that had gotten on his nerves and just missed her easy ways. He supposed it was what a square would call "love." Certainly he wouldn't think of marrying anybody else. But she kept on with the John, and he tried not to think about it; he had to play it cool.

Things got hot in Manhattan, which helped him ignore the thing about Irene's John; there was a series of raids, rough ones, and everything shut down. Connections disappeared. Narcotics men were everywhere, and he and Irene were in trouble. When they got really sick, she got hold of some yellow-jackets, just Nembutals, to see them through a couple of bad nights. She told the John her mother was sick; she couldn't let him see her feeling the way she felt. She was in bad shape, and Charles couldn't stand how she was suffering. He knew it was foolish for him to show on the street but after the second day of Irene's being so sick, he went out. He hunted down all the connections he knew, moving carefully, but everybody was busted. He went into strange territory and made a connection; the price was twice as high and the stuff was bad, but he brought it home. He was all nerves, sure that a bust was coming. But every day he was driven out again to score. He could get only one supply at a time, and finally the connection said money wasn't enough; he'd have to make some deliveries too, and do some chefing for strangers. He couldn't turn it down. He was hooked and Irene was hooked, and while it wasn't like being hooked on H, it was very bad.

He called Irene at her John's and told her he had to make a delivery way out at the end of Harlem. She didn't sound worried—she just laughed and said, "You gonna try passing?" So he went, fighting down fear.

Walking along the dark strange street, he could feel somebody behind him. He kept going, and his eyes were watering and his nose was running and his hands were shaking and his insides shook too, but he kept telling himself it was just fear. Then suddenly he heard that extra footfall behind him on the empty street and he knew this wasn't nerves; he'd picked up a

tail. When he got to the next alleyway, he made as if to go
past it, and then ducked into it and spun around.

There were three of them. It was a hijack operation and
not cops at all. At first he was enormously relieved that it wasn't
The Man, but then he suddenly perceived that these were three
mean-looking cats coming at him and he probably didn't have
a chance. He took out the packet and threw it on the ground
where they had to see it, saying, "There it is, you mothers!"
and as one of them scooped it up, he started to turn and run,
but the other two were coming at him anyway, the biggest one
first. Charles pulled his knife, but one of them slammed him
before he could bring it up, and the other one got the shiv
away from him and he was down. They ground his face into
the sidewalk and stomped his kidneys and he heard himself say
into the dirt, "Please . . ." and again, "Oh, please . . ."

They cut him and kicked him around and as the big one
came at him for the kill, there was a shout and scrambling and
they were gone. He heard the siren of a prowl car, low and
growling, looking for him like a hunting dog. He pressed his
hand into the cut place on his neck that was spouting blood,
and got to his knees and saw the packet on the ground where
the stupid mothers had dropped it when they split.

He grabbed the packet and got up and began to run, staying low and close to the buildings, heading for a lighted burger
joint up the street. The prowl car was behind him, but not far.

He looked at the spade counterman when he came in; he
looked hip and Charles took a chance. He said, "I'm hot."

The customer at the counter didn't even turn his head and
look at him. The siren was coming in louder and lower.

The counterman said, "You *know* it, Jack. Make a phone
call." He jerked his head toward the side door, and Charles
ran for it while the counterman began wiping up the blood. Outside, there was a nice green public phone booth in the lot of a
deserted service station. He got into it, not daring to close the
door all the way because that would make the overhead light
go on, but pulling it as close as he could. He pressed a quarter
into the phone and dialed Irene.

By the time she answered, his legs had gone soft and he'd
slid down the length of the cord onto the floor. The door had
moved shut, but the light didn't go on; it was fixed. He told her

where he was, and that he still had it, while the fuzz car oozed ominously along the block and stopped at the restaurant. She said she'd send someone, sounding very cool, but he was losing blood so fast now he didn't have much hope that she'd make it on time. He tore off part of his shirt—it was hard to do . . . his hands were weak—and held it in a tight bunch against the bleeding place. He dragged himself up, bumping up along the wall to get the phone back on the hook, because he was sure if the counterman didn't cover for him, the cops would come out here and notice that dangling cord and look in. He held the packet of O tight under his arm and then, because if they did pick him up, they'd search him, he took the bloodstained shirting away from his neck long enough to stuff the packet inside it. He could throw away the bloody cloth and the chances were they wouldn't look, unless they'd been tipped to get him by someone who knew he had it. He didn't think it was a frame, because those guys had been amateurs; the odds were on some neighbor having put in a disturbance-of-the-peace call. Hunched there among the old gum wrappings and peoples' spit and cigar butts and dirty paper, he kept telling himself he'd be dead in a few minutes, and trying to believe it and be sorry about it . . . but what he kept thinking of was how, when his face was shoved in the dirt and he'd been knocked around—he'd been knocked around before in his life, but there'd been a difference—he'd said *"Please,"* to those mothers. Twice. It made him ashamed; it showed him how hooked he was and what it was doing to him, being hooked. He wanted to call Irene again and say, "I love you, baby. Let's kick this bad scene. Let's get married. Brush off the John." He'd much prefer dying after saying that, than dying with the taste of blood in his mouth, and the curdling memory of shame. What he actually said was the bitterest word he knew. He said, "Charlie, you are a *loser*, man," and he closed his eyes on the tears that slid through his lashes.

Irene did the sharp thing. She didn't come herself; she sent two guys, crew-cuts, wearing fruit-boots, who looked nothing at all like anybody hip to any action. He was almost unconscious when they got there. One of them said, "Wow!" when he saw the blood, and they wrapped towels on his wound and got him out of there and into their Jaguar sedan, and one of them worked over his wound and bandaged it while the other one drove. They propped him up between them in the front seat and slapped a beret on his head and an ascot tie over the bandage, like he was a goodtimer or somebody from the Village. They pulled up next to a prowl car at one light and the college boy crew-cut at the wheel made jokes with the spade cops and Charles had to keep smiling like it was all fun while he was fainting.

He said, "Hey, I think I'm all out of blood," and passed out, and then he was on a narrow table looking up into a big ring of bright light and a young doctor was giving him a shot of Demerol. It wouldn't do much for him but it was better than nothing, and then he was being sewed up. The crew-cuts were gone and when it was all over, the doctor said, "There's a cab outside. Take it," and faded into a back room. All alone, Charles got shakily to his feet, buttoned his coat up over his bare chest, shoved the bloody shirt with the packet of O still inside it up under the coat and walked out of there on rubber legs, smiling foolishly.

At home, he couldn't stop shaking until after he and Irene cooked up the opium and gonged with it, and even then it kept happening over and over again in his mind, the footfall, the dark street, the knife, the alley, the phone booth, the counterman saying, "You *know* it, Jack . . ." his own voice saying to the hijackers, "Please . . ." like he never said it to anybody in his life. She held him, easy and cool, and he said something about getting married. She patted his cheek—was her hand clean?—and said, "Later. We'll talk about it later."

But they never did. The heat lifted a little and he was able to go out and chef again, but he was sure now he was due to be busted. He spent every minute waiting for it. He was right. Three nights later, a half-hour after Irene left, he got it.

Nobody could get him out of jail and he kicked, the worst way, cold turkey. Irene got money to him and the jailer promised and took the money but wouldn't deliver, and he almost died. When he came to trial he was still a very sick man. It was his first offense and they had him for possession, not pushing, and because he'd been a Marine, the judge offered him Lexington instead of a sentence. He took it.

He'd been scared enough and sick enough that he tried to go with what the quacks said, but he couldn't. He did the group therapy thing and listened and said the right things, but no change came inside him the way, for a while, he'd hoped it would. Like most of the hypes there—all junkies but him—he had the conviction which no quack could shake, that there just wasn't anything life could offer him which was as fine as getting high.

He played drums . . . they encouraged that; they said he had talent. There was a tenor man in there, great in the way Charles knew he never would be great himself, and they enjoyed working together. The quacks explained to him that he was extremely rigid and moral. "How about *that*?" he said to the doctor. His compulsive cleanliness, the doctor said, was a guilt reaction to his addiction. The doctor talked about his morbid hunger. Charles said, "Man, it's nothing like that—I told you—I just get hungrier than other people." The doctor tried to help him find something he would like to do which would be satisfying. He told him if he could make up some of the gaps in his education he could go far. (To what? A square job? Wife and kiddies? Car payments? A house in suburbia and getting on the lush in the approved way, just before dinner?) The doctor suggested that when he got out, he should not go back to Manhattan, but move some place else, say, perhaps to Los Angeles . . . a brave new world, away from his evil companions and vicious associations. He pretended to buy the dream this good square was so earnestly trying to sell him . . . It was easier that way, for everybody.

Back in New York, it took him two hours to find Irene. She had a new John and now her connection turned out to be Mary Lou, who was no longer a call girl because she was too thin for it; Mary Lou had only one John and she did occasional modeling for fashion magazines and she pushed. The three of them lay down together and had the biggest high he'd ever known, and it was like his whole soul came out of a cramp it had been in for a year. That high, all by itself, made all the kicking worthwhile . . .

Three months later the dreams about being hijacked and busted came back again. He could feel the bust coming. He moved. He moved again. Then one night, coming home loaded with snow for him and Irene, and loot from a big delivery, he spotted the stakeout in front of his apartment house—the Men in the Hats—and farther down on the other side of the street two guys idly standing on the corner, as unmistakable as if they wore neon signs saying "T-Men." He knew without looking back that there'd be somebody behind him. They had him. He couldn't go forward and he couldn't go back and he couldn't stand still.

He paused and his eyelids drooped and he could see it all, how he was on the books as a hype not only to The Man but in life, and to himself. He knew he was very strung out now, using more hop all the time, and now he'd get the cold-turkey cure again and at the end of it there'd be no Lexington this time; he'd be up for one to ten years just for holding. If they got him for pushing too, which was likely, that would bring more than the maximum ten, more than the minimum one. He wouldn't make it through a whole year in the pen. And he'd have two convictions so if by any miracle he did live through it, the next bust after this would be for life. The bust was here, and he had no hope and absolutely nothing to live for. Maybe he should flash the shiv and get himself shot . . . dead . . . and solve everything.

He began walking slowly toward the bust, sliding his fingers over the handle of the knife, moving on his toes like a cat, trying to tell himself in a minute he'd be dead, so look at the night sky while you can, and breathe the nice sooty New York air while you can, and don't look around at the two behind you, and be glad at least that you're not sick, that you're high when you're going out because that's one thing opium is great for . . . even squares got it when they were dying, the stupid bastards . . .

A girl's voice said, "Hey, sweetie . . ." softly, and he didn't turn his head but his eyes shifted and he saw the car moving beside him along the street. It was Mary Lou, and he didn't want her to come into the bust with him so he pretended not to know, but then she said, "Irene sent me," and he knew that she knew anyway. He looked again, and she had the passenger door of the car open, and she said, "Come on!" kind of desperately, and he turned suddenly and got into the car and she roared away from the curb, made a U-turn with the tires screaming, and jolted forward so fast he was thrown forward against the dash. He didn't hear any shots, and she spun the car onto a side street.

"Go," he said. "Don't hang around. Is there a tail on us?"

"Not yet," she said.

He was keeping down low in the seat, hoping they wouldn't

radio a description of the car, and hoping if they did, seeing
Mary Lou alone in the car would throw them off for a minute.
He kept smiling, because he wasn't dead yet and he should
have been and because he was high, a little high and calm. He
said, "Let's make it to the Holland Tunnel."

"I don't like that," she said.

"We're almost *there*," he told her. "How did Irene know?"
he asked her.

"She was going to your pad and she spotted the fuzz. She
called me from the drug store." She was beginning to shake.
He could see how her leg shook when she stepped on the gas.

When they were near the tunnel, he said, "Mary Lou, pull
over. Ease out, lose yourself for a while. If they pick up on you,
say I forced you. They've got it written down I carry a knife. So,
say that."

She shook her head admiringly, "Wow," she said softly.
"How cool can you be?"

He smiled at her in his high way, a big grin. He said, "Ool-
ya-coo to you, Mary Lou."

At the curb she leaned over and kissed him. "I didn't do it
for Irene," she said.

"No, baby," he said.

"Where you going?"

"Away," he said. "I'll write Irene."

She got out and gave a little wave at him, and walked away,
and just by the way her skirt swung, he could have seen she was
a hooker even if he didn't know her.

He was almost too high to drive. It wasn't till afterward
that he remembered about shifting gears on account of the noise
it was making. When he realized he'd had it in second for
forty miles, he laughed out loud.

He knew he could never make it into Canada . . . that
border was too rough, and besides he couldn't turn north. Ever
since the Arctic he'd gotten depressed whenever he even faced
the North. But he had to get out. The only place was Mexico . . .
everybody made it to Mexico and you could get marijuana there
easy and some hypes had told him you could get O or anything,
only cheaper than here. He had enough on him still to get him
down to the border and across if he rationed it, so that he
wouldn't be trying to kick and make it out of the country at the
same time. Once he was across he'd head for the village. It was

The Place in Mexico where the hypes were all beginning to go. He'd find people there who knew him and not be alone in a town full of squares.

The car was hot, he was sure, even though no cops paid any attention to him; he wanted to be with a crowd on a bus where he'd not be conspicuous, so he junked the car in Texas. Bus travel slowed him down, and by the time he got to Brownsville he had used up his last fix of opium. He picked up a six-months' visa for Mexico and got on a bus that shuttled back and forth between Brownsville and Matamoros with a lot of workmen on it, going home. Inspection was casual and he was over, looping high and cool on his last toy of hop, and that was so groovy he thought the whole thing from there on would be a cinch.

But that was just his "high" thinking for him. Matamoros was hot and dirty. He began to get the first withdrawal symptoms in the bus station waiting to get out of there and head south, deeper into Mexico, and with the first watering of his eyes and the cramps in his legs, he began to get unsure of himself. He had written a letter to the Veterans' Administration office, giving his change of address, naming the village as the place he would be. Now he took the letter out of the envelope and stared at it, wiping his eyes. Did it look as though he'd been high when he wrote it? Did they already know he was running . . . had the local cops gotten in touch with them? He never decided about it. He just put it back in the envelope when the bus was loaded and ready to go, and mailed it off. He walked on buckling legs to the bus.

The trip got mixed up with the whole phantasmagoric nightmare of kicking. It was like being in the movies and dozing off so that the shouting voices of the drama merged with dreams and he didn't know what was happening and what wasn't. When he began to get the heaves, he didn't dare get back on the bus. In El Mante he scored for some marijuana. They gouged a high price out of him for four lousy sticks, but it took the edge off the top and he was able to get on a bus again. After that he walked some of the way, hitching rides on trucks so he could lie in the back writhing with cramps and nausea and not be seen. In one town he tried to get lushed. It almost killed him. He couldn't understand how people could juice; he had never understood it. He drank a pint of tequila. It didn't help, didn't give him any high or make him feel safe. It just made him soggy and sick.

But he couldn't eat, either, although he tried if only to have something to throw up. His throat was raw from retching up nothing.

He could never remember the sequence of the last half of his journey. He was lying in a field one night, with his arms wrapped around a cornstalk, trying to get up, not trying any longer to get to the village but so strung out all he could think was of getting back into the States and getting a fix. Toward dawn he did get up all the way onto his feet, and, stumbling and reeling and doubling over with cramps which seized him and rolled him on the ground like a cat dying of distemper, he made it to a town . . . It was the wrong way for going to the States, but a town, and he got into a doctor's house to ask for help, planning to steal some morphine. They always had morphine. The doctor, like some insane part of another dream getting into this dream, turned out not to be Mexican, but a blue-eyed Irishman named Nolan, who knew in the first sharp flashing look at him what it was, and who asked him what he took, and when he said O, said, "All right, ye miserrable sick thing ya, just stay quiet and I'll give you something."

He did. There was no soar to it, no bang, nothing, but the cramps eased and the crazy weakness eased and his head began to feel softly full of something instead of roaringly empty and terrifying. Out of this relief, slowly loosening up his fingers and letting his body sag, he looked up at the white-haired, blue-eyed man and saw him.

The doctor said, very sadly, "Lad, you're just a poor fool, runnin' crazy and sick through the night. I feel that sorry for you. I've written the names of some medicines you can get in this country without prescriptions. They'll not be givin' you one of your good times, you know. But they'll help a little." He smiled kindly. "How are ya fixed for the ready, eh?" he said and took a bulky wad of pesos out of his pocket.

Charles shook his head. "Don't know, man," he muttered. He was beginning to get the yawns and he kept rubbing his hand over his numbing face. Then that blacked out. He never could remember whether the doctor had given him money or not, but after that he kept moving deeper into Mexico, buying two Seconals a time at a drug store—they'd give him that much without a prescription—taking one an hour, and taking Bellergal, and Veganin, which was made of aspirin compound with minute

amounts of codeine in it, and if he took enough he *almost* wasn't
too sick to make it . . . He kept muttering to himself when
nausea rocked through him, "With Bellergal and Seconal, a man
can almost make it all . . ."

By the time he reached the village, he had to have help getting off the bus. The Mexican passengers assumed he had dysentery like all the other *gringos* they'd ever seen, and they were
kind. He did have dysentery, along with a lot of other things.
The first American he saw in the village, when they propped
him up against a wall and the bus drove off and left him, was
Meg, a crazy broad he'd known in New York. She wasn't a friend
but she was a known hype. He saw her, with her face looking
like Mickey Rooney's, the dark glasses making two big circles on
it, as he slowly slid down to his knees on the street. She got
some Mexicans to carry him to her pad. He came to for a minute, saw how cool and dark her house was, and slid out again.
When he woke up, shaking and writhing, it was night and there
was a record player going and he was hearing Shorty Rogers
like he had come back into the world. Meg gave him a light fix,
and another the next day, enough so he could hang onto the bed
and talk. She asked him questions. Did he have money, besides
what was on him? He explained about the VA check coming in
and she nodded and said she'd stake him till it came, and if it
was late, Harry or Jim or somebody would help him. She rented
a house for him and moved him into it. One thing she couldn't
go through was him kicking in her house, she said.

He locked the door on the world, and went down into the
pit of kicking day by eternal day, night by interminable night.
When his check came, Meg brought it to him and he signed it
and she cashed it for him and took her share of it. She was leaving town, heading for the border with a big score of heroin.
Later he heard she was nailed as she crossed and got one to
ten years. Poor junkie, he thought, more compassionate about
junkies now than he'd ever been . . .

He was in terrible shape. He hid from the world and tried,
when he wasn't too sick, to think. That was almost as bad as
being sick. Because thinking brought him to a recognition of his
own emptiness. He used to try to fill the empty place with food,
and later filled it with opium. Now, as gradually he was getting
the monkey off his back, the emptiness was there again.

He lay in bed and thought about Irene saying, "New York's

my town. I swing in New York," and he tried to miss her. He tried to think of getting well and sending for her and helping her lose the habit, too. He supposed if they were other people that then they'd get married. He thought about that and it seemed crazy to him. All he'd cared about all this time was kicks, and what was there to life without them? What were you supposed to do? How did you live, and why?

If only Mary Lou hadn't come along, he could have walked into the bust and gotten himself killed. He would rather be dead than face the emptiness in himself. It was unbearable, and the only thing that would fix it was opium and he couldn't let himself have opium. So okay. But what did you do then? How did people live, with nothing? Or did they all have something, feel something he didn't feel or have? Would he find it after a while when the kicking was over?

As he got better, he came out of the bedroom more and more and looked at where he lived. He'd been thinking of it as a kind of shelf he was lying on, all alone, like something in a laboratory not quite alive yet. The house was clean and each individual room was large. It was made of adobe bricks plastered over and painted white, and the ceilings were made of bamboo and the floors were shining clean tile. It was cool. There was, besides the big bare bedroom, a furnished *corredor* which was the dining and living room, all open on one side, and there was a kitchen and a patio. The outhouse was in the *corral* in back of the patio.

Meg had told Harry, Jim and Abel about him, and they came to see him. They weren't squares and they didn't bother him the way squares would, but it was hard for him to be with them and he found when they went home that he was shaking and couldn't sleep and had to hit the Seconals again. Jim had a supply of Seconals and he was willing to sell them to Charles on condition that Charles would score for the next supply. Harry invited him to move in with them at the Posada of the Tres Marías, explaining how much cheaper it was.

But he had to be alone, and then after that he discovered he liked his house. It wasn't a bad pad and it was his and he hadn't been alone enough since he'd met Irene. Harry had a set of drums some junkie had left behind him in the town and he brought them over to Charles and they set them up in the little back room behind the kitchen. It took him a while to get up the courage to walk in there alone and begin to flex his wrists and drag the wire brush. But after a few weeks he could do it, not well, but well enough that Harry began to bring his tenor or his clarinet over and blow with him a little. Harry was patient most of the time, but he made it clear that he didn't think Charles would ever be much on the skins. Charles knew it himself. He kept working the cymbal to cover his lack of ability.

Harry said to him, "You no Shelley Manne, you know, sweetie," and he just nodded. He didn't say "And you no Stan Getz, Jack," which was what he thought, because the difference between himself and Shelley was far greater than the distance between Harry and Stan. That was the night they blew a lot of pot and decided that what the back room needed was a big picture window like in *House & Garden* magazine, or *Living* for Young Homemakers. They got swinging with this idea and went and brought Jesús back to measure the wall and make a wooden frame. When the frame was ready, Jesús and the other *mariachi*, Nicolás, came over and they all knocked out the adobe wall and set the frame of the picture window in its place. It was handsome and all it needed was a big pane of glass puttied into it.

Somebody had to go to Guadalajara to get the glass and he couldn't go because he knew he'd walk into a connection, get some O and there he'd be, with the kicking to do all over again. Jim couldn't go because his visa was five months overdue, he said, and he didn't want any city cops seeing his face. It figured to be more than that with Jim. There was probably a big Federal rap hanging him—something like desertion or draft dodging or something wild—so he was afraid to be seen or go back over the border. Every time anybody said anything about traveling, Jim got stoned and stayed stoned, silent, smiling that smile which wasn't a smile, until he stiffened out and thudded to the floor. He had a brand of solitude all his own, whether he was straight or strung out, with people or alone, that nothing interrupted. Harry told him that sometimes he was afraid of Jim, that he thought living with him was exactly like living with nobody, only sometimes there would be a look on Jim's face that was crazy.

"Like he could be a killer, you dig?" Harry said.

Charles just laughed because once Jim had said the same thing to him about Harry, and the kick was, they were both right.

Harry said he would go to Guadalajara to order the glass. But every time he was going to go, he got too smashed ahead of time, readying himself for the ordeal of the trip, to get on the bus. Once, because this was the third try, Charles pushed him up on the bus anyway, even though he was too juiced to stand. But Harry got off in San Juan, as he said afterward, to smoke a little pot, and when he came back, somebody recognized him as belonging to the village and hoisted him on a bus going back there.

They gave it up then, and Harry said that the window was more successful without glass than it would be with it. "Man, it's a true picture window, just right for the bourgeois mind . . . of nothing, through nothing . . . Besides, you won't have the smell of tea staying in the room this way. You got ventilation. It's functional, baby."

The picture window got talked about. The Mexicans talked about it—they knew everything the foreigners did anyway—and made excuses to come and see it. When he was out Josefina would conduct the tour back to the room and they'd stand and smile at it. Josefina, that poor ugly broad, was proud of it. It was the first thing in her life besides her bad skin which gave her any distinction at all. After a while the foreigners came to see it too, and Charles began to feel as though he had some very rare treasure or was curator of a museum.

He began to take walks in the mornings, and to build himself up with food and exercise. But he felt better and that was all. The town was empty, like him, and he couldn't stand to be with the squares so he spent most of his time with Harry and Jim and Abel. They bugged him, but there wasn't anybody else. He couldn't leave there, although after a while he got so he could go into Guadalajara with Jackson Garth in his truck . . . just as long as he stayed away from the bus station where the connections stood around . . . Jackson, that mother, made him pay, not only his fare but a percentage of the wear and tear on the truck. He was beginning to think, since he had to stay here, that he ought to try to do something besides just stay alive and off O, but he couldn't think of anything he'd like to do. He tried to draw but when he got done, it looked like some child had done it; it was flat and exact as though he'd done it with a ruler. He tried to write, but he hadn't had enough education for that and the words all misspelled embarrassed him. He showed one paragraph he thought was petty good to Jim, because Jim used to do some ghost writing before he was a hype, and Jim read it and smilingly told him, "Forget it, dad." He went back to the mournful drumming as often as he could stand it. But how could you keep doing something you knew you'd never be any good at? Practice doesn't mean anything if you just practice your mistakes and never get any better.

Usually he went into the back room and practiced in the morning, but this morning, waking up with the yens so strong, he knew that was out. He blew a joint and had some more of that tarry coffee Josefina had made. Maybe she put tobacco in it. She must put something in it . . . even she couldn't make it that poisonous without *adding* something.

He decided regretfully that Josefina would have to go on The Bus. It was not a real bus, but an imaginary one, part of a game he played with Jim—a fantasy bus on which he put all the people that bugged him, the losers, the squares, the righteous. In the fantasy, Jim was going to drive the bus; they would announce a picnic up at the waterfall and load up the bus with everyone he and Jim hated, and then Jim would get in and drive it up the mountain to the cliff, set it in low gear, and jump out to safety while the bus shot out over the cliff and crashed at the foot of the mountain with no survivors.

He got up, yawning . . . and yawned again. With the yens bad, numbness and yawning came back like this . . . He'd better get out of the house, find somebody to be with, not stay alone.

The best part of the bus game was his secret. When Jim tried to open that door to jump, he'd find out that he was a passenger, too. The door wouldn't open. He smiled. Like he'd told the Garth broad, a junkie is nobody's friend . . . and neither is a hophead.

He wandered to the door and looked out at the street in the late morning. He saw the red flag was up at the butcher's. Women were turning out of houses all the way down the hill, all the way to the lake's edge, twitching their *rebozos* back over their shoulders, carrying empty soup plates, obviously going to the butcher's. He turned back to call to Josefina and then remembered that he had sent her to San Juan. He pulled the door shut after him and stepped down into the street, walking along in big, greedy strides. How swinging if the butcher had killed a

cow, and Josefina scored for pork in San Juan! He'd have two
kinds of meat in the house on the same day . . . it was practically like living in the States. He'd been eating canned fish for
a week—mackerel in tomato sauce, and *atún*—and wasn't it
like these stupid bastards who had to end every word in an "a"
or an "o," to translate a word like tuna, which sounded Spanish
in the first place, into *atún* . . . ?

Outside the butcher shop, he saw that an ear and a tail had
been flung to the dogs. He leaned over as he passed and looked.
Good. It was beef.

He went up the two steep steps into the dark shop. The
carcass hung on a great hook and blood dripped from it onto the
stone floor. There was a hot sticky smell in the small room.
Flies moved, like a row of distant tanks, black, slow and steady,
over a white shining loop of intestine. The women stood patiently in the store, holding their empty dishes. When it was his
turn, Charles asked for liver. The butcher, Armando, raised
his heavy black brows at him, because liver was a delicacy and
greatly prized, and Charles said quickly that he would also take
a kilo of stew meat. Armando swung around with his big knife
and hacked at the carcass, then wrapped the meat in an old
sheet of newspaper and handed it to him. Charles paid him
and ducked under the low doorway and came down into the
white blinding sunlight again.

He hurried up the hill to Mariano's store. The only potatoes
Mariano had were small greenish ones going soft, but he took
them. Mariano, standing there chewing on the end of a long stick
of sugar cane, watched him as he picked out some little tomatoes,
not much bigger than marbles, and sorted out two handfuls
of sandy spinach, and got three onions.

He said to Mariano jubilantly, "*Hombre*, I am going to
feast!"

Mariano grinned and pushed the sugar cane around in
his mouth. "You have hunger?" he asked rhetorically, grinning.
The Mexicans called Charles The Empty One, and laughed together at his frenzied, constant, and sometimes unavailing,
search for food. They all watched him with this same grin, never
tiring of the joke, as he went in and out of the small, poorly
stocked stores of the village. They discussed what he bought
and decided for the hundredth time that it must be because of
his absurd height that he was always so hungry. Maybe that
was it, for all he knew.

He had forgotten to bring a basket and there were no paper bags, so he stuffed the potatoes and onions inside his shirt where they dropped to the belt line. He put the spinach in the back pocket of his pants, and took the tomatoes in one hand and the meat in the other. Now, after paying centavos into Marino's outstretched, dirty hand, he rushed out, heading for the baker's for some crisp, fresh rolls. Maybe this once he'd take a chance on real butter instead of margarine. It wasn't safe of course, but hell, it wasn't safe to breathe . . .

Crossing the street, he saw Carmen running toward him, calling his name. He looked at her and noticed that her usually pretty young face was tear-streaked.

"What's the matter?" he asked her when she got to him.

"El Viejito," she stammered and suddenly was crying. "Señor Ramsay . . ."

"What about him?" he said.

"I think he is dead, señor," she told him.

"*Sí?*" he said.

She explained in a rush that when she had come to clean his house she thought he was asleep and then later in the morning she peeked in at him to see if he wanted coffee, because she thought he had gotten drunk last night and was sleeping it off, and then she had left him quiet because he did not stir. But just now she had gone in and looked at him and his face was a dead face.

"Did you touch him?" Charles asked, not sure of his tenses in Spanish, so that he might have said, "Are you touching him?"

She shook her head.

Charles looked longingly at the baker's. In the dim cave of the shop he could see the trays of sweet rolls and the tiny loaves of bread. Soon now they would be all gone and there would be no more till tomorrow. The baker never made enough bread . . .

"I will go with you," he said grudgingly.

He followed her along the Calle Morelos, thinking about how he was walking farther and farther away from the baker's, and how people died down here. Just died. Not the way they died at home, with a surprise about it, or having been sick a long time so there was no surprise about it, but, nonetheless, with ambulances shrieking them through the streets to hospitals. Here they just went home and died. Or walked along the street and died.

Two weeks ago he had seen the old huarache maker lying face down in the street in front of his sandal shop and he had said to a passing Mexican, "What happened there, *hombre*?" and the Mexican shrugged and grinned and said, "Drunk, believe I." But later that day his wife turned the shoemaker over and they saw that he had died, on a corner with the sun beating down on him, and people walking past all day, smiling tolerantly at his dead, drunk-looking body.

Carmen pushed open the big door to the House of the Bells, and as he stepped into the cool shade of the plant-lined vestibule, the bells in the church tower next door clamored hideously and he stood still under the sound, hunching his thin shoulders under the weight of it. Everyone had congratulated Carmen's mother when she had rented the house to El Viejito because, oh miracle, oh goodness of God, he was *a deaf*. A deaf *gringo*, *fíjase*!, who would pay a high rent and not move out when the bells wagged their great swollen metal tongues . . .

When the bells stopped clanging, he followed Carmen into the wide patio. She drew her *rebozo* over her face and pointed shakily at a closed double-door. Charles set the meat and tomatoes down on the plain board table and went where she pointed.

At the moment he stepped into the dark room with its heavy curtain waltzing with the draft against the shutters, someone turned on the loud-speaker system in the Plaza, and in a shower of static, an American jazz record blasted the quiet. The voice of Jimmy Rushing shouted, coarse and vital, "I want to see my baby, see my baby, ba-ad . . ." and Charles remembered that before she left, Meg had given the Mexicans a stack of blues and bop records and told them to play them on their daily noontime concerts, in between their own ranchero songs. He went to the window, not looking at the bed, pulled the curtains and swung the shutters out. Light came harshly into the big high-ceilinged room and the music was louder.

Charles turned slowly, seeing out of the corner of his eye the motionless outline on the bed; he looked across the room to where Jerry Ramsay had put a pole on a wooden standard. Here his suit hung, double-breasted jacket soiled and spotted, trousers bulging round at the knees. One necktie hung over the pole, the maroon one he always wore, and one white shirt with the starch holding its frayed collar rigid on the hanger. On a straight chair his velvet-collared overcoat waited, and beneath it on the dirty floor were his good black shoes. But he had no socks. Charles remembered, although he had never thought about old Jerry Ramsay much, that seeing him dressed all the time in his navy suit, he had always been distressed to see his bare, white-skinned ankles.

He glanced out the window and saw Harry strolling along the other side of the street, his too-big jacket drooping off his shoulders, his glasses riding low on his nose.

Charles put his head out through the folds of the curtain. "Hey, man," he called over the music. "Come here."

Harry looked at him, pantomimed elaborate, stagy surprise at seeing him, and then shook his head. "Going to eat," he said and kept walking.

Charles said, "Hey!" and when Harry looked over again, made a gesture for him to come into the house.

Harry stood still, thoughtfully considered Charles' waving arm and then the little bundle of manure in his path on the cobblestones. Then he turned and crossed the street.

Charles pulled his head in and stood there listening as Harry's huaraches slapped their slow way up the *corredor* and Harry's voice said hello to Carmen in the patio.

Harry said in the doorway, "What's the chick got her face covered up for?"

"Come in, will you?" Charles said, suddenly impatient. Harry came a wary step deeper into the room. Charles pointed to the figure under the blankets on the bed, watching Harry all the while. "Old Jerry," he said. "Carmen says he's dead."

Harry's mouth loosened. His color changed and he put his hand over his stomach and pressed in, hard, as though he had a pain. "Yeah?" he said, but not asking a question, just stalling. His skin had gone slack and he hunched up his shoulders.

"Take a look, man," Charles said.

Harry inched forward and pulled back the ragged blanket. They looked at Jerry Ramsay's old face. It was not pink as they were used to seeing it, but blue-gray, and its expression was petulant.

Harry let out his breath unevenly. "He is . . ." he said finally, "the deadest." He drew the blanket up so it covered the staring eyes, and backed away from the bed. His color was still bad. He pulled his loose collar away from the moist skin of his neck and forced his shoulders down and schooled his face into a blank expression.

He looked around as Charles had, at the curtain's stately dance, and the coat on the pole swaying slightly, and the typewriter on the desk and the papers littered beside it. The jazz record ground along on the Plaza and neither of them spoke through the tenor sax solo.

"That wasn't 'Prez,' " Harry said at the end of it. "That was Herschel. Lester never got over his death. I knew Lester . . . if anybody could know him." He looked at the bed again. "This old cat used to bug me. I hated the way his vacant face would light up when he saw me, like he'd hit a switch that said SMILE, like he always figured we were pals." He pushed his glasses up, and his broad face in the hard light looked haggard and pouched. "I guess now he's dead we're supposed to say 'He was a grand old fellow.' " He drawled out the word "grand" again. "Gra-a-and."

Charles closed the curtains and the room was shadowed again. The jazz record went off and the Mexicans put on a ranchero song.

The onions under his shirt scratched against Charles' stomach and he shifted them around. He said, "I hate these squares running around with their hats pulled down over their ears, and their crappy music, and the stupid way they live."

Harry said, "He could have died up in the States, too."

They arranged with Carmen to guard the house and they took the meat, soaking pink through the black of the newspaper, and Harry put the tomatoes in his jacket pocket. They went to the telegraph office where the telephone was. Charles put in a call to Dr. Obregón in San Juan and explained, and the doctor's wife said he'd be right over after he finished his *comida*.

When they came out Charles said, "An ambulance would take off and be anywhere in Manhattan in three minutes. These squares got to finish eating *comida* first." He shifted his voice higher, mimicking. "*Despues'n la comida, señor*," he said.

"Take it cool," Harry admonished. "The cat's dead and the quack's hungry." He chuckled. "*You* ought to dig that."

"Listen," Charles said. "Eat dinner with me. I scored for some liver." He could hear how his voice didn't sound right. In a way he hoped Harry would notice it enough to say yes so he wouldn't be alone right now, and in another way he was ashamed for Harry to know he was in bad shape.

But he could see that Harry was going to say no. So he added, "I'm sick today, man, you know. Nervous."

Harry looked toward the Posada, and Charles supposed Elinor Garth was going to be there or something, and he was embarrassing Harry. But Harry said, "I'll just step over there and tell the Doña she can give my share of the burned lard to somebody else today." He smiled and gave a little frisk in the street. "I will also," he said, "get my mellow bottle of juicy."

A passing Mexican jostled Charles and apologized softly, with a smile.

Charles said bitterly, "Will you look where the mothering square is wearing his goddamned hat? Down over his goddamned ears!"

He couldn't get the *carbón* fire started in the stove. He tried like a boy scout, but it wouldn't take. While Harry sat in the *corredor* and drank, he went out to see if he could find someone to help him. His hands were shaking and he was so hungry his stomach hurt.

The only one he saw was Victoria's *niña*, and he called to her. He asked her to come and start his fire and then she could go to her Señora and tell her to come to take *comida* with Harry and him.

She nodded in a businesslike way and came in. Her wise-child's face did not change expression nor show amusement when she looked at the shambles he had made of the stove. She set to work, and Harry lounged over to the doorway to watch, still holding his bottle. She was brisk and efficient, and in a few moments, when the fire had really taken hold, she stepped back from it, a little like a magician, and turned up her smudged hands in a gesture which said, "It was nothing."

Harry said, "You can be *sure* . . . if it's Westinghouse."

The *niña* wound her *rebozo* about her head. "My Señora is working," she said, "at the machine. If she speaks to me, I shall tell her you invite her. But I am not permitted to speak to her unless she speaks to me."

"Is there food cooking in your Señora's house?" Charles asked her.

She looked at the floor, obviously not knowing how to answer. Then she said she did not want to discuss Señora Victoria with others, but she knew that the Señora had eaten very little for days . . . some tortillas and some fruit, nothing more. She had been fierce, with her hair in disarray, and she muttered and talked to herself, and clacked at the machine all night and only stopped when she was alone and then wolfed down a little of the food left for her. She did not look well, and now it was said that Señor Ramsay, the old deaf, had possibly died from not eating because nobody had sold him any food for a long time . . .

"I shall invite her," the *niña* said, and walked quickly away.

12

Victoria

WHEN Victoria came in, Charles was just putting the plates of food on the table. Harry lounged in a chair in the sunlight with a drink in his hand and the bottle on the table in front of him. It was perfectly evident that there was no emergency here, in spite of what the *niña* had said to her. She took off her dark glasses, but the *corredor* was bright and glaring and she put them back on. Charles told her he had cooked for her too, and that one plate was hers, and because she did not want to be rude to Charles and this was Charles' house, she hid her reluctance to stay there, and thanked him and went to the table. The *niña* had actually said in words only that the Señora must hurry at once to Charles' house; she had not said

why. She had believed herself urgently summoned . . . otherwise the *niña* would not have interrupted her work.

Charles said, "We're scoffing high today, Vickie. I scored
for some liver."

She looked at her plate. It looked appetizing . . . Charles
must have cooked it himself.

"Keeping your teatimers on, chickie?" Harry said in a
slurred voice. He was drunk, thick-tongued, pale. Teatimers . . .
that was what they called dark glasses because when they
smoked tea their eyes were sensitive to light.

She nodded. The food was very good. Charles was eating
with relish, but Harry had not begun. He sipped at his drink.

"The chick's dragged," he said.

"Come on, man," Charles said. "Will you eat the damned
food before it gets cold?"

Harry obediently took up his fork and stared at it as though
wondering what he was supposed to do with it. He put it down
again.

"Jesus!" Charles said.

Harry began to push tunnels into the mashed potatoes
with his knife. He stared at her.

"Let's talk some trash, Vick," he said.

She said, "I have nothing to say."

He looked away then, but it was not like having somebody's gaze lifted from you. The weight of his attention, like a
mantle, was still on your shoulders. Her shoulders ached anyway from the long hours at the typewriter. It was important to
relax them, to think about relaxing them. Harry had changed
since the last time she'd seen him. When was that? Weeks
ago, but when? Now he looked ill, and his eyes seemed smaller
than they used to. Smaller and meaner.

She ate. The man selling Popsicles labored up the street
outside with his cart rattling over the stones, calling out,
"*Paletas!*" and naming the flavors he had left. There were children's voices beneath his, and the sound of children's feet hurrying over the stones after him.

"Slush," Charles said. "You ever eat one? Like if they
bottled slush off the sidewalk in Manhattan . . ."

"Clean like that, too," Harry said.

"He's got one flavor that he calls 'nut.' How about that?

Not pecan or almond or anything. Just '*Nuez*' . . . It's gray."
Charles laughed. "Sometimes it's got pieces of straw and dirt
in it."

"Hair," Harry said.

"Yeah, but cold hair," Charles said. He had finished eating.
"I'm still hungry," he said plaintively.

Harry said, "Have mine."

Charles looked at Harry's messy plate. He said, "I'm hungry,
man. Not blind."

"Have mine," Victoria said. She had eaten only half of it.
Charles took some from her, and some mashed potatoes and
spinach. Then Harry got two hand-rolled marijuana cigarettes
out of his shirt pocket and handed one to Charles. They lit up,
leaning back in their chairs. The smoke smelled bad; she lit a
Casino to smoke with them.

Harry said, "That ain't going to get you nothin' but lung
cancer, babee. No jivin'. If you're gonna smoke, you might as
well smoke pot. Kicks before cancer."

Harry took a long sucking pull on the marijuana. There was
a frantic quality about the noise he made pulling the smoke into
himself, and holding it. She looked at him, saw how his pale,
wet face reddened. He lifted the glass of tequila so that the instant he was forced to exhale, another anodyne was at hand. He
was infantile, oral and greedy. His eyes blanked and softened as
he drank, getting rounder, so that he looked like a blank bare
soft baby, defenseless at the breast.

Charles glanced at her apprehensively; she had made a
choking sound, and abruptly she saw before her eyes a newspaper column she had read, with its title in big black letters:
IF YOU WANT TO BE ATTRACTIVE TO MEN, DON'T MAKE NOISES
IN YOUR THROAT.

"Jerry Ramsay's dead," Harry said, testing the words. "How
about that?"

Charles said, "I'm going to clear these plates away. They
bring flies."

"Leave them," Harry said. "They draw the flies away
from me."

"Yeah," Charles said. "But more come."

"Come one, come all," said Harry. "You know about Jerry?"
Harry asked her.

"Yes," she said. "My *niña* told me."

"We put this big value on life," Harry said. "What's wrong with the long sleep?"

Charles was gathering the plates and she helped him. Neither of them answered him.

"I think I'll slit my mothering wrists," Harry said.

"You keep promising," Charles said, "but you don't do it."

"Yeah, well, you know," Harry said. He looked sad.

She helped Charles carry the things to the kitchen and then went off to the *excusado* in the *corral*. It was dark in there, restful after the glare of afternoon light in the *corredor*. The walls were plastered-over adobe and scrupulously clean. Everything in Charles' house was clean, except Harry. Now she knew why they had wanted her to come to dinner. They had been affected by Jerry Ramsay's death . . . unlike her. All she had thought was, he's dead, so what? and gone on with her work . . . It was Jerry they wanted to do something for, and because it was too late, she had had to be the substitute. Jerry had been a soi-disant writer . . . she was a writer. Ergo, she must be given food and kept alive. The *comida* had been a bribe to the God of Death.

She washed her hands and, because the water was cool and clean, her arms and her face. But concentration was still on her face when she was done, like cobwebbing, and she did not feel alert to the present. She was enmeshed in the work now that, at last, it was beginning to feel right. These days she never really got out of the work, no matter where she went, no matter what happened. That was natural. It was, although Harry put such a low value on life, a testimony to life that she could have survived and was even now recovering.

Ned had been genuinely pleased with the last rewrite and, because he was generous, he had told her so, eloquently and specifically. It had been an extraordinary experience after the weeks of working without hope. She had dredged up the rewrite out of the very bottom of her being, thanking God that there was someone besides herself to please, since it had become so hard now to please herself. Ned was remarkably understanding and patient, and he had been all along. In fact, incredibly, when she had first gone back to him, in humility, to apologize, she found him not angry with her, as she had expected, but tolerant and detached. He had smiled at her, and

his eyes were kind. He had waited for her to say whatever it was
she had come to say. This self-control, this superhuman self-
discipline which was his, struck awe into her. He was painting,
and she stood in the studio and watched him. He wore the big
rubber apron, like a blacksmith's, which he wore when he
worked, and which had spots and smears of paint on it, and
his hand—that destructive vicious hand—was steady holding
the brush. He was silent, and she couldn't speak for a while, and
then she had watched his hand moving and it had calmed her,
almost hypnotically, so that when she did finally talk, her voice
was no longer the croak it had been, but was low-timbred and
reasonable. She promised then to try to behave better, and she
said she knew it would be difficult for her because the book
was not a reasonable thing to her but blood of her blood and
bone of her bone, her child, a creature to whom she had given
birth in anguish.

He nodded, paying her no great heed, and later when she
listened to more criticism from him and felt the top of her head
beginning to grow cold and her mind pinwheeling off into many
fragments, she had held up her hand like a policeman, and he
had obeyed the traffic signal and fallen silent. She had gotten up
and stalked away, and mercifully, that time, the explosion came
when she was at home and alone again. But she had gone back
and back, because she had to know every word he would say.

If it was hard for him, he didn't show it. He was as stolid,
relentless and impersonal as a tank. Like a tank he overrode her
feelings, her arguments, her furies. But even if he had been less
phlegmatic, she would have had to go on, probing into him for
every disapproval he might have, because only in this way
could she learn her own opinion. If he disliked a phrase, or an
image or a metaphor, she made a point of prying the reason out
of him, many times when he did not himself know what the
reason was. Probing in this way, actively, was the only course of
action possible to her. If she ignored what he said, as she was
determined to do in the beginning when the blow of his criticism
had first fallen, she found that she could not work. When she
was able to listen to what he said, to attend to his criticisms and
suggestions, she discovered that he had marvelous insight, an
artist's intuitive insight of what she wanted the book to be. No
editor, no one, had ever been so genuinely helpful and wise. It
was his *wisdom* which amazed her. He was brilliant and clever,

which other people could be too, but it was his wisdom
which was so important, and so rare. She found that she could
rely on his wisdom, and gradually as the work got better and
better, she became happier, almost exalted sometimes. The book
became new to her again, and she felt a great surge of the
enthusiasm with which she had started it in the first place . . .
That and more, because now her pleasure in the achievement
of it was confirmed by his approval and his satisfaction with it.
She had never been so happy with her writing before.

Ned had crossed the moat of her defenses and entered into
the castle where her creative being had lived so morbidly alone
all these years. She did not feel alone any more, and when,
sometimes, there was a whisper of warning against him—for
human beings create in solitude—she listened to it and went
more cautiously . . . but cautiously forward, for now there
was no turning back.

Chicharras were clacking in the trees. It was unseasonably
hot today. Perhaps that was why she had stayed here in the cool
dark, that and a reluctance to go back out there and see
Charles and Harry and say good-bye to them. They were such
miserable children. Once she had visited a home for retarded
children, and she had had that feeling, and afterward one of the
parents had told her that the children were really very happy in
their world—in their potato and turnip world of physical comfort—without joy, without fear. There was that one little girl,
fat, gray-faced, who had come close to her to touch her, and
stand near her, and the child had smelled bad, and her hair
was without luster, and her eyes were smeary with tears and
her smile was a parody of a smile, as an idiot's smile must be
. . . and she had turned and run, only to remember the child
forever and to think of it—lumpily, wetly, like a being made
of mucus—still waiting for her. Sometimes she had had that
feeling with Harry, that he was, in spite of his brilliance of mind,
retarded like that gray child, smeary-eyed with tears . . .
Today, probably because of the marijuana and tequila, he was
like that, sickeningly pitiful. But . . . he could be mean. He
could be many things. He was a vessel of despair seeking a
harbor.

A chill struck her and she shivered—the cool room was
full of death and shadows and fear . . . there was no energy
burning in her blood. She would go out of here and go back to

them and thank Charles for the *comida* and go back to her house
and her work . . . Leave the miserable, despairing children to
cry . . .

But the chill stayed with her even when she was in the
sunlit patio, roughening her skin, making her teeth chatter. She
rubbed her elbows and hugged herself and looked at the sky and
saw the vulture wheeling there, lying on the wind, looking down,
and behind the bird and over the mountains was the dark cloud.
It would rain then, perhaps by tonight. It was not only the
thought of death which made her cold, but a subtle shift in
the wind.

Harry said to her, "You going home to work, Vick?"

She nodded and turned to Charles to thank him, but he was
groping to his feet, looking in a surprised way beyond her, and
she turned to see what it was.

It was Helen Rogers, coming briskly up the *zaguán*,
smiling, heading straight for them.

"The pot, man," Charles said without moving his mouth.
"Hey, Helen," he called out, trying to smile.

Harry crumpled the small butts of marijuana into powder,
shoved the powder into his pocket, pushed the torn matchbox,
which had held the roach, to one side under his hand. "Cool,
pops," he said, and slid that into another pocket.

"Hello," Helen said to them and dealt out three smiles,
like cards, one for Victoria, one for Harry, one for Charles.

Harry slouched to his feet and bowed, and his open shirt
hung loose in front of him, and he wrapped it coyly over himself, like a fat woman in a kimono.

Helen was carrying some stained, greasy-looking notebooks.
She set them down on the table and brushed her hands together.
She smiled again . . . one for you, one for you and one for you.
No one smiled back. Charles was waiting for an explanation of
her visit, and Victoria was staring at Helen, seeing her with
extraordinary clarity. She had never noticed before that
Helen's hair had a wispy, rusted-wire look to it, as though she
had brushed only the top straight strands and left the bird's-nest
snarl underneath. Her face powder, which was too white, like
the rice powder women wore at the turn of the century, was
casually dusted over a rather dirty neck and a pink-wrinkled
face. Her eyes were large and round, opened like an ingénue's,
and her relentless smile was in place. She always behaved in a

scrupulously genteel manner, as though her husband, Carl, were not a boor, and as though they both were landed gentry and had just stopped in at the tenant farmers' cottages with a charitable gift. She had become so accustomed to this behavior that she did it now, when Carl was not with her . . . She was intrepidly elegant. But no, you could see . . . this was a milk-weed flower of a woman who could be dismembered by a harsh wind, blown away in many parts and pieces, leaving no trace of herself.

Helen was talking to her. ". . . . would be nice if you went through these books of Jerry's, Miss Beacon, and chose something suitable for Charles to read at the burial . . ." She turned her head and aimed the smile at Charles. "You have a good voice for reading," she said. "Carl talked to the Consulate in Guadalajara, and I've talked to Dr. Obregón. Burial must be at four . . . eighteen hours after death in the tropics, you know. I've sent Freddie Sutton to the coffinmaker at Jocotepec. He'll be back in time with the . . . casket."

Nobody said anything, and she tapped her thumbnail against her teeth. She told them the Padre had said he was unable to conduct the funeral because he believed that Jerry was an atheist. She looked at Harry, her round eyes traveling up and down the swaying length of him. "Harry," she said very slowly, as she would speak to someone just learning English, "would you play something on the clarinet?"

"Play?" Harry said. "Play?"

She nodded briskly. "We need a prayer, a reading and music. Will you play music?"

"No, man," Harry mumbled, lurching down into his chair. "No, man."

"Miss Beacon, will you see to it that Ned attends? That would be a great help." She turned quickly, not waiting for an answer, gave a brisk clubwomanly wave of the hand, and walked through the sun-filled *corredor* in her hand-loomed sagging skirt. There she paused, looking back, her smile still in place. "The cars will be lined up at the Plaza at four," she said.

Then she was gone.

Charles said, "You see she has legs? You see those drumsticks on a square, civic-minded broad like that? You never think they *have* them, man."

Harry poured a drink and kept trying to button his shirt,

not noticing that the button was gone. "Jesus," he kept saying. "That was terrible, man. Jesus."

Victoria said, "It was hard for her. I think perhaps she is a nice woman."

Charles said, "Yeah. With a dirty neck."

Harry said, "A 'nice' woman." His voice changed and he talked like W. C. Fields. "A nice 'woman,' yapping like a spayed poodle, ready to maul you to death but genteel-like, you dig? Broads interpret everything . . . that's the difference between a male mind and a female mind. The broad interprets every-thing . . . that's what she calls thinking. A hand on the arm becomes . . . a tender gesture, a caress, the cruel grip of a tyrant . . . whatever suits the broad's neurotic need."

Charles frowned at him. He picked up one of the greasy notebooks Helen had brought and opened it. "A hand belongs to somebody, man," he said indifferently. "On the other end of the hand there's a person, like, and the way it grips you means something . . ."

"My hand on an arm is only a hand on an arm," Harry said. "'. . . a little touch of Harry in the night.'" He smiled at Charles. "Jeannette," he said softly, "will you marry me?"

Charles looked at him steadily. "Sniffing C brings out the fruit," he said.

Harry laughed.

They had become unintelligible. She took one of Jerry Ramsay's notebooks and began to look through it. It was en-titled *To the Hussies of History, A Volume of Verse.* She leafed through the pages, skimming, and learned that to Jerry Ramsay, perhaps because he was deaf and because alcohol stood like thick glass between him and reality, there were no divisions of time, past or present. Last year and fifty years ago and two hundred years ago flowed together into one time. He wrote of the eighteenth century in Paris, of historic quarrels among the literati and how those quarrels had affected him, reminisced his way into rooms which time had sealed against him, kissed lips which time, before he was born, had blanched white and pulled back from skeletal bone. He told of romantic duels he had fought for the favors of "masked" or "veiled" or "dimpled" ladies, rebuked Balzac and chided Proust as if they were erring classmates to whom he wrote in the first years after graduation.

She said, "Listen," and she read to ᴛhem where ɴe ʜad writ-

ten, "Huxley, F. Scott Fitzgerald, Michael Arlen, James Branch
Cabell, Honoré Balzac, Heine, Schiller, Goethe and the divine
Tolstoy . . . I knew them all. We were an illustrious company,
and I was one of those Glorious Boys . . ."

She lifted her head and looked at them, and her voice
came out hollow and now the cold gripped her; it was the cold
knowledge of death, and she was cold for Jerry. She said, "They
were his friends. That lonely, lonely man. Do you think of that?
How lonely one is . . . how bitterly alone, once a child, and
then young, and then abruptly deaf, lost in a maze of alcoholic
mirrors, the funhouse, you know, macabre, wandering through
the mirror maze seeking a friend, choosing such a company of
friends . . ."

"Yeah," Harry said. "I guess he was one wigged old cat."

"How old was he?" Charles said.

Harry said, "He was about fifty-five. He'd juiced so much
he seemed older . . . or maybe he didn't know any more. He
still had big eyes for chicks, but all he did was juice." His voice
sagged. "He's dead. He'd dead and my old man is alive. My old
man is fifty-five. Why doesn't he die?"

Charles said, "Ah, don't drag me, Harry . . ."

Harry said, "Why? You so high, sweetie, you don't want
me to bring you down talking about my old man? My old man is
a very interesting character who should be dead. He was born
in Chicago in a flat on a street with soot and snow coming down
outside, black and white rain, a million miles from Texas, but
if you saw him, you'd say he was a Texan. He's a self-made
Texan, and that ain't easy. Man, you should see him in one of
those big pearly white hats with the string band around it,
and his big red neck and his low-swinging belly and his pile
of sawbucks . . . Man, the loot that grows for him . . . the
world gushes gold for him, rebop! . . . you'd say, 'Look at that
mothering Texan.' You would!" He laughed unhappily. "In
school when they asked me what I wanted to be when I grew
up, I told them I wanted to be a disappointment to my old man."
He closed his eyes and his mouth drooped. "I made it," he said.

"I guess if Jerry was so wigged," Charles said to Victoria,
"there won't be anything in these I could read."

"Why not?" Harry said. "You think any of those studs
—Balzac or Fitzgerald or somebody—are going to be in the
cemetery and going to object?"

Charles shrugged, "It's wild jazz to read at a grave, isn't it?"

"Who the hell are you reading it for? Helen Rogers and
Biddy and Deetsy and the Prince and the rest of the righteous,
whiteous sepulchres, for Christ's sake? Or the old dead stud in
the grave? Don't you think old dead Jerry's got some rights?"

"No," Charles said. "And that's a fact, man. He's dead."

"I don't mean rights like can he still vote," Harry said. "I
mean, he wrote this crap. He's got a right to hear it."

"You know something, Jack?" Charles said angrily. "You're
always bugging everybody about death, you love death and
Baudelaire and all that funk . . . you're gonna die swinging
and why should you live, and you know something? You don't
believe in death." He shook his head. "Man," he said, "that
body's decomposing right this minute. *That's* death."

"So's yours and so's mine," Harry said.

"On you I can see it, junkie," Charles said.

Harry smiled. "That's right, hophead," he said.

"I'm clean." Charles had begun to shake. His eyes looked
blurred and he was moving toward Harry with his fists clench-
ing.

"Clean *now*," Harry said. "But sick, man, sick."

Victoria stood up and put her hand against Charles' chest
and pushed a little. "The man's dead, Charles," she said sharply.
"He's dead. It's his death you want to fight, not Harry."

He stopped and in a moment his shoulders sagged and he
breathed out. "Don't do that again, sweetheart," he said to her,
"unless you want to get knocked around."

Harry's voice was musing and tender. He was talking to
himself. "Death comes, *she* comes . . . I believe Death is a
woman. She loosens, *gently* loosens, the cartilage in the nose and
the knees and the ears and the joints . . . with a light touch,
like the brush of a bird's wing, like a petal floating off a breeze
. . . and a little dirt, the first little shower of moist dirt spills
down on the rigid, blue-frozen fingers . . ."

"Jesus!" Charles said. "You are going to bug me today."

She discovered as his voice rose that she was shaking. She
stacked the notebooks one on the other because now she must,
really *must* get away from them. They could drive you mad. They
could, with their bickering endless destructive talking, work like
worms in your blood until life muffled you about the mouth and
you began to smother because there was no air not filled with

words . . . They filled your brain with words . . . with worms.

"I'm going to Ned's," she said. "I'll see you at the Plaza . . ."

She walked quickly to the *zaguán* and when Charles said, "But what will I read?" she did not turn around but kept going, saying only, "I'll find something . . ." getting away down the *zaguán* and out into the street, holding the thought of lonely Jerry to herself, thinking steadily not of Harry and Charles but of Jerry, thinking if she could find a white plume for him, she would bring that to the grave instead of flowers . . .

At five minutes of four it was still hot. She walked briskly up the hill, ignoring the heat and the glare, to the Plaza. The sun beat down on the assembled metal of the cars lined up facing the road out of the village. A beer truck stood at the head of the procession, and a man wearing a white coverall, which said on the back of it, *"La Cerveza Mas Suave en Todo El Mundo"* in red letters, fussed with the tailgate. When she came nearer, she could see that, in the truck's platform, beer cases were stacked to one side and the coffin, new pine, with a spray of bougainvillaea and two bunches of wilting roses atop it, had been pushed into place on the other side.

Helen Rogers stood in front of her. "Is Ned coming?"

"No," Victoria said, giving no reason.

Helen said, "Then you will ride with Harry and Charles in the Delegado's car." She pointed delicately. "There."

"Thank you," Victoria said.

She had been going to tell her she wouldn't go, until she saw the beer truck. Now she could not refuse. She walked through the heat to the car.

Charles said, "How about that? The beer truck?"

Harry said, "The liquor company owes him a ride."

Jerry's maid, Carmen, no longer crying, but smiling and waving at her mother who stood proudly watching from the doorway of the House of the Bells, climbed eagerly into the cab of the truck.

The Delegado, Gordo, came over to his cab, touched his sombrero to her, shifted the toothpick in his mouth from one side to the other, so there was the flash of his gold teeth in the bright light. "Señora," he said. *"Qué triste, eh?"*

"Sí," she said.

He got into the driver's seat.

Charles said, "We should get in, I guess. Ned coming?"

"No," Victoria said.

"Not his kind of thing, old boy," Harry said to Charles.

They got into the car and the procession began to move slowly over the rough street. The church bells pealed out a string of flat notes. The truck just in front of them made a whining noise in second gear.

The beer truck emphasized the barbarism of this hypocrisy . . . She was, exactly as Ned had said, a fool to be here at all. "Of course I'm not going," he'd said. "I didn't know him. When I saw him on the street I avoided him. Why should I attend the burial of his body just because Helen Rogers—that Tennessee Williams faded flower—asks me to? Ridiculous! Don't try to tell me that old wino meant something to you . . ." "He was a writer," she'd said, her mind full of the curiously moving phrases she'd seen in his book. But as he continued to refuse, her decision to go lessened, and she realized that it was foolish of her, and worthless. But, when Ned closed his door on her and she stood alone in the hot street, the unbidden thought came to her that one day, if she didn't get out of Mexico, make a successful life for herself in writing again, she could be where Jerry was now, going unmourned into a foreign cemetery, unknown. Even so, to go for this reason was not to go for Jerry, and that was why she was going to tell Helen, until she saw the beer truck. Something about that . . .

Charles kept flipping the pages of a prayer book and clearing his throat, preparing to read. She gave him the obituary note she'd scrawled on the back of an envelope, and he read it, saying the words over softly to himself. Out of reverence to the occasion, Harry bent far out of sight of the other cars when he took a drink from the bottle of tequila he carried. His clarinet, in its case, lay across his knees.

Charles glared at him. "Jesus, man," he said. "I hate lushes."

"Jerry didn't," Harry said, wiping his mouth with the back of his hand. "Besides, I'm a troubled soul. Old Oedipus complex is rexing . . . traumatic wish for my father's death . . . All that."

"Ugh," Charles said. He wiped his streaming forehead with a clean handkerchief. " 'The Lord is my shepherd,' " Charles read in his radio-announcer voice. " 'I shall not want.' "

Harry said, suddenly chuckling, "Oh, Jerry wanted! Poor old bastard. He wanted. How about some of those lines of his? He wanted 'thy dovelike breast, thy lustrous eyes, thy evil heart . . .' "

"*Probecito viejo, verdad?*" Gordo said in a sad voice, hearing Harry laugh, and reminding them of the corpse, which bounced in new wood over the truck's floor as the flowers shook off it onto the roadway.

The cemetery was on a hill. The sun was on the side and, now, in the far south, massed dark clouds made a solid wall behind the blue mountains. The lake shone, small as an amethyst, between the spiked groves of the papaya trees. The sun on the grass and the moving wind playing silken over the green lent a reminiscently holiday feeling to the hill, and it was hard to remember, even among the gravestones, and before the open pit of earth, that this was not a company picnic, to which some of the employees had come in a company truck.

Four Mexicans lifted down the coffin and set it on the flat stones placed beside the grave. One of them lifted the lid and fastened it back. All the Americans except Victoria came forward, some of them reluctantly, when the Delegado beckoned, and when he looked at her again and motioned for her to come along, she shook her head and stared at the ground. Charles did not want to go, you could see that, but he went with the others finally, and dutifully filed past the coffin, looking down at Jerry's once pink, now gray face, and saw the white hair plumed into unusual order on the black satin cushion.

When Charles looked, he went pale and lifted his eyes in a shocked way at the others. It was hard to know what it was which was upsetting him. She had known that Jerry would be dressed as he was dressed on the street, in all of the clothes which the Mexicans were used to seeing him wear. Perhaps they'd put his black velvet-collared overcoat on him; they were honest, scrupulous people and they did not rob the dead. But the sight of that would be enough to sicken Charles. He looked as if he were nauseated, about to faint, passing his hand over his forehead like that. Maybe they had not put socks on Jerry and he was lying there in the overcoat and his double-breasted suit and he had his shoes on but no socks. They would not steal his coat, and they'd prove it by burying him in it, but they would not have bought socks to put on his white glistening ankles

. . . Yes, that could be it. No matter how they did it, no matter how careful they were, there was always some macabre note like that, which they would not notice and which would sicken an American. They are braver about death than we are, more callous. Also, they believed, accepting death as a part of life, that the more *típico* the corpse looked, no matter what his particular typical appearance was, the better the job they had done. Had he gone about the village in Bermuda shorts, they'd have buried him in those. In Oaxaca she had attended a funeral of a wealthy young man who had been seldom seen without a yo-yo to play with; his family put a silver one with the rosary in his clasped hands. Seeing it, recognizing it, she had almost laughed aloud. It was a shock, and she hid her laughter behind her shocked face, until suddenly she discovered that it had made her sick and that she was about to faint. It did not do, you know, to go and look where they pointed and told you to look; it was most unwise.

The Delegado nodded to Charles and he began to read aloud. His voice, faltering at first, grew stronger and more forceful, and listening to him you would have thought him a strong and learned man of forceful character. But then he had told her once he had been a radio announcer, and many radio announcers, who work only with their mouths, develop their speaking voices remarkably. Singers, too, if you really watched them over the years, seemed to develop strong jaws, an unnaturally widened smile . . . as though the lower part of the face did all the work; it was especially unfortunate in women singers, that hard line of the lean jaw jutting forward. Charles' voice moved on the warm wind, carried past the listening gravestones and the reverently bowed heads of the Mexicans. They understood death and reverence; they bent their heads to it.

She looked at the Americans; there were about twenty of them lined up together. How strange they were . . . all of them, including herself. Elinor Garth was crying a little, and that embarrassed Jackson, who did not hide his embarrassment but kept shooting annoyed glances at her. She was also a little flushed and slightly drunk . . . Maybe she had liked Jerry. Or he represented someone or something else to her . . . her father perhaps, or a lonely uncle, or herself. Biddy stood close to the grave, leaning on her cane, examining the hole in the earth, knowing one waited for her . . . Abel was beside her, but nervous, turning his narrow head this way and that, most often coming back to look at Lucy. Lucy stood near him, like a little girl at a school function, holding in her pale hands a bunch of dark green lemon leaves, ready to lay them against the headstone . . . Looking at Lucy, it was possible to think that this was the tomb of the Unknown Soldier, or Arbor Day. Lucy surely had no connection with Jerry, no more than Ned . . . than she . . . Carl Rogers bit hard on the stem of his pipe. You could see his yellow, unbrushed teeth, and hear him breathing. There were black hairs standing down stiff from his nostrils, giving him the look of a wild boar; he puffed the smoke out of himself in an angry way. He was an angry man, with welts on his arms, and beside him Helen wore her socialite smile, more adamantly refined than ever. The Mexicans and the Americans were apart, lined up on either side of the grave.

Deetsy stood between Clay Patton and the new woman in town, Margo Whitman. Deetsy kept whispering to Clay, and because he was so tall and she was so little, she pulled at him, until he bent his head to listen to her; his lowered head made him seem like a handsome, once wild, now broken, horse. Deetsy had said many times she thought Clay was "cute," when he was Annie's cavalier. Feeling suddenly glad it wasn't the admiral, that good man, being buried now, as it so easily could have been, she knew she was glaring at Clay Patton because he was not grieving for Annie. Clay found life comfortable with Deetsy. His face had filled out, gotten the fullness at the chin line which comes with good living, and the fine pinkish tan that comes with good drinking. Deetsy took care of him. "All you can eat, for a dollar and a quarter." That was the look he had, of a man passionlessly, stupidly, sated. Deetsy was a long way from being a beautiful girl with shining hair who thought you were a young god, but she was, by the American colony standards anyway, rich.

We are disgusting. All of us here, for our reasons. Jerry Ramsay had been an old bore, an old wino, a drifter, a scrounger, a bum who turned his autumnal lechery into bad poetry. And we who have come to attend his interment are failures who have come to watch the burial of one of our own kind, paying him mock respect to bribe similar respect for ourselves when the day comes . . . Failure had a long hand, it could reach past money and fame and effort and take its choice. It was failure which was being mourned here, by those who saw it coming toward them.

Not me, God damn it. Not me. I shall not fail as a human being, and be shoveled into the ground, spuriously mourned by wretches who never even knew me. If I died here . . . which one of these has known me? Not one. Each one of these has seen himself in me, nothing more . . . I renounce them, every one.

She bent over, pulled up the back strap of her shoe which had crept under her heel. Margo Whitman was watching her, staring directly at her. She met the look, saw the cat's eyes, large in the bright light, grow paler still and lighter, as though they had no pupils, no darkness anywhere, as though the mind behind the eyes was ice-white, glacial. Now Margo looked away and then went and stood beside Hanschen.

Hanschen did not look very drunk yet and he had carefully stayed apart from the Americans so that now he was next to Don Eliséo and the other members of the Junta, who had come to pay honor to the dead *gringo*. He turned his head when Margo Whitman stood beside him, not touching him but just standing there, small and slight. Obviously it was an effort for him not to move away; as it was, his body, slightly drunken, swayed away from her, as though he were saying, "I am not of these, not one of them. I am Mexican."

It was the first time she had seen Hanschen since his own near-death, and remembering that, and how he had looked then, pitiful and frightened with his head rolling on the pillow and the crimson line the rope had burned on his neck like a thyroidectomy scar—no, it was too high for that, well above the thyroid . . . but still a crescent as such scars are, like another, lower smile, more timid perhaps—remembering that, it seemed absurd that he should be alive now, and this old man dead. Perhaps he thought so, too, and that was why he had tried to align himself with the strength of the Junta.

Too late, my boy. The days of safety are gone forever. He had come too close to death ever to feel completely at home in life again, ever to be able to take life for granted, which was what living was. Or was it youth? Yes, it was youth. There was that; he looked older. But she did not feel sorry for him, really; she could not. To be utterly honest, the only thing she was sorry about was that she had seen him, that she had gone with Ned after the party to Hanschen's house, and been a witness to that ugliness.

She could begin earlier with her regrets; she had never wanted to go to Ned's party in the first place, and she had refused the invitation. But the day of the party Ned had sent a note of apology, ending with "Please come, Ned," and when she did not reply, sent another note saying, "I don't care if you come or not, you impossible girl, but the Old Poet will be here and Manuél and lots of people you'll like and I'm sorry I said bad things, Ned." They had had a ghastly fight the night before in which he had abruptly lost all control of himself and become cruel. She did not answer this note either, and then there came the final one saying that if she did not come he would never forgive her and never speak to her again, so that she had finally, helplessly laughed, and discovered that she could not remember, incredibly enough, what that fight had been about, except that, to prove a critical point he was making about her manuscript, he demanded that she listen to a recording of Edith Sitwell's *Façade*, which she hated and which he knew she hated. But she had been the one who was wrong; she had retrogressed to her old resentment of his criticism and at that moment her nerves were raw and even when she was serene she hated to listen to poetry being read by its authors; they weren't any good at *reading*, any of them, and besides it was a monstrous irrelevance at the moment and had nothing to do with her or her work. But he had meant well and the truth was that she had behaved like a bad child in a tantrum. She had screamed at him and he had screamed back. While the record played, they had gone into vituperation and villification so loud and so angry that Jovita had come crying into the room to interrupt them, saying she was frightened. The rest was a blur, a remembrance of fury turning the world red and hot, but there was no real memory of what specifically had given this reddened tint to everything. If she could not remember it, it seemed unnecessarily vindictive not to accept his invitation.

She had gone to the party. It was about to rain and the street was dark and cold under a rain cloud. At the door of Ned's house, there had been Hanschen, somewhat drunk, his blond hair blowing about his big pink face, playing the buffoon sentry, pestering the guests who were invited to the party. Before her, two young Mexican men bowed to him with cold formality, pointedly not speaking to him, and then they had gone in.

"You're invited?" he'd said to her, swaying toward her. "What do you do for him? What obscenity do you do for him? He would not invite you unless you served some purpose . . ."

There were many cars parked along the street and, from within, the sounds of a party, a decorous one. She said to Hanschen, "Don't bother me. Don't bore me."

Hanschen nodded solemnly. "Yes, he has told me I'm a bore," he said.

She knocked at the door and, for the first time, was struck with pity for him because he was a creature obsessed. She turned and looked at him. Self-pity gave him a wet, dropsical look, "Go home," she said. He laughed and rolled his reddened eyes at her. Jovita opened the door to her and she went in.

The beautiful living room was crowded. Ned welcomed her, kissed her hand and led her around to the guests. The Old Poet was sunk deep in the couch, with his loose silk jacket rumpling up around him and his pleated white Mexican shirt belling out like an accordion. His delicate hand with its ruby ring flashed fire as he gesticulated, and he extended the hand to her as though she might kiss the ring. He paid compliments to her writing, saying that he should rise in her presence but he was not well and she must excuse him; he had not long to live. "They worry about me so," he said, waving his hand to include the young men on either side of him. He introduced them to her and one rolled up his eyes in a girlish, pliant way and smiled, while the other scraped to his feet and gave two strictly polite Mexican bows.

Nothing Ned had ever said about Rudolfo prepared her for his extraordinary handsomeness. He was like a young god, an exquisite statue, beautiful in any time and any culture. The young god turned and fussed with the Old Poet, getting him comfortably arranged on the couch, smoothing his garments about him as though he were a great baby, while the Old Poet gazed up at his perfect face with gratitude and delight.

When she went to walk in the garden, Ned sent Manuél after her, to keep her company. She had admired his work, but now on first meeting, he was a disappointment, a dull young aristocrat. He walked beside her, talking, and she did not listen but watched the lilac shadows streaking into purple under the swaying, agitated trees. A storm was coming. The swallows, alerted by the coming gale, swooped in to their nests in the ceiling of the *zaguán* like line drawings, brief and bitter.

He was talking about Spain, saying he liked Spain as he liked his mother, with respect and fear. "It is relentless," he said. "Austere. Like my mother. I used to think my mother had no lap and when I was small I always wondered how it was that other children's mothers had laps they could scramble into and feel safe. I have read of soft-bosomed women whose eyes are moist and sympathetic. But my mother was not one of these. And Spain is not such a country either, but like her instead."

A gust of wind put an end to his declamation and they went inside. Ned asked her if she had liked him, and she told him that such talk as she had heard from Manuél was all very well for psychoanalysts perhaps, who could hear the word "mother" without being at the mercy of pitiless associations, but not for her. Ned had laughed at her and hugged her and told her she was a "package of confusion" and charming and that's what was so endearing about her and why it didn't matter what she wore, because she was unique and marvelous and that was what really mattered.

When Muffin came in, she watched her. Muffin was a floury-faced Englishwoman with sharp separated teeth meant for eating small-boned creatures like birds and mice; she had thin, small-curled hair with pink scalp showing beneath its ridged waves, sparse eyebrows of yellow and silver, full pale cheeks and a twelve-year-old, barrel-shaped body encased in a tight print dress. She was a widow, famous for her shortbreads and pastries, an amiable giggler whom everyone there seemed to enjoy. She drank enormously, and Ned had said that she had drunk her last husband to death; after he'd been forbidden by the doctors to drink anything, Muffin was always pouring a liberal jolt for Carter, with no visible qualm of conscience. Carter's purplish tint deepened with every drink until, like an overripe plum, he fell soggily from the branch of life and his life juices drained out of him. It was interesting to look at this female murderer and wonder that it had not been a double death. Muffin drank steadily until, with no preliminary, no staggering and no thickened speech, at a certain moment in any party, she simply stiffened out and fell over, backward or forward, it hardly seemed to matter. It was expected of her, forgiven and even maliciously enjoyed.

Victoria watched as Muffin's doughface lit up with simple-minded pleasure when Ned gave her a drink. It was a martini and she tossed it off like a straight shot and held out the glass for a refill. There was a smattering of laughter and somebody gave a half-hearted cheer, as though now, officially, this was a party. Experiencing a subtle wave of revulsion and the desire to dissociate herself from Muffin, she set her own drink down untouched.

The newest arrival in town, Margo Whitman, was being introduced to everyone. She was graceful, small-bodied, handsome in a bony way. Her face was a little like Katharine Hepburn's, and therefore beautiful, but not enough like it . . . There was not the shimmer of tears quick behind the eyes, nor the look of nervous, friable compassion. Her mouth was cruel and fish-like. She was chic and immaculately groomed, her dress elegantly simple, elegantly worn. Her sandals were made of fine strips of leather, binding small delicate golden feet, somehow Biblically attractive, so that you thought of a lover holding them in one hand. At the moment Victoria was thinking this, Margo's golden head turned and she looked directly at her. She was unsmiling, and her eyes, pale lavender, appeared, as she stared, to become steadily lighter. Involuntarily, with Margo's eyes on her, she stepped backward. What was this Fury doing here, masquerading in modern dress, pretending to be like other people?

Margo Whitman's voice was startling, a throaty whispering imitation of Katharine Hepburn's.

"What will you have to drink?" Ned said to her.

"Straight gin, please," the husky voice said. "No ice."

Manuél said to Victoria, "It is said that she is buying up the town, the Posada and many houses, quietly, making no announcement of the purchases. She is insane, I think."

". . . people always think I'm imitating Hepburn," Margo was saying, "when they first meet me. I have no choice. This is how I happen to look and sound. Did you ever think how dreadful it would be to turn out to look and sound like someone else?" She took a swallow of her drink. "Excellent *ginebra*," she said. "Looking like someone else used to make me want to

hide. But hiding takes money, and making money brings you
out of hiding, doesn't it?" She spoke rapidly, her voice hardening,
going quickly and freely from one thought to another, not ex-
pecting interruption. Everyone listened, there was a compulsion
to listen to that voice, with its husky grating insistence, its
broken-glass laughter. "Once I went on a hunting party at the
lodge of a very famous American family, comparable to the Du
Ponts or the Rockefellers in wealth. They were the kind of terribly rich people who go in for philanthropy and art-buying and
backing plays . . . That was why I went. I needed backing for
a play. They go around in dowdy clothes, mending their socks,
making the laundress patch sheets, making do in the New
England way, and the amount of money they have is unimaginable."

"What happened?" someone said. She had waited for the
question.

"They shot at me," she said, her pale eyes widening. "They
were trigger-happy . . ."

The room was hushed; everybody watched her.

"I came out of the lodge after breakfast," she said. "Breakfast was buffet . . . I was last downstairs and I ate alone. Then
I put on my jacket, I was going to take a walk in the forest. It
was a beautiful morning. The Adirondacks are wonderful in
the early fall. The minute I came out the door a shot was fired.
A bullet zinged past my head and hit the doorframe. I fell to the
ground and I distinctly heard someone laughing . . . a whispery laugh in the forest, with nothing maniacal about it, just
amusement. Whenever I tried to stand up, there was another
shot."

Muffin said, tittering, "My dear gel, did they kill you?"

Margo did not so much as glance at her. "I knocked at the
door but no one answered," she said. "Then I crawled on my
stomach along the ground, like a snake, and got into the cover
of the trees. Bullets followed me, tearing into leaves, ripping up
the ground. I dug a trench with my hands and pulled leaves over
myself and lay still until dark . . ."

Ned said, "You couldn't dig a trench with your hands . . ."

Margo smiled. "Desperation gave me strength, pet," she
said. "At dinner that night I told my story. Everyone affected
disbelief, naturally. The would-be murderer—or murderers—
I've never known whether it was one or all of them—suggested

that I wear a red hat next day as a protection. They insisted that someone had mistaken me for a deer." She laughed, the broken-glass laugh, without enjoyment. "They pretended to think it likely that a deer would be coming out the front door. Anyway, next day I wore a red hat and next day the bullets came closer. I buried the red hat in the forest and got back to the house and I did not go out again until the week end was over."

At that instant there was a rush of moist air at the windows and the drapes sucked outward with the draft. Lightning flared; thunder cracked, rocking the house. Rain slammed down in a torrent, beating like many hands upon the roof. The record player faltered, the lights dimmed as the sound dwindled, and the lights went out. The wind whistled at the corners of the house and Ned struck a match and lit the two crystal candelabra.

The talk began again; people turned to each other and Margo was left alone, smiling still, in the center of the stage, with no audience.

Victoria had pitied her momentarily but afterward she was sure that Margo had, with a madwoman's capacity to evoke an answering madness in others, plunged the pretty party into chaos. She might even have said something to Hanschen on her way in, which precipitated the subsequent episode with him. Who knew what she had said, and how Hanschen understood her?

Muffin had been for some time trying incompetently to mimic Deetsy's Southern accent and swaying walk, and suddenly Rudolfo jumped up as though inspired and said, "I'll show you Deetsy . . ."

He borrowed Muffin's lipstick and applied the purplish pink to his own chiseled lips. He took off his jacket, opened his shirt and dropped it over his shoulders, very décolleté, and wrapped Muffin's *rebozo* about his waist for a skirt. He leapt up and with a great deal of jiggling did a rather poor but certainly malicious imitation of Deetsy walking down the street. He looked extraordinarily like a girl. Muffin screamed with laughter, patting with a kerchief at her reddening throat; the poet's crowd tittered obediently, and Margo Whitman smiled and smiled. Rudolfo made his walk more broadly seductive, pausing from time to time to do a stripper's grind, and began a strip tease.

Victoria had not known until then what pinnacle of rage Ned could attain. He was gray-faced, and his eyes flashed. He ran to Rudolfo, grabbed him by the arm and rushed him out into the *zaguán*, seeming to fling him ahead of himself. The Old Poet's eyes glittered briefly, like a lizard's, but he said nothing. Manuél asked to be excused, saying, "Rudolfo can't help it, poor stupid; he's a transvestite. I'd better join them."

From that moment on, the party, which had been low-voiced, sibilantly rich with gossip, curdled and went wrong. Muffin pouted at the interruption to her fun, the Old Poet was soon plotting in whispers with two of his boys, and in the flickering candlelight she watched Margo Whitman watching it all, as though it were her handiwork. And so it was, in a mystical way, her doing. Madness was catching . . . just as anxiety was catching. If there was madness in you—and who did not have the seeds of it?—she called it forth.

Ned came back eventually with Rudolfo, the lipstick rubbed off his mouth and his clothes rearranged, looking ashamed and chastened. Ned was still coldly furious.

"I order you all out of my house!" he said, raging. "I've told you before. I will not have this grotesquerie under my roof. Get out!"

Confused, babbling to each other, the Old Poet acting like a rattly old schoolteacher, flapping his hands, saying, "Come along, chicks. Come along everybody . . . Too deadly this party . . . too deadly . . . Back to San Juan . . ." they began to rustle to their feet and look about them dazedly. Manuél chided Ned gently and Ned answered loudly, "I don't *care* if it's raining, for God's sake." Rudolfo, hearing this and looking Ned in the eye, deliberately nudged one of the crystal candlesticks to the floor where it rang out on the tile as it splintered and its candles' flames were killed. "Naughty boy," the Old Poet cried delightedly at him. "Come along. You need a good spanking . . ."

Frozen in rage, Ned watched them go. Muffin made the straggling group laugh in the *zaguán* when she said, "Good heavens, I'm leaving a party sober . . . I'm still standing!"

When everyone was gone and only Victoria and Manuél were left, it was astonishing to see Ned's eyes, a moment ago so cold with anger, fill with tears. He dashed his hand at them and said in a wretched voice, "I hate that . . . that disgusting case-history nonsense! It makes me sick. I've *told* them . . ."

He began picking up the pieces of crystal, brooding over

them. She and Manuél tried to console him but he was not to be
reasoned with; his anger rose and fell like a tide, breaking out
again just when he appeared to be slowing down, and Manuél,
obviously not enjoying this portion of the evening, announced
that he must get back to Guadalajara. Ned had let him go with
an indifferent wave of the hand, but he had held Victoria in the
house by gripping her shoulder very tightly, saying, "*Stay* here.
Don't leave me alone now . . ."

He talked continually, and kept drinking, and as he drank
and became more disordered, the sorrier for himself he became.
"That silly little faggot," he said. "How depressing! I hate that
camping. Screw the world! Everything goes wrong." When she
interrupted, his voice overrode hers. "Imagine a great talent like
the Old Poet going old and fat and befuddled, running a kingdom
of psychopathic hirelings . . . Never. Anything would be better than that. When you get ugly you should die."

Later, deeply depressed, he said, "I'm so alone. There is
no world in which I belong. I try to make a world. I am like the
chambered nautilus . . . and there is only room for one in my
shell of a world. So lonely! I'm always so lonely! Nobody belongs in my shell with me."

She had said, "You're wallowing in self-pity."

He got up and made another martini. "And liquor,"
he said. "Don't upbraid me. Just listen."

Finally she had stretched out on the couch in the studio
and, as his voice droned on, fell into a half-sleep, hearing words
but with years of silence passing between the words. He did not
notice. Afterward she realized she had not really been asleep but
that every word had creased its path like a bullet into her
brain, and some of it made sense and some of it was mad, and
Margo Whitman stood smiling and smiling there in her mind.

The commotion at the front door roused her and they went
together to answer it, thinking some of the party had come
back, drunk and belligerent, to beat on the front door and shout
Ned's name. But it was Hanschen's old father who stood there
with a group of Mexicans around him. Hanschen had tried to
hang himself. No, *Grüss Gott*, he was not dead. But possibly he
was dying.

"Get a doctor," Ned said furiously. "Why do you disturb
me?"

The old man's wide red face was wet with tears. The Mexicans pressed forward angrily, and the Delegado said, "Señor, one does not refuse the wish of a dying man, eh?"

"He's not dying," Ned said. "It's an act."

"*Gringos!*" the Delegado said and spat out the toothpick he'd been rolling about in his mouth.

Victoria had explained to Ned quickly that they were angry and unreasonable; he was in danger from them. "A mob," she said. "This is the beginning of a mob. He asked for you. You must go. I shall go with you."

They went, the two of them encircled by the Mexicans, just as the first fish-gray light of dawn rose in the east, as though they were being led to a firing squad. She felt that they walked to the sound of muffled drums.

Ned had his anger to sustain him but she would never forget the sight of Hanschen's bloated face on the dirty pillow and how he turned his great head and rolled his suffering, reproachful eyes on Ned and *apologized* for failing in his suicide attempt. Ned's face should have silenced him but it did not. He cried shamelessly, blubbering, reaching out to grasp Ned's hand. In front of Hanschen's father, and the Delegado in the doorway —who had had the courtesy to remove his hat and who, after a moment of watching Hanschen, put it back on and shrugged as though he was not now so certain as to the identity of the villain in this melodrama—Ned said in a cold choked voice, "It is a matter of indifference to me whether you hang or are cut down . . . if you live, if what you do on this earth can be called living, or if you die. You botched your death as you botch your life. I have no interest in you." He leaned forward, looking, for once, directly into Hanschen's face. "I have done you no harm," he said. "If you wish to do yourself harm, I don't care. I can say only . . . better luck next time."

He'd straightened up, turned on his heel and stared down the father and the Delegado. He took Victoria's arm and led her out of the room and the house, and the Mexican group which had escorted them there, now fell away one by one until, when they arrived at her door in the full sudden sunlight of early morning, they were alone. The streets, wet through the night, steamed in the abrupt heat. The world burning bright was something to be fled from, into the cool cave of her house.

There was no pity in Ned for Hanschen who was so abased that he apologized for being still alive. But no sympathy was

due a would-be suicide. Suicides were murderers . . . Hanschen had tried to kill himself as a way of killing the Ned who
lived in his mind.

She looked at Hanschen now, standing here at Jerry
Ramsay's grave . . . still alive. Life was the deal, the only deal
there was. Anyone who rejected it did a disservice to mankind.
Suicide was the only sin which could not be forgiven.

Charles closed the book and stepped back. Helen Rogers
nudged Harry, and he walked to the place at the head of the
grave, his step faltering and unsure, not looking at anybody. He
muttered to himself, bracing his legs wide apart so that he
wouldn't sway, and lifted his clarinet. The warm wind ruffled
his lank blond hair, blowing it back from his broad face, and he
closed his eyes behind their slipping, smeary glasses. As he
began to play, he became the one thing he could be naturally
—which gave him dignity, and which he was not very often
—a musician.

The song he played, "Here Lies Love," was not recognizable
as a song, but with reminiscent Bach phrasings, and Brahms
melodic lines, it became a theme of the loneliness of man,
compelling grief, evoking mourning, and the understanding that
a man was dead . . . a pitiful man was dead, and going down
into the earth, to be there forever in the dry seasons and the
rain, far from the place of his birth and the people who knew
his history, far from the world.

As Harry played, the Americans abruptly seemed more
alien in this place of death, more foreign to this moment. Perceptibly the Mexicans stirred, pulled a little farther away from
them, and the coffin was lowered.

Carl Rogers leaned forward, supervising the mechanical
activity with genuine interest. Elinor Garth let the tears run un-
restrainedly down her cheeks, gazing at Harry as though her
tears were for him . . .

In this moment, when Harry lowered the clarinet with the
coffin, so that at the end he was playing toward its closed lid,
sending grieving notes to Jerry through the dirt which fell,
heavily flung from a shovel, onto the new pine box, there was
a common rush of fear. People moved back, physically, from
the actuality of the interment, and it was necessary to force oneself to stand martially straight and hold off the thought of

one's own death . . . It did no good to think, to know that if
it were she, dead here and now, and going into Mexican
ground, with a jazz musician playing her requiem, and Charles,
the eternal stranger, reciting a Psalm over her, that she would
be tearlessly weeping in that box, pleading without voice for one
more little piece of time in which to live, be and create . . . It
did no good to know that. Knowing that made you suddenly
conscious of the grip of loneliness, made you want to run,
hysterically smiling, toward life, toward other people . . .
made you want to love them, and be loved by them, touched,
caressed, eased . . . no longer caring who they were, just so
they were warm animals, just so they could say your name and
admit that you lived by giving you a name and addressing you
. . . In such a moment, seeking life, you could think of Ramón
(because people died. Died!) forgetting what he was and had
been, and all that he had not been, and find it hard to remember
why you had left him, had run off to be alone in this village of
death . . .

They piled the flowers and Lucy's lemon leaves beside the
headstone. Forcing herself to go close to the new grave—they
were still shoveling earth upon the box—she stood still and
wished for Jerry Ramsay, not really in a prayer, but in a kind of
idiot restatement of what he had been trying to say, that he
would find now that timeless world he'd dreamed about, and
be welcomed by the Glorious Boys into the illustrious company
he had chosen for his own . . .

Dr. Obregón touched her elbow. "Señora," he said and
bowed, "may I drive you back to the village in my car?"

She looked at him and saw that the funeral party was
breaking up, turning away from the grave, guiltily, like people
defecting from a cause, straggling by twos and threes back to
the cars parked on the shoulder of the highway. The Mexicans
were politely somber, but several children who had been brought
along began to scamper and run on the soft grass of the grave-
yard. How well the trees grew here, how sweet the grass,
nourished by the human richness of the soil . . .

The farther the Americans moved from the grave, the
more briskly they walked. As though reminding themselves that
they were alive, they lifted their heads and looked about at the
dappling golden sunlight, the black chariot clouds rolling in from
the distant mountains, bringing the night's cold rain. They

talked, in low voices, their faces smoothing out, losing the anxiety which had been there before, so that they looked like people who had been to the doctor and found out that they were not seriously sick and would not die, and wasn't it, now, a magnificent thing to be alive, to be well? But it had been close . . . so they formed groups, the small groups joining others so there were large groups.

The Delegado came over to her. He nodded his head toward Harry, who was very drunk now and, even with Charles helping him, lurched as he walked, stumbled over hillocks and almost fell. "*Qué borracho, eh?*" the Delegado said, showing his gold teeth. He scratched himself and shook his head. "Little boys who play with toy soldiers should not drink," he said.

Dr. Obregón held his white sombrero in his hand and the moist breeze pushed at the silver swallow-wings of hair at his temples. "*Pues*, Gordito," he said. "Were you never drunk?"

"*Sí*," Gordo said instantly. "But a funeral?" He shrugged, let his hands drop. "It is a different *cosa, verdad?*"

The doctor ignored him, took her arm. "Come, señora," he said.

She went with him, because she did not want to embarrass him in front of the Delegado. But when she had gone a few steps, she paused and turned back and said to Gordo, "Harry is my friend, señor. You will take care of him?"

"*Pues, sí*," the Delegado said, as though nothing else would ever have occurred to him.

Willie and Sam Chester came along past her, and she realized they had been there, standing by the grave, but she had not really seen them. Partly because Sam did not look like herself in a dress instead of her usual leotards; the girl was spindlier than one remembered, more childlike in the clothing of a woman than in the playclothes of childhood. Willie's face was anxious and puffy.

She remembered one night Sam had done a dance around a burro in the street on the way home from a party. It was not a good dance—she lacked grace, her movements were twittery and jerky—but there was something in how she looked . . . the slim, long-haired girl in a leotard on the shabby, dark street, pale and pagan, dancing intently between crumbling, cracked façades, in and out of the moonlight . . . A bad dancer, but the dance was somehow memorable. It was her awkwardness which made it so. Sometimes skill vitiated intensity . . . a poem could be so skillfully written that you could not read it but swallowed it like flowing wine . . . sometimes clumsy art invoked reality.

The doctor drove rapidly, passing the other cars, feathering them with dust. She watched the grass and hills and trees go past, and wondered was he some kind of teen-age hot-rod driver at heart, showing off for her? But no, he drove this road so often, he was tired of it, and used to driving it in a hurry. There was something about the way he drove which reminded her of Ramón . . . and antagonized her. But he did not talk and she was grateful for that. This had been a day of many words, all of them trying to give the lie to death.

At her house he shut off the motor and turned to her. "May I come in?" he said.

She said, "No, Doctor. Forgive me. I must work, and then I go out."

"I have been thinking," he said, with difficulty. "I must talk to you, señora."

She said, "This is not the time." How like Ramón he was, really . . . stockier, a heavier-set man, but cut of the same cloth. "I have a headache," she said. "So I shall go into my house, if you will excuse me." When he did not speak, she put her hand on the door handle of the car. "*Con permiso*," she said.

He put his hand on her shoulder. "Look at me," he said. "Turn your head and look at me."

The sun shone warmly in the street around them, but there was a chill in the air. She jerked her shoulder from under his hand and opened the door. She did not want to look at him. But his hand cupped her chin, the fingers trembling hotly against her skin. He turned her head so that she faced him.

"I dare to touch you," he said.

His eyes blazed with a look of love and his dark skin was flushed with desire. His whole expression was of yearning and passion. "I am . . . like a crazy man," he said. "What am I to do?" He spoke in a desperate whisper. "I have never known such a feeling as this, never in my life. Now that it has come to me what it is, it is there all the time, day and night. I have no rest from it. It is impossible that I could feel so much and you feel nothing."

"*Eso es,*" she said. "I feel nothing."

"You lie to yourself, señora," he said.

"I do not," she said.

He held up his arms and looked at them. "They ache for you, do you know that?"

She shook her head. "I am sorry for you. I am sorry that your arms ache and you cannot rest, but I cannot feel what I cannot feel." She looked at him. "Must I say to you that you are a married man, Doctor?"

He groaned. "No, you need not remind me. Is Ned your lover?"

She opened the door of the car and began to get out.

"Please no," he said. "One minute. I didn't mean to say that. My jealousy of that *güero* maddens me. I say insane things. I insult you. But I am sick with love, you understand . . ."

She looked back at him, coldly, with annoyance. "I have heard enough," she said. "I am not in love with you and I shall never be in love with you. To me you are a bourgeois, a middle-aged married man with children, who lives in the small worlds of two Mexican villages. You do not attract me."

She got out of the car, closed the door smartly and went into her house without looking back.

After a while she heard his car start and roll heavily down the hill. She had told him the truth. The truth was alleged to set you free.

It was the village, living here. The life drained off all your patience and courtesy, and you had to be cruel.

She set her purse down on the leather tabletop. There was no nice way to say no, after all. No kind way. She would bathe and change her clothes and go to see Ned, be with him now in the serenity of his house, restored, a compensation for the ravages of the day. She would bring the pages she had finished and they would go over them together, if he was in the mood. They were good pages; he would like them.

She went to the typing stand and picked up the last pages and began to read them. They were very good, they really were.

She thought about Jerry Ramsay. The sun was going down; it would be night in the cemetery, his first night there, and it would be cold . . . just as cold if she thought about

him as if she did not. She must hurry now. Ned liked her to be on
time for supper. He was making a *quiche lorraine*. Thinking of
that, and remembering how little she had eaten at the *comida*
in Charles' house, she hurried to the bathroom and lit the
calentador. After a funeral, one needed hot water and warmth
and life.

13

Ned

AFTER A WHILE Ned realized that the energy
with which he was working so tirelessly was anger. It made him
clumsy, which probably wouldn't matter as far as crating the
paintings was concerned—it was hardly delicate work—but
he didn't want to damage his hands, they must be steady and
strong to paint. He lifted them, looked at them. They were shaking.

He lit a cigarette and went to the window and looked out at
the afternoon in the patio. It was December; the sun shone
brilliantly; the air was crisp and clear. It would be colder in
Mexico City. In New York, by the time he got there, it would be
freezing and there would probably be snow. It had been a long

time since he had seen snow. The memory of the squeaking
sound of snow underfoot made him smile with pleasure.

Why should he be angry? He was escaping something
which had turned ugly, getting away in time with no harm done
him, and the future promised nothing but good fortune. The
show he was to have in Mexico City, according to the advance publicity—which was, for once, well-handled—should
provide him with considerable money and attention; his subsequent show in New York would add to his prestige. Everything
was going fine.

After New York, there would be Paris again and the south
of France, and the Lido—why did everybody underestimate the
Lido?—and then Spain, and finally the villa he had arranged for
in Italy. The Italian town had an unlikely name and might not
yet be a tourist haven. Nonsense, the whole world was a tourist
haven.

He rubbed out his cigarette and went back to crating the
paintings. The one of the birds was next; he began to place
layers of corrugated paper in the box, looking at the One Bird,
the one most vivid of all . . . The Bird was all blues . . .
what he thought of as "medical" blues, with a lot of ugly damp
brown in them and cold gray going into muddy green, which
many doctors fancied and put in their offices. Perhaps they
supposed that such blues summoned peace, evoked serenity.
He smiled; this bird, this medically blue bird, was his answer to
the fumblers in the hospital; in particular, it was his answer
to the young doctor who—in bad clothing, sharp-eyed behind
glasses, knowing nothing, aside from his one studied memorized
science—had dared to tell him that he was not yet "well"
enough to be discharged from the institution. That doctor's
office had blue drapes of just this color, and a blue couch which
was even worse. He hadn't been able to force himself to paint
the bad blue of the couch, for any caustic reason of satire, because he could not have endured looking at it. The blue of the
couch was also the blue of the doctor's necktie, lumped thickly
beneath his larynx in a vulgar and obtrusive Windsor knot. The
blues had been compounded.

"God is everywhere," he said to the blue medical bird,
now half hidden in layers of excelsior. "You must not feel sad.
Every bluebird need not be the bluebird of happiness." Then he
pushed more excelsior over its blank, blue-black eye, its

machine-perfect blue body, stood over the crate and, although
the bird was now hidden, still saw in his mind the shiny eye, the
pale blue beak.

It was hard to go. Perhaps that was the root of his anger.
It was hard to sell the house—the almost perfect house—to
Margo Whitman, to listen calmly when she told him how she was
going to fix it for sale to American tourists. She would screen in
the dining room because tourists were afraid of flies around
food. Hideous! And imagine painting the walls of his living
room pink! This was to make it look cozy, she said. Who could
have guessed that she, who always looked so chic, would turn
out to have this macabre, nursery sort of mind? Of course,
in another way, she was a Medea who might just as easily
splash a bit of blood on the walls here and there to give the
place a "touch of color". . . But once he was gone, never to
come back, what difference could it make to him what color she
painted the walls? He'd remember the house as he had made it
and he'd have her money . . . as exchangeable as the money
of a saner, kinder, more tasteful woman; with that money he
could buy escape from this dreadful town, travel, find another
world in which he could live . . .

The village was impossible. He was tired of everything
. . . Manuél, whose liquid Spanish ran on and on saying as
little as a brook babbling over stones . . . Rudolfo . . . Maybe
in Mexico City he'd see Chloë and take her with him on part
of his journey. Her last letter had been desperate. It was time
again to play with silly Chloë . . . She could make him laugh.
But what had been here before in the village was now intolerable, and what was beginning to happen was going to be more
intolerable than that.

The signs had been there from the moment he came back
this time. His illness, with that incompetent Dr. Obregón
irresponsibly letting it drag on, and Victoria staying in the
house, hanging around to sponge up all she could of his food,
liquor, cigarettes and information, and beginning to look at him
with that soulful, and therefore alarming, soft expression . . .
She'd become all hungry eyes, all thirst and demand, ready to
devour him, soul and mind. Wouldn't you think she'd have
more sense? A woman of her experience . . . Those messy
things she wrote . . . the pages and pages he'd read, all of
them too strident, bold, emotional, *unseemly* . . . There was

no tracery in them, no pale blood tinting the thick bones, no tiny blue veins, no ivory of skin . . .

If other things had made it worthwhile, he might have continued to reason with her, help her with her writing; but other things had not made it worthwhile. Other things had gone wrong, instead . . . the Old Poet was angry and would never forgive the affront of having been thrown out of the house. That could be fixed only by his giving another party to make it up to him. But he could not do that; he could not endure the thought of one more of those harrowing, disgusting textbook episodes where men dressed up like girls and pranced around like living case histories. He knew quite well if he saw that again he would go berserk. He had come close last time . . . because it was Rudolfo. El Chiquito was too beautiful to perform like a burlesque queen for the laughter of cretins like Muffin and madwomen like Margo. Oh, there was no doubt that Margo was mad; you didn't need an M.D. when you looked into those wasteland eyes of hers, or heard the paranoid fantasies she talked, to know that she was mad; the way your hair rose on your scalp told you; the chill on your skin gave you an incontrovertible diagnosis.

Anyway with Manuél becoming an out-and-out bore, and the Old Poet's crowd lost to him, what was left? Hanschen? Since his buffoon suicide attempt, Hanschen spent his days trying to make friends with all the newcomers to the village, doing unasked favors for them in order to tell them his story about Ned. There was no mark of the abortive hanging upon him, except in his eyes, which looked as though finally they had seen where he was going, and seen that there was no other place for him to go. He cadged drinks, gave up painting, complained of mysterious ailments, which, by implication at least, he attributed to what he called "Ned's attempt to murder me." He expounded, to everyone who would listen, his theory that in some occult way Ned had hypnotized him into trying to kill himself.

Hanschen wandered around, telling people that it was Ned who had made a homosexual of him, babbling about how he had loved girls before that, and even once been married. Ned had stolen his manhood, his parents' little bit of property, and his honor. Worst of all, he had stolen his talent so that now when he went to paint, his hand stiffened and his brain emptied. He was convinced, he said with great satisfaction, that he had been bewitched.

It was disgusting, and it was going to be more disgusting before it was done. Hanschen had never been married, in the memory of anyone in the village. He told a thousand lies, and explained these with a thousand more. Ned had not "made a homosexual" of him, if such a thing could be possible, which it could not; Hanschen had never been interesting to him in that way; perhaps *there* lay the cause of these fetid bleatings upon the clear clean air. There had been no feeling between them, no touching, no contact more intimate than that with the grocer or the fellow student . . . Ned had not stolen his damned land; he'd bought what was offered for sale, received the deed to the property in good faith, and he was not any longer, although no one knew that yet, even the owner of that property; he had sold the corner lot, with Abel's Bar on it, to Margo Whitman. The land he'd bought from the Old Poet was paid for, and there were papers to prove that transaction, too . . . But, sighing, he decided that the worst of all the accusations was the one that he might have thought Hanschen's paintings or talent worth stealing. It was a mercy to the world of art that Hanschen's hand would no more pick up brush and smear canvas; however, it was not, in any sense, his doing. But something was achieved by the sheer volume and frequency of these allegations; people who neither knew nor cared to know the facts dismissed most of what Hanschen said, but still when newcomers met Ned at a party or on the street, they said to each other, with nudges and whispers, "That's the one."

Not that he cared. It was an added unpleasantness, another straw on the huge load of straw on his back, enough to make him happy to leave the area in which such a one as Hanschen could function and, however slightly, succeed. Aside from that, Hanschen was deteriorating rapidly, stealing, drinking an incredible amount, getting into fights in which the other man could only pinion his arms to keep him from hurting himself; one could see that sooner or later one of these eruptions would take him into court; he'd be charged, and he would certainly countercharge with some accusation about Ned, and then it would be very difficult to get away from here, because the Mexican government ground slowly, and inaccurately, in these matters involving foreigners who owned property. It was quite possible that although he was innocent, Ned would find himself smeared over the front page of *El Sol,* and very much poorer financially.

Almost every day he had to turn away a *mozo* who brought
a gift from Hanschen . . . today seven white roses. The illiterate note accompanying the gift hinted cryptically at some mystical insult. Ned sent no reply, only refused the roses. At other
times the gifts were, if less mystical, more openly hostile or
phallic . . . a knife, one day . . . a length of rope with its
end shaped into a noose, and a note saying "It's your turn,
Freund."

Aside from Hanschen, the town itself was becoming different, peculiarly frightening. He tried, as always, to shut it
away, but he had been finding it harder and harder to do that
lately. There were more and more hoodlums coming here all the
time—hipsters, people called them—vandals who roamed the
streets, without possessions, without manners, bums. They
grinned at him with evil eyes. He did not imagine it. He had
seen it, time and again. And Harry, that miserable vagrant,
was more openly bellicose each time he had the misfortune to
meet him.

Victoria stubbornly defended these creatures, saying stupidly, "Oh they're just lost boys! Have you no compassion?"

He had none at all.

Victoria, who was one of the main reasons he must go,
was also one of the hardest things to leave. Except that in the
long run it would be a favor to her if he did go now. If she'd
gone on with her own life as it was before, just seeing him now
and then, giving him something and not merely taking and
draining the life out of him . . . But she hadn't. She'd become a vampire, playing the ingénue, always looking up at him
trustfully, handing him her sheafs of messy, ill-written pages
. . . No, he wasn't being fair. They weren't ill-written; they
were . . . heavily muscled, that was it. But now that he had
taught her restraint, worked with her on the first three chapters
so they were now something they had not been before—pale,
quiet prose with its vigor controlled, a little like, he really
thought, Elizabeth Bowen—what more could he do? Discipline
was what she'd needed all her life, imposed from without, since
she could not impose it from within. She needed to put aside
the violent emotionalisms of her Slavic nature and use self-
control and reason instead. But now she had learned that lesson; certainly he was tired of teaching it. The chapters were
rewritten, sent off to the agent, and now Ned was tired of her.

He was tired of her face, of her gamin laugh—all of her—her
dreadful clothes, her unworldly mind, her self-deceptions. He
was weary of seeing her come in the door, of looking at her
across a table or over a martini . . . weary of the words she
used . . . *enchanting, artless, sim-plic-i-ty,* as though she'd
made them up herself. He wished she would not come to see
him with carbon stains on her fingers, and he wished she
would not play the pupil sitting at the master's feet, saying, yes,
yes, go on . . . no, no, tell me all of it, begin at the beginning.
Did she never want him to shut up? To begin at the end? Must
she swallow him alive?

She endowed him with godlike proportions; she was one
of the small ragged army of camp followers which wanders the
earth not knowing what it wears or eats or thinks, looking for
God. She met him and thought she had found, if not God, then
one of God's own teachers. It wasn't, he supposed, anything so
foolish as love. But it could be a kind of love. This was another
reason he must go. He did not want to have to hurt her, and
yet he could not be to her what she would eventually want him
to be, if she did not already want that very thing. And he did not
want to go through the painful experience of explaining himself, to her and to himself; the truth was he could not be to
anyone what was wanted; something had been ground out of
him very early in life. Beyond a certain limit, he could not go.
In a way, Hanschen's pursuit of him, his wild, witless, primitive accusation was true. It was impossible to deny responsibility, to answer the charge; the answer was only: Don't love me,
then.

It did not matter to him nor to the gods, who lay in pagan
comfort eating purple grapes on an Olympian hill, if Hanschen
suffered, or if one day he actually did take his own life. But
Hanschen represented an entire force of people, of whom Victoria was one, who followed after him, denouncing him because he could not love them. How many times must he hear
. . . "You're not human! You love only yourself!"

He stood utterly still, listening to the suddenly loud cicadas
in the trees, the murmurings of the village, the waves of the
distant lake. It was tragic, he supposed, although he really
wasn't sure what the lack of love meant, but he could not love.
Love was an absurdity anyway. But life without love, without
that capacity for feeling, was like living on a series of shallow

porcelain planes, in which desire for conquest was the highest
emotional achievement of which he was capable. Hanschen,
slobbering drunken fool that he was, probably could not love
either and mistook his *idée fixe* for love; that must be a comfort,
but such miscalculations were not tenable for him. He had never
imagined himself in love with Rudolfo for example; that was
just a stupid pretty boy to be had, to be enjoyed, to be cast
aside. Chloë . . . would always be too much a child to know
that sensuality was not love, and pleasure not love. He was different; pleasure and sensuality might be all he got and gave,
but he did not delude himself that these together added up to a
third thing called "love."

He felt guilt toward Hanschen . . . not for the crimes
Hanschen ascribed to him, but because he had only used him
and given him nothing in return; Manuél, too, in his European
false cynicism, nonetheless dreamed out of his eyes at him . . .
waited for love, striving for it as silently and quietly as he
could . . . Seeing this, he had an impulse to yell at Manuél,
"It's gone as far as it can go!" as though he were talking of a
train which could climb no higher than it had. Manuél did not
demand . . . he merely put himself in a position where, at
some fortuitous time, Ned might show genuine affection for
him. But being unwilling to pretend to a fraudulent depth of
feeling, he had been forced to appear insensitive to Manuél's
mute appeal, and that was wearisome.

He flung himself down on the couch. He was not so much
angry, really, as depressed . . . Didn't he always get depressed
when it was time to give up one life and start another? Of
course. Because he knew, quite well, that the new life, like the
old, must end on a series of light shining porcelain planes . . .

The world was shrinking around him, becoming uglier all
the time, its corners crowded with infantile hoodlums, who
soiled the earth by their existence upon it. The whole colony
here, the foreigners, the scum which floated down the continent
to snag against the last rock of Mexico and remain, stagnating
in pools, until at last the odor of their decay was a stench in
the nostrils . . . were they everywhere? Was this what life
was, now? How was he to live beside this corruption forever?

He should have been a priest . . . There was cleanliness,
order, and even in a strange medieval way, sensualism in the
ascetic life . . . But he had no faith. No matter. Did Richelieu

have faith? Could one not possibly be a better priest without
faith than with it? He closed his eyes on the peaceful vision of
a monk's immaculate cell . . . Strains of Mozart and sunlight
streamed into the narrow room, blessing his tonsured head . . .

He could tell Victoria that he had that in mind, that he
had found his "vocation," and it would, if he told it to her cor-
rectly, fill her with awe. She would release him . . . bowing
to a higher claim. But why should he lie? Let her fall, let her
crash; what right had she to demand sustenance from him? She
should have known that he had already given her all he could
give, and that she was now to him a bore, a gadfly, a tick working in his skin. He took his hand from his eyes and let the light
daze him a little. "I'm sick of her," he said.

She imagined herself to be a bottomless well of feeling.
Maybe she could be persuaded to go back to her Mexican husband? Or perhaps a little push would shove her into the short,
sturdy arms of Dr. Obregón? No, she must just be left, coldly,
abruptly . . . dropped back into the confusion from which he
had lifted her when he found her.

But she had saved his life. (Nonsense, she saved her own
. . . which is all that sacrifice was, if you analyzed it.) She had
come to him openly with her offerings, her pages, her thinking,
her feeling, her clumsy, child-awkward honesty. Maybe she
would be better for him, in the long run, than selfish Chloë?
No, no. Probably he would not have Chloë either; he'd be alone,
as he always had been. There had been interim periods of com-
panionship in his life, but these were not by any means the
fabric of his living. He'd known very early that he was alone in a
peculiar way; he had not fought it. It might have been possible
for him to have lived an ordinary life, stayed in Dakota or its
equivalent—Ugh!—fought down whatever homosexual im-
pulses appeared, which was what most men did, or else indulged
them furtively behind the cloak of heterosexuality. He need not
have followed his soul, as Victoria would put it, wherever it led
him, into madness and out of madness and then into the clutch
of idiots Mexico had turned out to be. But he had chosen when
he was young; he had turned his back on the ordinary and
pursued the chimera of beauty. However, admittedly, it was
more than beauty he pursued now. He burned with ambition; he
wanted to carve his name into the world as the few great ones
had done. Let lesser men love each other . . . he would paint.

This restatement of values did not now relieve his tension; he was still disturbed over Abel's visit this morning. That was when the tremor and the anger had begun. When Jovita said, "*El Negrito, señor*," he'd sent her back out into the *zaguán* with the message that he had no business to discuss with him unless Abel had come to pay him the rent money he owed. But Jovita then stood stock-still, twisting her apron in her hands, not refusing to go, but just not doing it. "What good are you to me?" he'd said to her, and she'd shaken her head. "*Pues*, no good, señor." And then she'd asked him, please, it was a very hard thing for her to have to say . . . She liked Abel, and he did not owe *her* any money—how could she say a hard thing? —and again she would not move.

One had no choice with these servants . . . one worked for them, damn it . . . only the deluded could imagine otherwise. Coming along the *zaguán* to meet Abel, he'd begun to limp, the way he did sometimes going toward someone he did not want to see, or toward a moment he did not want to experience. Abel had remarked on the limp immediately, but he'd brushed the question aside as being too personal and unimportant to answer. Abel did not look well. His skin had an unhealthy sheen to it and his eye whites were deep yellow and clouded. Even the black irises seemed clouded over. He saw this in Abel but he ignored it. He flatly put the question to him about the back rent for the bar, without preliminary.

"I'm hard up for loot, man," Abel had said. "I haven't been making much in the bar, and the Mexicans have increased the bite. I'm going to get the money. I just . . . haven't got it yet."

"None of it?"

"No, man."

"Then why do you come to see me, Abel? You've owed me a lot of money for a long time . . ."

Abel's head went back in a tic, as though it had been jerked, as though he'd felt a short rein pull up for the first time, and then his face got a blurred look, uneven, bewildered . . . He said, "Things aren't the way they seem, Ned," in a soft voice.

Ned said, "Oh, but they are. They are just exactly the way they seem."

The eyes flicked fast from one side to the other, and Abel seemed abruptly taller, moving toward him, noiselessly as a cat. "Margo Whitman now," Abel said in a tight, soft voice, "she's

going around telling everybody that you sold her the bar, and
she's going to take it over . . . The Kraut says it's true, too,
but Hanschen don't ever tell the truth. But this time, it sounded
like true, Ned, you know? Now you tell me what seems true is
true." He stood very still, staring at him out of cloudy eyes. "I
want to know," he said. "You don't be a bastard now, Ned. You
hip me to what's happening. Truth won't hurt you to tell. But
it's going to hurt me *not* to hear it. You level with me, Jack."

He spoke quietly, but the way he stood, light, lithe, head
pulling down so his jaw was tucked in . . . shoulders tightening . . . was a fighter's stance . . . quite beautiful in its way
. . . but possibly a killer's stance. Ned could not tell this killer
the truth. So he'd lied. Who would not lie? He'd said that certainly he had *not* sold the bar to Margo, and that he would have
told Abel if he had. He said he wasn't a businessman, he was a
painter. He said he needed the money . . . he wouldn't need
it if he had sold the bar, would he?

Abel had stepped back then, his body relaxing. He said he
had a headache. He said his headache was bad and he needed
to rest. He put his head in his hands and groaned.

Abel had gone soon after, giving a big wave of his hand,
shouting good-bye to Jovita in the kitchen.

Then, when he was alone, Ned had felt the cold perspiration start out on his forehead, and he'd gone into the studio and
lain down. Better to lie and live, to escape, to get out of this
crazy place. He had a right to sell his property if he wished, and
he wished, and to tell only whom he chose to tell. But life in the
village was intertwined with other lives; he was enmeshed in
those strands too, enmeshed but alone.

He took off his glasses and put his arm over his eyes. It was
as though his soul had many shells around it and that, unper-
ceived by him, they had cracked one by one, so that now he had
no protection and his soul was exposed, blinking on a bright
day. In spite of all he did to make life beautiful and secure, it
was a hopeless affair. He felt sorry for himself; no matter how
hard he tried, or where he went, or what he did or said or
painted, life was a joyless march toward the insipidities of old
age. If only he were not what he was! If only he could be totally
different, one of the smilers, one of the easy ones . . .

He thought about the fact that he was crying for himself,
grieving for himself. Why not? Wasn't it bitter to know that no

one else would ever weep for him? Only he would ever know that life was and would be an imitation, a facsimile, for him. The truth was, that under his helping Victoria to live, there had been a deep hope that she, of all people, might be able to help him. Now he no longer had that hope.

Margo Whitman sat lightly on the bench at his worktable and watched him sealing up the crated paintings and address-ing them. She seemed like a small thin cat, not so much to be sitting on the chair, but to have paused there, weightlessly, dis-turbing nothing.

She said, "Why do you address them if you're taking them with you, pet?"

Ned glanced at her. "Haven't you ever traveled on a Mexi-can train? You know how easily they could be lost."

She smiled, but not with humor. "I've traveled a good deal on trains. But I usually take a *mozo* with me and I won't let the porters touch my things. Do you have a compartment?"

"Yes," Ned said. He looked at her again. The white shark-skin dress she wore, a simple sheath, was immaculate, whiter than one could imagine white, and the skin of her bare arms and legs was golden against its light. Her delicate white sandals moved on the tile floor, but soundlessly. She was in every way very light and still. He knew that she watched him take inven-tory of her; it was her eyes which were frightening; the rest of her was small, compact, delicate as a feather. "You look very nice today," he said. When she made no answer, he added, "Abel was here. Please don't say any more to him about having bought the property from me. I'm still trying to get the back rent he owes me . . . I won't get it if he knows I've sold it to you."

"You surprise me," she said huskily. "What optimism!" She smiled again, humorlessly. "You'll never get the rent he owes you. Don't you know that? I know it, and I've known him only a short time; which is why, of course, I won't have him running the bar at all."

He looked at her. "That's Abel's sole source of income," he said.

She shrugged. "Then he'll have to get another. He shouldn't be here anyway if he's that improvident, don't you agree? I sup-pose he'll have to be sent back to the States."

"Off with his head," he said musingly. Conversation with
Margo took on this Alice-in-Wonderland quality. She said ap-
palling things tonelessly, like a poor actress, giving no conviction to the lines. It was difficult not to stare at her. His eyes
returned to the sight of her again and again, as though if he
did not look at her often, he could not believe in her at all.

She stretched her slim arms, flexing the thin fingers like
claws. He had heard of many pieces of property she had bought,
not only the bar and his house and the Posada, but countless
other houses and a couple of grocery stores. He wondered if
she knew that she had made an amusing mistake renaming the
Posada? She called it La Casa Margo, or Margo's House. The
Mexicans had made a pun of it; they called it La Casa Amargo
among themselves, which meant The Bitter House. The Mexicans did not like her; they feared her and made ironic jokes behind her back. The bitter house . . . they expected no good
will from her apparently, and planned to extend none to her.
She sat there twisting a strand of her blond hair.

He said, "I didn't like having Abel call on me this morning
all worked up into a state of frenzy. And this afternoon Jovita
asked me if it were true that I had sold my house to you. I don't
want this gossip going around."

"What difference does it make?"

"I told you it was no deal unless it was kept secret. I don't
want to go through scenes and reproaches."

She looked at him. "You've probably told people yourself.
Victoria, for instance."

"No," he said. "I don't want her to know."

"All right," she said. She yawned. It was not unattractive;
she stretched a little, gracefully, like a cat. "I couldn't sleep last
night," she said. "I was up at three-thirty in the morning
wrapped in a *serape*, sitting on my veranda awaiting the dawn."
Her face brightened, going a little pink with excitement. "I must
tell you what I'm doing about the Embezzler," she said.

"Doing *about* him?" he said.

"I have reported him. He'll be deported in a day or so. My
attorney is probably the only lawyer in Mexico who can make
the Federales hurry. They'll take him to the Texas border and
by then I'll have the American officials at customs informed
that he belongs in an American maximum security prison." She
smiled again, placidly. "What *are* you staring at, pet?" she said.

"You," he answered. "You mean the Embezzler really *is* an embezzler?"

"But of course," she said. "And there's some question of defrauding through the mails, too, you know. It was fortunate that I kept the letters he mailed to me in the States, making such fabulous promises about my stay at the Posada. It's a Federal offense, defrauding through the mails. Then there's Lola—his shall-we-say *secretary*?—the Mexicans are willing to deport him on grounds of contributing to the delinquency of a minor." She shrugged and sighed and gave him a clear cold look of innocence.

He said, "I don't believe in you. You're not real. I never really believed he was an embezzler either . . ."

She laughed, the broken-glass laugh. "Nobody's here without a reason. What's yours, love?"

"What's *yours*?" he said, without smiling.

"This place needs me," she said. "I intend to turn it into a gold mine. Tourists will be breaking records to get here . . . Ned, there's nobody in this whole town able to *do* anything, except you." She flicked a quick finger at the crates of paintings. "All you care about are those daubs of yours . . . and Rudolfo, I presume. A terribly handsome boy. I must say I can't blame you. Does he ever show any interest in girls? Or are you taking him with you?"

Now he smiled, very carefully. "So many questions," he said in a gently chiding way. "Come along into the bedroom while I pack my things. Would you like a gin and soda?"

She said, "Yes. Gin. Straight gin, please. And I shall come into your bedroom with you."

The flat way she answered him made him uneasy. He said, "*Just* while I pack."

She laughed. "I'm not interested in you that way. I'll leave that to Victoria."

"She writes marvelously, you know," he said.

In the bedroom, he set up his various suitcases and trunks. She lounged in the chair under the window, sipping her gin and watching him. She did not remark on the painting, the one Victoria called The Icicle, but when she glanced at it, he remembered that he had promised to give it to Victoria. As he moved from closet to luggage rack, he felt more and more a curious sense of complicity. He felt like a conspirator against

Abel and the Embezzler, as though by having sold his property
to Margo, he had helped her seize the town. But that was absurd. Her buying the Posada—oh, Bitter House indeed—had
nothing to do with him. Selling her the bar and the house
. . . yes, he could be charged with these crimes, and the
thought of Abel fighting her made him feel oddly sick, as though
it mattered to him that Abel was doomed to lose . . . Nonetheless, as she had said, Abel was improvident.

That was different. Abel was an artist of talent whose feeling for art was right and whose drive to paint might propel him
into superb achievement one day. After all, Abel was a fellow
artist. The Embezzler meant nothing to him . . . here or in
the States; he had no reality, no humanity actually . . . Who
cared if he lived, died, got imprisoned, deported . . . he was
not an artist. But how far did his responsibility toward Abel go,
anyway? Was it up to him to support any talented but improvident painter who came along? Ridiculous. He was free to sell
his property to anyone he chose . . .

It would have helped if she were not quite so ruthless.
She was too much of a megalomaniac for a small village to handle . . . She needed a whole country. But perhaps only ruthless
people had that kind of money, and only such a one as this
could ever have paid the full price for his house. Besides, he was
probably attributing to her too much strength; her madness
was a sickness after all, and the mother of her destruction was
within her, in a hideous gravidity; Mexico was an incubator in
which such life burst out of its confines and enveloped its car-
rier with tropical rapidity.

The image of the malignant growth was so vivid to him
that when she spoke he was startled and could not hear what
she said at all at first, having to go over to her and say, "What?
What? I can't hear you . . ."

"I said," she told him, without raising her voice but enun-
ciating elaborately, "I don't understand about you and Hanschen. He's a cretin and a bore, but I can't understand how anyone as smart as you could let the business with Hanschen get
to be such a mess that it hurt you."

"Oh, that," he said. "It didn't hurt me. I'm a painter. I'm
not in the real-estate business."

"But it's made everybody hate you, darling," she said.
He smiled.

"Where there's smoke, everybody says . . . you know?"

He said, "Where there is smoke, there is smoke. Everybody doesn't hate me."

She fingered the white starched cotton curtain beside her. "I'll have to replace these with hand-loomed colorful stuff. People are afraid of white."

"Don't tell me all the gruesome little ways you're going to mess up my house, will you?"

"Come off it," she said calmly. "You won't be here. You won't see it. But . . . everybody does hate you." She tilted her glass so that the last crystal drops of gin ran down the glass to her thin lips. "The Mexicans don't like you . . . you make the mistake of taking them seriously. They despise you for that. They don't love you, Mr. Grasshopper; they think you are ridiculous."

"Do you think they will like you?"

Smiling, she shook her head slowly from side to side. "All they know is slavery," she said. "It is all they have had. These poor people . . . no, they are not rich enough to like any one of us. Slavery makes them hate."

He said, "Mexico's culture is a far older one than ours and, in some ways, a wiser one. Mexican-Indios are not just a childlike people who set off firecrackers at dawn, as you will find out." He smiled at her. He disliked her very much. "I shall make a prophecy," he said. "You will die here. Mexico kills its would-be conquerors. Your bones and your body will enrich the Indio's tortillas someday when Mexico has held you in its earth a while."

"Do you think so?" she said softly. Her eyes were extraordinarily light; they looked liquid.

"Yes."

"What will kill me?"

He faced her. "Quetzalcoatl," he said. "The Serpent God of Mexico. I don't know how . . . maybe with dysentery or hepatitis . . . or maybe more directly with a knife. Your Mexican slaves carry knives, you know. Quetzalcoatl kills those who come to Mexico only to plunder her."

Her smile dwindled and she nodded thoughtfully. It gradually resembled the head-nodding of a much older woman, and it made her youth and slimness seem an obscene trick, as though she had been exhumed from an ancient tomb, bloodless, mummified, and disguised as a golden-haired, lovely, power-mad child. "I shall not die here, *amigo*," she said. "I shall defy your superstitious prophecy." She looked up at him out of the cold wasteland of her eyes. "How nice you are to me," she said sweetly. "Is it because you like me?"

He looked at her and looked away, at the painting on the wall which Victoria loved so much and which Margo had not even seen. "No," he said, as if her question had not been ironic. "No." He was not nice to her; he did not want to be. He was not nice to Abel either, or the rest of the town, to go away and leave them at the mercy of this woman, unwarned, unprovided for . . . It clouded his going, this knowledge that the village would become different when she owned it all and that he had helped her to own it. It spoiled his going in a way, forced him, in his complicity, to keep it a secret until the last moment. He disliked her a good deal more for that. "No," he said. "You know, I don't think I like you at all?"

"That's all right," she said, smiling. "That's perfectly all right. You don't have to, pet."

14

Victoria

VICTORIA sat in the corner of his bedroom in the low white chair. The late afternoon sun came brazenly into the room and brightened the painting on the wall, The Icicle, and she found that she kept turning her head and looking at it. It seemed, in that glow, to produce its own cold light, like the glare that came off snow and could blind you. How many times when he was sick, and she was taking care of him, she had looked at it, studying it, finding him in it, somehow. Now that seemed very strange, and as though it had never happened; he was different now . . . almost deliberately so. The painting was the same.

He handed her a drink and lifted his own to her. "*Salud*," he said.

"*Bon voyage*," she said, sipped the drink and set it down.

He turned away and went on with his packing. She used to notice how much he looked at her, so now it was marked that he did not.

"I think you should say '*bon voyage*' only when someone is taking a sea journey," he said.

"And you are not?" she said.

"To Mexico City?" he said. "Hardly."

He folded and refolded his Chipps suits over the ingeniously constructed suit-hangers until they were perfect, wrinkle-free. He was patient, smoothing them out again and again. She looked at the matching jars of lotions, oils and colognes, waiting to be clasped by the rich leather straps of the suitcase. She remembered how she had gone with him to the post office in Guadalajara to shop for stamps. He examined all the issues to see which went best with his stationery. Everything had to be perfect, every little thing.

"I'm going to miss you," she said.

He stood there, musing over two racks of neckties. "No point in taking all of these, would you say?" He shifted a handful back onto the rack he was leaving. "As long as you have enough black ties, you don't really need many of the others . . ."

She was silent and then after a moment she said again, "I am going to miss you." It sounded forlorn and she hastened to make fun of it by exaggerating it. "What am I to do without you here? You, my sanctuary, my oasis, my corn in Egypt?"

He smiled, but he did not look at her. "I forbid you to get Slavic about this," he said. "You know I'll be gone for only a few weeks at the most. I'll have my tiresome show and come back with my clipping books full of clichés, and while I'm gone you're not to let yourself slide back into one of your evil Balkan moods, do you hear? I forbid it, Victoria. No listening to Chopin, no wallowing in emotionalism. Nice bright hard Mozart is my prescription . . ."

She tried to smile but she could not. She felt deserted.

"When I come back, we shall celebrate together," he said. "Think about that."

"Of course, of course," she said.

"You'll have had word from your agent by then . . . maybe even an advance. We'll sit around and feel successful

together. I'll bring back some French champagne and a tin
of caviar . . ."

He was altogether too cheerful. She almost said, "I've
had champagne in my life, son. It's not a big thing to me . . ."
She watched him being cheerful and preoccupied, not looking
at her, and she felt odd, dislocated, as though the room had
tilted slightly all of a sudden, as though a temblor had churned
deep in the earth, jumbling up the room, time and the world,
just a little. But no, the room was neat as always. The room
could not tilt; Ned would not permit it.

He was different. It was hard to know, watching him,
whether he had ever been like this before, making false, cheerful noises at her, or whether she was just noticing it now. It
could be that he simply *seemed* guilty to her, because of the
question in her mind and because she looked at him to find the
answer to that question in his behavior. Would he permit his
behavior to tilt slightly, to be just a little off-balance, if he
would not permit the room to tilt? No. But it could be that he
thought he was acting the way he always acted, unaware that
doing consciously what had been done before unconsciously
was a degree removed from reality and made him less credible.

Imagine packing like that to go somewhere. He would arrive at his destination, pristine, beautiful, without wrinkles.
When she traveled . . . ah, but that was another matter. Her
two tin suitcases were thrown onto the top of a second-class
bus; she rode all day and all night, almost prostrated in the
tropic states, rumpled and soaked in perspiration, and then later
in mountain country, shivering with cold, sitting next to some
dreadful old man, a primitive *tipo*, who reeked of *pulque*, and
belched, and snored the hours away.

But what happened to her simply could not happen to
Ned. It was impossible to imagine him, for instance, at the bus
stop at Ciudad del Maiz, sitting at the long board table with the
other passengers, eating the hot ears of corn, and being *grateful*
for it—although it was fit only for horses—because it had been
boiled in the big tin *botes* and you would not get amoebic dysentery from it, and because it filled you, and what difference did
it make that it was tough and tasteless! She could imagine Ned
only on a train, strolling into the dining car for supper and having *chocolate* and fresh rolls with sweet butter.

"I'll bring you something smart from Mexico," he said. "A

surprise. Maybe a hat. Would you like that? Something expensive . . ."

She looked at him scornfully. "No," she said.

"All right," he said. "What would you like?"

"Nothing," she said.

He looked at her and looked away. He took some of his drink, and she lifted her glass, too. Out in the street the milk boy was passing. She could hear the clopping sounds of the horse's hoofs and over that his thin, urgent cry, "*La leche!*" Jovita would be running out to him with her pitcher to be filled.

"My husband has been telephoning me," she said. She was amazed hearing herself say it. She had not known such an idea was in her mind.

"Oh?" he said. "Which one?"

"The last one. Ramón. Begging me to come back to him. Begging me to let him come here to woo me." She rolled her eyes at him. "You can imagine how much work I'd get done with that going on . . ."

"What a bore!" he said.

"Dreadful!" she agreed.

He went into the bathroom to get more supplies and she closed her eyes tightly. Why had she told him that lie?

He laid out soap and toothpaste on the table. He said, "I can't trust Hassan to Jovita again. Last time I was away she neglected him horribly and he was thin and sickly when I got back."

She looked at the cat as it lay in the far corner of the room. It was a king of cats, large, deep-voiced, graceful, with cocoa tintings and blue eyes. "He's beautiful," she said, vaguely.

"It's only for two weeks, I think, really. Or three at the most," Ned said. He looked at her.

She raised her eyes to him and slowly it was borne in upon her that he was asking her to care for the cat. She turned her curling finger in at herself questioningly, because he must have noticed that she had never at any time touched the cat, or gone near it, and she shook her head in disbelief. "Oh, but it would be an honor, you know," she declared. "An *honor*. But I cannot believe you ask me . . . ? No, you know I know nothing about cats. Nothing. I have never touched one. Are you asking me to keep the cat for you?"

He laughed, and put his shaving kit down and came over

to her and drew her close to him and kissed the top of her head. "You're a funny one," he said, and gazed down into her face. "Would you? It wouldn't interfere with your work? He's very well trained."

She got up, looking into his blue eyes, bright behind their spotless glasses. "I feel so strange," she murmured, and found that she was pressing her hands together agitatedly. "Everything has begun to seem a little strange to me. There is . . . something about this. As though it were not just my keeping the cat for you." With a little gush of laughter she said, "Do you know this is exactly how I felt when I decided to get married?"

"Which time?" he said.

"Every time," she said.

They laughed together.

"The cat won't be as much trouble as your last husband," he said.

"Him!" she exclaimed. "He's spoiling every day with those phone calls. I have to run to the telegraph office, and today we had a poor connection with the Mexico City operator cutting in all the time." She pinched her nose and did an imitation, " 'Bueno, eso es Mehico. Bueno, Guadalajara? Bueno?' and there he was pleading and shouting that he *loves* me and he can't *stand* it without me, and you know how fiercely proud a Mexican is about an operator hearing something like that." She stopped. He did not look very interested. She said, "It was mad, boy," finally, and sat down, her performance over.

"Forget about it," he said briskly. "It depresses you. Have you got a pencil? Let me give you Hassan's routine and what he eats and how to take care of him."

She got a stub of a pencil out of her shoulder bag and jotted down on an envelope the details that he considered essential.

But while she did this, writing and listening to him, her fingers holding the pencil were cold and the room seemed more tilting than ever, and she could not stop wondering why she had lied to him about Ramón . . . lied, and embellished the lie with acting, with a complete performance. Maybe, feeling betrayed by him, she was trying to betray him too . . . No, she was not sure that his behavior, which seemed to be labeled *guilt,* was actually guilty at all. Not knowing was strain enough to explain her fear . . .

"I *wish* you weren't going," she said and kept herself from crying.

"Oh my God," he said. "I'm not being sent to prison for five years, you know. I'm going to Mexico City for three weeks, and then I'll be back."

"Will you?" she said, staring blindly at him. "Will you?"

He did not answer. He looked away, but not before she had seen how his mouth tightened.

She said, "I think something is about to be broken, don't you see? It will never be the same again."

"You'd better come along if my going away is all that catastrophic," he said.

But it was ironically said. There was impatience in it. And he did not mean it. She said, "No, that would be a difference, too. Your going, right now, is the end of a time. Everybody has times in his life which look as though they're going to last forever, and they never do. If you're standing outside them, you know they won't last. But if you're inside them and they have been good, you tell yourself they'll go on forever."

"Has it been a 'good time'?" he said. "I don't think so. It's been a difficult time, but in it we've become friends. If my going to Mexico for two weeks or three or whatever it turns out to be, puts an end to that . . . then it wasn't much of a friendship, was it? Nonsense. We'll be friends forever."

She shook her head. She was trying to rub a carbon stain off her little finger. "Once a doctor told me I had t.b. He said I must let them collapse one lung so that it could rest. I must move to Switzerland . . . I was in Paris then . . . Or, he said, I'd die. I refused the operation. But for many years it was as though I had a string, with one end tied to the lung which had the crater in its wall, and the other end tied to my brain. I was aware, every second, of this string of fear, of consciousness, *acute consciousness* from then on, of the danger of hemorrhage and death. Don't work, don't run, don't breathe fast, don't stay up all night, don't drink . . . Any moment, it could happen. Death, like a clap of the hands."

"The Beast in the Jungle," he said.

"In a way, except that Henry James' beast was almost exclusively cerebral. Mine was a betrayal of the body; it was my body which wouldn't let me live. Five years later the crater was healed, there was no hemorrhage, and although there is a scar, I have not had active tuberculosis since then. The string, you see, was cut. And do you know that I didn't know what to do? I wasn't glad; I was confused. I had lost something. The string which tied me to death, had also, in a way, tied me to life. Without it, I floundered. It was the end of a time . . . not a good time by your standards perhaps, but the end of a time. Do you see? I have the same confusion now. It will never be the same again."

"Not Henry James at all," he said lightly. "It's Kafka."

She watched him snap a suitcase shut with no straining or pushing or having to sit on it and then stare worriedly at its bulging sides wondering if it would fly apart and regurgitate his belongings into some public scene. No. His suitcase had been expertly packed, and now, to her everlasting awe, she saw him produce exactly the right keys for that suitcase and turn them in the locks. Imagine! She had a box full of suitcase keys and no idea any longer to what suitcases the rusty, scummy things belonged. But even though the suitcases to go with the keys must be gone by now, she was afraid to throw the keys away simply because they were her keys. When she packed, she tied up her tin suitcases with stout rope and prayed that God would keep their eccentric fastenings holding the multitude of unsorted garments she had crammed into them; that was what she called packing.

When the suitcases were locked, he came to the table to fix his drink. "So that's how you will miss me," he said. "The way you missed the crater in your lung. Marvelous compliment." He laughed and poured a little more gin in her glass. "You're morbid. This is not the end of us, Victoria."

She looked up at him. "Do you know what people are saying?" she said.

He shook his head.

"They are saying that you're selling your house and the bar and you're going away. That you're leaving Mexico. They say when you come back from Mexico City it will be just to pack up and go away forever. Is it true?"

He did not say anything, and she waited.

She said then, "*Is* it?"

He said, "No."

"Because, boy, you would owe it to me to tell me this first,

not to deny it. Not to leave me here and have a stranger tell
me you had gone and I would never see you again."

He stood very still, not even blinking, looking at her. He
had never been so motionless before. "I told you it wasn't true,"
he said.

"I am very fond of you," she said.

"Inordinately?" he said.

"Inordinately."

"And so you should be," he said. He was smiling again, at
ease. "I am a very charming fellow. You will take good care of
Hassan and when I come back, we shall celebrate."

She drained her glass, set it down and stood up. "I have
a poem for you," she said. "It's not a very good one. I haven't
written much poetry lately . . . but it's the only good-bye gift
I have for you." She fished into her shoulder bag and brought
out the crumpled piece of paper and handed it to him.

She saw how reluctantly he took it, as though it might get
his hands dirty. It was tacky-looking with a lot of cross-outs
and erasures. He began to read it. Seeing that his mouth continued small with distaste, she wished she had at least re-
typed it.

> *The dream in the night*
> *Has a rough hand, gropes*
> *Into the dark box, passes*
> *Tremulous fingers over the blank*
> *Blind papers . . . rattles the few*
> *Small beads, which lie, forgotten there,*
> *Bright, eye-winking in the corners.*
> *The dream can run. It runs swift*
> *Along the wet-stoned passage;*
> *Dark cape flutters, dips, hastens*
> *With a rushing birdwing sound.*
> *A lantern flashes bright*
> *Turning a corner, blazing up,*
> *Guttering down, till night*
> *Regains, reholds the corridor.*

He looked at her. "I don't like it," he said. He sat down on
the corner of the bed, looking at it. "There's something intesti-

nal about it. Were you being Freudian? What were you trying to say?"

She snatched the paper away from him and stuffed it back into her purse. "You're impossible," she said. "I shouldn't have let you see it."

He laughed. "It just needs reworking," he said.

"I'll burn it."

"You wouldn't have put it back into your purse if you were going to burn it," he said. "You'll reread it and when you're done hating me, you'll work it over."

"To hell with you. I'm going home," she said.

"All right," he said. "I'll write to you."

She looked at him.

"Don't look so forlorn," he said. He stood up and put his arm around her and gave her a hug. "Do you think you might take Hassan with you now?" he said. "I'm leaving very early in the morning. Why don't I find his leash . . . and you can walk him home with you . . . ?"

Although she warned him in her choked voice that she didn't know if she would do very well with the cat, never having had one, but she'd try, the next thing she knew he was handing her the leather leash and she was walking down the *zaguán*. He kissed her and said, "Rewrite the poem, dear. I shall look forward to reading it," and the door closed on the blurred sight of him.

There was still a ragged banner of crimson in the sky from the sunset, which was edged around with dark. The night's chill was already coming on. The cat strolled along before her at the end of its leash, in a measured way, as though it were accustomed to such promenades. Some of her distrust of it ebbed away; it would be nice if the thing's behavior was predictable and she did not have to worry about it all the time.

Smoke puffed out from the eaves of the houses, hazy and blue and smelling of corn. The church bell clanged a summons to the Angelus, and in the Plaza a ranchero song resounded against the empty evening walls. Naked light bulbs burned weakly on their corner poles and the mountains were enpurpled by the descending dark. Three women were walking toward her, up the hill to the church, and they looked, in the soft blue light, like three black *rebozo*'d Madonnas. When they were closer she saw that one of them was One-Eyed Lupita, who just

the day before yesterday had deliberately tried to cheat her on
the weight of a pound of sugar. The sugar was gray anyway,
with bits of dirt in it; she bought it from Lupita only because
she felt sorry for the woman. Well, that taught you to be sorry.
In her fury she had said, "The least you can be, since you are
stupid and incompetent, is honest." But now because Lupita
turned her sightless cheek into the fold of her *rebozo*, lest the
look of it offend, and softly called out, "*Qué pasé buena noche,
señora, eh?*" she forgave her and gave a sweet answer. Poor
woman . . . what were a few centavos one way or the other?
It was a village sport to try to cheat the foreigners, and why not?
The foreigners, comparatively at least, could afford it. But the
reason behind her sharp speech to Lupita had been a dislike
that day of everything Mexican, since she had only just then
learned the Mexicans' name for her . . . not from someone
who could not resist the joke of telling her as she had once expected, but she had overheard a conversation about her. They
referred to her as *La Hormiga Brava* . . . The Fierce Ant. The
kind of ant they called *brava* was a large shiny black automaton
which toiled ceaselessly, carrying over its head a leaf three
times its size, and which was indomitable, indefatigable and
ineradicable.

She hated the name, and the thought that this was how
they saw her—of all the creatures on the earth which she might
have been named after—made her hate them more than ever.
She often called them "subhuman" when she was angry with
them, and that was wrong, too. But the point was, that this
name they had given her was not given in anger, but was an
amiable and, to them, amusing description of her, spoken in
good humor and regarded as a *bon mot*. While they seemed to
accept you completely, while they play-acted that you were part
of their life and the life of the village, when they gave you
such a name, they told you, if you had forgotten, that you were
still the stranger, the outsider, come to live on the edge of
their lives. She'd meant it when she said to Ned that he was
her sanctuary, her oasis, her corn in Egypt. This was exile in
Egypt, a land of famine; she could die, her heart could hunger
and thirst itself to death in these barren wastes . . . He was
all she had for the nourishment of her soul and intellect and
being . . .

The cat paused, abruptly coming to a halt and looking

ahead. She stopped, too. Perhaps it was tired. She could see no reason for its stopping, but then she did not know how to make it go on again until it wanted to anyway. The thing to do was wait, as if stopping had been her idea. The *niña* would be pleased to have the cat in the house; she admired it greatly.

But the *niña* would not be at the house at this hour; since the *niña's* illness she had insisted that the child go home at sunset, and stay home, resting beside the *brasero* she had loaded with *carbón* and given to the *niña's* mother for this purpose. She told the woman how important it was, in these cold, frosty nights, for the child, if she must sleep on a mat on the ground, to be kept warm. She had threatened, if the mother did not do this, to keep the child in her house at night instead, where at least she could sleep in a bed. The mother was stubborn; she was one of the old-time ones who thought beds were unhealthy and weakened those who slept in them instead of naturally on the ground like all other of God's animals, and, *pues,* when you looked at *gringos,* who could argue? Were they healthy?

"I am," Victoria had said glaring at the woman. "I have health. I sleep in a bed. I am a *gringa.*"

"Yes," the mother had said, "but my child is not, and for her a bed would be unhealthy."

The cat moved, again without any visible reason, and as it strolled on, she followed. The *niña* would not see the cat until morning. It would be a good surprise for her. Extraordinary how fond of the little pest she'd become since she was sick! From the very first, when the *niña's* little brother had beat on the door in the morning and told her that the *niña* could not come to work, she'd been possessed by a peculiar, maternal fury. She'd gone, as soon as she was dressed, to the *niña's* house, and the instant she saw her, she knew she must bring her home and nurse her or the child would die. The mother, that slovenly cow, had stuck a leaf on the *niña's* forehead and made her cups of jamaica tea. She had gone to the church to pray, and came home to sit waiting for God's miracle. If the Christian God were tardy, the mother would take the *niña* to the witch doctor in Ixtlahuacán . . . the one who had managed to kill Chatta's brother Cirilo with such admirable dispatch . . .

This country did not deny the new, did not surrender the old, but accepted both, to its detriment. New gods, old gods

. . . it made no difference. New drugs, old drugs . . . a leaf on the forehead and an incantation cost less than penicillin, and there was a man in Jocotepec who had died of penicillin poisoning. Nobody died from a leaf on the forehead . . . and the leaf, which did not kill, also did not cost a month's wages . . .

She had had to be very tactful to get the *niña* away; she said it was the other seven children in the house she was thinking of protecting, and of helping the mother, the poor, tired, overworked *mamacita*, who could not possibly spare the time to nurse one sick little girl when she had to care for such a large family.

She'd picked up the *niña* in her arms, and felt the fever burning its way through the blankets, and carried her home. The child was almost unconscious; her breath was foul, her cheeks sunken. There was the dry, desperate smell of fever. The smell filled her with rage, because it was the smell of death. It was the closeness of death to the child which infuriated her, while its mother prayed and waited for God's miracle.

She'd worked over the *niña* all that day and night, trying to break the fever. She piled blankets and quilts and coats on her, and pulled the couch close to the living-room fireplace where she kept a big fire going all night. The *niña* was in a delirium. She unwound the blankets and bathed her with alcohol and then rewrapped her in the cocoon of coverings many times until at last at dawn the fever dropped slightly . . . But not enough.

By then the child slept, too deeply, exhausted, scarcely breathing. She could not rouse her to get food into her and she sat for two hours with her hand on the *niña's* wrist, fearfully clocking the failing pulse. It was weak; it fluttered like a maimed insect, hopping up agitatedly, falling back to lie for longer and longer times motionless on the floor of the vein. She dared not leave the child, even to get help, but when she heard Charles' voice outside, she dropped the *niña's* wrist and hurried to the door and dragged him into the house.

"You must get Dr. Obregón . . ." she said.

Charles took the message she wrote down for him, because she knew how bad his Spanish was, and hurried off with it. A half-hour later, Harry knocked on her shuttered window and called through it, "Vickie, the quack's coming." He told her that Charles could not put a phone call through, because the line was down, and he had taken a car and driven to San Juan. Later she found out that Dr. Obregón was ill and in bed, but Charles had pushed past Señora Obregón, ignoring her protestation, and delivered Victoria's message.

When Dr. Obregón arrived, she was shocked at his appearance. There were shadows under his eyes and, because he had been a stocky, full-fleshed man, this thinness now seemed to have happened inside of him, making him smaller, so that he was, in his skin, like a man in somebody else's clothes. His eyes were hollow and he walked carefully, doling out his strength in careful portions, but when he looked at her, light came into his face, replacing the in-looking dark of sickness, and passion blazed up in his eyes again.

"What is it, my friend?" she asked him, frightened.

"*Pues*, nothing," he said.

"You must tell me," she said.

"After I see the child," he told her.

His examination was quick and efficient. He sent out for Charles, who waited in the car, and the three of them together rigged up the glucose bottle with one of her belts thrown over a beam. "*Salmonella*," Dr. Obregón said to her. "Paratyphoid."

She nodded. That was what she had thought. Charles went out again, not looking at the sick child. Dr. Obregón took vials of chloromycetin from his bag. "I don't like to use it," he said heavily. "Sometimes it causes internal bleeding. But . . . I have no choice. You will give her these pills."

He gave the *niña* an injection, too, and then he handed Victoria a syringe and some needles. "You can do it?" he said. "Give the injections?"

"Yes," she said, so then he wrote down his orders.

He stood up, wearily, and passed his hand over his wet forehead.

She said, "I am sorry you are ill. What is it?"

"My temperature goes up and down every day . . . not too high, not very low. I keep thinking of bacterial endocarditis, but Dr. Gomez Parra tells me no. He says it's Malta Fever—brucellosis. I trust him, as much as one doctor can trust another. He is a fine doctor, but I am apprehensive about my heart."

"You're frightened," she said. "It has frightened you."

"Yes," he said. He sighed. "I am like any layman when I

am sick . . . Suddenly I cannot think. I know only that I am
sick, and that frightens me." He smiled at her. "Do not concern
yourself, señora," he said. "It is nothing."

"Who takes care of you?" she said.

"My wife," he admitted. He looked ashamed then, and confused. "She is good to me," he added, as though someone had
said she was not.

In the *zaguán* he said, "You understand that you take a
chance, nursing another woman's child? If she dies here, they
will blame you. A *Mexican* child, señora."

"What can I do?" she said. "Leave her lying on a mat on a
dirt floor with a leaf stuck to her forehead? Let them feed her
beans and tortillas and with this fever have her running to an
outhouse every ten minutes? She would surely die."

He took her hand and she felt how his palm was hot and
dry. He said, with an expression of great sweetness, "The
thought of you supports me and gives me strength. Everything
you do . . . Like this, like this taking care of the *niña* . . .
everything you do makes me love you more." He put his hot
finger against her opening mouth, preventing her protest. "*Por
favor, no me digas nada,*" he said. "Tomorrow when I come to
see her, I do not say anything foolish. Do not reprimand me."

That time, she had felt more respect for him than before.
She had believed that he would keep his promise, and he had.
He called on the *niña* every day for two weeks and never again
mentioned love to her, nor would he discuss his own obviously
failing condition. Shortly after that, when the *niña* was out of
danger, she had heard that he had gone to Mexico City to con-
sult with a specialist there, and everyone said he was afraid,
and that he insisted something was wrong with his heart when
no other doctor agreed with him. The Mexicans said he was
guilty, because he had fought the Padre, and because he had
chosen to serve the *gringos* and make money, instead of helping
his own people. The Americans said he was having a nervous
breakdown, and that he was a hypochondriac . . . "So American, he's as neurotic as we are," they said, and smiled. All his
patients made unkind diagnoses of his troubles; no one helped
him, and the day he left San Juan, his drug store was broken
into and a supply of narcotic drugs stolen. After that, Federal
soldiers paraded before the broken door all night and the next
day. Dr. Obregón's wife hired an armed watchman to stay in

the pharmacy at all times. There were no more robberies after that.

During the time the *niña* had stayed with her, Ned had not come to see her. He had sent flowers, but he said it was a pest-house and he would not come until the danger was past. By the time he visited her, the *niña* was convalescing and there was no danger of contagion. He had looked at the wan little girl propped on pillows in the sun in the patio, and though his eyes softened for a minute, he deliberately stiffened his back and turned away. The *niña* had not minded. She'd been playing with the dreadfully homely doll which Victoria had fashioned for her out of bits of ribbon and cloth, and which was, the *niña* confessed, her very first doll. The child kept the doll with her all the time, talking to it and kissing it. After the *niña* fell asleep, Ned lectured her on the folly of yielding to pity in a Mexican village . . . "You can't afford it, my dear. Where would it stop . . . ever? There is no end to the pity one can indulge here . . ." While he lectured her so, he straightened the clothes on the doll and painted it a new face, which was really quite beautiful, and reshaped its peculiar body so that it did not look quite so lumpy, and put it back into the little girl's arms again.

"You have begun, though," Ned said sadly. "Now how can you keep pity out?"

Because of his efforts with the doll, she did not answer him, as she would have answered anyone else, sharply and suc-cinctly; she did not say that had it not been for pity, she would not have stayed in his house and nursed him through his illness either.

"Pity takes all one's life," he said. "You would do better to choose loneliness."

She had smiled at him. "You call it 'loneliness,'" she had said. "You don't say 'solitude' or 'isolation,' or 'self-exile.'"

"I admit what it is," he said. "I choose it as a lesser suffer-ing to pity, and a less costly self-indulgence than pity." He looked at the doll. "I didn't fix this for her," he said. "Nor for you either. I fixed it because it was ugly. Why add to the ugli-ness of the world?"

She never told him that when the *niña* awakened and saw her changed, prettier doll, she had cried for the only time in her life. She wanted the old ugly doll back again, because it was hers. Ned would not have understood how that could be . . . that an ugly thing could be pretty to you because it was your own. She and the *niña* erased his improvements, and then the *niña* was more content, but never again quite as happy as she had been; never again was the doll so completely her possession. If she had told Ned that, he'd have sighed in despair; it would only prove his theory that people resented help, fought education, resisted culture. "Damn democracy!" he would have said. "I am living in the wrong century."

He was. Much of what he said was true . . . charity righted no inequities, and kindness was a weak virtue . . . no more than a prelude to inevitable betrayal . . .

But could these two inescapable facts in any way justify a lack of charity? That righted no inequities either. And was unkindness a better prelude to betrayal?

Betrayal . . . There was something wrong about the way Ned had said no when she asked him if the gossip about him were true. He did not blink. He stopped blinking when he answered. He was absolutely motionless, as though he stood in a moment of deciding something.

She was walking slowly now, remembering how he stood there, and the cat was pulling on the leash a little. Too bad. Too bad, cat; I waited for you a moment ago . . . Now you wait for me.

Ned had stood there as motionless as the symphony conductor stands in the full fifty seconds before he brings his baton down and the musicians play. Always just for long enough that you wondered incredulously if this time he really were not going to start them, after all. Or, once when she had seen an operation—Jack had been going to do a play about doctors and he prowled hospital corridors, dragging her with him to sit in the amphitheater and watch how surgeons behaved, memorizing their gestures and the tones of their voices; the surgeon came in, gloved hands in the muff of a sterile towel, and as the towel dropped away and the assistant handed him the scalpel, he had looked, motionlessly like that, at the exposed abdomen, and there was the silence, the staring, somehow listening silence, as though he wanted, not to hear the anesthetist's report, but the song of the sickness in the abdomen before he cut . . .

Yes, Ned had been like that. But he had then said no . . .

the symphony conductor had begun . . . the surgeon had made the cut . . . Why would Ned have lied to her? She had not known him to lie before. He did not bother to lie. He did not lie about the poem, and it would have been easier for him just to say he liked it and send her on her way than to endure the sight of her unhappiness and listen to her abuse. Besides, if he had really sold the bar and the house and if he were going away from Mexico, why should he lie to her? He owed her nothing. Also, he would know, surely, that she would not tell anyone a secret of his . . .

The cat tugged at the leash, and she walked, more briskly now. Her reason argued that Ned had not lied, but her intuition, in a smaller and smaller and finally hushed voice, insisted that it knew he had lied. Her reason pointed out the fact of the cat to her intuition. It was an alive, walking fact, evidence that he cared for her, trusted her and was coming back to the village . . .

She should have told him when he urged her to choose loneliness, that if he could have stood it himself, he would not have needed the cat. Everybody needed something to love . . . not necessarily to be loved by . . . but to lavish love upon, because otherwise it was not possible to be sure that you were alive. If a man cannot have anything human to love, he will love a mouse, a bug, a blade of grass.

When she got to her house, the cat sat and waited while she turned the key in the lock and then when she had the door open, the thing still sat and would not move. She tugged at it with the leash, and finally dragged it up over the high sill. Maybe she was supposed to say something to it. Maybe it was used to being called by name, given orders. Now it sat in the *zaguán,* facing the street door as she closed it, not looking at her. It was hard to touch it . . . to touch fur . . . but she got the leash unhooked from its handsome leather collar, and stood back waiting. After a moment, it was apparent that it wasn't going to bound joyfully about the house; but was it going to sit there facing the closed door until Ned came back to take it away again? Her voice sounded false in her ears when she spoke, but she said, "There you are, Hassan." Its ears twitched but it did not move. "Rooty-toot-toot, Hassan," she said, because if words didn't mean much to it, sounds would do. When that got no

reaction, she walked away from it. Maybe it was, like a bad
child, better ignored; it hadn't much sense of humor.

The electricity came on, and music burst from the throats
of many nearby radios. She switched on the light in the patio
and looked at the walls to make sure the cat would not be
able to get out of there, run off, get hurt. It looked safe enough.
Anyway, Ned had an open patio with walls no higher and it did
not run away from him.

When she got back to the *zaguán,* the cat was still there.
It was lying down now, with its four paws tidily placed beneath
itself, facing the door. You'd think that instinctively it would
investigate its new surroundings, look for pleasures or search
out dangers. But it did nothing. It was not even asleep. It was
simply *there,* with its eyes open and slightly crossed, looking
at nothing. Was it just going to be *there* the whole time Ned
was in Mexico City?

Then it must be just in the house, not in the house of her
mind every minute, or she'd go mad. There were voices in the
street, and she could hear Harry saying, "Like, you know,
baby . . . ah . . . Lawrence Welk. You can't groove behind
that . . ."

Charles' voice, a little louder, said, "Junkie, junko."

It made you lonely, hearing people go by, even people who
were incomprehensible. If it had been Charles alone, she'd have
opened the door and said, "Come in, come in." But not Harry.
These days Harry was frightening. There was a greasy look to
his skin, and he perspired a lot more than he used to—and it
wasn't even hot now—and his eyes were peculiar. More than
anything, he laughed badly, as though he could hear himself
laughing in a tunnel and strained to keep the laugh-sounds going loud, long after mirth was gone . . .

Last week she had met him in the street. She had seen him
in the distance, drifting down the street toward her with
Charles beside him, and she waved and would have turned off
on another street, but Harry called out to her to wait and then
when he got to her he rested his wrists on her shoulders and
gazed down into her face, pretending delight. His face was clay-
white, and the gray smile on it was frightening and she could
see how angry with her he was. It had been a long time since
she had been to see him, or invited him in . . .

Harry smiled wistfully at her in that gray smeary way and said, "Chickie, you used to be an itty-bitty buddy of mine . . ."

Charles cleared his throat.

"We're still friends, Harry," she'd said. "I've been working."

"Yeah?" he said with terrible earnestness. "You been writing? What? Words? Numbers? Stories? Love letters?"

"No numbers," she said. He was leaning heavily on her.

"Did my mother tell you I was a junkie and you shouldn't talk to me?"

She shook her head. His mother?

"S'all righ'," Harry said thickly. "She told everybody. Man, everybody hipped me how she came here the other night and warned all the good folk . . ." His eyes gleamed. "Didn't she warn you? Maybe she doesn't know you are one of the good folk?" he said.

Charles said, "Oh wow, man! I told you that was a dream about your mother." He said wearily to her, "This is a big talk-day for him. Today he digs talking."

"I dig oral activity," Harry said, wiggling his eyebrows like Groucho Marx, "with all that implies."

"Come on, Harry," Charles said. "Let's split."

Harry said, "Come to Charles' pad, Vick. He's going to give me a shower. Me and Jim. He's going to heat buckets of hot water and pour it on us and make us clean . . . Saved, washed in the blood of the lamb . . . Then we're going to blow some sounds." His face was too close to hers; her eyes were straining to see him, and his cheeks looked balloon-wide and pale and his breath was bad in a sweet way . . . "I dig you, Vickie," he said. "I've got my chick, but Vickie, I love *you*. Do you know why?"

"Let me count the ways," Charles said.

Harry straightened up like a sinner testifying at a revival meeting. "I love you because you are an original," he said.

"Thank you," she said.

"Unlike anybody else in the whole stinking world. Your destiny is not to be prophesied. Lunacy? Probably. Greatness?" He shook his head and his glasses slipped on his greasy nose. "Greatness or Grapenuts . . . who can say? You watch me, you think I am mad, but still you listen because somewhere in me, in the unclean depths of me, there is a shaft of light and

purity and prophecy and you know that. Now you take our
Neddy-boy. Ned doesn't know that. He can't see beyond my
body's dirt to the cleanliness in me. Neddy-boy is not an original. He is a facsimile, a virginal facsimile, his ilk is legion, if
not American Legion. My father belongs to the American Legion, did you know that? He puts on a little hat sometimes and
shouts about the Reds and the Negroes and the Jews and the
Catholics, and the Pope . . . and he whispers jokes about
everybody who is not what he is, and he laughs in a dirty-old-
man way at those jokes . . . Oh yes, behind the shout there
is always the whisper; bigotry comes in the economy size, a twin
package, a double-header, a parlay across the board . . . And
do you know what I see Neddy-boy doing? I see him trying to
make my Vickie, my original, over into his own mold. He is fash-
ioning, as though he were God, another little Neddy-boy. Now
that might be all right, but not when he uses my Vickie, my
original, to do it. Not when he gets into my Vickie and begins
to change her all around . . ." He gripped her shoulders
tightly and his face came closer to her. "Have you sold your
soul to him, Vickie, because his fingernails are clean, because
he shaves twice a day, because he is lovely, lovely, lovely . . .
Have you?"

Charles pulled his hands away, saying apologetically that
she shouldn't mind him . . . he was drunk, lushed up, not
knowing what he was saying . . .

But, "*I know, man,*" Harry said insistently. "I'm not lushed
and I'm not high. My fix has worn down to where I'm just
straight, that's all. I got to lay it on Vick about Ned. She'll get
lost . . . He changes you, trying to make you be like him,
Vick, because he does not love you as you are. You are an offense to him. He sees the cords of your neck standing out in
tension, your anxious face, and your thinking, despairing eyes
. . . He sees how time is making the skin of your neck crepey
and loose . . . He sees that you are a woman, and that reminds
him he was born of woman and he hates women, you dumb
broad, can't you see that . . . ?"

Charles pulled Harry's hands off her shoulders, and she
broke away then and hurried down the street away from them,
hearing Charles reasoning with Harry, and hearing too, inexplicably, the sound of Harry crying. That made her pause, and
she looked back at them and would have gone back, except that

Charles, seeing her hesitate, waved her away and went on
arguing with Harry, pushing and pulling him up the street. She
ran home then and got into her unmade bed and lay there
with her clothes on, breathing hard, frightened, thinking Harry
had really gone over the falls, that he was really going insane or
had been, in those moments, insane . . . which was what, she
now believed, she had seen in his gargoyle face that night at
the Garth house in the lamplight, except that that evening,
when she thought about it, it seemed hilariously funny instead
of tragic, whereas it was tragic, and beneath all that consideration was the fear that came because in the chaotic mixture of
his babbling there had been a fragment of truth here and
there. Her shoulder muscles ached where he had grabbed them
so tightly, and she found that she kept putting her hand to
the skin of her neck, feeling it, saying it wasn't crepey, wasn't
loose, didn't feel old. She wasn't old, didn't look old. . . .
Harry's eyes had been like caves, where tigers lurked, pacing,
ready to spring at her, maddened and murderous . . . He was
sick, he was insane, he was on dope, he was crazy with
dope . . .

He was honest. She had felt his honesty. He had tried hard
to reach her, to say something to her which he felt, whether
it was crazy for him to have felt it or not, and she respected
the effort . . . But what was she thinking? If you meet a
madman who says the sun is shining when it is shining, does
that make true whatever other gibberish he says?

It was that gibbering, insane Harry who went by her door
now, and not the Harry she used to think she knew; you did
not invite him into your house, and you did not ask for more of
his chaotic, dope-spun truth. You preferred to stay alone, even
in the specifically alone way which Ned's going away gave you.
She had washed back and forth between Ned's world and
Harry's world for a long time. With Ned gone, there was no
Ned's world to run to, and Harry's world was in ruins. Dr.
Obregón was in Mexico City, not that she'd have tried to put him
between herself and her new aloneness, but losing the possibility of doing that removed even an implausible alternative.
Abruptly, she was utterly alone, and not sure of how this special aloneness had come about; nor was she sure why this
aloneness was different from others she had known. The house
would hold herself, the cat, and, during the day, the *niña*. It

also held her work. What else? What had been there before
which was not here now?

She looked toward the typewriter, as though the answer
might be there. But she felt nothing, no rush of emotion, joy-
ous or furious, because she had sent off the three chapters and
was waiting for an answer from the agent, and if the future of
her work now came under the umbrella of a specific doubt, so
the present was umbrella'd by that same doubt.

Was it Ned's departure? In his house, she'd had a sense of
the world tilting. Her life had been, in these last weeks,
more and more circumscribed all the time, as though somebody
had tied a rope around the middle of it, and tightened it every
day. But Ned had not done that. Who had done it to her life?
She had been busy; she had thought her days were full; she
had had time for no one, except Ned, of course, and the *niña*
when she was sick. Now she was alone.

There was the cat. It was not a little thing that Ned had
asked her to care for the cat; it was as if he had entrusted a
portion of himself to her . . . not in all ways as she had gradually come to entrust herself to him . . . but in one way. She
would look at the cat.

Every day the cat strolled around, looking at things but not
nosing into them. It inspected her couches and chairs but it did
not jump on them, and time and time again, it went back to
the *zaguán* and lay down in the shadow, facing the door.

Crouched over her typewriter each day, she observed the
cat, seeing how when he lay down, he tucked his paws in under himself and wrapped his tail in an even curl around himself, as though making his own pedestal; he looked Egyptain.
"He's so tidy," Ned had said. "It's one of the things I love about
Hassan." The cat moved beautifully in languor, his muscles,
thickly padded with fat and fur, rippling under his glossy coat.
Sometimes she spoke to him, as she would to any guest she did
not know well, but the cat never turned his head and looked at
her at such times. She did not even feel that she had interrupted
him, since he ignored her entirely. She looked at the cat but the
cat did not look at her. A cat may look at a queen, but then
again it may not.

In the nights when she was sleeping poorly, she often got
up and sought out the cat. Usually she found him lying on the

cold tiles in the patio, a noiseless, living shadow on the moonlit floor. His eyes opened sometimes and gazed at her with no
surprise, and closed again. She went back to her couch, wondering why she had gone to look at him.

Hassan was different with the *niña*. The child made a game
of chasing the cat, playing *torero* with him, whisking the dish-
towel before his eyes in a dazzling *veronica,* and sometimes
trying to lasso him as she had seen Gauchos do in the movies.
It was surprising how tolerant of the games the cat was, and
how willingly he played with her. After a while he would get
bored and stalk off, to sit down alone, staring phlegmatically at
the door again until the child captured him. He permitted the
niña to lift and carry him, nestling his head into the crook of
her arm and staying beside her when she was in the kitchen.

The cat would not eat *caldo michi,* probably because of the
vinegar in it, and she told the *niña* to get some extra fish heads
from the fishermen and give those to the cat. But the cat would
not eat these either, and there they were on a plate in the cooler
for two days, staring many-eyed at her whenever she opened it
to look for something to eat herself. A plate of eyes staring at
her. She told the *niña* to take the fish heads home to her mother,
who could make a stew of them. The *niña* was pleased; the
head had most of the *vitaminas* in the fish, she said; her mother
had told her that.

The *niña* took the fish heads away and they bought stew-
ing beef for the cat. The arrangement was morally wrong but
then the cat would be hers for only a short time anyway, and
she owed it to Ned to keep him healthy.

She did not become used to the cat; on the contrary, she
became less accustomed to it with each day's passing. Why did
people have cats? What did they do? They didn't guard anything.

The cat stared, yawned, rolled onto its side, strolled in and
out of rooms, wandered silently into the patio and sat down, doing nothing. The concept of its vacant mind, a mind therefore
incomprehensible, began to plague her. She bent down and
peered into its face, as though, if her head were close enough to
the cat's head, she would know what went on in it, but she
learned nothing. She tried, because this behavior was foolish,
to keep its presence out of her consciousness. At times she was
persuaded she had forgotten it and was proud of her triumph,

but once, in the midst of one of the days when she was sure she was not aware of it, she found herself whirling on it, screaming at it in a witch's voice, "What are you thinking, for God's sake?"

Another time, sitting at the typewriter, worrying only about not having heard yet from the agent, she saw one of the swallows which nested in the ceiling of the *zaguán* flutter down to the ground and hop along, snatching at crumbs. She watched the cat excitedly to see if it would hunt. She knew it could not get the swallow—the swallow would be too fast for it—but she waited to see if the cat would stalk the bird, since cats hunted birds, as everybody knew.

Hassan ignored the bird, as he ignored her. The cat turned its head and watched the bird hopping along the floor, but it did not move, except to stretch and yawn. Was it an abnormal cat? Were its instincts lost in the centuries of domestication, so that it had forgotten things like hunger and the fever of the chase? Or did it simply have no reason to hunt the swallow when it had already dined on beef?

If another cat came along, a female, would it bestir itself to pursue that, or had it settled for the sexless pattings of human beings as all the love it needed? She thought about Ned and wondered in just what way he loved the cat. She put out her hand once, overcoming her reluctance to touch fur, and stroked the cat, but it got up and walked away from her outstretched fingers, twitching its rich tail. Then, free of her, it bathed itself, with its own tongue.

It was a horrible creature . . . a creature-possession.

One night it leapt to the top of the bookcase and lay there. It was a cold evening and she had a *rebozo* wound round her shoulders as she sat at the typewriter. But the cat could not know, could it, that it would be warmer higher up in the room? Could it think? She stared at it and the cat stared back at her, in cross-eyed indifference. After a moment—and she was aware that a lot of time passed this way, hypnotically, with her staring at the cat and the cat staring back at her—it reached out with its paw and pushed at an envelope which was on the shelf near it. The cat did not watch the envelope flutter to the floor, as she did. But wasn't that proof, since it was a deliberate act, that the cat must have some thought, some reasoning process? Then what could its reasoning process be?

Several times, because it must be wrong never to take the

thing anywhere, or Ned would not have given her a leash, she
tried to take the cat out with her when she went to the post office
to get the mail. But it did not want to go. It resisted her; she had
to drag it up over the doorstep and down into the street, and then
it sat down, or humped at the sight of a dog a block away, or
hissed and spat when there was a burro or a cow nearby.

But not taking it out did not help much. There was a
nagging feeling of having left a responsibility behind her, and
against her will, she would hurry home again, not lingering to
watch the sun set, not daring to go as far away as the lake shore
for a walk and a change. It was ridiculous to feel so housebound,
and no one would know that better than she . . . It wasn't a
newborn baby she left, helpless in a crib, after all. But it was
the cat's very lack of helplessness which prodded her homeward.
Because, always fearfully, she began to wonder what it would
be doing when she was not there.

But the cat-worry was only one circle within other ever-
widening circles of worry. No letter, word or postcard from Ned
was a worry, and the gossip the *niña* repeated many times,
that Ned would come back for the rest of his clothes and then
leave Mexico forever because he had sold his house and the bar
to Margo, became a ringing worry which she jumped through
every day. Her intuition that this was so, was something to
be contended with daily, and the last evening when he had stated
to her in so many words that it was *not* true, had to be remembered, felt over for the texture of truth, found again among
so much that was forgotten, and revivified. When she had
gone through that hoop of worry, there was the next hoop
waiting for her . . . the way shiny-costumed girls used to
appear on vaudeville stages, smiling, holding burning hoops for
the tumbler to jump through . . . Later, one of them would lie
down in a box and be sawed in half, only to leap up in more
smiling unreality and pretend to be alive a few moments afterward. When she was a child, although it had been explained
to her that the man did *not* saw the lady in half and she must
not scream, there was always the certainty that *this particular
time,* the lady had not gotten out of the box and was being
sawed while the audience watched in complacent certainty
that it was a trick—and if it was so surely a trick, why did they
want to watch it?—and she watched for a gush of blood to gout
out of the box and listened for the screech of the saw on hard

bone, and the terrible scream that told everyone this time it was
a mistake. Her father had to take her out of the theater.

She passed from the hoop of worrying about Ned, into the
next hoop of worrying about why she had not yet heard from
Cushman. It was not like him not to have written her by now;
unless, of course, he had not read the material himself, but had
sent the manuscript off to the publisher directly to get the advance. She'd made it clear in the letter about needing money
and needing it now; she'd told him that after it was accepted
and money was sent from the publisher, he could pick and poke
as much as he liked, but not now.

However, each day when there was no letter she worried
a little more. It wasn't like him. He must have read it. By now,
it must be with a publisher.

Of course, he might have been away when her manuscript
arrived in New York; he might have been on a vacation; he
might have a new secretary who did not know how important it
would be to get in touch with him wherever he was; he might
be sick! He might have written weeks ago, and the letter be
lost somewhere in this abysmal country, this huge dead-letter
office.

The final hoop was that the publisher had not liked it, but
in that case, Cushman would have written her to say so, and
moved the manuscript along to one of the others. She'd been
published by three good houses in the past and left on good
terms with each one. She had no enemies. There was no doubt
of the value of her work, nor any real possibility that the publisher would not like it. There was no danger of rejection. She
need not come to that final hoop and jump through that.

In the afternoon she heard the three o'clock bus from San
Juan rattle past the house, and decided to go at once to get the
mail. The *niña* was off on a day's holiday and would not be back
until sunset; by then the post office would be closed, and she did
not want the *niña* to be out in the streets when the evening chill
was coming on anyway. The child looked better, but toward the
end of the day, her cheeks got a rosy flush that was worrisome,
and her forehead often felt warm and dry to the hand. It was beginning to look as though there might be a tubercular sequel to
her illness; as soon as Dr. Obregón came back from Mexico City,
she was going to have the *niña's* lungs examined. She did not

cough, but then coughing came later. It was as though after
these many years, because she had gotten foolishly fond of the
niña, the string which once had been in place between her own
mind and the crater in her lung, now traveled from her mind to
the *niña's* lungs. She bought extra milk and insisted that the
niña drink it. The child wanted coffee instead; every day there
was an argument.

In the bathroom, scrubbing her face and arms and neck, she
saw that her eye-whites were gray and she looked tired. Today,
surely, there would be a letter. She dabbed on some lipstick . . .
The container was nearly empty and she could not shape a
mouth with it very well, but it did not matter. The town was
full of people, but there was nobody who mattered to her. She
put on her dark glasses, and fastened the fraying T-straps of her
old shoes, and grabbed up her shoulder bag. When she got to
the *zaguán,* the cat was sitting there, facing the door. Probably
she should drag it along the street with her, give it one last out-
ing. Ned was due to arrive tomorrow or the next day. But the
cat did not look at her, and she hated the back of its head. She
walked past it, stepped out into the street and locked the door
after herself.

Did it cry in there? Was that a cry she heard? Listening,
she shook her head. It never cried. And if it cried, what was
there to be done for it?

When she got to the corner of the street and started up the
hill toward the post office, the straggling group of Americans
was moving away from the open window. Good. When she got
there, Don Eliséo would just reach into her box and get the letter and hand it to her. She would not have to talk to anyone . . .
Helen Rogers had an armload of mail. Who would write to
Helen Rogers? What would you say to her? Am fine, how are
you? Wish you were here? No, it was probably business . . .
orders for her handwoven goods.

She stood at the window and Don Eliséo shuffled over to her
and looked into her face, and she said irritably, "You know me,
you know me," to him. Then he went off to her box and took an
air-mail envelope out of it, examined it in slow motion and came
to her with it, like a man carrying a ton of stone. "From Nuevo
York," he said.

"*Gracias,*" she said and snatched it out of his hand.

It was from Cushman. She turned away from the window

and stood still as she opened it, aware of the thick beating of her heart and a sudden rush of nausea so that her throat and mouth filled with an ugly metallic taste.

First she saw the check, for five hundred dollars, signed by Cushman, and with the relief of seeing that, could not see anything else for a minute, but stood there in the suddenly blinding sun, sighing out a long-held breath as though she had not breathed for weeks. It was an unlikely sum, but it must mean that he'd gotten an advance or a definite promise of one, and was sending his check first on the strength of it because she'd told him she was broke. Broke! Not even a whole ten-cent-store lipstick left . . . nothing. But it was surprising to feel so relieved. She hadn't really known until now that she needed relief so badly . . .

Half a block later, she began to unfold Cushman's letter.

"Dear Vick, in spite of your instructions, which I considered unreasonable, I have had three readers read your ms. and without looking at their reports, read it myself. Then I read the readers' reports and I agreed with them. I regret to say that I am not going to submit this material or any part of it to any publisher whatsoever."

She stumbled on a jagged piece of curbing, went then to the adobe wall and leaned against it while she read on. "Everything you have written," he wrote, "sounds as though somebody else wrote it. It is dead. It is dull. It is affected. It has no life. The people are not real and not human and I do not care about them. Having known you these years, and believed steadfastly in your talent, I cannot believe that you wrote this one hundred and fifty pages of nothing. These pastiches from you, of all people? *Impossible*. What has happened to you? There was more life in the letter accompanying this manuscript than in any page of the ms. itself. What in the world do you think you are writing? What is this pretentious nonsense about? What have *you* got to do with this snobbish, pretty-pretty set of people who are positively *cute*?

"I regard you as a friend, one of my few good friends in the literary world, and a rare talent. I am enclosing my check to you, which is a loan, and I implore you to get out of that miserable bottom-of-the-world resort which is destroying you and which, I assume, has cut you off from reality. Victoria, don't you think it is about time you stopped running away? How many years has it been? How many years do you think you have? Please use the money for fare, and come home where you belong and where you can write as you used to write . . ."

She jammed letter, envelope and check into her purse with shaking hands, and with rage turning the street red in front of her, turning the world into a roaring hollow in which the teeth-grinding, water-racing sounds of rage were all there was to be heard, ran toward the telegraph office.

At the telephone, putting through a call to New York, shouting information in two languages, yelling from a throat choked with fury, scarcely able to hear Mexico City but hearing the New York operator, beginning again with the Guadalajara operator, who seemed more distant still, on a line that crackled and wheezed and clacked like an animal greedily chewing up the words . . . she gripped the phone, set too high on the wall, and glared into the yard of the family who owned the telegraph office. She recited to herself, as though it were a disciplinary task, meant to hold her together, what she saw so that it seemed to have be stated to be seen, memorized to be real, while rage bubbled up and burst within her in a succession of explosions: the yard is of packed dirt; it has been recently swept; the marks of the coarse broom are on it, making wave patterns; the wall surrounding the yard is made of adobe; the wall is littered with a profusion of vines; the hens stalk in and out of the yard and the house in a constant, panic-striken search for food; out of sight but back there in the yard some place beyond the well, a small goat bleats insistently in a small voice.

My God, now I have lost the Guadalajara operator and I am getting the Jocotepec operator. This will never end. This is desperate. I am desperate. I shall get a gun and go there and shoot him and have it done, and his blood spilled before the call is completed.

All the work . . . and now charity from an old friend!

For this moment she had striven, starved, slaved, gone without, dressed like a fugitive from a rummage sale, deprived herself of life, robbed herself of time. For this moment she had written and rewritten days and nights, endured misfortune, self-doubt, hideous depression, hysterical joy, delusions of divinity.

No, this was intolerable. *It was intolerable.* There was the

moment where, if one could still speak, one said, No, I shall
not endure this.

Why did she cry? What did crying have to do with rage?
Why were there tears running out of her eyes? They did not
have to do with anything. Now she had gotten the Mexico
City operator and by-passed the Guadalajara operator and kept
yelling and swearing and crying, and she could feel her face
swelling up.

A child of the house stood over by the well in the yard, hiding slightly behind its stoned circle, watching her. It meant
nothing. Nothing had meaning, except to reach that nasal,
empty-minded, brain-no-bigger-than-a-worm's, agent, not a critic,
not her friend, not worth knowing, of no value. He had never
known anything, not even what he was told, and he knew less
now than before. He was a pompous hireling who must be destroyed. But when the call went through at last, rerouted twice
through Mexico City, there was no answer. Time and the Mexican telephone system had won out and in New York there was
an empty office and a telephone ringing in an unpeopled room,
its sound clattering urgently against filing cabinets and a water
cooler and a closet door left open by a last departing secretary.

What time was it in New York? Six . . . seven? Was it
Saturday, or Friday . . .

See the small-headed hens? See the vines, unpruned, tan-
gling over the rough bricks at the well's edge? See the child
watching you, with its dirty thumb in its dirt-ringed mouth? See
the empty office in New York? See the letter in your purse? See
the telephone?

Without deciding to do it, not even conscious of doing it,
she put in a call to Mexico City to Ramón.

When he answered, she sobbed out his name, suddenly
weakly swaying away from the high mouthpiece of the telephone, saying, "I am desperate. I am a failure. Oh what shall
I do?"

"Victoria," Ramón said. "What are you saying? What is
the matter?"

"I am a failure," she said. "Oh my God, you must help me,
don't you know . . . ? I am all alone . . ."

There was a silence and his voice said, "Do you mean you
want money? I am in a business conference. *Mire,* there are
people in my office, talking business . . ."

"No, I do not want money!" she cried. And she slammed down the receiver.

Out into the dusky street again, full of the sweet burning corn smell. There was the long, cobbled road to her house. There was the Coca-Cola sign at the *pura esquina*. Two dirty little children ran in a circle, playing a game, wearing nothing but little shirts which hiked up above their protruding navels. A burro cropped at the sparse grass growing between the stones of the street. There was the lake, mauve between sun-stained mountains. There was an old crone with a small blanket spread out on the ground before her door, and on the blanket little mounds of peanuts for sale, their shells blackened.

"*Cacahuates, señora?*" the crone whined as she passed.

A man passed her, touching his fingers to his sombrero, saying, "*Buenas tardes, señora.*"

She glared at him and she could feel how her lips pulled back from her teeth like a wolf's, and she saw how he halted, startled by the look of her, and then hurried on.

A fierce ant, was she? methodically plodding along, a tiny, ugly automaton, carrying pages over her head, lifting ideas and carrying them to other ideas, struggling along a narrow track, capable of a small bitter sting. But of no consequence. Of no consequence! Even to them, even to these, she was of no consequence.

She turned into her house. She went through the dimness past her typewriter and the stacked yellow paper beside it, and went to the red-painted cupboard Ned had given her, and got out the brandy bottle. She wheeled with it in her hand and went out into the patio and stood in the clustering dark and drank a great swallow from the bottle. It burned. She coughed, gagged, held it down. She went into the kitchen and found a glass and brought it back and filled it to the brim with brandy and stood there drinking it, not throwing up, but almost throwing up. Stand in the dark and drink the brandy. Look at the mountains' deeper dark against the sky, and drink the brandy. It is possible not to think at all. People who said there was never a time when your mind was empty of thought were wrong. She was empty of thought and feeling. There was only the brandy burning in the emptiness of her mind like a great hot coal.

When the brandy was finished, and before she was drunk, but knowing that very soon now she would be drunk, she turned to go in, into the deeper darkness of sleep, and stepped on something and stumbled.

The cat screamed out hoarsely and rolled under her foot and clawed her ankle.

Ablaze with fright, she kicked out at what clawed her, viciously and wildly, and struck at the cat's body.

There was another hoarse scream and the cat sprang into the air and, with its tail hanging like a loose rudder, loped over the stones, leapt to the patio wall where it stood silhouetted for a second, like a panther, and then it was gone.

She looked for a while at the place where it had been. Then she went into the living room and lay down on the couch and took off her dark glasses. She lay flat and still with her clothes on, waiting to be asleep, to be away in sleep.

At four in the morning, a weight came down on her mind as her eyes opened. What was it? But almost before she asked the question, the knowledge was there. Cushman's letter. It was the way you wake up after a death, when they have given you something to make you sleep and for that space of lost time you do not grieve, but when you awaken, the weight of death is there upon you, to be lifted again. She got up and took off her twisted clothing, and put on her old bathrobe. By now the infant next door was awake and crying, and the maternal hands were slapping tortillas rhythmically in the kitchen. Sandaled feet moved in the dark street outside the windows and small voices spoke hoarsely.

There was not much boiled water in the *olla*, but she took what there was and made a pot of black coffee. While it cooked, she went to the bathroom and dashed water on her face, without looking at herself. Then she came back, poured a mug of coffee, spooned some of One-Eyed Lupita's sugar into it and brought it with a lighted candle into the patio and sat there. She drank the coffee, and listened to the village sounds and stared at the first pale blue of the dawn. By the time she had drunk all the coffee, and smoked her first cigarette, the sun had vaulted brilliantly into the sky. She blew out the candle.

She cleaned up the living room and then the bathroom, hauled up some pails of water and bathed herself. The sun was bright but the morning air was cool. She brushed and braided her hair, dressed, and when she got her old woolen skirt on,

saw that the zipper was broken. She held the waistband together until she got the leather belt clasped around it, and then
tucked the zipper into a fold of the cloth. She came back into the
patio and sat down and looked at the morning. There was the
day in front of her, like a pan with nothing in it.

The *niña* came in, tiptoeing at first in case she was asleep,
but when the child saw her sitting there, she pattered over to
her, smiling, saying, "*Buenos días, señora,*" and waiting. It was
best to say nothing, not even turn and look at the child. That way
she would know to leave her alone.

The little girl withdrew, tiptoeing again, into the kitchen
where she stood looking out the window, gnawing on a stale roll
. . . Twice she called the cat. But the cat did not appear.

The *niña* boiled water for drinking and while it boiled, she
made many unnecessary trips out of the kitchen through the
patio and into the living room, looking for the cat and hoping
not to be observed, glancing first at Victoria to see if she were
watching and, when she decided it was safe, making little sh-sh
sounds and peeking behind bushes.

Victoria sat there throughout the morning, unmoving, not
thinking, staring. Her eyes kept looking at the same thing and
she, behind her eyes, did not think, did not let thoughts come
like birds to twitter and chirp through the twilight wastes of
her mind, and also, did not see whatever it was her eyes saw.
She heard sounds, but they were not recognized. You could say
it was a kind of sleep, a desert, a sand plain of sleep, and the
only thing which ever appeared upon it was her shoulder bag.
The shoulder bag appeared, closed, hung in the limbo of mid-
air over the sand, and when that happened she blinked to make
it go away.

In the afternoon, the shoulder bag appeared more and
more persistently, and when she saw the envelope's corner, now
apparently forcing its way past the clasp, she knew that the
time of her withdrawal was almost over. Reality, in the shape of
Cushman's letter, crushed into her shoulder bag, would not be
denied much longer. There were, after all, only the two things
. . . reality and insanity. Both were painful.

Ned called at the house at sundown. He was still wearing
his city clothes, a dark gray suit, an immaculate white shirt, a

narrow black tie. He carried, though there was not a cloud in the sky, his long black umbrella in its silken sheath.

He came in briskly, tossed a package he'd brought onto the chair near her, came to her and kissed her forehead.

"There you are," he said. "I'm home, as I said I would be! And the show was a success and when you come to the house I'll show you all the nice things the critics said. I sold lots of paintings, although everybody says it's been a bad season for American artists. I was really awfully lucky! Of course, I don't charge enough for it to matter, really . . . as far as the money is concerned . . . There were some Americans and they insisted on buying The Icicle, but I told them it really belonged to you and if at any time you wanted to buy it, they'd have to sell it to you. So it's on loan, you might say . . ." His voice died and he stepped back and looked at her. "Oh, God," he said. "You're in one of your *things!*"

She could see the flash of light from his spectacles as he turned his head and looked around as though he might find some explanation of the trouble, and then came back and stood before her again, and peered into her face.

"Not one word for me?" he said, raising his eyebrows.

The silence stretched thin between them. He straightened up, sighing. He said, pointing to the package, "That's a present, as I promised."

He went and opened the door of the living room and looked in there and then closed the door again.

"I brought Chloë back with me. I thought maybe you'd come over for supper. You'll like her. And we'll have our champagne and caviar as I said . . ."

Because she had not spoken since yesterday, her voice had a dry, rustling sound to it. She said, "The cat's gone."

"What?" he said.

"The cat's gone."

"Gone where?" he said.

"Gone."

He looked all around him, and then he looked back at her, and the silence now went into him and became his, not hers, and now his eyes were going bright cold blue and his mouth was stiffening. Just slightly to the left of his head, above the arid sand dunes where he stood, her shoulder bag with Cushman's letter hung, swaying in the limbo breeze of the angry silence. He did not know that, but he turned his head nervously as though he thought something might be there. Then, when he did not see anything, he looked back at her again, with his lips opening spitefully, about to speak. . . .

That would not do. No.

She rose and lifted her right arm and extended her hand with the forefinger pointing at the door to the street.

"You will please to leave my house," she said.

He gazed at her, his mouth rounding with surprise and disbelief, losing its shape of spite. He looked at the door to which her finger pointed, and looked back at her again. A little puff of incredulity came out of his mouth, but he began to back away from her, and his eyes were believing her more all the time now, looking more frightened than angry, believing and disbelieving, but with his body backing away, which was an act of belief. When he got to the small step, he turned and stumbled down in a disordered way. He went along the shadowed part of the *zaguán* and at the door he looked back at her again, at her rigidly pointing finger and her face, and he looked away and went out the door. The door closed after him. She did not hear his footsteps on the street outside, but he was gone.

15

Harry

THERE WERE FIREFLIES going around in circles, traveling fast, flashing red and yellow, and it took a while before he realized that they were following the sounds of the voice which went around and around in the same way and, in fact, was what *was* going around. The fireflies were made of sound and that was what lit them up and flashed them on and off. There was something pulling at his blanket and his own hands were too weak with sleep to hold onto it although he was trying to hold on, while at the same time he followed the fireflies around their circles . . .

"Come *on!*" the fireflies flashed. "Harry, come *on!*"

One eye opened itself and drowned in the light and he shut

it as quickly as he could. Some of the fireflies were forming words very rapidly saying something about Jim—that Jim was gone?—while another set of fireflies insisted that he open his eyes. He allowed both eyes to slit open, letting in the lash-fragmented line of light to see if it could be endured. He turned over and burrowed his head into the dark self-smelling pillows and that drove off the fireflies, but then the pillows were jerked from under his face, and his nose was pressing against the hard mattress. He rolled over.

He said, with his eyes still shut, "Will you bug off?"

"It's noon," Charles said, and pulled the sheet away from him so cold air ran over him with little furry feet.

"You and your lit-up tails and your cold, furry feet," Harry said. He sat up and opened his eyes and the light hit him like a shovel being slammed against the side of his head. He sat there, rocking a little, feeling bad, blind from the glare, with the cold paws of cats walking on him.

He opened his eyes and held them open, with his hand. He looked through his fingers at the other end of the room. His clothes hung there on a rope in a row, like the story of his life run backward, because it started at the end with the first band jacket, and all of them were hung on there chronologically, band jacket after band jacket, just the way he had gone from big band to big band wearing those big drapey coats which were all too big and saggy on him in the beginning and worse now that he was so much thinner. It was the story of his life as a musician since the end of the war, but backward, because the last band jacket was hanging near the table where the toy soldiers were all set up, there by the window, and that was the war and should have been the beginning, not the end, because the toy soldiers had more reality, with their pennants and tanks, and horses and ambulances and nurses and chow trucks, than the war had had as a war. *This* was a war on the table. The war, it-self, had not been a war. It had no strategy, no grandeur, but was instead a dreary personal experience enlivened only by the discovery that he could not, no matter how foolhardy he was, get himself killed.

You could tell to look at the table that Jim wasn't gone. That must have been a dream about Jim. Jim was set up for his first victory over Harry. He had Harry's troops flanked in a pincer movement and today Jim was going to capture two di-

visions. It was the last thing Jim said last night, that he was going to take those two divisions today, and that was what Harry
wanted because he was bringing in his aircraft, sucking Jim's
troops into the vulnerable terrain where he had been pocketed.
But Jim wasn't a smart enough stud to figure that out; he'd
never have gone away today because this was to have been
V-Day for Jim . . . after a two-week war of defeat.

He groped on the bedside table for his glasses and almost
knocked over the tequila bottle, but he grabbed it just as it was
going over. He got his glasses and put them on. They were
dirty and they blurred out some of the wild light in the room.
The coughing started then, rattling and wheezing, making the
lobes of his lungs ache deep in his back. He set the bottle down
on the bed beside him and pressed his hands against the ache.
Sure was low. Maybe it was his kidneys and not his lungs at
all. Whatever it was, it ached. There was a mouthful of tequila
in the bottle and if he could get that down it would loosen up
the cough, but lately he hadn't been able to hold the mouthful if
he hadn't had the fix. With Charles in the room and the
cough this bad, he'd have to try without the fix. He uncorked
the bottle, tipped it up and poured the tequila down his throat.
When it came back, he swallowed again and waited.

Charles stood with his back to him, looking out the open
window. That was where all the goddamned light was rushing in
from. "Shut the window," he said.

Charles said, "It stinks in here, man."

Harry said, "I don't like to start my day with you, mother."

Charles said, "Those sheets are crummy."

The tequila was not resting easy. It was fluttering around
in there in a very disgusting way. He got up and got his feet into
his huaraches, and then took them off because he had to get
his pants on first. He groped around on the foot of the bed till he
found his rolled-up trousers, and then he dragged them on and
put his huaraches on again. He didn't have time to pick up a
shirt. He grabbed the first one of the band jackets and got into
it. He was shaking. He saw Charles was watching him shake
like that. "Going to the *excusado*," Harry said.

Charles said, "I'll turn my back. Have your fix here,
junkie."

He grabbed up the shaving kit and hurried, although the
jogging footsteps hurt his head, out of the room and across the

patio to the john. The Doña called out something at him, but
the tequila had come up in his mouth now, and he couldn't stop
the retching that had begun, like waves, combers, rolling up
his body from the groin to the mouth . . . Once in there, he
just opened his mouth and it happened. After the first mouthful
though, and Christ how it burned his throat, it was just dry
heaves. He got off his knees in a few minutes, but he was shaking, and he had a bastard of a time getting his hands to hold
stiff and still enough to make the fix and set the needle in the
vein and then remember to go slowly, not slam the stuff home.
Once it was in, and the first impulse to flash was over, so that he
just retched a couple of times but not hard, he waited, putting
the string back into the shaving kit, squirting alcohol through
the syringe because there was a lot of hepatitis around, and he
had enough going for him without that. Fever was a gas, and it
might be a way down and around to finding that sweet dark tunnel where it would be always serene, but it might also bring
a doctor who would keep him from his fix and that would be another thing, something else. He put the syringe back in its metal
case, and checked his supply, because if Jim had gone away,
he'd have taken some, but it was all there, enough for the rest
of today and tonight and tomorrow morning. Mariano had promised him that by tomorrow noon he'd have a new supply. He
was able to straighten up now; there was a rush of heat through
his cold body, and his stomach was beginning to get quiet and
soft like he had nothing hurting him in there any more, but
just layers of soft stuff, and soft stuff was moving over his
nerves, sheathing them so they didn't pull and jerk and he was
definitely getting straight. The thought came, as it always did
before the straight was entirely there, with one jab of surprise
and fright as he believed it, "I'm really on this now." But he
waited through that, and when the straight was fully all over
him, he knew he wasn't on it at all, really, not hung up, or hooked
or anything, just . . . using something to get comfortable.

"I've got a terminal illness, baby," he said to his yellowing
face in the mirror. "I've got life."

When he came out he saw Charles talking with the
Doña María, bugging the old lady about the sheets and like that,
but actually she hadn't been able to get into the room to touch
anything and it wasn't her fault, only Charles' Spanish wasn't
good enough for him to dig what she was saying. But when you

looked at the old doll, even if you were supposed to like her and
sometimes he pretended he did, you didn't really. A landlady was
a landlady and this one deserved to have her wrists slit for
Christmas.

He went on into the room and there was the bare mattress
stripped of its sheets and the blanket. He usually put his shaving kit under the mattress, but that wouldn't do now, because
she'd find it when she made the bed; he'd have to find a new
place.

He stood looking at the toy soldiers, trying to see how Jim
could have gone away when he was on the verge of his first
win, and feeling cooler all the time, more and more straight, so
his mind was clearing now, but he did not have a good feeling.
Maybe on account of Jim. Maybe because of the way the day
started. He liked a day to start itself; that was best. Charles
was coming back now, he could hear him.

Charles had a tin tray which had a picture of a bottle of
Coca-Cola on it and a girl's face, mostly chipped off. The tray
held coffee and a plate of eggs and bread. He set the thing
down on top of the bureau and then began to fuss with the salt
and pepper.

"You going to eat that?" Harry said.

"You are," Charles said, but he didn't look at him or smile
or anything. There was nothing loose about Charles today.
He was all nerved up.

"Charles-baby," he said. "I'm not hungry. I got no eyes."

"Quit weaving around with the shaving kit in your hand,"
Charles said. "Man, look at you! You're flying. How much are
you using?"

He didn't answer any of that. Charles brought him the
coffee and pushed him down in the chair. That was all right.
No matter how much old Hophead Charlie Beauregard pushed
him around and dogged him around, he still did not know how
smart Harry was. Nobody knew how smart he was. "Don't dog
me 'round," he said.

"Drink it," Charles said.

He tasted it. "Pemex," he said.

While he drank the coffee, Charles told him that Margo
Whitman had turned the heat on Jim. She'd found out about
the big rap hanging over him in the States, that he was wanted
for pushing and that it was the *third* time, which would mean

life; Margo hollered cop and Jim flipped when the Federales came for him, and double-flipped so nothing would hold him but a strait jacket and four guys to hold him after that. It was so real . . . it was real. So he'd probably get put in a VA psycho hospital when they got him back in the States . . . for life.

"Margo Whitman?" Harry said. " 'La Belle Dame Sans Merci.' "

"She said Jim was giving *her town* a bad name," Charles said. "That broad is buying up the place. Like it's hers, man. The Posada, this place, my house, Abel's Bar, Vickie's house, Ned's . . . just name the place and she's got the papers on it." He leaned forward. "The broad is after you, too, Harry," he said. "I been hipped that the Federales are coming back . . . for you."

He drank the rest of the coffee and handed Charles the cup. The coffee was sloshing around in him, but he was going to be able to hold it. He had a bad, bitter taste in his mouth. Charles ate the breakfast so the Doña wouldn't have to see the eggs left untouched and know that Harry had not eaten his breakfast, because everybody was hip that it was hard for a junkie to eat. That was the reason Charles gave for eating it, but you could see that besides all that, he had eyes for the food. While Charles ate, he talked. Dozing, Harry listened, and sometimes when he went off down the narrow velvet path to find the waterfall in the deep green mossy jungle, Charles pushed at him and woke him up.

Then Charles found a shirt and started to put it on him. He looked at his arms carefully first and then he said, "Where do you shoot it, junkie?"

Nobody would guess where he put it. He was very cool. The Feds could examine his arms forever and not find needle scars; he'd thought that out in the beginning.

But Charles found it right away. He just looked at the vein in his ankle and said, "Don't you think the fuzz will think of that? We got to find you some socks, man."

There weren't any socks. That mothering Jim had stolen them all. Charles sat down and took off his own socks and put them on Harry, but that ankle was red and swollen and Charles looked at it and shook his head. He got up and went out and when he came back, he woke Harry up, taping and bandaging the ankle.

"Hey," Harry said. "How do I get at it?"

"You don't," Charles said. "It's infected. You sprained your ankle, man."

"But later," Harry said. "When it's time for the fix, I mean?"

Charles said, "I told you . . . it's infected. You need a new vein." He stood up and looked at him. "You got to remember to limp."

He went to the window and looked out again and then he came back. He found a rum bottle in Jim's cupboard and soaked Harry's lapels with it and made Harry wash some of the rum around in his mouth, so he would look and smell like he was drunk because everybody knew no junkie was a juicer.

"Maybe the stone goddess won't want any lushes in her town either," Harry said. "What do I do for Margo then, mother? Join A.A.?"

Charles said, "We are going to take a little trip, Harry. You and I are going out of this town and you won't be holding when we're on the move, either. We're going to San Miguel till the heat dies down. This is a big bust that's coming . . ."

For a minute it came at him through his straight, and he got scared. Sweat tickled on his scalp and he could hear how noisy his breathing was. He said, beginning to panic, "Now, don't hang me, man . . ." and he was looking around the room for a place to stash the shaving kit, saying, "Go home, square. Go home."

Charles said, "No place in this room is going to do, Harry. You got to lay it on me. I got this planned."

"No, man," Harry said.

"When are you due for it?"

"Four hours."

Charles had a cloth *bolsa* full of vegetables. He took the stuff out of it, and put the shaving kit on the bottom, then he piled the lettuce and tomatoes and beets on top of the shaving kit.

"What month is it?" Harry said. "If it's still December, I got time. I'm not due at the border for a month . . ."

"It's December." Charles took two visas out of his pocket. "I got us both, baby," he said. "I'll carry them."

Blinking at Charles in the glare of light, saying, "But where's Annie, man?" he was thinking that this was really getting to have the sound of trouble and his damned mouth was too dry and Charles talked like he didn't know how his voice

could file down on your teeth and your nerves until you wanted
to get away from him no matter how, and if it was real trouble,
why, Charles was nobody to hang on. You needed somebody who
could really help you then, didn't you? The only one he could
think of was his father, like always when it was on the level, so
he said, "Telephone him. Telephone my father. Tell him it's real
trouble, you dig? So he'll come and get me out . . ."

"They won't let me call," Charles said. "The phone is restricted to military personnel."

That didn't mean anything. "We at war?" Harry said.

"I told you. Martial law," Charles said. "Curfew. Shoot on
sight after nine o'clock at night. You finally going to pick up on
what's happening?"

"Man," Harry said. "Why don't we kill that broad, Charles?"

"We'll put Margo on The Bus," Charles said.

Later when he looked around, explaining that he meant it
and The Bus wasn't real—it was only a fantasy—Charles was
gone. He had a flickering memory that Charles had said something about finding out what times the buses left Guadalajara
for San Miguel, and what time buses left the village—yeah,
that was it—and then he'd gone. After a while the Doña was
standing there with the clean sheets, her old crone's crackling
voice going, and he got out of the room and stood around at
the well, waiting, while she fixed the bed. He'd forgotten to
limp.

It didn't matter. It was December and he was going to slit
the Doña's wrists for Christmas. Get your Christmas-slitting
done early. Maybe, if he was going to kill anybody, it should be
the stone goddess. Would Margo bleed? "If you cut me, don't I
bleed?" Not you, you miserable broad. Pebbles would fall
out of your veins . . . stones, pebbles, frogs, bugs . . .

The idea of bugs made him crawly and he was shaky anyway. He wasn't going any place. He couldn't go so far from
Mariano. Besides he had hepatitis. He was sure of it. He might
die of that. He couldn't go to San Miguel, unless Mariano came
along with him, and brought his supply of Nice White with
him. Rinso-white, that's what it was, whiter than snow, and
pure . . . until lately. Lately it felt like Mariano had been cutting it . . . He'd needed more all the time, like now was only
an hour or two after the fix and he was still strung out a
little.

He went back into the room and drove the Doña out, shut

the window and got into the bed she hadn't finished making, lying down in his stinking clothes, shivering with chill. He
pulled the covers around himself and lay his head on the clean
white pillow and flaked out through the velvet drifts of dark and
when he found the rich purple surfboard, he caught on to that
one and stretched out for a long ride-out, and he began to think
up tenor solos that traveled farther out than Bird or Coltrane or
anybody . . .

In the dream he was a small boy again, and somebody, not
Charles, was putting his socks on. He'd been sick, and he was
sitting in a big chair that had wings on the sides, as big as ele-
phant ears, and it had always been his favorite chair because
it was so safe, because he thought nobody could see him when he
was in it. It was a servant helping him, wasn't it? A nurse or a
servant or something . . . then it had been, but in this dream,
it was his mother, when she was younger. His eyes opened and
the dream merged into the memory of her talking to him, telling him to try to get along with his father, but she didn't understand that his father hated him, and looked at him with hatred
when his mother wasn't around. His sister said he looked at her
the same way, but he'd never seen it. His sister said it wasn't
hatred, that the old man was afraid of them; to him the two
kids were like little consciences watching him and knowing
somehow, with the hip-wisdom of children, that he was mixed
up in a dozen shady deals. That was the first he'd heard of shady
deals. His sister said he was lucky, because as long as he didn't
know about them, the better he could get along. But his mother
was respectable in all ways. Cold eyes, cold mouth . . . an ex-
piano teacher, religious-minded, and fond of her daughter. She
always looked at *him* in an exasperated way when his father
yelled at him or hit him, and he got the feeling that she was saying, He's not mine, not like me. Neither of them seemed to like
him. But he couldn't blame them. He wasn't very likeable.

He wanted them to like him in the beginning, but when
they didn't seem to, he gave up that idea. The old man hated him
and he tried to hate the old man back, but he didn't have a reason. So he stayed out of the house and it got so he didn't see
much of them. He was always with the gang, with Ollie and
Greg mostly, trying not to seem any richer than they were, while
the old man was sporting flashier clothes and houses and cars
all the time. He just wanted to be like the others.

Greg and Ollie liked him. The rest of the gang liked him.

He got along with boys, and with men, all his life. But with women, he was always afraid and he didn't know what to do with them, and so he chased them when the gang did, but otherwise, and underneath, he was still afraid of them. The only girls he wasn't afraid of were the ones who had something wrong with them.

In the Army, when he got all the medals and made it so big, he figured that ought to change the old man's opinion of him, but it didn't. When the hero came home, he just stood around the big damned ugly mansion in the middle of a desert, and his father was always surprised to see him there, like he'd just been born, and like he was learning to hate him all over again. It was absolutely impossible for him to have a conversation with the old man, which was what made it so wild when other people said to him that his father was witty or clever or kind or bright. He always thought: He is? Are you sure? The old man had no word for him and he had none for the old man. His mother too, fussing over the wedding stuff for Betsy, didn't seem to know what to do with him. When Gerald—How about that? Betsy marrying a guy who was not only named Gerald, but referred to himself as Gerald. "This is Gerald Stoneham speaking," he'd say on the telephone—asked him to be best man, his mother said, "Harry? You want *Harry*?" as though Gerald had asked for the butler or the plumber to stand up for him. Then later Betsy told him it was all right with her, but Mother was afraid he'd get drunk and ruin the ceremony. "Then they can throw me out with the rented gilt chairs and the hired harpist and the potted palms next day," he said. "What is this wedding? A goddamned opening night or something? Think I'll keep the show from being a hit?"

Betsy, filing her nails, had looked up at him, smiling in that sad way which made him remember that she was older than he was. He had seen that smile many times and never known what it meant.

That night Betsy came into his room. She brought a bottle of Scotch with her and a couple of glasses. She was already a little bit lushed, and it was the first time he had ever seen her that way.

She made the drinks and they were strong ones. She said, "Have you got any reefers? I've never smoked one, but I know you do. I'd like one."

He said, lying, "No, baby. I wouldn't turn you on."

She sat on the foot of his bed and looked at him. He could see how miserable she was. She wasn't used to lushing and she couldn't look cheerful the way she usually did. He said, "What's the matter, Bets?"

She shook her head.

He said, watching her drink, "You got no eyes for this cat?"

She looked straight ahead for a minute down a long, lonely avenue. "No eyes at all," she said.

"Then the hell with him," he said. But she wouldn't answer.

They juiced awhile with him doing most of the talking and her not answering any questions until they were both pretty loaded. She began, quietly, to cry, making such sad, sighing sounds, it was like when she was a little girl and it broke his heart.

He said, "Bets, don't marry this square. You don't have to marry him. Wait till you find some stud you flip for . . ."

"No," Betsy said. "I never will. I never have and I never will." She said in a muffled voice, "You know why, Harry. You've just made yourself forget it, that's all."

He honestly didn't know. When she said that, there was something and it made him uncomfortable whatever it was, but he didn't remember. He took her in his arms and held her and she cried there. Finally she got up and walked across the room. When she turned to him her face was bleak. "I like girls," she said. "You know it. You've always known it. You remember . . ."

He said, "No. Oh, no." He stared at her, across the room. She looked like a child. "That boarding-school stuff . . . But that was a long time ago, Bets. That's not *now* . . ."

"It is . . . now," she said.

Pretty, clean-faced, wholesome, clear-skinned, light-eyed, curly-haired, sexy . . . He couldn't believe it. He couldn't stand it and he couldn't believe it.

She said, "Please don't hate me, Harry. I'm doing the best I can." When he didn't say anything, she came over to him. She dried her eyes. "I don't want to be the way I am. But I am." He still couldn't say anything. "Don't worry," she said. "Gerald is going to be very happy with his wife. I'm smart. He's never going to know the difference." She went to the door and opened it and looked back at him wretchedly. "But I'll know it," she said.

His mother was right. He did get drunk at the wedding. In fact, he was stoned out of his skull long before it, and a nice safe sober fellow took his place. They threw Harry and his medals out with the rented gilt chairs and the harpist, when it was over.

That didn't bother him. But it rocked him to know how wrong he'd been about Betsy, and it frightened him, because finding out Betsy was like that, he wondered if he was, because they were a peculiar damned family and nothing was the way it seemed with them. He wondered about that for a long time, and studied about it. He got pretty well educated on the subject of personalities and he discovered that he wasn't a fag . . . he was a baby. He'd never gotten beyond about four years old emotionally, if he was that old. So, he chose the cripples of the world for his playmates . . . they were ever-young . . . and with his tenor and his clarinet he played his cripple's music and now he had a bandage on his ankle to cover the swelling and the bruise where the needle-scar was infected, and he had a fever and he was shooting heroin and on his way into the black woods of death, because this ache which had started in his back and which was coming through the straight and spoiling it, was also in the front, and his eye-whites were yellowing and he burned with fever and had hepatitis. Today he was sure. The skin on his hands was yellow. There was only a chance it was the needle infection. There was a much bigger chance it was hepatitis.

So he wasn't going to go anywhere with Charles, and he wasn't going to be extradited, or deported. He was going to die right here in this bed . . . after he'd slit the Doña's wrists.

Everybody had a place in him, burning or ashen, where he lived, where his hope for life lived, where the starving-eyed child in him looked out. He'd seen those eyes, the special eyes of that place in everybody many times. Charles' eyes got like that about O, and Vickie's when she said, "I'm working you know. Writing." She was going to be just a poor old doll as soon as she got the shaft from Ned . . . not the shaft she wanted, but the one that told her she was a poor old doll who had fallen like a plumb line for a screaming faggot. Poor old doll.

Elinor was a born poorolddoll. There was that thing in her, he'd seen it there more often than in other people, but it was harder to remember it was there because the chick was so

dumb, yet it looked out like a deer at a forest fire, eyes wide
with panic. Life was a forest fire to her. Jackson knew that; that
was what he hated about her. He didn't want to look at the forest
fire all the time, be reminded of it. The fire was out in Jackson
and the burning place in him was ashen, gray, as beaten and old
as if he were seventy right now. He wasn't going to get any older,
as long as he lived. He was *there,* now.

That look in Elinor—and the broad in Indiana, what was
her name? Mary Jane . . .—that was the look that made him
feel something, more than pity, pure noble lust, and in that
kind of love he found more jazz. He was the lazy kind of sadist.
He needed them to be already beaten by somebody or something
else, looking at him with hope reborn. There was no hope. But
these chicks, with that hopeful hungry look, they couldn't bear
for you to say that there was nothing but kicks. No chick could
live that way, even though some of them pretended they could.
It was biologically impossible for them to live with the truth.
They couldn't live knowing nothing was coming but death and
that all you got was the kicks you put in between you and that.

Death has a black carriage, a brougham, with silver fit-
tings, and black drapes at the windows, and the black horses
wear black plumes and their hoofs are shod with shining steel
so they strike sparks on the stone street, and the black glossy
hides of the horses shine with grooming, like they were polished,
and their flanks glisten. Behind the drapes Death wears black
satin and a black lace veil, and behind the veil is a smiling,
fleshless mouth with exposed white teeth.

"Whatcha say, mamo?" he said.

He could overshoot. Suppose he loaded up, jammed it home,
fell out that way so there would be no more waiting and worrying, no crazy broads like the stone goddess to hunt him down.
That spade horn man on the ship to Hawaii, Dickie—but all
horse and no blow and he knew it, man, he was hip to how he
sounded—going into the head and locking the door, and they
heard him fall against the door. Dickie didn't want them to
blowtorch him out of that john. He'd even planned how he'd
fall. When he'd gone in, all twitches and sniffing like any
junkie, he'd stopped a minute at the door and given Harry a long
look. He let me see. Man, I knew what he was going to do. I
wasn't surprised when I heard him fall. I just sat there and
blew pot.

But you die a junkie death and everybody remembers that
and forgets the rest. They'd forget the medals and the brain, the
IQ higher than any of theirs, the boy who should have
written poetry, who should have painted like Leonardo, who
should have written like St.-John Perse, who had it in him, all
those things, but who was fatally in love with his own death
and who was only four years old.

Life got to be sour in your mouth and kicks came harder
and harder. What was it he used to be like? Because it was
gone now, that memory. Maybe if he tried to be the way he was
before the world looked like an empty rotting unfurnished
house to him . . . Marrying Carmela had been the mistake
maybe. No, she happened after the mistake. He was the mistake. She wasn't a bad chick and the baby wasn't a bad baby if
you dug babies, but all that stuff about its future was the bug
that flipped him out, and her *trying* all the time to do and be and
feel . . . what you were supposed to do and be and feel *without* trying. The minute you tried, impulse was gone, spontaneity
was gone. What was I like before I lost my *joie de vivre?* He
knew damned well Carmela didn't want to go off with that
square in the Chevrolet coupé, as Slimovoutee would say. She
looked back at him, standing in the rotting empty world, one
last time, with the hungry eyes, so he waved her away. Get off
my back, chick. Take your square and go.

Betsy had said, "I like girls."

Betsy with two kids, looking sunny in the kitchen, smiling
through the P.T.A. meetings, her blond hair always combed
and perfumed, never wearing slacks, but those full skirts, a little
short, and the wired brassières so she looked like she should
look, clear-eyed and young in her thirties but beginning then to
make jokes about feeling older . . . and Gerald never did wise
up, never hipped to Betsy's "girlfriends" and the wild Mexican
maid that was around for a year or so. Wow. Betsy looking at
Carmela, and there was the hungry look for her and he saw it.
But Carmela wouldn't have believed it, even if Betsy and he together had told her about it. Only once she looked funny, when
she was in labor and Betsy held onto her through one of the
pains, and when Betsy pulled back and away, Carmela looked
at her and shivered and said, "This twilight-sleep stuff is . . .
mixing me up. . . ."

It wasn't about Betsy that he'd gotten this way, the way he

was. The poor flip broad had to do something. She was a good mother, and a good wife, and if she got too much out of the girls, what of it? Everybody digs something.

At first, Gerald thought Betsy had had the accident deliberately. Genius Gerald said she was too good a driver to wrap the car around a tree the way she did, unless she did it on purpose. Maybe. So what, if she'd had enough of it? Carmela thought it was deliberate, too. There was another brain for you. Carmela said, "She did it on purpose and I know why." "Why?" "Because she was in love with you, Harry. Betsy was in love with you."

He said if Betsy was going to do it, she'd have done it a way that was sure. Hitting a tree at ninety miles an hour wasn't sure. You could be crippled and spend your life on your back begging for every swallow of water.

He lay there, staring up at the dirty ceiling. "You waiting for me, Bets?" he said.

There was no answer, no feeling of an answer. She wasn't anywhere, waiting. She simply wasn't.

That was the thing about death he always began to feel, how it could be that you could simply not *be* so you didn't even know you weren't being, so that there wasn't any you any more to be or not to be. Like Alice, he looked down the rabbit hole, tempted to fall, but not able to believe . . . That was what Charles said one time, "Man, you bug everybody about death and you know something? You don't believe it."

How could he believe it? Nobody believed it. Asylums were full of people who'd gotten a glimpse of it, just enough of a glimpse to know unalterably that it was there, until that knowledge got shocked out of them. Then, like babies, they thought they were immortal again. But it is the fact in life that we live with, it is the hand reaching for our hand, "all the time, Mama, all the time . . . Well, I drink to keep from worryin', and I smile to keep from cryin' . . . and to keep the public from knowin' what's on my worried mind." He liked that line.

"Someday, someday, Babe . . . I'll be six feet in my grave . . . I won't be around, to be treated like a lowdown, dirty slave, no Mama, no, no. Baby, no no. Oh, no!"

Or, "If you live, your time will come."

You said it, Mose. You said the word. You laid the word on me. You and Marcus Aurelius and Epictetus, and Kant and—

not Aristotle, Aristotle was a fink—Kierkegaard and Sartre. Don't give me your No Exit philosophy, you studs . . . I'm proving it for you. Who was the cat that did the *Noctes Ambrosianae*? When somebody went to the border, he'd ask him to get those, bring them back. Would they have those books in Brownsville, Texas? He should send Abel for him. Hell, they'd rather he married their sisters than ask for something like that in a Texas bookstore. Lynchville.

Maybe he could get in blackface and go to Brownsville, go to the bookstore. That's a way to die, for a cause. I go no cause to die for. But I got cause to die.

Right in the middle of the Paul Desmond solo on "Take Five," which was playing in his mind exactly as it played on the record . . . and the big vamp the drummer did while Brubeck would *not* meet him on the ¾ time . . . so it was like standing at the wrong kiosk waiting to meet a friend and, like anybody waiting to meet a friend who didn't show, the drummer began to get nervous and drop bombs . . . "Prez" always said, "No bombs, man. Make it pretty." Anyway in the middle of all this action with the tenor and the drums and Brubeck on the piano there was Jackson Garth, and at first he thought it must be Charles, old Mother Beauregard, come back to see him again; but it wasn't. It wasn't a dream either because it really was Jackson Garth sitting there and he really had been here for some time now, hadn't he? Whenever he'd opened his eyes in the last few minutes, hadn't he seen old whey-face, gray-face Jackson sitting there, looking like a graduate of the narco squad . . . a fink, a born goddamned fink—you could smell it if you couldn't see it—telling him all this wild jazz about how he was going to wrap Elinor around his neck and he tried to listen, to pick up on what Jackson was saying, and stall so as to keep Desmond going on tenor . . .

And he said, stalling, "You know, sweetie, why I never liked you or trusted you . . ." all the while talking carefully so as not to interrupt the rhythm in his mind, Algerian like they never made it in "Night in Tunisia," but still having to get on top of what Jackson was saying out of the pious mouth, no matter what, because, man, I mean that was a nightmare and a very bad thing . . .

"I never liked you," he said to Jackson, "on account of all the time you been here on the big goof-off, man, you never fixed the license plate on your truck. Now, yeah, it's a little thing and you can say I have a small mind to sift out a small thing . . . So say that, man, lay the word on somebody. You're *nouveau head*, you know that? But that license plate banging on your truck, making that *noise*, man. I mean, if you were a *musician*"—letting his voice drop when he said "musician" like he was saying "saint"—"if you were a *musician*, that sound would have bugged you. I mean . . . no, man. I don't want to ride anywhere with you in that truck with the funky plate banging around all wrong, like 'Used to it, used to it, ch . . . ch . . .' You know the old joke about Lombardo . . ." The joke was a gas, but Square John Jackson hadn't heard it and he was too high to worry about sharing his pleasure in it. He just laughed alone. But Jackson was coming on very hard now with the righteous con about she's your chick and I know you wouldn't have betrayed me, baby, if you could have helped yourself, and she's yours. It's not only bigger than both of you, it's bigger than the three of us, junkie. So she's yours.

But you know that I told you it was time to do something. Only it looked like too late to do something. Hey, now what had been happening? How long had he been asleep?

Harry said, "Jackson-baby, you know I got hepatitis? You know you're visiting the sick?"

Jackson smiled.

"You sit around here long enough, sweetie, and like the song says, it could happen to you. Highly contagious, this infectious hepatitis."

"I wanted you to know why I wasn't taking you and Charles out of here, Harry," Jackson said. "It's because I'm going alone. Just me. Down to Yucatán."

"You ought to do something about that license plate, you know? It makes a bad impression."

Jackson laughed. He didn't laugh much lately when you thought about it. But now he was the gray man anyway, made of ashes, no burning place in him, no hunger.

Jackson said, "If I took you away, what would Elinor do? Elinor needs you, Harry. Every afternoon she's been needing you. So, she's yours. And Ricky, too. Yucatán is no place for a kid.

That's hot, miserable country down there, and that poor little son of mine shouldn't have to go . . . and be so far from his mother."

Jackson got up and walked over to the door. He stood there, looking short and square and ugly.

"You've flipped, Jackson," Harry said in a mumbling voice. "I been playing toy soldiers with your chick, that's all. That's all, pops. You can't hang me for that."

Jackson smiled. "I know all about it, junkie," he said. "She's yours. I told her she was yours and she wept with gratitude." His smile broadened. "It's a happy scene. Jackson's gone and the lovers united at last. I've waited a long time for some sucker to come along and take that broad off my hands. Lighthorse Harry of the Horse Marines!" He laughed.

That was an unfortunate remark for a Square John to make. Be all right if *he* talked about horse, but not Jackson. Not when he was *on,* and Jackson was *off.* But it would be better not to pick up on that. He made a show of drifting off to sleep again, but Jackson kept talking in that square way out of a tight throat. He was bugged, you could hear it in his voice, and there was a pain you could hear in his laugh, somewhere, like he'd got everything worked out to hang it on Harry and in a way he was sorry.

"Hey, man," Harry said. "What do you say?"

"All the world loves a lover, Harry," Jackson said. "But *nobody* ever loved a lover the way I do . . . you dig? I used to go around wondering, Loverman, where could you be? And here you are."

He was gone. The gray son-of-a-bitch was gone.

Charles was right on time. You could count on a hophead to know what time meant. Charles would know how Harry'd been looking at the clock, like he didn't already *know* the time in his legs and arms and stomach. He used the other ankle and then Charles looked at the place and when the bleeding stopped, pulled the sock up over it.

"That's what's bad with that," he said. "You bleed too much there. In your arm you can stop it easier."

"But they . . . won't . . . look there," Harry said, slowing down, with everything turning into velvet again, softer than velvet, with all his nerves putting on their smooth suede gloves, with all his muscles easing up, so he could stand, so he could look at Charles and see his old yellow punkin head. He said, "About Jackson, man. He came to see me, came into my pad . . ."

Charles said, "I know. Forget it, forget Jackson."

"Yeah, yeah," Harry said. It didn't seem so bad right now. There'd be a way to fix everything. "I don't trap easy," he said.

Charles laughed. "Lying in a bed, junked up, you don't trap? Look around, man. You are trapped." He shook his head. "There's a bus leaves Guadalajara tonight for San Miguel, but there's no bus going out of here before that. We can't make that. There's another one in the morning. I'm trying to get us a way into Guadalajara tonight . . ."

"Call a cab," Harry said and laughed, and laughed.

"You gonna light that cigarette you're smoking?" Charles said, and yes, he did have a cigarette in his mouth. He looked at it. It would taste very, very good.

Charles said, "You know, that's not a bad idea? Call a cab . . . I'll talk to Gordo, maybe I can make a deal with him. I'd better leave the snow with you, baby. I don't like walking into the Delegado's office carrying it . . . You just stay here, quiet and cool now, Harry," he said.

Then he went away again.

Sitting there, bombed out, he made lots of plans this time, hilarious plans involving his father and Elinor and Ricky. He could use them. He'd just go to Texas to his father and hand them over and say, "Here you go, Dad. I brought you some more." His father had made such a big deal about paying the settlement Carmela asked for, and paying for the baby's education and all that jazz, and after Betsy's death, Genius Gerald had decided to fall apart so the two little girls lived at home in the big ugly palace in the desert with their granddaddy and their grandmommy. Gerald cut out, wandering around the world, explaining to everybody about Betsy and why it had to be an accident, until somebody said, "Bellevue for you."

If Charles got out, if the two of them got out . . . He ought to get swinging, go find Mariano. Charles wasn't going to be worrying about keeping Harry in H . . . he wasn't hooked. That was up to Harry. "All right, Harry-baby," he said to himself. "Go get some." But then he fell out again, for a while. He must have.

Because when he opened his eyes a minute later, there were lots of cigarette stubs on the floor around him, smoked, and one was burning his hand. He smelled it burning before he felt it, and then, looking at the burn, he didn't like that. He'd better not keep cigarettes around. He could set himself on fire this way. That's how Wild Bill Dickenson had gone. Just burned a hole in himself . . .

He got up and poured some rum on the burn and he could feel that, but it was a matter of disinfecting it first whether it hurt or not, and then he went to the shutter and opened it very carefully and peeked through the crack at the street. It looked cold. There was something frightening out there, not specifically, but something which changed the look of the walls and the cobblestones and the sky. The sky looked like painted tin with a phony sunset on it like you could get at some kindergarten where the teacher had said, Now children we're all going to paint sunsets on these pie plates, isn't that bee-yooo-teeeeful?

He closed the shutter and backed away to the bed. He sat there, twisting his hands, looking at how yellow they were, and discovered that his fly was open. Yeah, well it had been a little drafty. It probably had been like that since before Jackson was there.

Wasn't it peculiar that he should suddenly be afraid? What was he afraid of? It was . . . He used to think he was afraid of Jim. Jim was so crazy, the way he'd lie in the bed and not get up and not blow or anything, just change his shirt once in a while and look out at everything with that blank look. At first he thought he was very cool, but then he'd gotten so he was afraid of him because of that stoned-out, skull-eyed look he had, and he always wanted to get away from Jim, but now that Jim was gone, he was still afraid of Jim, so it couldn't have been Jim, could it? See, you've got a pretty good mind, you can still think, you can outthink them all if you have to. Like you can face that it wasn't just Jim you were afraid of. It was "crazy" you were afraid of. And "crazy" is still there, so you hung it on Jim, but it's still here and you got nobody to hang it on . . . except y-o-u. But if it's crazy and y-o-u you're afraid of, why wouldn't you want to go out on the street? You'd want to get away from y-o-u and crazy, wouldn't you? But he did. It was just that he was afraid to. He was afraid of both. Afraid to walk under the pie-plate sky, afraid of a bust, afraid of everything. A bad scene. It was, all of it, a bad scene. Afraid to stay here. Alone, like this, but afraid of anybody who would speak to him.

He got up and walked around. He walked all right, better than after too much tea. Nobody would be hip that he was on. Nobody would be hip that he was only four years old.

He peeked out of the shutter again, but there was a mean shadow spilling down over that wall over there, that moved, like smoke. He closed the shutter, saying, so everybody would know he was kidding about being afraid of a shadow, "Only the shadow knows." That would be a good record title. He went to the other side of the bed and got his horn and got the reed set into it right and turned on the tape-recorder, and got his lips right and began to blow, warming up, after a while knocking himself out with the sounds.

When it was done, he listened to the playback. It was just his axe, nothing else, so the beginning wouldn't sound good. You wouldn't expect it to sound good. He listened all the way through, and then he set the tapes on erase and erased it all. There was nobody in the world he would ever want to hear that . . . including y-o-u. Because that was not just far out, that was . . . b-a-d.

He had stashed the shaving kit in the *excusado* behind the loose adobe brick . . . that was dumb, but it was still there, wasn't it? He took another fix. Ahead of time. Okay. He'd just had a traumatic experience, and now he sudsed the blood in the syringe to jolt it home with the H, and it almost knocked him on his back.

Leaving there, he was walking funny and he knew it. He leaned against the wall, and there was a kind of darkness. When he opened his eyes, the Doña was yelling at him something about urinating in the well. She was what was c-r-a-z-y. He'd just come out of the *excusado,* hadn't he?

There was a long fall-out after that, all velvet slopes and pale clouds like streamers, turning pink, and there were no mean shadows and nothing ugly. Somebody touched him once and he came out of it and back into time and the room and saw that it was Elinor and her hand curved under his chin and her eyes looked into his face and she said, "Are you sick, Harry? Your forehead is hot." He said, "Yes, man. Sick. Fever. Fever's a gas." She said something about a doctor and he moved his chin out of her hand. "Get away," he said, "you'll get it. Hepatitis. Split, chickie. Just wander down that grassy slope over there and find the running stream at the bottom of the hill . . ." He heard her go out of the room and stand talking with the Doña outside, and the Doña was telling her that he was just drunk—Christmas is coming, Doña María . . . and you know what that means!—but anyway she made Elinor go away and that was better. When he was sure she was gone, he went down the grassy slope himself and found the stream and saw how it sang over rocks and made little sparkling pools; Elinor had gone away to wait until he sobered up, and he put his two hot hands into the stream and that turned the water yellow but it felt cold. It wasn't jaundiced; it was full of gold, like in the Big Rock Candy Mountain . . . like his daddy's life, full of gold and grassy slopes and streamer clouds and velvet, and his hand on a cool ivory breast moved, found it was made of stone, and he ran screaming, because it might be the stone goddess and to look upon her was to die, to touch her was to die a long time. Margo looked, when you looked at her, like his mother. Only his mother wasn't paranoid, and Margo was the original Mrs. P., and without the help of alcohol or junk or anything, except that somebody said he'd seen her sitting on her veranda looking at the lake one morning about four o'clock, getting blind on martinis all by herself. But his mother had never tasted a martini, nor wine, nor any kind of "spirit." She was pretty proud of that. Never just said, "No, thank you." Made the point. "I have never . . ." she said. Always made it funny when he shambled in, foully drunk.

But the time she read that notebook of poetry he'd written . . . you wouldn't think she'd understand that, would you? With a mind an inch wide? She understood it enough to stand up and give him one across the honker and go out to the backyard and make a fire and burn it. Two years' work . . . burning. But he was too ashamed to admit he cared about them. Anyway maybe she didn't understand them at all. That was right after he and Ollie and Greg had gotten expelled and she would think that whatever was there was something putrid with sin. Funny about that with Ollie and Greg and that little jerk who tagged after them—whatever his name was, Al, or something . . . He had never really wanted to cut the Assemblies at school, but he couldn't admit that. He had to go climb up onto the roof of the auditorium with those other clowns and get big kicks out of smoking until finally they got caught and it wasn't even marijuana.

What his mother didn't know and what the Army didn't know and what everybody didn't know was that he was weak. Smart but weak. He couldn't stand alone against the gang. He couldn't wear brown shoes if the gang wore sneakers. He never had that kind of courage. He was always folding himself into the background trying to be invisible, imagining he was invisible, with this cry rising in him all the time to be heard, listened to, taken into account. Nobody took him into account. It wasn't too bad until he began to hear himself in the bands, playing hard, which he wouldn't have admitted because it was safer to knock down on the job because you had an out when you got chopped, and he began to know, himself, that he was not original. He could not stop imitating; no new ideas came into his head. For a while on tea he thought they did. He thought he was getting to something, but then he knew that last time, stoned as he was, that he was third-rate, a Getz imitator, and no farther along musically than he'd been in the beginning. He didn't learn. He didn't feel. What he said in his music was somebody else's story. He wanted to tell his own story, but he had no story to tell. God damn. And that mess he'd played today. Man, that was the worst. He wouldn't hire himself as a sideman. So all this time he'd been trying to be something he was not and never would be . . . Wow. You are one depressing bastard, Harry. You are beginning to bug me like I have never been bugged . . .

For his life and himself to mean anything, it had to be the music. But not just because he'd gotten on H. That was thinking backward. Some ways he'd like to have been a teacher, live one of those relaxed easy lives, walking around among the trees digging the chicks on the campus, looking at life, digging life, not blowing his brains out of his mouth all the time and trying to say everything in the restricted forms of music. Who *thought* music? Thing was, he reacted to music. He reacted to life. He was a reactor, not an actor, not a doer, not a thinker, not a feeler on his own.

Once he'd been on a panel discussion, with some other musicians, and the d.j. was asking, if they had sons, did they want them to grow up and be musicians. And somebody young there said, "Man, a musician is the greatest." That was a piano player though, and they don't think like other men. Anyway, another guy said, "You haven't got anything to say about it, Jack. If he wants to be, he will be." And everybody but Harry had said that in one way or another the kid should be a musician if that was what he wanted when he grew up. And Harry said he thought he could be a musician, a jazz man, only if he *didn't* grow up. And they all glared at him, except for the famous one, who said, "Yeah well, it's not what you call easy-go. I had a hard time." But even he looked at Harry like he'd said something evil and un-true, or something he didn't understand. The famous one kept looking at him. Then he said, "I'm still having a hard time. Is it easy for you guys? What life do you have?" And the bass-man, ex-junkie, off H but having kicked it only once, and later he was to get on again, said earnestly, "It's a creative life." How about that? Creating what? Imitating Hawk, imitating Prez, imi-tating Getz and Bird and now everybody on the Coltrane kick. I'm on a cold train, mama. Who was laughing? He was laughing. What did any of it have to do with him? He was no jazz man. That was the truth. He could play as written, play as heard, reproduce sounds and that was all. Harry will now give us his impression of Lester Young for the next five years.

Okay, so he was no Bartók, who was?

No, but he wasn't even interested in being a Bartók. He wanted music in his life, all he had to do was play records. He'd hear better than he could make every time. Too bad he didn't just start off doing imitations, like the rooster at dawn. Wow, man. And now Littul Harry is going to give us his impres-sion of . . . himself.

Everybody thinks I'm evil. Everybody has always thought I was evil. But I never thought I was. I'm weak, and if you're weak and you got nothing going for you, evil is the easiest way to play it. It's just one step in deeper than saying I-don't-care. And it's one way to stay ahead of the crowd.

But I had a brain. I had an IQ of one hundred and sixty-seven. They told me in school I could be anything I wanted to be . . .

I wanted to be rotting in Mexico, loaded with heroin, burn-ing up with fever, having some other guy's broad and a kid wrapped around my neck, a paranoiac chasing after me with the heat, and my only friend Hophead Charlie trying to get somebody to help him get me out of town . . . keep me alive . . .

Open your eyes, Harry. Live a little. Swing a little. It's almost over. Yeah, but all the heroin in the world, white mountains of it, can't keep me from dying sad the way I've lived, can't make me smile inside of me at anything. This why you hit the tree, Bets?

And he was so deep in playing the evil way of life, he couldn't get out. He was hooked on that before he got hooked on alcohol. Like now, it comes to me maybe I'll take that dumb one-legged chick back to Texas with that hellcat child of hers, and maybe I'll make her happy. How's that for a twist? It was too late. He didn't know how to play it that way. The thought of seeing her all the time, listening to her, looking into even her beautiful face the rest of his life—even if it lasted only five minutes—was too much. He couldn't make it. Besides he'd have to turn her on H anyway, so she'd understand he couldn't do *that* any more. Turn her on, and next step would be, turn her out, because his old man wasn't going to put up the bread to buy H. A lot of sick cats might dig balling a chick with one leg— like him—but that made him sick. *"Let 'er go, let 'er go, God bless her . . . She'll never find a sweetman like me."*

So die in your bed, Harry, your dirty bed at the bottom of the world. You never lived.

Charles said, "I brought my skins, man. We leave early in the morning. I worked a deal with the Delegado. He's going to lend Armando the butcher one of his trucks, and he'll get us out in the morning. The Feds won't come back till tomorrow, so we're clear tonight. You got a joint? I need a blast . . . where are they, Harry?" He was setting up the drums in the corner of the room and he joggled the table where the toy soldiers stood, and he could have been killed for that, only Jim was gone and the game was over. He pointed to the mountainous terrain where his fourth division stood, because it was under there that the reefers were and that was what Charles wanted. "Let's jive some," Charles said.

16

Victoria

OVER THE LAKE you could clearly see the Southern Cross, if you cared about things like that. Victoria did not care very much about it. She had not come out to look at the sky. She came out to be out. Here you stayed "in" or you went "out."

Ahead of her in the street was the policeman in his poncho, making his unofficial rounds, from cantina to cantina. He stumbled a little, his worn huaraches slipping on the stones. He was already a little drunk, but there wasn't a crime wave going on and it hardly mattered. The town was under martial law. Mexicans stayed "in," out of danger. At the military barracks ahead of her, two soldiers in wrinkled blue uniforms leaned against their bayonets, scratching themselves and talking. One

of them watched her approach. It was not nine o'clock yet; the
curfew was not in effect until then. But it would not be beyond
the soldiers to take a shot at her if they felt so moved; they
were bored, and they were stupid; therefore, they were dangerous.

Coming close to them, she lifted her hand in salute. *"Buenas
noches, señores,"* she said, then adding in English, "You miserable morons," pulling her mouth into the grimace of a smile.

One nodded; the other grunted a reply. She passed them.

If they had asked her where she was going, she would have
told them, *"Al centro."* It was the standard answer and therefore
acceptable; I am going to the center. The center of what? The
center of the nothing which this village is, to the center of nothing, you morons. The ancients said the self lived in the center
of the body. I am going to the center of myself, which is also
nothing.

At the corner of Ned's street she slowed down. There were
cars parked in front of his house and all the way down to the
edge of the lake. Music came out of the house, and laughter,
distant and polite. There was Manuél's white Cadillac, the Old
Poet's polished antique Buick, and other cars she did not
recognize.

Margo Whitman had told her that Ned and Chloë were
leaving for New York in the morning and that they had announced that they would be married en route. Margo was slyly
amused. "Do you think he will marry her? You know him best,"
she had said.

She had stared unseeingly at Margo, not answering, and
not even listening when Margo went on and talked about raising her rent. Margo was saying something about getting more
for the house after Victoria had moved out and she had a
chance to remodel it. She had made her eyes focus then, made
them see this Fury with the girlish manner. "Get out," she had
said. But with no fire, no rage. Wearily she had said it. "Just get
out."

Hanschen was leaning against Manuél's car. He had a bottle
of tequila and he tipped it up and let the liquor run down his
throat. His face, when he lowered the bottle, was boiled red and
his eyes were bloodshot, his smile a smeary display of neglected
teeth.

"Welcome," he called out to her.

She could go over and hit him, pound him over the head
with her purse. But that would be like hitting a child because
it soiled itself and did not know enough to be ashamed. Just get
by him, leave him behind. Everyone left Hanschen behind; even
people who went nowhere left him behind because he was falling
backward so fast. Too bad they had cut him down, too bad he
wasn't dead; he had showed good judgment in trying to kill
himself; he had picked a worthy victim.

She climbed along the street toward the church, with his
drunken shouts following her. She must pry him up out of her
mind. He did not belong there. He belonged where he stood, out
side Ned's house, standing there forever, even after Ned was
gone, hating the house in order to keep from hating himself too
much.

At the corner she looked up one street and then the other.
There was nothing happening on the left, nothing happening on
the right. Go back down the hill, walk out on the pier? You
could stumble over a sleeping drunk, or step into something
foul . . . rotten fruit, excrement or garbage. There was not a
wall in the town which had not been stained by someone's urina-
tion. It was an ugly world, defaced by animals and human
beings.

She leaned against the church wall. She was out of breath.
That was curious. She had never before been out of breath from
this climb. The wall was cold, with paper-dry bougainvillaea
scratching over it in the wind. She was all alone. She had no
one. No one. No mother, no father, no husband, no lover. Her
sister was dead. She had no friends, no life. She looked around
in wild terror for a second.

There were little gray toads hopping in the street, hard to
see in the low light of the bulb at the corner, but moving, as
though stones jumped. You could step on one in the dark. Would
it croak, or lie there crushed into silence so you would never
know if your shoes were stained with blood? She was afraid to
leave the church wall.

The black wave of loneliness swept over her. It was over-
whelming. It had been happening to her all week, the black wave
rolling over her, sealing up her mouth and eyes, flowing
through her hair, weighing heavily on the top of her head. "My
God, my God," she groaned and when she heard herself crying,
she dabbed at her eyes with the corner of her *rebozo*, the tears

flowing faster than they could be wiped away. She turned toward the church in which she did not believe, and under the onslaught of darkness, prayed . . .

She turned her face into the wall, crying against it, helplessly, more alone than she had ever been in her life. Everything had been stripped away from her. There was nothing left.

The bells clattering in the tower startled her. She pulled back from the reverberating wall, began to run away from the din. It was intolerable that close, as though she rode the clapper and struck the side of the bell herself . . . But, running, was she stepping on the toads!

She stopped, halting abruptly, breathing hard. Behind her she heard footsteps and when she looked back, she saw two Mexican soldiers patrolling the street. It was nine o'clock now. That was why the bell had rung. She must get indoors quickly, away from the soldiers; she must not be on the street, like a whore, after the curfew.

She turned left at the corner. Even when they had orders to kill the dogs, the roving starved mongrel-packs of Mexico, they could not hit them squarely, so that the dogs took a long time dying, and their howls and writhings filled the dark hours. She must not be accidentally and poorly shot down like a dog, to howl and writhe.

She could not go to Abel's Bar, because now it was Margo's and she had not reopened it yet. She was close to the Posada of the Tres Marías. She did not want to see Harry, but he was someone. Anyone was better than no one. She could not go home to her house now, to staring through another night, another day . . . Harry might just let her sit there if she did not say anything. Maybe the Doña would have some coffee and some *sopés* left over from supper. She had eaten nothing since yesterday morning. She hurried, terrified of stepping on the toads, but hurrying.

There were two soldiers, one of them carrying a swinging lantern, coming toward her. She went fast to get to the door of the Posada before she met them.

She pushed open the big door and walked up the *zaguán*. The green plants showed satin in the electric light and now the moon came out from behind the cloud and silvered over the patio. She stood in the *corredor* beside the oilcloth-covered table and looked at the picture of the tomato-cheeked girl on the calendar which hung over the Coca-Cola box. The kitchen was dark. There was no line of light showing under the Doña's bedroom door. There was no food to be had. She leaned against the Coca-Cola box. She was still crying; tears ran down her face.

It seemed to happen without her knowing it, or feeling it. She wept for herself, because there was no one to say, Stop that nonsense now; get on with your life. There was no one to tell her what to do.

The black wave was coming back, to overwhelm her again . . . again . . .

Coming from Harry's room now, there was music, a clandestine, soft jazzy rhythm on the drums and Harry's tenor sax rising above that, breathy, hushed . . . as though it were telling a secret the world must not hear. She went quickly to Harry's door, and wiping her eyes with her *rebozo*, and then rubbing her hands against them and pinching her cheeks with her fingers to make color and feeling come back into them, she stood, listening to the music. Harry was not alone; someone played the drums. It was probably Charles. She lifted her hand and rapped timidly on the big door.

The music stopped, and then Charles' voice said cautiously, "Yeah? Who's there?"

"I am," she said.

There was a silence. Their eyes would look at each other and one of them would shrug. She must charm them, enchant them so they would let her stay.

Charles opened the door. "You better not come in, Vick," he said. "The heat's on us." He saw she didn't understand. He said, "Cops after us. The Federals."

"They're not coming till morning," Harry's voice said from deep in the room. "Let the chick in, mother."

Charles shrugged and opened the door wider for her and stepped back.

"Let me stay a minute," she said, when she was in the room. "I won't bother you. I need to be with people." Her voice shook; she could hear it herself. She made herself smile. "It is one of those evenings, you know," she said, "when Mexico is horrible. When the world is empty and sick."

Harry came shuffling over to her and put his arms around her. He held her close. "Hello, orphan," he said. The smell of him was indescribable; she held her breath. "Mexico is always horrible," he said, "and the world is always empty and sick."

"Can I sit here and listen to you play? May I?" She gazed at them, beseechingly. "I won't bother you."

"You been crying, Vick," Harry said. "Sure, sit down. CharlieHopheadBeauregard and me are just knocking out some easy jazz. Real easy and cool."

She sat on the straight chair near the table with the toy soldiers on it, and Charles began tapping the cymbals with his wire brushes, just a little, with his wrists flexible, so that the beat sounded like another pulse in the smoky room, as though life made a noise you could hear. It was reassuring. She leaned back and closed her eyes and listened as Harry came in on the solo, and she was not so alone. The sounds filled her for as long as they played. How lucky they were to be musicians. A writer could use only words, the words he used himself every day, all the time, to describe himself and other people; the words were not sacred and saved exclusively for writing, as notes were saved and used exclusively for music. You could not leave yourself out of your work, for this reason, among others, and then when somebody turned down your work, he had turned you down, said no to you, told you he didn't want you and nobody would want you. Nobody wanted her, her body, her mind, her words, her writing.

The music stopped.

"Very nice," Charles said to Harry. "Man, I didn't think you could blow any more."

"Thanks, clyde," Harry said. He turned and looked at her. "Ned's leaving, yeah, chickie? You crying for him?"

Victoria said, "Please, Harry. Just let me listen."

"*Yeah,* but I *know,*" Harry said. "He shafted you, didn't he?"

She spoke with her eyes closed. "You get what you ask for," she said. "I made it very easy for him. In fact, I made it inevitable."

Harry nodded. "I dig," he said. "So now you come to me. I guess I'm Big Daddy. I'm a very handy Big Daddy, too, sweetie. And I'm no fag."

Charles said, "No, man. Not *even.*"

Harry glared at him.

"Where's Jim?" she said. "And Jackson and Elinor?"

"Elinor was here but she's gone," Harry said, and laughed. " 'She done been here and gone,' like Little Jimmy Rushing.

Jackson? Well, Jackson is nowhere, like always, you know? Like Jack the Bear, nowhere. And Jim is in good hands. Dr. Kildare's got him." He took a narrow, homemade cigarette out of his shirt picket. "I'm going to blow some pot, Vick. You want some?"

"No, no," she said. She smiled. "No, thank you. I don't, you know. I'll have a drink if you offer me one."

"Yeah," Harry said. "But you know, Vick, you drag it a little when you sit here and you don't blast with us. I mean, I got no juicy to offer you, so how about a little . . ."

"Harry," Charles said, interrupting, "send the broad home."

Harry looked at him, his eyes slitted. "You go home, Charles," he said. "I been telling you all day. Like, later, I said. I think Vickie's due for a moment of truth, like in the *corrida*."

Charles shook his head. "Don't do it, man," he said.

"You know you're curing my Oedipus complex?" Harry said. "I'm sick of you, MotherCharlieBeauregardHopheadStud. You make me wish I'd dug my old man instead. I mean like, this is life. You worry about tomorrow. I got today, man, just today."

"Today has been going on for fifty years," she said. "I'm so tired."

"I hear you," Harry said. "You're ready. Old Harry's going to turn you on. Old Harry's going to lay some sweetpeace on your soul."

"Sweetpeace," she murmured. It sounded wonderful. Harry lit the cigarette. The smell of marijuana was foul. She said, "Harry, I don't need . . ."

He was holding the smoke in his lungs. When he exhaled it he laughed. "Don't lie to Big Daddy," he said. "You *need*. You *need* to be turned on . . ."

She laughed, too. "That's how I am . . . like a light bulb which has not been turned on . . ."

"This will cool you," Harry said. "It's cheaper than liquor and it doesn't rot your brain and make you soggy. You been listening to the liquor lobby all your life. Nobody ever got cirrhosis from smoking tea, baby. One drag or two will ease up your nerves, make them like velvet." He turned to Charles. "Dig this vicariously, sweetie. Virgin kicks. Wow."

Charles said, "You're talking while it's burning." Harry handed him the cigarette and he took a drag so the cigarette glowed bright red. "It ain't O," Charles said in a sepulchral voice, "but it helps."

It was her turn. She hadn't decided to actually, but they acted as if she had, and then she thought she could just take a little. If you breathed all that air in with it the way they showed her, it couldn't do much to you.

She took it and a great gulp of it went burning hot into her lungs and she coughed and they looked at her in dismay. Next time she did better and they nodded approvingly. She didn't feel any different.

They began to play again. "I dedicate this homesick blues to this village," Harry said. "I dedicate it to the rectum of the world."

They seemed to play much better than before. She enjoyed the sound more, devoted herself to listening more, and as she did, she decided that they had never played this well, ever before, because the music said so much to her now, about writing and Ned and Ramón and herself. Suddenly everything seemed comprehensible, and no longer frightening. She could even imagine not minding her terrible aloneness. Maybe the next time that black wave of despair broke over her, she'd be able to fight it back.

"See?" Harry said. "You're cooling it."

"But this feels marvelous," she said and discovered how dry her throat was. She could hardly talk. Harry gave her some water before they lit up the next one. The water was delicious, crystal cool as though from a mountain tarn. "Marvelous," she said, taking a big drag on the cigarette. It smelled wonderful to her now.

In between she smoked regular cigarettes and drank water and once she found that she was talking out loud at the same time Harry was singing, but she was perfectly all right, clear-headed, really.

He sang a marvelous line about "I got a brand new gal that walks the block . . . won't make a quarter for watching the cop . . . That won't get it. No, man. That won't get it. " And then in a minute, " 'I got another gal, just stands in the door . . . how she makes so much money, damned if I know, but that'll get it. Yes, man. That gets it."

Charles said, "You . . . that little girl with the red dress on . . ." and they both laughed.

It was funny. She couldn't have said why, but you should already know it was funny without being told. There was a sound like many bees buzzing and, somewhere, high-pitched laughter.

Later Charles said, "Hey, man, you countin'? Vickie's stoned."

She would have told them she wasn't, if she could speak, but she couldn't. It didn't matter. It wasn't necessary, all the talking people did anyway. It was better to listen to the music. They weren't playing now, though, except it was still playing inside her head. She had her own concert.

"Vivaldi," she said.

"Thank you, madame," Harry said, and that was hilarious too, except that she cried about it instead of laughing. She couldn't explain how it was that the tears were just there anyway, waiting, and she had to use them. It was all right. They didn't seem to notice.

"Stoned, skullwise," Charles said.

Sitting here, twisting the cloth of the skirt into pleats, retwisting it when the fingers were dissatisfied with the pleats, looking at the floor, she could hear their voices. *She* hears them; I do not. I am dissociated from her. I have no feeling of the continuum of myself, as it has been from the beginning, was, is, and will be. I do not know who I am at the very moment that, in my dissociation, I watch myself. My face there in Harry's mirror does not relate to me, is not my face, except that I have a sense of responsibility for it and I know it is not Harry's nor Charles'.

It does not exist separately, nor does my face float, but it is as though I have gone away from behind it. My body is separate within itself, so that my arm, resting on the table, does not rest there knowing that my foot rests on the floor; when my eye looks at my foot, it does not also know that my arm is leaning on the table. My body not only has no connection with that face in the mirror, it has no connection with pain or pleasure either. But at the same time I know that its throat is dry and it aches somewhere. I think, She has an ache. Her throat is dry. Also, she is numb at the same time that she suffers, trembles, cries and feels the ache; there is, simply, a short circuit. She is made of short circuits and blown fuses, so that no impulse travels very far.

I exist in confusion, a confusion which is vast and spread out all around me. Having no sense of self, I am now without memory, without past, but not newborn, not new to life. As we live, we die. But the confusion is frightening, because it should not be so, that I should be here not knowing who and what I am. Nothing is possible.

I knew a girl, a child really, who, when she was fourteen years old, stole letters out of people's mailboxes. Afterward they asked her why she did this, why she read their letters, even dreary business letters and advertisements and bills and public announcements and governmental forms. They asked her why she kept these things, what did they do for her? The child could not answer because she did not know then that she was looking for an identity. And anyway, if she had answered them that, she would have been asking a graver question than the question she was trying to answer, which is the way with all wise, true answers, the way with all truth. The child wanted to be somebody reading letters.

I was that child. I am not different now. I could steal letters for the relief of seeming to be a person whose arms and legs existed in consciousness of each other, who had a mystical sense of identity, which is the mystical substance of life, all of life we can tolerate and the part of life we cannot do without. Even someone who has amnesia has an identity as a person-who-has-amnesia, because to have amnesia he must have something to have forgotten.

I am what the Chinese call "an old soul." I am persuaded of this deeply, although I do not know altogether what that means. My experience now is Jungian, mystical; I experience only the hidden, unconscious knowledge of my species; I have then the species-unconscious, but none of my own. I do not contain myself. I have lost myself somewhere on one of my soul-journeys; I have not come back to myself yet, and there is nothing for my disconnected, short-circuited body to do but wait for a self to come back to it.

I left myself in another reality. That is a risk we run, we Old Souls, when we project ourselves, empathize ourselves into another person's reality. It is dangerous; you might stay there and then you would be like someone who died, as though the soul had leapt up from you, gotten caught like a silk kite on a sudden wind, spun, whipped away, turning many circles, revolving in sunlight until the string breaks and it is gone from you. But it is not a conscious decision; it is something that happens.

You look at someone and you do not know it, but the blue silk kite of the soul springs up, whirls on the wind.

I think I must have left myself in Ned's reality, looking at life from his eyes, instead of looking at my own life from my eyes. Wait, what is it like, the soul I left with him? Does it sing, does it moan? Is it caught there, dancing in a pale and luminous agitation behind the small windows of his eyes, hearing dimly through his ears?

Harry and Charles—they behave as though you are here. They talk to you. They see the parts of you all connected, as if the switchboard were governing all calls upon the different parts of you, integrating them all, hooking them up. They do not know that you have left yourself, and that you have no Central Government and the soul of you is giving off an effulgence of light, milky like a pearl's light, in Ned's reality.

But I have had some kind of shock, haven't I? Yes. Some kind of shock has happened to me, and there are reverberations of it still; they impinge against me, disturbing the china cabinet of my head with plate rattlings and crockery noises, and there are also supersonic concussions striking against the seismograph of my skin. But there must be some remnant of mind left me to think with: maybe being an-Old-Soul, I have left to me the Old Brain, the hypothalamus, which is not very smart and knows only simple things and is like the janitor of the building, who knows how to regulate the boilers and the furnace, because that has been his job for centuries, but who cannot add anything to what he has already learned to do, nor know any other thing. I am thinking, perhaps, with that vestigial mind.

If I have this much of my mind still with me, there must be some attachment of soul to this Old Brain; there must be some mechanism at work so that I can think not her, but me. Not she, but I. If I can think "I," perhaps it will be all right and then she can wait until I get the rest of myself back.

But I cannot move.

I cannot stand up.

I cannot move.

They have come over to me now and they are looking at me and they say I have been talking. She didn't know I was talking. But they were listening. Charles looks frightened.

Harry pried up one of her eyelids. He said, "Stand up."

Long, flowing thoughts came in the wake of what they said as though their words were ships.

Charles said, "God damn you, Harry, I told you . . . Come on, baby, get up."

She floated down onto the soft, cloudy floor.

Charles picked her up and set her back on the chair. Her eyes were closed, or somebody's eyes were closed, so that no one could look in and see that no soul was in the person.

Harry said, "She's got the horrors. Man, she needs some food."

Charles said, "Where am I going to get food in this mothering town? It's a long way to the Stage Delicatessen, baby."

Harry said, "She's a poorolddoll, maybe it doesn't take much. You can't die from pot, man, you know that."

"Maybe *she* can."

Harry sighed. "Man, I'm falling out," Harry said. "Let her sleep."

"Come on now, Vickie," Charles said. "I'm going to get you some food. Take it easy."

Charles went out. Harry stood there, sighing, scratching his head, scratching his chest, scratching his face.

Charles came back. "Nothing in the kitchen," he said. "I couldn't even find any old tortillas."

Harry said in a whining voice, "It's getting to be *time*, man."

"Ah, you hooked junkie," Charles said.

Charles tried to get her up again, but when her legs buckled he sat her down and held her there, looking into her face, with his face frightened.

"Let's take her to Elinor," Harry said. "She'll have food in her house."

"The curfew, you bugger," Charles said. "Soldiers in the streets and you want me to carry Vickie to Elinor's?"

"You'll have to make it to your pad and get food and bring it back, then," Harry said. "I'll hold her on the chair."

"Bustville," Charles said. "But I'll go. Look, she's falling off the chair, man."

"Put her to bed," Harry said.

They lifted her and put her down on the bed and then Charles was gone. She could see what was happening and know what was happening but it wasn't happening to her, as though she were an intelligence floating off somewhere up high, watching, watching, bumping around on the ceiling like a balloon . . .

Harry got a syringe out of his shaving kit and a paper of white stuff. What was he doing? Was he going to give her an injection of some kind? He was very intent. He heated some water, by holding a lighted candle under a metal box. He balanced the box on a tablespoon. The flame came up around the sides of the box. Then he set it down and his back was to her, and then he mixed the water with the powder and drew it up into the syringe. It was pearly white, like her lost old soul. He tied a string around his upper arm, like a tourniquet, with a pencil in the string holding it tight; flexed his hand, slowly pushed the needle into the vein at the inside of his elbow, waited, with sweat running down his forehead, pulled blood into the syringe, sudsed the blood in and out of the syringe with the pearly soul-stuff, flipped off the string, took the needle out, brought his arm up tightly, fell against the wall. In a minute he slid over to the side so he was half lying on the table, half lying on all the toy soldiers, making a stertorous grunting sound of pain and pleasure, swearing a little in a whisper . . .

Hear him whispering. His breathing was funny. He sounded like an animal. He was muttering in between the gasping breaths. She could not move. She could not even frown. She tried to frown. There was a wild animal in the room and she could not move to save Victoria, Vickie, Vee.

"I love you, habit," he whispered. "Man's got a habit, he's got the world." He stood up, fell against the wall, slid down along it to the floor and he was out of sight. "Oh God," his voice said. "I got hepatitis. I'm sick. Because when I'm straight, I'm still sick and my mind is blowing out on me."

He scrambled around on the floor and then pushed himself up so that he was standing and then he went reeling around the room, bumping against things, like an animal in a small enclosure, and then the only sound was his breathing and the slap of his huaraches on the tile floor, while time telescoped, growing big, growing small.

There was a clandestine knocking and a voice at the door, not Charles. Harry did not answer. He went to the cupboard and took out a knife. A *knife? Why?* He put it under the paper mountains of the toy-soldier tableland, handle ready. He came to the bed, pushed the shaving kit against her side, covered it with the blanket, saying, "Vickie gets the bust, wow," then hurrying away to reel against the door, lean against it, listening.

The door rattled, pushed in with Harry backing up with it. It was Abel. He said, "What's happening, man?"

"Hey there, Crow-Jim," Harry said. "You're intruding."

"What's the matter with her?" Abel said.

Harry laughed. "Turned her on and man, she flew— straight out."

Abel said in a low shocked voice, "Turned her on *what*, Harry?"

"Just pot, man."

"Not you though, Harry-baby," Abel said sadly. "You're turned on more than tea."

"Yeah. Verily. I got hepatitis. I got a terminal illness . . . I took some aspirin for it."

"You spell that with a C or an H?"

"Yeah, you know it," Harry said. He rubbed the back of his neck, rubbed his nose, pushed at his nose with his thumb.

"Man, I got to talk to you," Abel said.

"Sure, man," Harry said.

Abel sat down on the chair and Harry leaned against the wall and Abel talked, in a low slow voice.

"Yeah, yeah," Harry said. "It's depressing. You talking in that swing-low voice all of a sudden . . ."

"It's because I need help, Harry. I'll pay you back. I swear it."

"No," Harry said. "It's no good you coming in here talking quiet, buddying me up. I'm not the White-Negro. I'm a poor sick junkie and the heat's coming on me tomorrow and I got to get out and I got no money *left*. It's all gone on H, and I got hepatitis, I told you, and I got Jackson's old lady hung on me and her kid besides . . . Jackson's cut out. And I got Charlie-HopheadBureaugard and that stonedoutpoorolddoll there . . . I got no friend, nothing, nobody . . ."

Abel said, "I hate to do this, Harry. But if you don't lend me the money, I'm going to have to take it."

Harry laughed. "Take a freedom-ride, spade," he said.

"Easy," Abel said. "Cool, now. Think, Harry. I got nothing to lose, you dig? A hundred pesos. Make it seventy-five. I'll go on seventy-five. That's not even ten dollars American, man."

Harry shook his head.

"One more time, Harry," Abel said. "I ask one more time."

Silence. She had to move now, lift her hand, speak, tell Abel he could have her money . . . the way it happened before. Lift your hand. Make a noise. *Make a noise.* No noise? Can't move: *Move.* Oh . . . Harry jumped on him and they are on the floor, they crashed onto the floor and they're writhing, and I can hear when they hit each other, and they kicked the chair over now, and they struggle and Abel is pleading with him and there is that terrible sound when they hit each other and Abel is crying, saying, "I don't want to hit you, Harry. Don't!" And Abel is getting up, and dragging Harry up with one big hand, and now Harry is saying please, and Harry is reaching into the toy-soldier mountains *for what*? For money, and he has it and Abel is letting go of him, and Harry is slowly counting out the bills into Abel's hand, but I thought there was the knife in there, that was where he put the knife, and I thought he was going to stab him, but Harry isn't a killer, and he knows Abel is crazy, and he knows . . . *The knife? The Knife?* Warn him! Scream! *Warn Him!*

"Abel . . ."

No sound?

And the knife, going up, not down, up, up from the groin, and Abel, sighing, and blood spilling on the floor . . . sighing Harry's name, holding himself together, and Harry backing off while Abel stumbles forward, sliding down to his knees, sliding out of sight, and the watery sound which must be blood spilling onto the floor . . . And Harry gazing down on him, his hand bloody, his face pale yellow. Sick, he's sick . . .

This is the worst dream I have ever had, to be paralyzed while Harry murders Abel, while blood gouts over a knife onto a tile floor and Harry bends down and pulls money out of a bloodied hand, and wipes the blood off the money, mumbling to himself, wiping the blood all over himself, his jacket, his pants. But why would I dream of Harry doing these things? Why do I dream of these things? Why doesn't the dream *end* now? It should *end* now. Holy Father in Heaven, Listen to Your Daughter. Make the dream end, Holy Father. Make it . . . end.

What I think is happening cannot be happening and I must be catatonic because I cannot make a sound, cannot warn, advise, protest, cry out, cannot move, am paralyzed, the paralyzed witness to a nightmare. In many nightmares one must run and

cannot, move and cannot, and I am having one of those nightmares, only part of it is thinking that I am catatonic too, you see.

Is it possible that Abel is not dead? If I could move, I could
find out.

Now Harry is beginning in this dream to figure out a way
of getting rid of Abel, so nobody will know he killed him, before
anybody comes here and finds him. He is going from Abel's body
to the door and looking at the distance, and measuring it and
figuring on the blood spilling, because he's gotten a towel now
and has bent down to staunch that blood. How long does it flow
after death? Till it's all gone? The next time I dream this dream,
I must be able to move because I am in danger too, because I
saw the murder . . .

Now he is opening the shutters and looking down the street
. . . for Charles? Is he looking for Charles or for the patrol?
Who is Betsy? . . . over and over, mumbling and mumbling
like an old man. I have seen old men mumble like that . . . an
old man on a bench in a park in Paris one time . . . an old man
in Hong Kong . . . An old man's mumble sounds the same in
any language, and Abel would never, after this dream, live long
enough to mumble like an old man, never be an old man, because in this dream he is dead. I want to stop dreaming this
dream, now. I cannot endure it any longer.

Now he's decided how to do it. He's taking one of his jackets
off the hanger and sliding it under something on the floor . . .
do you feel as though you hit an electrified guardrail when he
bends over that *something which you know is Abel why don't
you call it Abel? Abel's body?*

I shall be able to recall every single motion he makes,
everyone makes, every word everyone says, all of the sounds
of this night's dream, including that rooster crowing somewhere
off down the shore of the lake, and the soft distant voices of the
soldiers talking Spanish . . .

He's dragging it now in its sling of coat. Dragging what?
Abel's electrified body? No, it is the guard against the idea which
electrifies you every time because it means that Abel is dead, that
he has been murdered before you . . . as Harry in his way has
been murdered before you. You have seen him take his drug.

Now Harry was dragging the body up to the sill and everything was getting red paint on it, but he was working, pushing
and pulling, ignoring that, even taking the red towel out of the

wound, dumping the body out of the window, pushing when the hips wouldn't go over the sill, pushing and swearing with his red-dyed hands, until there, it was gone, and now he was sagging against the wall again, gasping and gasping, sweat running down his face, cutting pale lines where there was blood. Somebody had bled a great deal, and a great deal of blood had gotten on Harry. It should be possible to smell it, but she did not smell it so it must be paint.

But fear like twin blue sharks nosed along the bottom of the brain saying Blood, saying Murder, saying Death, saying darkness and death and devil . . . and she tried very hard to scream as the sharks turned upward nosing up toward the distant surface of her consciousness but it was not possible to scream, and still she screamed and screamed within herself and would not forget that she screamed tomorrow when she was awake and the dream was over, would not ever forget how she had screamed . . . and how nobody had heard her; would not ever forget how she had tried to scream a warning to Abel and how no sound had come from her mouth, as no sound was coming now . . .

The woman came to the door at four o'clock in the afternoon and announced that she was there to take possession of the house. Her tone of voice was belligerent and her eyes were small behind thick glasses, as though there were not one eye behind each glass, but several, as though she were a new, extra large species of fly, pretending to be a schoolteacher on leave, in a heavy coat, pretending to have driven the station wagon which, loaded so that it sagged on its axles with her belongings, stood now just beyond the door of the house, in the street.

"What did you say your name was?"

"Winifred McCluskey. Miss Beacon, I can show you the signed rental agreement with Miss Whitman."

"No, no, don't bother," Victoria said. She did not smile at the fly. She said, "The rent for this day is paid. I shall leave the house at five o'clock. No sooner."

The woman wanted to argue. It was necessary to shut her out so that what she said in that brain-addling voice did not stay in your mind. She held up her hand. "Five o'clock," she said.

Miss McCluskey's small mouth formed an unpleasant smile. "What am I to do for an hour?"

"Go away," Victoria said. She shut the door on the woman and bolted it against her.

She walked back up the *zaguán*. The house, now that she had distributed everything she had brought into it, was as bare and cold as it had been the day she had seen it first and said, "I'll take it." She had given the orange-red cupboards, which were Ned's gift to her, to Charles. Charles persuaded Jesús, the *mariachi*, to come with him and the two of them carried them away, to set them up in the room with the glassless picture window. Most of the rest of her things she gave to the *niña's* mother. The *niña's* mother accepted every gift with delight, not increased nor lessened a jot by evaluation; anything was welcome.

Probably the *niña* would work for Miss McCluskey and lavish her childish love upon that creature as she had lavished it on her. But, the *niña* would miss her. Children had long memories, although people imagined otherwise. One day, she would send for the *niña*. She had not said anything of this to the child, because who knew whether it would be possible? Who knew what was coming now, and how it would go? One had no right to hold out a promise to a child and then fail to carry it out. It was quite possible that she would not be able to carry it out, quite possible.

Her belongings still fitted into the two tin suitcases; she had not added to her wardrobe, nor given up any of it, either. It was only, like herself, a little shabbier. Going away, she would take what she had come here with . . . the two suitcases and her typewriter. Oh, yes . . . and the pages Cushman had sent back. She had those . . . her accomplishment.

There was a grave difference in the self she was taking away. It had been two weeks since Ned left, and two weeks since the murder, and one week since Harry's death. In that time she had learned not to tremble, not to wring her hands, not to cry. She had learned to seem more balanced than she felt, and if she did not manage to appear serene . . . well, nobody expected it of her. But there was no place in the village she could bear to look at one more time.

Abel had said that. "*One more time, Harry.*"

Remembering, like a religious saying a rosary, she made her silent, ritualistic statement to herself of blamelessness: I could not move. I was anesthetized, paralyzed, immobilized. I could not stop what happened. Even if I had not smoked all that marijuana and gotten so benumbed, there was nothing I could have done, just as Charles said. If I had gotten up, shouted, warned Abel . . . the murder would have happened anyway; it is possible that I might have been murdered, too.

But now comes the mocking voice of one of her critical selves saying cruelly, like a twelve-year-old boy doing a falsetto imitation of his older sister, "Oh, are you going to turn me on, Harry? Like a light bulb?" . . . The aging ingénue, ignoring all you knew of how crazy Harry was, because you were alone . . .

As alone as I shall be at the moment of death.

That was why the village was no longer to be borne. It encompassed the greatest loneliness of the soul; it left you finally, no matter how you thrashed against its bonds, utterly alone. It was a village of destruction and Americans should not come here.

Oh, there were some who could come. But most should not. Not because you couldn't run away, but because you could. If no one betrayed you in this village—and if you stayed long enough betrayal was inevitable—finally, you betrayed yourself.

I don't shake now, thinking about it. I don't tremble even when I am alone. And the murder does not keep endlessly happening in front of me. But, it is possible that I shall never recover from all of this. Quite possible. I am determined to recover, even while I suspect that determination is not enough.

Harry said once, "You've really got a heart as big as a peanut . . ."

Her own sighing breath in the cold room was the only sound to be heard . . . and now a burro braying far away along the lake . . . Lonely sounds in a lonely town.

She had loved Ned. She had written poems about him. And to him. She had opened the casement and invited him into the chamber of her work, a more profound invitation than inviting him into her bed, and one he could accept. But she did not do these things for him; she did them for herself. It was a mistake.

Ned said once . . . "I am a chambered nautilus, alone in every section of my shell. There is room in here for only one."

Charles said that Harry was a killer, had been a killer in the war, killing unnecessarily, that it was not heroin which had made him kill. Charles said that if she had not already been upset, the marijuana would not have affected her so . . .

Charles, that opium-soaked gangster, was he so wise?

He had been heroic. He had saved her.

He got you out of there, carrying you, running with you on his back through the dark streets, past the shouting soldiers, ducking and dodging and breathing short whistling breaths from your dead weight on him. But getting you away from the bloody room . . .

What if he had not come back just then, bringing food for you? He had seen Harry dump the body into the street. He had seen Harry close the shutters. He had gone around to the back of the Posada and climbed the wall and gotten in. He grabbed Harry, dragged him into the *excusado* and left him there, came back for you and picked you up and pushed you over the back wall, jumped after you, picked you up and ran with you to safety. Then he came back for Harry, cleaned the blood off him, dragged him out through the *corral* and stashed him in the first car he saw. He drove him to Guadalajara and put him on the bus for Morelia, came back and parked the car again where he had found it.

Harry's father kept the Mexicans from making a fuss. He did not speak Spanish, but he was generous with money. After Harry's suicide in Morelia, they had no one to prosecute for murder anyway. Harry was not listed as a suicide; the autopsy showed that he had been very sick, that he had a severe hepatitis. Harry's father said several times that in a delirium people killed, and sometimes killed themselves. Harry's father had looked around the village in a bewildered way, his eyes bloodshot. "I guess the fever was what did it," he said. "That and the delirium."

"Sure, sure," Charles had said. But Harry's mother kept muttering, "Both of my children, both of them," in a tone of shame, as though one suicide to a family was enough.

Charles had also helped Elinor Garth pack and follow Harry to Morelia, knowing that what she was doing was wrong, but not arguing with her when he saw how determined she was. Letting her go, letting her go to Heroin Harry was had killed Abel.

"Why?" Victoria had said to Charles, still shaking, still all nerves in the first week.

He'd shrugged. "I'm not God," he said. "What do I know? I'm a hophead."

"Why did you save me, then? Why do you not save Elinor?"

He'd looked at her twisting hands. "I don't know, Vick," he said. "I don't know. Like, with you, it was a reflex, I guess. I didn't think about it. There wasn't time." He'd laughed suddenly. "And . . . I hate a bust," he'd said.

Now it was said, *se dice*, that Elinor and Ricky had gone to Yucatán, looking for Jackson . . . That made Charles laugh, too. "*'Take me back, baby,'*" he'd sung. "*'Try me one more time.'*"

There was a beetle, heavily armored in shell, moving stately and clumsy as a battlewagon, across the tile floor. Look at him. She leaned forward. What say you of the night, beetle-bug, beetle-bug?

The beetle-bug could say that it was a long night and a bitter one. It had been. When she walked out the door, there would be an end to the long and bitter night, a final end to a time and a place.

If Margo had not come here, bought up land and houses, hunted down human beings, run them to ground, played the catalyst . . . No, it was not so simple. Only a lie was simple. The truth was always confused, complex. We are all catalysts engaged in catalysm. We are all catalysts engaged in cataclysm.

All of us. We have run each other to ground.

But so we go. Back. Forward. To the side. Imagining we have a choice of direction and movement, telling ourselves the walls around us are not there . . . like rats in a maze, seeking doors, but never looking up to see that we are enclosed, imprisoned, confined, repeating the patterns laid out for us until we fall gasping onto our sides and die.

"What are your plans, Charles?" she had said to him.

"For what?" he said, with his eyes squinting.

"For now. What are you going to do . . . ?"

He stared at the floor, still squinting. "No plans, Vick," he said. "There's nothing to plan for. I can't go back to New York . . . yet. Later, maybe. I can't stay here. This is no place, man; nobody can stay here. A friend of mine is coming down in a week or two . . . a nice guy . . ." He stopped and looked at her and then suddenly he had laughed. "No," he said. "*Not a* nice guy. But I know him. We'll blow some pot together . . . and, like that."

The beetle had fallen onto its back and lay there, helplessly waving its inadequate feet in the air. It was not to be endured. Once you read Kafka's story you could not see a beetle on its back, for then it was a man on its back, unable to save itself. From the crack in the tile, a small shiny black ant emerged, coming near to the beetle, looking at it, walking all around it, returning to the crack to tell the others. After a while the beetle, immobilized like that, would be dead. And then they, the others, would come to it . . .

She got up, took the poker and turned the beetle over. As she did, she saw that it was already host to many small parasitic bugs on its underside. She shuddered, and went away from the sight of it, out into the graying patio, and stood there in the cold.

First, she must go to Cushman and apologize to him. Without his money she could not be leaving here. That was not quite true. One way or another she would be leaving now, leaving to go back into what was called "her own world," which she had been so long away from and still could not define. Then she would get a job. She would work, and make the money to support herself while she wrote. She would be in her own country, with its physical comforts and its bourgeois moralities. In the end, she would work at her book until it was what she wanted it to be . . . if she could make assets of pain and distortion and wretchedness. All men lived in pain. Show me a middle-aged face, which, in repose, does not look melancholy. We all carry the mark of disappointment on us.

When she could afford it, she would send for the *niña* and after six months with her, if it worked out, she would adopt her. But not to find joy in the child; she was no child-worshiper, not one of the ones who said, my own life is terrible so I shall make a new life for a child and it will be happy. She would not delude herself with ideas of making anyone happy. She would not delude herself with ideas of making herself happier.

Happiness has nothing to do with life. It is an insane concept.

She would never send for the child. Six months and the child would be forgotten.

She would write. She would begin again, look anew at fa-

miliar things, examine the cloth of life, feel with her fingers its
tight-knit seams . . .

Cushman had said, ". . . How many years do you think
you have?"

How many times was she going to try to evolve a formula
to live by? Life was life. Life was the deal and you went looking
for it. This village was not life for her, nor for any of them;
it brought death rushing toward you, hurried it, urging it along
the path to you, a jumble of bones in a wheelbarrow . . .

The church bells began to ring . . . the giant dishpan
sound which was firmly fixed in her ears and forever to be a
memory of this place and this moment . . . It was quarter to
five. She turned her back on the sight of the darkening mountains and went down the *zaguán* and there paused, took up her
shoulder bag and put its strap over her shoulder, picked up the
two tin suitcases and the typewriter, left the big key in the
lock and opened the door, not looking at Winifred McCluskey
who waited in her station wagon.

She walked alone down the cobbled street to the pure
corner where the bus would come, and set her bags down and
stared for a last time at the battered tin sign which said
MEJORAL, *Para la dolor en la cabeza*, and at the two Mexican
men in cartwheel hats who stood outside the cantina, not touching each other, not speaking, merely standing there, observing
her out of ancient Indio eyes.

The church bells continued to clang their dissonant summons to the Angelus, and down the way she could see the milk
boy on his horse, handsome, with two great shining milk tins on
either side of his pommel.

It was a beautiful village. It was an ugly village. It was
filthy. It was clean. It was pulsing with evil. It shone with
virtue. It was foreign, it was familiar . . . it contained as many
contradictions as life itself and trembled with its gravity of
turbulent life . . . It was Paris, Rome, New York, Mexico, the
world. It was a dot on the map of Mexico. It was, as Charles said,
"No place, nowhere."

The bus turned the distant corner and lumbered toward her,
wallowing in the deep ruts of the road, loaded down with luggage, crowded with people who carried string bags, baskets,
live chickens, bottles of tequila . . . people who would talk
and make jokes on the long trip into Guadalajara . . . There

would be a plastic statue of the Virgin of Fatima, or Guadalupe,
one or the other, on the bus dashboard and, if the driver had a
devoted mother, a small vase of fresh flowers strapped down before the statue. The driver would wear a St. Christopher's medal
at his throat, and he would joke with his passengers and drive
like Beelzebub while the flowers shook in their vase and the
Virgin extended her plastic hands in irremediable acceptance.

A car rattled down the hill behind her and she did not turn,
because it was probably the new tenant, McCluskey, with something unpleasant to say . . . or it might be Dr. Obregón, hurrying back from Mexico because he had heard, the way such
things are heard in Mexico, that she was leaving, to plead with
her once more, one last time . . .

One more time, Harry, Abel had said.

But a man's voice said, "Miss Beacon! Victoria!"

There was something at once familiar and strange about the
voice so that she turned hesitantly, and looked at the car, just
as the bus rattled up in front of her.

It was the admiral. He was driving the car. There was no
one with him. That was what she had heard in the voice, the
buffalo note . . . the memory of torment . . .

"Where's Annie?" she said.

He stuck his head out the window, and his fine weathered
old face was smiling rather timidly and his white hair was
whiter now, with less gray, less black than before, a purer
white. "I left her," he said.

She stood motionless then, hearing him say that, turning
the words over and over in her mind, the most surprising
words he could have said.

"Where are you going?" he said.

"Home," she told him.

Two boys leapt off the thick rail at the back of the bus
where they rode, and each took one of her suitcases and threw
it up on the roof where a third boy battened them down with the
other luggage. She held on to the typewriter. That she would
carry with her, all the way. She moved toward the opened door
of the bus, toward the statue of the Virgin and the nodding,
wilting flowers placed there by devoted maternal hands . . .

"But wait," the admiral said. "I want to talk to you."

He shut off the motor and he was opening the door, getting out of the car. She did not answer him but when he looked

at her, she slowly shook her head, because there wasn't time
to explain. Suddenly, there was no time at all. Time was gone.
She stepped forward and climbed the two steep steps onto the
bus and took the fare from her pocket and gave it to the bus
driver.

The admiral had come to the door and he stood there now
as the door closed upon him, and the wind ruffled the pure white
of his hair and his eyes sought her out among the passengers,
urgent, trying to say something.

Somebody made a joke about it, about the lover who was
left behind, and there was a little smattering of laughter as
the bus jolted into life and began its rocking journey along the
rutted street. One of the boys standing on the back rail of the
bus banged his hand twice on the metal chassis, and the bus
driver looked up into his wide rear-view mirror over the statue,
and grinned satanically at his reflection as he slammed the gear-
shift into second, and the bus lurched forward with a whine,
accelerating jerkily.

Remembering how the admiral had loved that girl, the picture of his divorcing her would not come, and memory insisted that Annie had divorced him and he was lying about it.
Annie had found somebody else. Annie had learned again that
he was ". . . so old, so old." But there was strength in his face,
and a look of having resolved something, as though he had been
moved finally to weigh love and youth and beauty against self-
respect, and to choose self-respect as a more fitting companion.
He looked at ease with himself, as he had not looked before,
and he looked well. There was enthusiasm in his voice and,
oddly, youthfulness in his eyes. (Harry staggering around Abel's
bar with a tattered bandage on his head calling, "Where's
Annie?" in that wounded-buffalo voice.) Well may he ask.
Where is she indeed? She had been wrong there too, protecting the admiral from what he must one day find out, endorsing
his attitude toward Annie, and believing with him that Annie
was necessary to his survival. It was the reverse; Annie, having
Annie, was killing him. Now, he had saved himself, and that
meant that he could always have saved himself, and she had
chosen wrong.

She looked back then, and saw him standing there beside
his car looking after her, watching, as the bus disappeared, and

then she could see him no more. Finally the bus labored its way onto the rise of the highway and roared with sudden incredible speed around the first turn, so that all the passengers were jounced against each other, and when Victoria looked up again, the village was gone.

About the Author

EILEEN BASSING was born in Boston, Massachusetts, and was educated in New York, Ohio and California. Her first published works were the four *Jamie* books, written for children. These were followed by a number of short stories which appeared in magazines and quarterlies. Some time ago she moved to Mexico with her husband, also a writer, and their two sons. During her three years there she wrote her first novel, *Home Before Dark,* published by Random House in 1957 and later made into a successful motion picture. At present she lives in Malibu, California, where she has a new novel in progress.